PORTRAIT OF AN
UNKNOWN WOMAN

VANORA BENNETT

Portrait of an Unknown Woman

HarperCollins*Publishers*

HarperCollins*Publishers*
77–85 Fulham Palace Road,
Hammersmith, London W6 8JB

www.harpercollins.co.uk

Published by HarperCollins*Publishers* 2006

1

A catalogue record for this book
is available from the British Library

ISBN-13 978 0 00 722492 0
ISBN-10 0 00 722492 3

Typeset in Sabon by Palimpsest Book Production Limited,
Grangemouth, Stirlingshire

Printed and bound in Great Britain by
Clays Ltd, St Ives plc

The family of Thomas More after Hans Holbein the Younger.
Private Collection. Photograph © Bridgeman Art Library.

Sir Thomas More and His Family by Rowland Lockey after Holbein.
The St Oswald Collection, Nostell Priory (The National Trust).
Photograph © NTPL/John Hammond.

Map of London by Ralph Agas c. 1561 © City of London.

This book is proudly printed on paper which contains wood
from well managed forests, certified in accordance with
the rules of the Forest Stewardship council.
For more information about FSC,
please visit www.fsc-uk.org

Mixed Sources
Product group from well-managed
forests and other controlled sources
www.fsc.org Cert no. SW-COC-1806
© 1996 Forest Stewardship Council
FSC

To Chris, with love

Many more people than the writer find themselves working on an unfinished book. I am enormously grateful both to Susan Watt and her team at HarperCollins for their wonderful editing, guidance and even a desk to finish the writing, and to my delightful agent Tif Loehnis and all her colleagues at Janklow & Nesbit. I'm no less indebted to my family. My sons Luke and Joe have been extraordinarily patient while I shut myself away to finish my chapters. Their nanny Kari has kept the house going while my parents offered all sorts of moral support. My father-in-law George has turned out to be a superb marketing manager. And I owe more thanks than I can find words for to my husband Chris for all the brilliant story ideas he came up with while reading many early drafts and chapters in whatever spare multi-tasking minutes he could make between legal cases. Most of all, though, I'd like to express my gratitude to Jack Leslau, whose lifetime's work – the development of a fascinating theory about John Clement's true identity, based on his study of Holbein's paintings – was the starting-point for this book.

CONTENTS

Plan for FIRST PORTRAIT OF THE MORE FAMILY by Hans Holbein the Younger, painted at Chelsea in 1527-28, destroyed by fire in the 18th century.

Elizabeth   Margaret   Sir John   Anne   Sir Thomas
Dauncey   Giggs   More   Cresacre   More

PART ONE

Portrait of Sir Thomas More's Family

1

The house was turned upside down and inside out on the day the painter was to arrive. It was obvious to the meanest intelligence that everyone was in a high state of excitement about the picture the German was to make of us. If anyone had asked me, I would have said vanity comes in strange guises. But no one did. We weren't admitting to being so worldly. We were a Godly household, and we never forgot our virtuous modesty.

The excuse for all the bustle was that it was the first day of spring – or at least the first January day with a hint of warmth in the air – a chance to scrub and shake and plump and scrape at every surface, visible and invisible, in a mansion that was only a year old anyway, had cost a king's fortune in the first place, and scarcely needed any more primping and preening now to look good in the sunshine. From dawn onwards, there were village girls polishing every scrap of wood in the great hall until the table on the dais and the panels on the walls and the wooden screens by the door alike glistened with beeswax. More girls upstairs were turning over feather pillows and patting quilts and brushing off tapestries and letting in fresh air and strewing pomanders and lavender in chests.

The hay was changed in the privies. The fireplaces were scraped clean and laid with aromatic apple logs. By the time we came back from Matins, with the sun still not high in the sky, there were already clankings and choppings from the kitchen, the squawked death agony of birds, and the smell of energetically boiling savouries. We daughters (all, not necessarily by coincidence, in our beribboned, embroidered spring best) were put to work ourselves dusting off the lutes and viols on the shelf and arranging music. And outside, where Dame Alice kept finding herself on her majestic if slightly fretful tour of her troops (casting a watchful eye down the river to check what boats might be heading towards our stairs), there was what seemed to be Chelsea's entire supply of young boys, enthusiastically pruning back the mulberry tree that had been Father's first flourish as a landowner – its Latin name, *Morus*, is what he called himself in Latin too (and he was self-deprecating enough to think it funny that it also meant 'the fool'). Others were shaping the innocent rosemary bushes, or tying back the trees espaliered around the orchard walls like skinny prisoners; their pears and apples and apricots and plums, the fruits of our future summer happiness, still just buds and swellings, vulnerable to a late frost as they took tomorrow's shape.

It was the garden that kept drawing everyone out, and the river beyond the gate. Not our stretch of wild water, which the locals said danced to the sound of drowned fiddles and which was notoriously hard to navigate and moor from. Not the little boats that villagers used to go after salmon and carp and perch. Not the view of the gentle far shore, where the Surrey woods with their wild duck and waterfowl stretched back to the hills of Clapham and Sydenham. But the ribbon of river you could see from Father's favourite part of the garden, the raised area which gave the best possible view of London – the rooftops and the smoke and the church spires – which used to be our home until we got quite so rich and powerful, and which he, almost as much as I, couldn't bear to pass a day without seeing.

First Margaret and Will Roper came out, arm in arm, decorous, stately, married, learned, modest, handsome and happy, seeming to me, on that scratchy morning, unbearably smug. Margaret, the oldest of the More children and my adopted sister, was twenty-two like her husband, a bit more than a year younger than me; but they were already so long settled in their shared happiness that they'd forgotten what it was to be alone. Then Cecily with her new husband, Giles Heron, and Elizabeth with hers, William Dauncey, all four younger than me, Elizabeth only eighteen, and all smirking with the secret pleasure of newlyweds, not to mention the more obvious pleasure of those who had had the good fortune to make advantageous marriages to their childhood sweethearts and find their new husbands' careers being advanced by regular trips to court and introductions to the great and good. Then Grandfather, old Sir John More, puffed up and dignified in a fur-trimmed cape (he'd reached the age where he worried about chills in the spring air). And young John, the youngest of the four More children, shivering in his undershirt, so busy peering upriver that he started absent-mindedly pulling leaves off a rose bush and scrunching them into tiny folds until Dame Alice materialised next to him, scolded him roundly for being destructive, and sent him off to wrap up more warmly against the river breezes. Then Anne Cresacre, another ward like me, managing, in her irritating way, to look artlessly pretty as she arranged her fifteen-year-old self and a piece of embroidery near John. In my view there was no need for all the draping of her long limbs and soft humming in her tuneful voice and that gentle smiling with her lovely little face that she did whenever John was around. It was obvious. With all the money and estates she'd been left by her parents, Father would have John marry her the day she came of age. What would be the point of bringing up a rich ward otherwise? Of all his wards, it was only me he seemed to have forgotten to marry off, but then I was several years too old to marry his only son.) Anne Cresacre didn't need to try half so hard. Especially since you could see from the doggy way John looked at her that, even if he wasn't very clever, he knew enough to know that he'd been in love with her all his life.

The sun came out on young John's face as he came back, better dressed now for the gusty weather, and he screwed up his eyes painfully against the harshness of the light. And suddenly the peevish ill-temper that had been with me through a winter of other people's celebrations – a joint bride-ale for Cecily and Elizabeth and their husbands, followed by Christmas celebrations for our whole newly extended family – seemed to pass, and I felt a pang of sympathy for the newly man-height boy. 'Have you got your headache again?' I asked him in a whisper. He nodded, trying like me not to draw anyone's attention to my question. His head ached all the time; his eyes weren't strong enough for the studying that made up so much of our time, and he was always anxious that he wasn't going to perform well enough to please Father or impress pretty Anne, which only made it worse. I put a hand through his skinny arm and drew him away down the path to where we'd planted the vervain the previous spring. We both knew it helped with his headaches, but the clump that had survived was still woody and wintry. 'There's some dried stuff in the pantry,' I whispered. 'I'll make you a garland when we get back to the house, and you can lie down with it for a while after dinner.' He didn't say anything, but I could sense his gratitude from the way he squeezed my hand against his bony ribs.

One moment of kindness reassured him; and it was enough to add honey to my view of everything too. When Dame Alice came back from her own spontaneous little stroll in the garden, rejoining the crowd gathered as if by chance and staring towards the spire of St Paul's, I was touched to see our stepmother – Father's second wife, who'd married him just before I'd come to the house, and looked after his four children and the wards he'd taken on, as sensibly and lovingly as if they'd been her own – had been quietly taking trouble with her hair. She always laughed robustly but she didn't like it when Father teased her about the size of her nose. Her great beauty was her beautiful broad forehead, and now she'd brushed her hair – with its stray streaks of grey blackened with the elderberry potion she liked me to make for her – back off it to show the unlined, luminous skin at its best.

Father's teasing could be cruel. Even Anne Cresacre, who had nerves of steel, wept with frustration over the box he gave her for her fifteenth birthday. She thought it would contain the pearl necklace she'd been asking for for so long. But it turned out there was nothing in it but a string of peas. 'We must not look to go to Heaven at our pleasure or on feather beds,' was his only comment, along with that quizzical, birdlike look from far away that reminded you he wore a hair shirt under his robes and wouldn't drink anything but water. At least she had enough presence of mind to overcome her disappointment and say to him at dinner, as prettily as ever, 'That is so good a lesson that I'll never forget it,' and win one of those sudden golden smiles of his that always made you forget your fury and be ready to do anything for him again. So that time it came out all right, and anyway Anne Cresacre could look after herself. But I thought he should be kinder to his own wife.

Dame Alice could do what she liked to her hair on this day, anyway. Father was the only one who wasn't here. He was away somewhere, like he always was since we'd moved to Chelsea. Court affairs; the King's business. I lost count of what and where. Even when he reappeared, looking tired, with the new gold spurs that he didn't really know what to do with clinking uselessly against a horse's muddy sides, and we all rushed out to see him, he just shut himself away in the private place he'd built in the garden – his New Building, his monk's cell – and prayed, and scourged himself, and fasted. We hardly knew him any more. But I had heard him promise Dame Alice when he last set off that he'd be back as soon as the painter arrived. And I happened to see that morning that she'd laid out some of his grandest clothes – the glistening fur-lined black cape, the doublet with the long, gathered sleeves of lustrous velvet attached that were long enough to hide the hands whose coarseness secretly embarrassed him. He liked to believe he just wanted his portrait painted to return likenesses of himself to his learned friends in Europe, who were always sending him their pictures. But being painted in those clothes spoke of something more. Even in him, worldly vanity couldn't quite be extinguished.

And so our eyes devoured the river. I could almost feel the pull of everyone's waiting and wishing. Longing to display ourselves to Hans Holbein, the young man sent to us from Basel by Erasmus – a living token of the old scholar's continuing affection for us, long after he stopped living with us and went back to his books abroad – in memory of the good old days when Father's friends were men of the mind, instead of the spare-faced bishops whose company he'd come to prefer these days. In those times ideas were still games, and the worst argument you could imagine was Father's with Erasmus over what he should call the book he was writing about an imaginary nowhere land (which had ended up being as much of a best-seller as any of Erasmus' works). We were longing to show ourselves as the accomplished, educated graduates of an experimental family school that Erasmus had always, in his almost embarrassingly flattering and charming way, praised to the heavens all around Europe as Plato's Academy in its modern image. And longing to be back, at least on canvas, in a time when we were all together.

Except me. Even if I was staring upriver as longingly as anyone else, I certainly wasn't looking for any German craftsman bobbing up and down in the distance with a pile of travel-stained boxes and bags bouncing around next to him. He'd be along soon enough. Why wouldn't he, after all, with his way to make in the world, a recommendation in his pocket, and the chance to make his reputation by painting our famous faces? No, I was waiting for someone else. And even if it was a secret, childish kind of waiting – even though I had no real reason to believe my dream was about to come true and the face I so wanted to see was truly about to appear before me – it didn't lessen the intensity with which I found myself staring at each passing boat. I was looking for my teacher from the past. My hope for the future. The man I've always loved.

John Clement came to live with us when I was nine, not long after my parents died and I was sent from Norfolk to be brought up in Thomas More's family in London. John Clement had been teaching Latin and Greek at the school that Father's friend John Colet had set up in St Paul's churchyard, and Father and Erasmus and all the other friends of those days – Linacre and Grocyn and the rest – had made their passion.

They were all enthusiasm and experiment back then, all Father's learned friends. When the new king was

9

crowned, and the streets of London were hung with cloth of gold for the coronation – a sure sign that there'd be no more of the old King Henry's meanness – they somehow got it into their heads that a new golden age was beginning in which everyone would speak Greek and study astronomy and cleanse the Church of its mediaeval filth and laugh all day long and live happily ever after. Erasmus once told me that the letter his patron Lord Mountjoy sent him, telling him to come to England at once and sending him five pounds for his travel expenses, was half-crazy with happiness and hope about the new King Henry. 'The heavens laugh; the earth rejoices; all is milk and honey,' it said.

It would surely have curdled all that milk and honey they were swimming in back then if only they'd known how quickly everything would go wrong. That within ten years their playful shared mockery of the bad old ways the old Church had got into would have turned into the deadly battle over religion that we were living through now. That one of Erasmus' European disciples, Brother Martin of Wittenberg, would have pushed their notion of religious reform so far that peasants all over the German lands had started burning churches and denouncing the Pope and declaring war on both their spiritual and temporal rulers. That Father would have responded by giving up his belief in reforming Church corruption, taken court office instead, got rich, and been transformed into the fiercest defender of the Catholic faith against the radical new reformers he now called heretics – an about-face so dramatic that we didn't dare discuss or even mention it. That Erasmus, the only one to preserve the memory of those hopes that we'd all entered a more civilised age of debate and tolerance when the new king came to the throne, would leave our house and go back to Europe, from where he'd spend his old age wearily mocking his greatest English friend for becoming a 'total courtier' and wondering at the evil real-life form his gentle dreams had taken.

But even back then, the happy humanist throng couldn't just sit around all day laughing at the wonder of being alive in their land of milk and honey. They had to do something to mark the start of the golden age. First there was the school at St Paul's. And then, when Father realised how many children he'd gathered in his own house, his four and the orphans like me and Giles and Anne, he persuaded Dean Colet to let him hire away a teacher from the school and set up his own personal humanist academy.

John Clement's chambers were up at the top of the old-fashioned stone house we were brought up in in London, which had so many creaking wooden floors and dark little corridors and hidden chambers that it could easily have been a ship, so it was natural and pleasing that its name was the Old Barge. He lived at the other end of the corridor from our rooms, next to Erasmus and Andrew Ammonius. If we were playing in the corridor, we had to tiptoe past the grown-up end, shuffling our toes through the rushes, so as not to disturb them while they were thinking.

John Clement was big and tall – a gentle giant with an eagle's nose and long patrician features and a dark, saturnine aspect that could easily have lent itself to looking bad-tempered if he hadn't always worn a weary, kind, rather noble look instead. He had black hair and pale blue eyes with the sky in them. He was Father's age, though taller, with broad warrior shoulders. You could guess at his physical energy – he strode off down the paving stones of Walbrook or Bucklersbury on great impatient legs every afternoon, instead of sleeping after dinner, and he taught us our Latin and Greek letters by pinning them to the archery target in the garden and letting us shoot them through with arrows. We were city children, being raised in a mercantile elite of burghers and aldermen who only kept bows and arrows gathering dust on a hook because they were obliged to by law, and would never raise a sword, so that was our only experience of the aristocratic arts of war. We loved it. Dame Alice raised her eyebrows at John Clement's preference but Father just laughed. 'Let them try everything, wife,' he said. 'Why ever not?'

Despite his long, athletic body with its muscles and quick reflexes, there was nothing in John Clement that signalled any wish to fight. He had a natural authority that commanded our respect, but he was also very patient with us children, and always ready to listen to other people and draw stories out of them; a comforting paternal presence. He wasn't like the other adults we knew – the brilliant talkers and thinkers who came to Father's table – because he was shy about talking of himself. He read a lot; he studied Greek in his room; but he was modest about sharing his thoughts with adults, and especially quiet and respectful around the great minds Father gathered around himself.

It was a different story when he was alone with us. He was so good at playing with words that we children hardly noticed we were also learning Latin and Greek, rhetoric and grammar. To us it was all a great game: verbal melodies and counterpoint in which every voice was always on the verge of laughing and one voice, his, was shaping the jokes.

Of all the games, the one he played best was history. Our serious rhetoric lessons – we studied rhetoric and grammar for several years before moving on to the higher arts of music and astronomy – were drawn from the history games we played together. So were our Latin translation lessons and our first attempts at Greek. He took snippets of street stories about the long-gone wars and embroidered them into tales of derring-do that made it easy for the youngest children in the group to enjoy themselves as much as Margaret and myself. We would put whatever had struck us most in our own lives into the story, then translate the latest bit of play-acting into Latin and back into English. One day, when I was still young and greedy and letting my mind wander to the strawberries ripening in the garden, I even put my gluttonous wish to eat them in. I made the wicked King Richard III pause before some villainous act and tell the Bishop of Ely: 'My Lord, you have very good strawberries at your garden in Holborn. I require you to let us have a mess of them.' It made everyone laugh. Father came into the classroom and helped us write the episode down *exertationis gratia* – for the sake of practice. One day, he said, he'd write a proper history of Richard III, and publish it, and it would be based on our games and the similar ones John had played with the boys at St Paul's school when he was teaching there. And there was a dish of strawberries on our own table for dinner that day.

But it wasn't all laughter and strawberries. There was always something sad about John Clement too: a sense of loss, a softness that I missed in the bright, brittle Mores.

He found me alone in my room one rainy Thursday, crying over the little box of things I'd brought with me from Norfolk. My father's signet ring: I was remembering it on his little finger – a great sausage of a finger. And a prayer book that had belonged to my mother, whom I'd never seen, who died when I was born, but who my father had told me looked just like me – dark, and long-legged, and long-nosed, and creamy-skinned, with a serious demeanour but the hope of mischief always in her eyes. I didn't remember much about my real father (except the official fact that he was a knight who left me just enough of a dowry to put me on the market for adoption by rich

13

Londoners after his death). But I still felt the warmth of him. He was a bear-hugger with a red face and a shock of dark hair. And when he had you inside one of his embraces, half-stifled but happy, you knew he'd always keep you safe. In his arms, talking about the person we'd both lost, so gently and fondly that our yearning for her almost re-created her. She would be kneeling at her prayers, with the book in hand. (That was the only way I could imagine her – like she was in the effigy in the chapel – impossible to picture what it would have felt like for this perfect woman to have touched or talked to me.)

My father and I were united by this love. So nothing prepared me for them bringing him back from hunting one morning on the back of his horse. He'd broken his neck at a jump – a foolish sort of death. No one comforted me. You're not really a child any more at nine. I dressed myself for his funeral, and dropped my own handful of soil on his coffin, and began several years of quiet life in corridors: watchful, eavesdropping on the lawyers and relatives as they made plans for me; picking things up, magpie fashion, storing away my few memories and what tokens of my parents I could before I was sent away to be watchful in other people's corridors. My mother had known Thomas More long ago, in London, before her marriage. It was a whim on his part – a kindly whim – to take me. But he wanted me to think of him as my father from now on. He told me that, with a sweet look on his face, when I turned up at the Old Barge.

Of course I knew nothing back then about how famous this man's mind had become all over Europe. And I had no clue that, because of my proximity to him, I too would now be moving in the kind of exalted intellectual circles where you could find a man of genius in every room in the house, with one or two to spare on a good day. Or that we girls – I was to have several new 'sisters' – would

14

be trained up to be Christendom's only women of genius. All I noticed on that first day was that the stranger I was to call 'Father' had a gentle face: kindly, with its dark features full of life and light. I warmed to him at once, to the face and the smile, Thomas More's compact body and the sense he gives everyone that only their wellbeing is important to him. Even if this stranger never quite replaced the memory of my real father, Thomas More's presence was comforting and flattering enough that the country child I still was then found herself eagerly trying out the word 'Father' as she looked at him, full of a hope she was too young to understand.

Life with the Mores had turned out to be many kinds of joy I could never have imagined at the age of nine; and now I couldn't think of living any other way or being anyone except a bit-player in this familiar company of mighty intellects. But the reality of my relationship with Father had never lived up to those first hopes. He was kind, proper, and distant. There were no embraces, no comforting, no special moments. He kept me at arm's length. He saved his hugs and horseplay for his own Margaret, Cecily, Elizabeth and John.

He saved his cheerful banter for their stepmother Alice, who came to him a widow eight years older than him, with her own estates and her own strong commonsensical views on life, just a year before I came to the house. Father's foreign houseguests found the new Mistress More harder going than the soft-spoken first wife. If you went along the upstairs corridor late at night and listened to what Erasmus and Andrew Ammonius were whispering in Greek, you'd always be sure to hear the words 'hag' and 'hook-nosed harpy' somewhere in the conversation. But More wasn't as delicate a flower as his learned foreign friends. He gave as good as he got from the Dame (we children all called her that, half-jokingly – the name seemed

15

to suit her). He joshed back like a real Londoner, enjoyed her plain cooking and ribald talk, and after his attempts to interest her in Latin had failed, he had some success in making her at least learn music. Father's new marriage seemed to suit something robust and down-to-earth in him, even if it coincided with – and perhaps caused – the end of some of his humanist friendships. In many ways it suited me and the other wards they adopted too, since no one could have been kinder or run a more welcoming home than Dame Alice. But no one treated me like a beloved child. And I'd have given almost anything for someone to act as though I was special.

For the first few years I was there I almost never dropped my guard except in the books I started reading (something I'd never have done if I'd stayed in Norfolk). Without feeling truly accepted by my new father, I found it hard to make friends with my new stepmother and sisters and brothers. An empty heart was safer than the darkness. At night I would wake up with jaws aching from not crying; eventually they put me in a room by myself because I ground my teeth in my sleep. Being by myself was both welcome and frightening: frightening because I didn't know what to do with the hot, dark, snivelling, smeary, gut-wrenching, dog-howling breathlessness of the misery that sometimes came to me now when there was no one to pretend to.

Until the teacher, with his big frame and his floppy dark hair, appeared when I was too lost in my feelings to stop, and stood in front of me with his own eyes filling with tears, just like mine. 'I understand how you feel, little Meg,' he said softly, understanding everything with so few words that my shame gave way to wonder. 'I lost my own father when I was a boy. I'm an orphan like you.' And he hugged me, and let me scrabble into the dark forgetfulness of his chest and arms like a lost infant and sob my heart out, then found a handkerchief for my eyes, and took me on his walk.

'Come on,' he said lightly – looking even a bit naughty and conspiratorial – as we slipped out of the front door while everyone else was sleeping off their midday meal. 'Don't let's wake everyone up.' It must have been when I was thirteen or fourteen; early in the year; cold, in that London way, with a fierce drizzle beating into our faces. Even so, when we started down Walbrook (paved over by then, already, but our house on the corner had been called the Old Barge since the days when it really had been a brook, and boats had come up it from the Thames), the street stank. Naturally, since the pissing conduit was only a few yards away. Equally naturally, neither of us much wanted to walk in that stink.

'Tell me . . .' John Clement began, with a furrow up his forehead. I thought he might have been about to ask me about my real father, but I could also see that my grown-up tutor didn't know how to continue or what comfort to give. I didn't want to encourage him to try; it was too private to talk about. So it may have been me who, taking a rare decision on behalf of someone else, pulled John Clement the other way, out of the odours of Walbrook and into sweet-smelling Bucklersbury Street and the shadow of St Stephen Walbrook – where the paving stones were newer and smoother and the smells were gentler and we were more sheltered from the fitful rain.

Some of the apothecaries and herbalists on Bucklersbury had shops, with scales in the window and herbs and spices and preserves on shelves behind. Some plied their trade from the street. We were followed the length of the street by a mad beggar with rolling eyes, yelling comically, 'Unicorn's horn! Unicorn's horn!', which made John Clement laugh and give the man a coin to go away; which only made the man, who said he was called Davy, follow us closer and louder than ever. It wasn't the unicorn's horn that John bought me in the end, or the dragon-water or treacle of the more respectable traders, or the dried crocodile hanging in the shop under the sign of the harp. It was a little bottle, painted sweetly with flowers, from an old countrywoman who had set up her stall on a wall away from the main rush of business.

'Good day, mistress,' he said courteously to her, 'I'm looking for heartsease,' and the wrinkled old white head nodded wisely at us both with a flash of pale eyes.

'Washes away your sorrows . . . raises your spirits,' she said knowingly. 'Add it to a glass of wine. Twice a day, morning and evening, six drops.'

He presented it to me with an adult's flourish; 'for sorrow,' he said lightly, and his favourite motto, 'never look back; tomorrow brings new joys'; but he didn't quite meet my eyes. It was as if this grown man, my teacher, had suddenly become just a little bit shy.

I kept the heartsease in its pretty bottle. (I couldn't bear to drink it. But it did its job even so.) It was only the first of my presents from walks in Bucklersbury, because we went back and back. That was just the beginning of our joint fascination with the secrets of the street. It wasn't just those two herbalists – Mad Davy with his unicorns' horns, pigs' trotters and tall stories, or old Nan with her pretty coloured potions – whom we got to know. They were my first favourites, but there was a whole crowd of other odd fish packed into Bucklersbury. Alchemists and barbers and surgeons and tooth-pullers; scientists and frauds and soothsayers. As the weeks and months went by, we got to know every wise man and eccentric in the place.

It was always on a Thursday, every week. It was our secret. I would put on my cape after dinner and be waiting for him by the door. ('You're like a dog, waiting

18

so faithfully, grinning,' Elizabeth said when she saw me there once; even at eight she had her sharp tongue. 'You make me want to kick you.' And she gave me a mean little smile. But I didn't care what she said.)

And every Thursday he'd give me something else for the medicine chest I was building up. When I was fifteen and Father asked John Clement to accompany him abroad for the summer and work as his secretary – on Father's first diplomatic mission to Calais and Bruges, a gesture of trust as Father moved into the King's circle that John said delightedly he'd never expected – John bought me a bigger present to remind me of our walks: a pair of scales to weigh the medicine I'd go on buying for myself and that I'd tell him about at harvest time.

But John didn't come back to us at the end of the summer. Father came back alone. He had no private explanation for me about what had become of John – as if he had never noticed the friendship developing between the two of us – just a bland phrase addressed to everyone present at his first dinner at the family table. 'John needs to broaden his horizons,' he said. 'I've helped him get some teaching at Oxford. There aren't many people there who know Greek.'

The looks Father gave me were as kindly as ever, the encouragement he gave to my studies just as heartwarming. But I knew he was more at ease with talk of philosophy and public expressions of goodwill than with private feelings, and I found that I wasn't brave enough to take him aside and venture into the personal. I couldn't find the courage to ask for more information about why John, the first adult I'd made a bond of friendship with – someone whose apparent warmth had reminded me of my country past – had vanished without a word. I retreated into my books and watchfulness again. But for all the sadness that went with that second loss of an adult I'd become close to, I found the strength in the end to take it philosophically and see some good had come of it. My friendship with John had been interrupted, but my fascination with herbs and healing continued. For the awkward, learned but slightly shy girl I'd become, hesitating over how to or even whether to expose myself by expressing an emotion, the ability to treat those near me for the small ailments of everyday life was, if nothing else, a release: not just my form of excellence, my small spark of genius in the great fire of mental energy generated by the More household, but, perhaps more importantly, my way of showing love.

Even though John never wrote to me in the years that followed, I kept an ear tuned for mentions of him in other people's conversation. That's how I found out that his first Greek lecture was the best attended in the whole history of the university. It's also how I discovered, a year or so later, that he'd gone travelling again – the kind of travelling that men in the More family's circle of people of genius did. He'd gone to Italy – Padua and Siena – to study medicine. He'd learned his Greek when he'd attended another university abroad, long ago, even before he started teaching; I thought in the Low Countries, though he'd never said much about it. Perhaps he just felt now that there was nothing to draw him back to London. No family. No close friends. He probably thought I was just a child in need of kindness, and forgot me.

We had plenty of other tutors after that, and we crammed our heads with so much geometry and Greek and astronomy and Latin and prayer and virginal practice that we started being trotted out in front of all and sundry as an example of the new learning. There was nothing private about our lives, even if once we moved to Chelsea we were far from court. We were always on display. Father took to publishing every scrap of work we

20

produced: all those daily letters we were supposed to write him through our schooldays, practising verse composition and disputation, translating our every thought from Latin to Greek to English and back again, were much less private than we realised. He sent the best ones slyly off to Erasmus, complaining that our handwriting was terrible, and waited for Erasmus to profess himself 'amazed' by our wit and style – which of course Erasmus kindly did. And even the letters Father sent us – Latin letters to the '*schola*', talking about how deep and tender his love was for all of us, how often he took us in his arms, how he fed us cake and pears, how he dressed us in silken garments and all the rest of it – got published too, and polished up and improved long after the event.

Yes, by the time the idea came up of getting our family portrait painted, Father had really got into the habit of dining out on stories of our brilliance. He loved to tell people that there was no reason why women's brains, even if they were poorer spiritual soil than men's, couldn't produce wonderful plants if they were properly tended and planted; or to boast that he was so soft-hearted a parent that he'd only ever beaten his children with peacock feathers. In fact, we'd set such a fashion that the Eliots and the Parrs also started copying Father's teaching methods. Little Katharine and William Parr were at risk of becoming as clever as us if they didn't watch themselves. Father had even got interested enough in my modest medical expertise – it was more than just herbal remedies by the time I grew up; of course I'd also started taking a look at some of the Galen and Hippocrates that I imagined John Clement to have been studying in Italy – to be begging the others to read more medical texts too.

Still, none of the tutors we had after John Clement had ever become my special friend. Nor did anyone seem to have remembered to look for a husband for me through all the alliance-making of the past few months, which had taken up so much of Father's time and effort on everyone else's behalf. That had left me all the time in the world to feel nostalgic about John Clement, who I still believed had loved me most, once, however impossible it now seemed given that all we'd heard about him for years was the occasional mention in a letter from Basel or Bruges from one of the learned friends who didn't come to the house any more.

Until yesterday. (It seemed incredible that it had been just a day, and here I was with my heart in my mouth already waiting for a sighting of him.)

Yesterday, when Elizabeth suddenly leaned forward at the end of dinner. It was a casual day; Dame Alice didn't bother so much about Bible readings when Father wasn't there, and Elizabeth's strangle-voiced new husband William had left the table to write letters. She gave me a meaningful look down her straight nose, and said, quietly, so only I could hear, 'I saw John Clement in London.'

I practically choked on my posset. But I kept my face composed.

'What do you mean?' I asked. 'He's in Italy, studying for his MD. Isn't he?'

'Not any more,' she said.

Elizabeth was one of those women I would never be: not a thinker, but small, neat and with alluring manners; catlike in the sense that she always landed on her feet and made it look effortless. She was the prettiest of the More daughters and the worldliest. She reeled in William Dauncey, with his Adam's apple and substantial income, on the basis of one evening at a court function and some demure-looking flirting; she got Father to place him in a sinecure job in the Duchy of Lancaster office right after their marriage and she was already fishing for better place-ments for him. I'd known from the first moment I saw her, when we were children, that we would never be close. I didn't like to think it was just envy of her milky skin and blankly beautiful features that made me imagine her as the kind of person who'd always get her own way, and who would be as spiteful as a scratching kitten if she didn't. I preferred to think that I'd spotted a deep-seated mean-spiritedness in her that I knew I could never love. And now it flashed through my mind that her meanness might just stop her talking if she saw me wanting desperately to know what she had to say.

Still, I couldn't resist trying. Casually, very casually, I asked: 'How interesting. What's he doing now?'

'He's a server in the King's household for the moment. He's been back in London since he qualified last summer.' She paused. She always knew the details of people's positions. 'He says Father got him the job.'

We both let Father's omission in telling us that important fact pass, and our shared silence drew us closer. Some things were best left unsaid. There had been a lot of eloquent pauses in our household since we moved to Chelsea.

'He was at a dinner Father sent us to last month, right after the wedding. Part of this plan to get William and Giles seats in the next parliament.' (I tried, not completely successfully, to still the twinge of envy that this casual mention of her wifely plans set in motion inside me.) 'We were in the Duke's chambers and Father was called away suddenly to read something for the King before we even went in to dinner,' she paused again, looking at her golden ring, 'and then John Clement turned up. I nearly died of shock . . .' She stopped and looked out of the window. There was sunlight beating down on us. 'It's hotter than you'd expect for the time of year, isn't it?' she went on, even though the inside of the room, bare of decoration still because there'd been no time to commission drapes and pictures yet (hence the Holbein portrait idea) was actually draughty and rather cold. 'He looks older,' she said, and there was something a bit wistful in her face. She twisted the wedding ring on her finger. 'I saw quite a bit of him after that, actually.'

She'd been back for three days. Father had sent her and Cecily home on Sunday evening, earlier than they'd expected, to help prepare for the painter's arrival. I'd hardly seen her. She'd kept to her room and her prayers and whatever whispered conversations young married women might have among themselves, but she hadn't sought me out. Why had she held on to this piece of information for so long? And why was she telling me now? I could sense that, in her devious way, she was probing for some reaction from me. Not knowing what reaction she could be looking for made me feel uneasy, and stubbornly unwilling to give an inch.

'He's not going to become a "total courtier" too, is he?' I asked. Eyes firmly down on my own ring-free hands. Erasmus' nickname for Father when he first saw him on the King's business had stuck. I laughed a tinkling girlish laugh, which sounded forced to my ears. Elizabeth didn't seem to hear its falseness, but she wasn't in a mood to laugh. She was looking gentler than usual, playing absent-mindedly with her spoon in the ruins of the dish of beef that (with more than her usual birdlike appetite) she had demolished. She just smiled.

'I don't think so – he can dance, though, did you know? – but he says he wants to practise medicine soon. He's trying to join the College of Physicians.'

'And does he have a family?' I asked. Holding my breath.

Perhaps it was a mistake to ask the question direct. Remembering to look modestly down at my hands again, I found they weren't where I'd left them. My fingers were plucking at my brooch. To cover my embarrassment, I took the whole thing off and put it down on the table.

She shook her head, and a little smile appeared on her face, like a fisherman's look as he starts playing the fish he knows is hooked at the end of his line. She bit her lip, then looked up at me, with her demurest public look. 'He said he would love to see the new house. He said he'd come and visit us.'

I waited. I'd gone too far. I wasn't going to ask when. I concentrated on the sunlight in the garden.

The silence unsettled her. 'He was asking after you, actually,' she went on, unwilling to let go, and under the flirtatious eyelashes sweeping her cheeks I could sense anxious, watchful eyes. 'That was when he said he'd come and see us.'

'Oh,' I replied, feeling my heart secretly leap, and suddenly confident too that I could get off the hook of her questions. I shrugged, almost beginning to enjoy the game. 'I doubt we'd have anything to say to each other any more, now that we've finished with school . . . though,' (and here I smiled noncommittally) 'of course I'd like to hear about his travels.'

'Oh no,' she answered. 'He was particularly interested in you. I was telling him how you'd become a medical miracle and practically a doctor yourself. I told him how you'd cured Father's fever by reading Galen. He liked that.'

I did cure Father once, a few years ago. And I did consult Galen. *De differentiis febrium,* the book was called; on the difference between fevers. It was when Father came back exhausted and hot and sweating and fitting from one of his diplomatic trips to France, and none of the doctors who came to the house could do anything for him. They all loved it when I pronounced that he had what Galen called tertian fever. But the truth is I couldn't appreciate Galen – what they called heroic doctoring, with lots of recommendations to purge and bleed your patient and show off in your diagnosis – it seemed like hot air to me. All I did was quietly give him a simple draught of willow-bark infusion that I'd bought on Bucklersbury. One of the apothecaries told me it would cool his blood. It did – he was up and about again within a day. I couldn't tell any of them how easy it was, though; they'd have thought me simple-minded. It was easier to let them go on believing in Galen's three-day fever.

'He said you were the one who got him interested in medicine in the first place. He said it was all because you used to go walking in Bucklersbury talking to the herbalists,' Elizabeth went on, and I was aware of her eyes on my face again, 'and how he'd love to see you again. And then he said, "It would have to be on a Thursday, of course." But he was laughing, so perhaps he didn't mean anything by it.'

Another silence.

I pushed my platter gently back.

'Well, it would always be good to see John again. I miss the old days in London, when it was easy for so many people to call by. Don't you?' I said finally, looking round for the brooch I'd put down and displaying so little interest in the idea of a visit from John that I could see her secret curiosity, over whatever it was, finally wane.

But of course I could think of nothing else afterwards. And I'd woken up this morning earlier than usual and full of hope – because today was Thursday.

It happened more awkwardly than I could possibly have imagined. When we finally saw a likely-looking wherry crawling down the edge of the river, we all poured out of the wicket gate like an overenthusiastic welcoming committee and rushed to the landing stage to freeze our spontaneous selves at the water's edge.

But there were two people, not one, arranged uncomfortably around the pyramid of bags and boxes stowed in the bottom of the boat. They didn't seem to know each other, or be talking. But both wore foreign clothes. And both began to gather their belongings about them as if they were going to get out.

Dame Alice was staring at them, perplexed, visibly wondering which was our guest and inspecting the packages for signs of paints and easels and an artist's paraphernalia.

One was a thick-set man of about my age, whose square face was covered, from head to blunt yeoman chin, with a layer of shortish, fairish, curlyish hair. He had eyes set in solid pouches of flesh, and ruddy cheeks, and a short nose. He was looking out with a stranger's hesitant hope of a kind welcome. The other was a tall man with an old dark cloak wrapped around his face up to the ears. It was only when he stood up, making the boat wobble, and jumped out on long, energetic legs, that I recognised his big hook of a nose and the indefinable sadness in eyes that reflected the sky. He didn't look a day older.

'John?' I said, questioningly. Then there was an explosion of sound from behind me.

'John!' Elizabeth yelled joyfully, completely forgetting the decorum expected of a married woman, and slid out from William's arm to rush forward into those of the tall man. He took a half-step back, then braced himself, caught her, and opened his arms wider as if to catch more children.

'Little Lizzie!' he called, putting a smile on his face, and looked round rather anxiously as though hoping that his other former pupils would join the embrace.

Then something went through the whole group. A shiver, as though they'd all come out hoping to console themselves with a taste of imitation happiness and had suddenly been offered a plateful of the real thing. They tightened around the newcomers like starving beasts of prey. Everything else they might have been out in the garden to do went clean out of their heads. Everyone was suddenly caught up in the old days. One beat behind their sister, Margaret Roper and Cecily Heron ran up to the newcomer. He looked relieved at the warmth of this three-woman collective embrace, so relieved that he seemed almost about to swing them all around in the air at once, but perhaps remembered that they were three young matrons now, and not small girls, or started worrying about the danger of flinging them into the choppy river in mid-arc. He let go of them all, a little suddenly.

'That's never John Clement?' Dame Alice said, and for a moment I thought I saw tears in her eyes. That was impossible, of course – she was always so brisk. But that moist glimmer I must have imagined did remind me how she and John Clement used to huddle together to discuss how best to handle the younger me. She never knew I was listening from the gallery; he probably didn't either, though I stopped being sure of that. I remembered feeling reassured that this forthright, no-nonsense woman worried over my nightmares and studied quietness back then; reassured too at how she trusted our first teacher, and at how carefully she'd listen to his slow, thoughtful responses. They were old friends.

'Clement!' old Sir John barked, looking astonished – the closest that the old authoritarian could get to being excited. And he began shuffling vaguely forward.

John Clement bowed low to Dame Alice (in his quiet way, he'd always had elaborate manners). He bowed lower still to Grandfather. But then his formality gave way and he put those long arms, which still waved more than most other people's, around both of their backs at the same time. I thought he was only a breath away from whirling them off the ground too.

There was a sudden babble of welcome. Voices testing their strength. Cheeks and hands and arms proffered in greeting. And all those insincere phrases people say. 'You haven't changed a bit!' 'You look younger than ever!'

But it stopped as quickly as it started. He was looking around, as if he hadn't seen everyone he was looking for. And then he caught sight of me, and I saw his face light up.

'Meg – I've come on Thursday,' he began. And this time his arms hung down awkwardly, and he didn't try and swing me round like a little girl. Feeling the happiness inside me surging out towards him, it was me who stepped forward.

But Dame Alice had recovered from her shock and got the measure of the situation by now, at least enough to talk properly to her surprise guest.

'Well, now, Master John,' she said playfully, stepping in front of me to give his cheek an affectionate tweak. 'What are you doing fondling all our daughters as if they were Southwark Queens? And what are you doing here anyway, turning up like a bad penny after all these years away without so much as a word to any of us? Not that it matters why – we're just all very pleased indeed to see you. No – stop – don't tell us anything here. Come up to the house at once, and tell us around the fire instead. We can't stand around gossiping on the riverbank. It's January, for mercy's sake. Whatever can have possessed us all to come out and hang around in the cold in the first place?' And she rolled her eyes comically and guided him away with a firm arm, still talking, with Grandfather and the rest of them streaming along behind, screeching like ravens. 'As if it were spring!' I heard her say from way in front.

Which left me alone, in the river breeze that suddenly seemed to have a touch of ice in it, on the jetty. Alone, that is, except for the boatman, now pulling boxes and bags out of the boat, and his squat passenger, who was looking as crestfallen as I felt as the crowd on the jetty disappeared.

The fair-haired man caught my eye. 'If it please you, mistress,' he said in halting English, fumbling in pockets and pouches. 'I am to put up at Sir Thomas More's house at Chelsea. Am I here?' And he pulled out a much-folded letter, which I could see even from a distance was covered in Erasmus' dear, cramped scrawl, and gave me a mute, pleading look from his spaniel eyes.

'Oh heavens above,' I said, struck with remorse. One of the items piled on the boards came into sudden focus for me – a long wooden frame tightly wrapped in woollen cloth: painter's tools. The poor man was shivering in his rough cloak. And everyone else had gone without him. 'You're Hans Holbein, aren't you?'

After a few minutes it stopped seeming such a messy encounter. 'I'm so sorry, I'm so sorry,' I was muttering, full of confusion and excruciating embarrassment, but the big man beside me just burst out laughing. He had a big laugh that came up from his belly; he didn't look a man to be bothered by embarrassment. He just looked capable and friendly, with big thick hands and fat spatula fingers, the muscular sort of hands you need to grind up powders with a mortar and pestle and mix them together. I didn't know much about painting, then, but I could already sense he would be good at his craft.

So I could feel the sunshine again as I walked up from the jetty to the house where I knew I'd find my family fussing happily around John Clement and where, sooner or later, the two of us would have a chance to talk again. I had Hans Holbein trotting beside me, trying to make his massive frame small in the manner of humble men, and the skinny boatman trotting behind, weighed down with bags and squawking, 'Thought it was the right thing to put them in together if they both wanted to come down here. Save them a few pennies, I thought, missis.'

With Master Hans beside me, with his easel balanced on his shoulder as if it weighed nothing, drinking in the vista unfolding before us, I saw it again myself as if for the first time. And it became beautiful to walk onto our land through the wicket gate (ignoring the gatehouse with the dark secrets whose windows I can't bear to look through), and up through the lawns and beds, which suddenly seemed full not just of withered trees and shrunken shrubs, but of tomorrow's berries and butter-cups and lilies and gillyflowers and sweet cabbage roses, and up the steps towards the dignified redbrick frontage Father had chosen for us all – a porch, two bays, and two sets of casement windows on each side. There were jasmine and honeysuckle stalks already growing over the porch. We planted them last year, when we moved into the new house, built to show Father's ever-rising status, and left our old London life behind. And one day soon we'd be seeing cascades of sweet-smelling colour coming from them.

'My English is not good, and I am sorry,' Master Hans was saying, slowly, so you had to concentrate on what he was saying, but I liked watching his sensible, no-nonsense face and the hearty voice, so that was all right. 'But this is a very beautiful house. Peaceful. So I congrat-ulate you. You must be happy living here.'

Talking to him was like dipping into a great vat of warming soup. Chunky broth with savoury vegetables and a meaty aroma – not the grandest of food, but more wholesome and comforting than the most elaborate dish of honeyed peacocks' tongues. Cheerfulness was spreading through me now, as I pushed open the door. 'Yes,' I said, feeling more certain than I had for a long time. 'Yes, we are happy.'

'Give me your cloak, leave your things here and come straight to the table – you must be cold and hungry,' I went on, smelling the food being laid on the table behind the wooden screens and hearing the murmur of voices. He paused. Suddenly he did look embarrassed. 'Mistress, excuse me, I have one question before we sit with your other guest. Tell me, what is his name?'

In what I thought was a reassuring manner, I laughed. 'Oh, he's an old family friend. He's called – John – Clement,' I said, pronouncing the words so clearly that even a foreigner could copy them, happy to have the chance to say the name. I began to nudge the German towards the hall, but Holbein didn't seem to want to move. He chewed on the thought, looking puzzled.

'John Clement,' he repeated. 'That is the name I remembered. I drew a picture once of a John Clement. A young boy who would be our age now. It was my first commission from Master Erasmus. Would he be the son of this gentleman?'

I laughed again. 'Oh no,' I said, shaking my head firmly. 'This John Clement hasn't got a son of our age. He's not married. It must be someone else, or maybe you mistook the name. Anyway, do come in properly, Master Hans. You might not believe it, but my family is very eager to meet you. And I can smell dinner on the table.'

'Yes,' he said, and met my eye, and laughed again. 'I must have made a mistake.' He let me guide him forward at last, and Dame Alice sent him to wash his hands and settled him at the table with a barrage of explanations and good-humoured apologies and expostulations and platters of steaming roasted food, and there was a lot of bowing and loud talk for foreigners, in clear, over-enunciated voices, and the kind of slightly forced good humour that

32

you get among strangers meeting for the first time. I watched her dash off a note to Father telling him the guest we'd been expecting had arrived – and a second unexpected guest into the bargain – and took it to find a boy who could go to town to deliver it. Everyone had packed in, among them Nicholas Kratzer, the astronomer, who had not yet managed to start talking German to his compatriot. By the time I sat down to eat, there was only one chair left – on the same side of the table as John Clement but at the other end. I could hardly see him, let alone talk to him. He had Elizabeth and Margaret on either side, and all I could really see was Elizabeth chattering excitedly enough for all three of them, with pink in her cheeks again. I didn't hear him say a single word through the meal – but there was plenty of chatter all around, and I couldn't really catch the drift of what they were talking about. My own vis-à-vis was Master Holbein, on the other side of the table. The German was a restful companion, wolfing down vast quantities of food in silence. But I also caught him doing something other than wiping up sauces at speed with great wedges of bread. Once or twice I looked up and saw him chewing on his bread, thoughtfully, like a cow on its cud, and giving John Clement long, slow, considering looks. Whatever the odd thought was that he'd had as we walked in through the door, he was still clearly turning it over in his head now.

2

After dinner – after the settling and snuggling of the midday nap had begun, after the merciful silence that descended on the house whenever Dame Alice fell asleep – I slipped downstairs and found my cloak and boots.

It was what I'd always done at fourteen, on Thursdays. But now I felt my hands patting nervously at my white ermine cap and pushing some stray black hairs back under it. My heart was beating faster than usual. It wasn't really just like old times. I had no idea what would happen next. John Clement had no bedroom door here from which to emerge, fumbling for his cloak, tripping carelessly against the banisters and cheerfully cursing under his breath. Was he about to come out from somewhere in this unfamiliar house, gangly and grinning, to sweep me off? And where would we walk if he did? Or would he not remember at all? Would I stand here by myself, feeling foolish, until there was nothing to be done but take my cap off again and go back upstairs?

It was completely quiet, but something made me look round. From the chapel doorway at the other end of the great hall, in the shadows under the gallery, Elizabeth was watching me. It was her eyes I'd felt in my back.

'Woof,' she said, with a nasty glint in her eyes, and retreated into the candlelit darkness. So she remembered. She knew. I could hear her husband William's nasal voice inside, raised in prayer, until the door closed.

I thinned my lips, determined not to be downcast. But suddenly I felt very alone in my cloak in the doorway, hot under its prickly heat, looking down the corridor and up at the gallery in hopes of detecting the sounds that weren't beginning. I could, I thought, take a turn round the garden by myself. No one would think I'd expected anything different (except Elizabeth). But I felt unsteadily close to tears at the idea.

Then I forgot Elizabeth, because the front door opened from outside. A roaring gust of air and sunshine blew in. And a pair of usually sad eyes, now filled with laughter, looked down gently at me. 'Come for a Thursday walk with me, Mistress Meg,' John Clement said lightly, in his magical voice. He'd been waiting in the garden. He was good at secrets. He held out his arm. 'It's been a long time.'

We walked in silence for a while, into the wind.

There were so many things I wanted to ask him. So many things I wanted to tell him.

But there was no hurry now he was here.

'Sometimes,' he said, more softly than ever, looking straight ahead and not at me. (A mystifying haze had come over us both; a glorious kind of embarrassment; we couldn't quite look into each other's eyes, and I was snatching sideways glances at him instead – committing to memory each feature and joyfully relearning the contours of cheek, nose, throat and chin as if I were caressing them with my eyes. His dark hair was just as I remembered it, though with a dusting of silver at the temples now. His eyes were the same: light blue and piercing, with that heartbreaking hint of learned sadness always in them.) 'Sometimes, it's good to be so at ease with a person that you don't have to say anything. I've missed that. I don't know many people this well, anywhere.'

At ease was absolutely the opposite of how I was feeling at this moment; but the wonder of this joyful embarrassment I'd been stricken with stopped me from laughing at the idea. I couldn't quite believe he was feeling so at ease with me either. He couldn't meet my eye even more than I could his. But hugging that secret knowledge to myself only made me happier.

He was matching his long, athletic stride to my shorter one. I could feel him reining back his legs. We were so close I could almost feel the muscles in his legs brushing against my skirt. I was half-turned towards him, against the wind, my arm hovering weightless and nervous above his, trying not to melt into the warmth we made together. But, all down the side of my body that was next to his, I couldn't help but feel the line and life of him, and rejoice in silence at the loveliness of it.

'I could walk like this forever, with you,' he said, almost whispering.

I made a small sound back; I didn't know what to say, because I couldn't say, 'I've been waiting for years for you to come back, and if I died now I would die happy just to have seen you again', but it didn't matter. Because I'd just half-seen him snatching one of the same glances at me that I'd been secretly throwing at him – memorising my features before turning away back into his silent contemplation of his memory of me – and a new soft little explosion of happiness was happening inside me.

He laughed. 'But it is cold,' he added. We were down by the river already, with a bank of snowdrops coming up behind us under the oak tree and a fierce glitter on the water, and the wind was coming at us hard and fast, snatching at his foreign-looking black beret. 'Shall we sit down somewhere, out of the wind? In one of the gate-houses – maybe this one right here?'

I didn't understand the surge of feeling sweeping me along. All I knew was that there was nothing I wanted more than to be alone with him, somewhere warm and still, so that I might at last be brave enough to look into his face and we could talk forever. I started to nod my head, feeling my body slide closer into his arm. Then I realised what he was pointing at: the westernmost of the two gatehouses. The place I never go.

'No,' I snapped, surprising even myself with the sharp-ness of my tone. 'We can't go in there,' I added, feeling his surprise and making an effort to keep my voice calm. 'Father's started keeping . . . things . . . in that gatehouse. Come away. I can't tell you about that yet.'

Urgently I pulled at his arm, aware with another part of my mind of the closeness of his chest as he laughingly surrendered and let me manoeuvre him away. It was three hundred yards upriver to the second gatehouse. 'But this other gatehouse is all right, is it?' he asked breathlessly, catching me up and sliding his arm around my waist now as we walked towards it. I could feel it across my back. Fingers on my hip bone, moving. 'What does he keep in here?'

What he kept here was his pets: a fox, a weasel, a ferret, a monkey, all on chains; rabbits in a wooden hutch; and a dovecote of fluttering white birds on the roof. Erasmus used to watch Father's doves with me, out in the gardens at Bucklersbury, long ago. 'They have their kind-nesses and feuds, as well as we,' he wrote afterwards. And he loved to tell how we'd seen the monkey, off its chain because it was ill, watching the weasel prising loose the back of the hutch. That monkey had run over, climbing on a plank and pushing the wooden back into a safe position again, saving the rabbits. Animal humanism – just the kind of story that Erasmus would treasure. Just the kind of thing that used to amuse Father, too, before his life took the turn it has now.

It was peaceful in the eastern gatehouse. It smelled of straw and feed and wood – calm country smells. We pushed open the door and sat down on a bench, side by side, with his arm still round my back, and listened to the wind on the water.

With his free hand, John Clement loosened his cloak, and turned to gaze down sideways at me. The arm behind me was bringing me round to face him, a process my body seemed, independently of my brain, to be joyfully helping. There was a little smile playing on his lips. He lowered his head and nudged his nose against mine. His eyes were cast down still, but his lips were so close now that he only had to whisper. 'So, grown-up Mistress Meg Giggs – what shall we talk about?' He smiled wider, and his smile filled my whole field of vision. 'I hear that while I've been away becoming a doctor you've been becoming one too.' His fingers were exploring my side, his arm was drawing me closer. 'And I want to know all about that. But first, I want to say,' he paused again, 'how beautiful you've grown,' and he looked straight into my eyes at last.

And then, somehow, we were kissing, and I was so dizzy with longing that I found myself clinging to him, aware of his cloak and the ribbons on his foreign-made jacket sleeves and the heat of my blood and – at the same time as losing myself in the bewildering mix of hardness and softness and wetness and roughness and gentleness and sensation on every inch of our bodies as they strained together – feeling touched to have the power to make his heart pound so audibly in his chest, and his hands shake so.

With a sigh, we came apart, and sat, rumpled and flushed, looking at each other from under our eyelashes, and laughing at our own shared confusion. 'Oh Meg,' John whispered. 'Now I know I've really come home at last. You've always been home to me.'

Which was just about exactly what I had wanted to hear him say ever since he went away, almost half my life ago. And just about exactly what I had begun to think that neither he nor any other man ever would say to me, while I passed my empty spinsterish days buried alive in the countryside, watching all the others get fat with happiness, and became more isolated and eccentric and embittered by the day. So almost all of me wanted to believe the wonderful words I was hearing now. But I couldn't stop myself also hearing another voice. It was Elizabeth's, and it was taunting, 'He's been back in London since last summer,' and 'Father got him the job.'

I looked up at him, hesitating over how best to put my difficult question, with prickles of frustration in advance at trying to believe the answer could only be simple and honest, and at the same time feeling almost dizzy with the desire to slide back into his arms and lose myself in another kiss.

'So tell me . . .' I began, feeling my way into a new kind of uncharted territory. I couldn't bring myself to say, 'You've been back in London for six months, just one hour's boat ride away, and never sent word; you went off abroad ten years ago; you never once wrote – and you expect me to believe you've treasured your walks with the little girl from all those years ago so much that you've always thought of me as your home?' So I started as gently as I knew how: 'What has it been like being the King's server for all these months?'

He met my eyes now with a different kind of look, a little wary. Then he nodded once or twice, as if he'd answered some mysterious question of his own, and kissed me chastely, a brush of lips on lips.

'Well, it's a sinecure; a place at court while I set myself up properly; your father's kindness to me for old times' sake,' he said. 'But I know what you're really asking. You think I should have done something better than just turn up out of the blue to see you after so long. You're asking for explanations.'

I nodded, relieved that he'd grasped my thought. He paused again. He was thinking hard. I became aware of the rabbits scratching around in their straw.

'Listen, Meg,' he said at last. 'I can't give you enough explanations to satisfy you completely. Not yet. But you have to trust me. The first time I asked your father if I could marry you was nearly ten years ago, when he took me abroad for the summer.' I held my breath. I hadn't expected to hear that. My heart started beating even faster, so fast that I had to make a conscious resolve to keep my face studiedly turned down towards my knees so he couldn't see my shock (though I was aware that his face was turned studiedly towards his own knees). 'But your father said no,' he went on. 'He said I had to settle myself in the world before I could think of marrying you. He told me that if I'd got so interested in herbalism I should go and turn myself into a learned and rational physician – get my MD on the Continent – and bring something new to the new learning in England. Well, I have. And I came back to England with you in my heart. I swear I did. The first thing I wanted to do when I got to London was to come to you.'

He sighed. 'But the problem was that your father still said no,' he said.

I couldn't stop myself looking up now. He must have seen a flash in my eyes. 'Why?' I said, and I could hear my voice – which I'd thought would come out breathless with a happiness I'd never even imagined might be mine – sounding hard and vengeful instead.

'There are things he wants me to be able to tell you,' he said. He stopped again. Looked down again. Took a big breath, as if making a decision, and went on. 'He says I have to become a member of the College of Physicians first,' he continued, and there was anxiety in his voice. 'Not just a member, but one of the elect. I'm doing everything I can. I'm talking to Doctor Butts, the King's physician. It's not easy; I've been away for years; I have to prove myself as a good physician to someone I've never worked with. But your father won't be swayed. He says I have to be able to tell you I've succeeded in my work.'

It was the More household attitude: everyone must bow to the things of the mind. Usually I shared it. I revelled in my knowledge of things no ordinary woman knew, and most men didn't either. But now, when the picture of a life of ordinary domestic happiness seemed both tantalisingly within reach and impossibly out of reach, Father's strict intellectual requirements of John Clement suddenly seemed unnatural and harsh.

'I shouldn't be here now, to be honest; I promised him I'd stay away. But when I met Elizabeth,' he looked down and scuffed the straw with a boot, 'and started thinking about how close you were here, just down the river, and I knew your father was away at court, and it was about to be Thursday – well, you'll have to put it down to a lover's impulse: I just couldn't resist coming to take you out for a walk.'

I didn't know what to say. His words and my feelings were going round and round, somehow failing to blend, leaving me speechless. I tried to control my spasm of anger with Father and concentrate on the happiness of being with the man I loved at last. He was looking searchingly at me.

'Say you believe me,' he said.

'Say you love me,' I heard myself say. With self-loathing, I heard myself sounding petulant. Like a child not understanding a story but wanting a happy ending.

'Oh, I love you all right,' he whispered. 'I've always loved you, whoever you were – the little orphan crying over your lost past, the bright-eyed child storing up everything the apothecaries could show you, the girl who couldn't stop asking difficult questions, the beauty you've turned into now,' and he stroked my black hair, exposed now, with my white cap gathering straw on the floor. 'And I always will love you. We're two of a kind. And even though I'm twice your age, and not quite settled in life even in my dotage – if you're willing to have me, nothing will stop me coming back to ask your father for your hand. Again and again. Until the time is right. Don't you ever doubt that.' And he folded me back into his arms so that his cloak covered us both, and moved his face over mine.

'Stop,' I said breathlessly, almost unable to pull back but with a new, more urgent question suddenly bursting through my head. 'Tell me one thing. Why are you letting Father just give you orders like this? You've known him for years. You know he loves a good argument. Can't you at least try and talk him round?'

I couldn't bear what I saw next. His face fell, and the lover's antennae I had just discovered felt him moving away somewhere very distant.

A defeated look came over John's face. 'I owe it to him to do as he asks,' he said, very quietly. 'I can't even begin to go into all he's done for me over the years. It sounds odd to say this, since we're much the same age as each other, but he's been like a wise father to me for most of my life. I can't start defying him now.'

'John,' I said, with a new resolve in my voice, groping

inside my head for a way of showing him how things were for us these days. 'Let me show you Father's new life.'

And this time it was my hand on the door, pushing it open into a roar of fresh wind and sunshine, and my strong young arm guiding this man with the troubled eyes out of our darkness.

3

'Listen,' I whispered, and tiptoed to the very edge of the gatehouse window, beckoning John forward.

I'd brought him to the western gatehouse again. He was hanging back, bewildered, clearly wondering why I wanted to return to this little brick building when I'd been so scared of it just an hour before. But it had become important to show him the truth. I took his hand and drew him up in front of me so he could peer into the darkness inside too, and the touch was a fresh revelation of how my skin loved being against the skin of those long, fine, delicate fingers. Regretfully, I put that private joy aside. This was no place to think of love.

In that stillness of bodies waiting, with the wind on our cheeks and flapping in our cloaks, we gradually began to hear the whispering from inside the window. Lost, hopeless, desperate; a thin Cockney chant. 'Lord of your endless mercy bring my body to death . . . Lord of your endless mercy bring my body to death . . . Lord of your endless mercy bring my body to death.' It had been going on from morning to night for the entire week that Father had been away. It had been chilling me every time I crept this way on my walks. I heard it in my dreams. All I could see of John was his shoulders and the back of his head, but I could almost feel the goose bumps rise on his flesh. Slowly he turned his head around towards me, and there was horror on his face, and his mouth was forming the silent words: 'What *is* it?'

'Look inside,' I mouthed back, 'but carefully. Don't let him see you. Don't scare him any more.' He peered forward. I knew what he would see when his eyes got used to the gloom: the wooden stocks, and the pitiful little stranger's figure with his legs and arms trapped in its holes, a living arc of thinly covered bones and torn clothes topped by two bloody eyes, half-closed, over swollen lips moving in perpetual prayer.

John stepped back quickly from the window and I came with him. He looked sick. He hurried twenty steps away with me trotting behind before he paused for me.

'A heretic?' he asked in a whisper.

I nodded. 'This one's called Robert Ward. He was a shoemaker on Fleet Street until last week. They arrested him as part of a conventicle praying in the leather-tanner's rooms upstairs. He has six children.'

'Why has your father brought him to your home?' I thought there was pity in the hush of his voice, too, and it gave me strength. 'What's wrong with a prison?'

'There've been half a dozen of them in the past few months. Father doesn't tell us anything about them, not even that they're here. But he told the gardener who feeds them that he just wants to talk them out of evil. I happened to overhear –' I felt my cheeks redden, though John let my blush pass and didn't ask how I happened to overhear a conversation so obviously not intended for me and how long it had taken to pick the mulberry twigs out of my hair afterwards '– him saying he'd brought them home to interrogate "for their own safe-keeping".'

'Well,' John said, stopping and looking straight into my

45

eyes, visibly trying to follow my thoughts, searching for an explanation to hold on to, 'perhaps he's right to do that. Someone's clearly been beating that man up. He probably is safer here.'

There was something comforting about hearing him say those sensible words. I liked the searching way he looked at me, really listening to my concern, trying to get to the bottom of what was on my mind. But it was too easy to cling to the belief he was offering. I hesitated, then plunged on. 'But what if . . . ?' I didn't know how to end that sentence. I tried again. 'He's been here for days. If he looks that way now, when was he beaten up?'

John looked even more closely at me. 'I'm listening, Meg,' he said seriously. 'Are you saying you think it's your father who's been beating him?'

'I don't know,' I confessed miserably. The darkest of the thoughts I'd been having seemed impossible now that he'd voiced my suspicion in that familiar, sensible voice – but not quite impossible enough. 'But sometimes I think it's possible. So many other things have changed that you don't know about.'

The sun was a deceptive mellow gold, but the lawn our feet was thudding against was turning hard as iron and John's breath was freezing to white.

There was more to show. He was shaking his head, looking too unsettled to hear everything at once, as I pulled him forward again. He certainly knew that Father had been at war with heretics ever since Brother Martin had declared war on Church corruption ten years ago and plunged Europe into upheaval. But he might easily not know how far Father's personal war against evil had taken him: that, as well as his liveried life at court as the King's most urbane servant – not just a royal counsellor and attendant, in and out of the King's chambers, but Speaker of the House of Commons in the last parliament, and, since last year, with a knighthood and the chancellorship of the Duchy of Lancaster among his privileges as well – Sir Thomas More now spent large parts of every day trying to stop up every crack through which heresy might seep into England.

It wasn't the Father we saw at home who'd become a persecutor of men. The man who ate and laughed and talked with us, only less often than before, was the same sunny wit we'd always known. I'd only become aware by accident – by stumbling on his victims – that he seemed to have become someone else too. A frightening stranger with a face turned towards the shadows.

The prisoners I'd been spying on in the gatehouse were the small fry caught in the net of Father's surveillance and entrapment in the gutters of London; the victims of his agents' creeping among the leather-sellers and the drapers and fishmongers of the city, hunting down evil in the shape of little men grappling with their consciences in back rooms, before bringing out broken prisoners with piles of logs on their backs as a symbol of the eternal fires they would have faced if they hadn't recanted.

I didn't understand the high politics of it. I couldn't see how the whole spiritual and temporal edifice of the Church of Rome could be threatened by these terrified tradesmen. I couldn't help but feel sorry for them.

Still, I knew that these humble men weren't the only ones Father was investigating. There were others in his sights who were far closer in their outlook and beliefs to the way we used to be. The men he was going for hardest these days, people were saying, were the bright young scholars at the universities, who he said were 'newfangly minded' and 'prone to new fantasies' and might corrupt the very sources of faith, like little Cuthbert Bilney, arrested after preaching a seditious sermon in London, or the six Cambridge students imprisoned in the fish cellar of their college for keeping heretical books. Perhaps these men of learning were genuinely a danger. But it chilled me to think that Father's new position in the world might be turning him into a defender of the worst as well as the best traditions of the Catholic Church, part of the sequence of foolish friars and grim clerks arguing about the number of angels you could fit on a pinhead whom Erasmus and he had once poked so much fun at.

'Of course I want to believe he's being kind,' I went on, breathless even though we'd stopped walking. 'That he's getting these men out of prison because they're in danger there. That he's trying to give them time, that he's reasoning with them and persuading them to recant, and saving their souls. But what if it's worse than that? What if it is him bloodying these men's faces out here where no one can see? What if he's worse than a "total courtier" these days,' – and I took a deep breath – 'what if he's started enjoying torturing people?'

John shook his head. 'Impossible,' he said stoutly. He stopped again and put reassuring arms around me. 'I can see why that idea would worry you, Meg, but you must see how fanciful it is.' Then, perhaps sensing that I wasn't relaxing and giving up my fancy as easily as he'd expected, he added: 'For instance, look how easy he went on young Roper. There are people who'd say that shows he's too soft for his job.'

I almost laughed with the shock of that thought from another, less worried part of my mind. I had no idea how John Clement had heard about Will Roper's brief love affair with Lutheranism a few months back. I didn't think anyone outside our family knew anything about how Will, just qualified as a barrister, had been hauled before Cardinal Wolsey for attending a heretical prayer meeting with some of the German merchants in London. It was all thanks to Father that Margaret's husband was sent home with nothing worse than a reprimand, when the other men arrested with him were forced to parade to Mass loaded down with firewood and jeered at by the crowd.

Officially, I didn't know any of this. But there'd been no stopping Will talking while he was in the grip of the new idea, telling us excitedly that it was corrupt to pay to pray for the souls of the dead, because Purgatory had never existed except in the minds of money-grubbing monks; nonsense to believe in the age-old communion of the faithful, living and dead, joined through time in the body of the Church, because faith was a private matter between God and worshipper; and that it was foolish to see divine purpose in the Church of Rome. Forget priests, forget monks; refuse to respect your fathers; break every tie with the past.

Will was nothing if not sincere. He'd argued with Father in every corner of the house and garden. And Father was nothing if not gentle back. I'd seen him walking in the garden with Will, an arm around the younger man's back, a sorrowful look on his face. 'Arguing with your husband has got us nowhere,' he'd told Margaret in the end, 'so I'll just stop arguing.' Perhaps it was his prayers for Will's soul, and his forbearance, that finally persuaded my brother-in-law to stop his flirtation with the forbidden and rediscover his passionate belief in a more familiar form of God (and his passionate admiration of Father into the bargain).

'That wasn't the work of a bigot, now, was it?' John was saying gently. 'No one could have been more restrained.' And he was encouraging me to smile, to wipe the fears from my heart. My mouth twitched back at him. It was a relief to remember that moment of sweetness. I almost gave in. But not quite.

'But it doesn't make sense,' I said stubbornly. 'How he behaved with Will doesn't fit in with the other things he's been doing. In the New Building, where we're not invited. And in London, and at court. That's what I don't understand.'

John was towering beside me, with an anxious look on his face again that probably matched the anxious look on mine. I felt disloyal to be snooping through the parts of my father's public life that he didn't tell us about at home, but I'd been a secret agent in my own home ever since we came to Chelsea. So I kept drawing on his arm, pulling him on through the garden. The only way I could show John what troubled me about the direction Father's mind was turning – how he was leaving behind the civilised thinking that had created our bookish, loving family; how he was now to be more feared than trusted or obeyed – was to show him what I'd seen.

We were walking towards the New Building – Father's sanctuary from court life: his private chapel, his gallery, his library, his place of contemplation and prayer, the place where he wrote his pamphlets. It had monkish bare walls, a single bench and a plain desk. He prayed, then he sat at that desk and poured out the filth of his public letters. I couldn't imagine how he could bring himself to even think some of the words he came up with, let alone write them, let alone publish them:

Since Luther has written that he already has a prior right to bespatter and besmirch the royal crown with shit, will we not have the posterior right to proclaim the beshitted tongue of this practitioner of posterioristics most fit to lick with his anterior the very posterior of a pissing she-mule until he shall have learned more correctly to infer posterior conclusions from prior premises?

I opened the door, brought John inside (he seemed taller

than ever, hunched inside its austere confines), and closed it, silently pointing out the brown-stained tangle of the scourge swinging from a hook on its inner side. The scourge was another new manifestation of Father's conscience: his protection against the bodily lusts that kept him from becoming a priest himself long ago; the weapon he turned on himself in his bigger war against instinct and unreason.

What private lusts, and for whose bodies, would made him flail his own skin until he drew blood? It hurt me to think of his poor innocent skin, already chafed and broken by his hair shirt, lashed into worse pus and scab by that ugly sliver of bloodied leather. It was almost as bad as seeing the tortured prisoners at the other end of the garden, to imagine him torturing himself, alone, in here.

He kept his pamphlets and writings in the library, along with the confiscated, banned and impounded books that he had special dispensation from Bishop Tunstall to read and refute. He had a complete library of heresy here, in his place of prayer, down to William Tyndale's New Testament in English – one of the few copies that had escaped the bonfire at St Paul's. Cardinal Wolsey had thrown the rest into the flames. Watching him were 30,000 cheering Londoners and my grimly approving father.

On the desk was last week's draft of the letter Father had been writing to Erasmus for so long, begging him to get off the fence and denounce Luther. I'd read it before, and been chilled by the fury of Father's phrasing: he wrote that he found all heretics *absolutely loathsome, so much so that unless they regain their senses I want to be as hateful to them as anyone can possibly be*.

Hateful indeed. I shivered. The word brought back the image of Robert Ward, the scared little shoemaker locked up in our garden, praying to die.

I knew Father was wasting his ink trying to persuade Erasmus. Nothing I'd seen the old man write suggested there was the least chance of him publicly supporting Father in any crusade against the religious reformers. He was too busy feeling disappointed, in Luther and Zwingli on one hand, in Father on the other. In everyone who'd once been a humanist but had since become a zealot.

Erasmus might have taken to calling the most ranting evangelicals 'rabble-pleasers', 'mangy men', and 'utterly lacking in sincerity'. But he was no more impressed with the 'uncouth, splenetic' style of Father's written attacks, which he said, 'could give Luther lessons in vehemence'.

I felt for Erasmus. Deserted on both sides by the former disciples of the new learning as they forgot the classics and rushed into their violent religious extremes instead. Sitting in Basel, looking forlornly round for intellectual playmates who might still enjoy Greek writings and Arabic geometry, or revel in moderation, mockery, learning, laughter, inquiry, beauty, truth and all the rest of the last generation's forgotten dream. The same dream that Father brought all of us up to be a living illustration of; the same dream that Master Hans would tomorrow start illustrating us as illustrating. A charming public image coming into existence of a private reality in danger of fading away.

'Look at this,' I heard myself whispering to John, pulling out one offending volume after another and opening them to the worst pages. 'And this. And this.' There was still enough January sunshine to read by inside. But he screwed up his eyes with a show of reluctance and took them to the desk, by the window, to see properly.

'Don't you see, John?' I pressed, and my whisper hissed against the bare plaster. 'He's lost his reason. We could wait forever for him to give us permission to be together. He might never do it. He can't think about any of us any more. He's too obsessed with this. He's gone mad with hate.'

I'd been thinking this about Father for so long, while

I'd had no one to share it with, that it was a relief to speak my doubt aloud, especially to the man I loved.

But John was squaring his shoulders, and giving me the same kind but unconvinced smile that my smaller self had seen whenever I offered the wrong answer in a lesson. He shook his head.

'It's his job,' he said simply, dropping the page of foul-mouthed nonsense about Luther's posterioristics. 'That's William Ross speaking, not Thomas More.'

Another neat commonsense blow at my fears; another sign that John knew a lot about Father's work. I had to admit that Father had been asked by the King – and not chosen himself – to reply to Luther's writings against the Pope. And it was true that he'd been ashamed enough of the crass language, zealotry and poor reasoning of the writing he was doing in service of King and country that he'd only published it under a pen name. It still made me hot with shame to read those words: William Ross was a bullying bigot, and everyone knew William Ross was Father. Still, if John Clement could separate the two names in his mind, perhaps that meant Father hadn't compromised himself as disastrously as I'd thought.

'He's not imagining the danger of heresy,' John said gently, sensing that he'd found a chink in my armour. 'I know that the man you showed me in the gatehouse looked pitiful. But we have to remember that he's not what he seems. He's part of the darkness that might envelop Christendom.'

'How can he be? He's just a skinny little cobbler from Fleet Street!' I said hotly, on the defensive again.

'But a skinny little cobbler from Fleet Street can be the darkness,' John answered persuasively. 'Or he can to most people. Look, you're young enough, and lucky enough, to have been brought up in a time of peace and in a sophis-ticated household where everyone has read about different peoples through the ages having had very different kinds of beliefs and lived in very different kinds of states and still prospered. Your head is full of Greek gods and Roman lawmakers and Eastern men of learning and stars moving in orderly fashion through the heavens. You think civilisation is everywhere. So you have a confidence that you don't even know is unusual. You don't live with the fear of chaos breaking through and destroying the way we live that haunts the rest of us. You have no idea how other people feel. Most people feel mortal terror at the idea of the unholy chaos outside, waiting to engulf them. And I don't just mean the poor and superstitious and unlettered, the people brought up without sucking in Seneca and Boethius and algebra with their mother's milk. I mean everyone brought up in the shadow of war. Everyone brought up before this rare time of peace and outside the very unusual household you're lucky enough to come from. I mean everyone older and less lucky than you. I mean people like your father and me.'

'But you and Father are men of learning! You know everything I know and more!' I cried, full of frustration that he wasn't following my train of thought.

'Ah, but we weren't brought up to it, and that's the difference,' he said, with a certainty that made me pause. 'We grew up in a world where there was nothing but the fear of the darkness. When death was waiting round every corner. When London could be surrounded at any time by an army threatening to string up every man and rape every woman and throw babies onto their sword blades and torch every parish church. When books were rare and locked up inside the monasteries, and our only hope of salvation was the One True Church and the priests who could mediate for us with God. Of course men of my age and your father's age fell in love with the new learning and the new freedom to think as soon as we had peace

54

and leisure enough to explore it. But we haven't forgotten the fear we grew up with. It's always at the back of our minds. And we can't feel easy when people take up arms against the Church. You can't expect that of us.'

He paused, waiting to see the light of acquiescence in my eyes. But I ploughed on, even though his assurance was beginning to make me feel I'd only understood part of the problem. 'But Father and Erasmus and all the rest of you used to talk about uprooting corruption in the Church,' I said plaintively. 'And none of you expected to be treated like criminals for it. So why is it so much worse if a few cobblers get together to pray in a leather-tanner's room?'

He sighed patiently. 'It's not just a few cobblers or a few prayers any more, Meg. It's not a bit of mockery at the table about crooked priests selling indulgences either. It's gone much further than that. What's happening now is an assault on God and His Church. It's armies of peasants running amok in the German lands burning down churches and murdering the faithful. It's rogue monks betraying their oaths of celibacy and marrying the nuns who've sworn to be the brides of Christ. It's the old chaos, the horror you've never known, threatening us all. Even if you did understand, it would be hard for you to see the danger from the calm of England, but anyone who's been in Europe in the past few years and knows the signs can see the darkness looming again all over Christendom. It could happen here. Your father is right to be frightened, and he's right to fight it. We couldn't hope for a better general than him to lead us in the war against the heretics – precisely because he is the same scholar and gentleman who brought you up. The same good, subtle, generous, wise man. Which is why nothing will make me believe what you're afraid of – that he could enjoy causing pain. You have to put that idea aside. It makes no sense.'

His certainty sounded stronger than mine. His loyalty to Father made me feel ashamed. I looked down.

'It's simpler than you think, Meg,' he said. 'You and I will find happiness together. Neither of us will ever be alone again. But we have to do as he says. We mustn't distract his attention. He's fighting his war on many fronts. It's not just cobblers who are a danger. There's worse elsewhere. There's heresy rearing its ugly head everywhere – even at court.'

He shifted his shoulders, looking around for the door, clearly unwilling to continue trespassing in Father's private place. And, taking my arm again as we stepped out into the clean light, he told me the secret of the King's Great Matter.

Henry VIII, in love with a lady-in-waiting. Henry VIII, in love with a lady-in-waiting at a court so full of rose bowers and Canary wine and dancing till dawn and flashes of leg and cleavage and canopied beds with feather pillows that it seems made for love. Henry VIII, so in love with the one lady-in-waiting who refuses to recline in any of the rose bowers or feather beds at the court made for love that he wants to get rid of his Queen and marry again.

The King is a glittering bubble of gold and bombast. He never takes no for an answer. He is being tormented equally by love and by the Book of Leviticus. 'If a man shall take his brother's wife, it is an unclean thing . . . they shall be childless,' says Leviticus. And Leviticus is telling the King just what he wants to hear, now that he wants to be shot of the Queen, because once, long ago, for a few months, the Queen was the child bride of the King's child brother Arthur, who died.

The Queen's first marriage has only begun troubling the King's conscience since he has begun to want a second marriage for himself. It didn't need to trouble anyone's conscience back when it happened, because back then the Pope formally pronounced that the first unconsummated

*marriage of children hadn't counted as God's holy union.
But now the King is full of doubts. As he dances atten-
dance on the scented girl with the pointy chin and the
witchy eyes and the fascinating mole on her neck, he's also
wondering: is God punishing him for his sinful marriage
by denying him a son?*

*Queen Catherine; devout, learned, Spanish, and in her
forties, with powerful friends at court and all round Europe
but just one young daughter to show for twenty years in
the King's bed. And worried.*

*And a clique of ambitious nobodies forming around her
rival: pretty, witty, elegant Anne Boleyn. The kind of
courtiers known collectively as a 'threat'. They're throwing
her together with the King; parting the tapestries with a
wink and a glitter of excitement.*

'I was with the court at New Year at Hampton Court,
and I saw them together myself,' John said sombrely. 'They
were in a group of maskers. But there was no disguising
the King. And no disguising what he felt about the lady
in yellow.'

'But what does the lady in yellow have to do with us?'
I asked.

'Don't be impatient, Meg,' he said. 'This is the point. The
lady in yellow is making your father's battle against heresy
many times more dangerous. She has the King's ear – and
she's flirting with the heretics too. At a time when the King's
of a mind to be interested in anything that undermines the
Queen, the Church of Rome and the Pope, she's poisoning
him in the most subversive way imaginable by giving him
the new men's books to read.

'If her influence grows, who knows how far the heretical
thinking might spread? And who knows what chaos we
might be plunged into? Peace is an illusion, an agreement
between civilised people, and something your father has
worked all his life to promote; but it's the nature of

humanity that the beast is always lurking somewhere beneath the surface.'

The phrases were echoing emptily in my head now. I pleated a fold of my cloak. I didn't understand. 'You're talking politics,' I said sulkily. 'Not ordinary life. Not us being in love and getting married.'

'But Meg, politics *is* life. If you lose peace you lose everything else: love, marriage, children, the lot. You should thank God you're too young to remember how things were before – in the time of wars,' he answered bleakly. 'But anyone a bit older than you will say what I'm saying now. I lost my family in that madness' – he shivered – 'and I know there can be nothing worse.'

Had he? He was old enough to have lost family in the wars, but he'd never talked about it. All I knew for sure was that he'd been taken into a family friend's household as a boy, after his own father's death. I'd asked him about his childhood once. He'd just shaken his head and twinkled at me. 'Very different from the way I live now,' was all he'd said. 'I like this way of life a lot better.'

'The best we can do, in the weeks and months to come,' his voice rolled on now, 'is to hope that the King's fancy turns elsewhere and this crisis passes. And meanwhile, try not to judge your father too harshly. Some of the things he's doing may look cruel, but it's up to him to root up the evil spreading over English soil before it starts clinging to the King. The only thing we can do is let him concentrate on doing his job, and wait for the moment to be right for us.'

He swung me round in front of him like a doll, lifted my face, and looked searchingly into my eyes. 'Oh Meg, don't look so scared. Have faith. It's going to happen. I'm going to marry you. I only wish,' he added, leaning down and kissing the top of my head, very gently, 'that it could be today.'

I stayed very still, looking down, treasuring this moment

of quiet togetherness, warmed by the sincerity in his voice and the folds of his cloak flapping in the rising wind, watching the shadow of the anxious clouds scudding through the deepening sky chase across the lawn at my feet. Still hardly able to believe that he could be here, saying he felt about me as I always had about him, still swimming with delight. And feeling half-reassured that he didn't think Father was becoming a vengeful, sadistic stranger, though not sure I completely agreed. Still feeling twinges of unease and uncertainty; but willing, more than willing, to do whatever John Clement said, because he said he loved me and because I loved him.

'You said,' I whispered, with my face so close to his chest that I could smell the warm man-smell of him, trying to focus on the questions I needed answers to but not sure any more what they were, 'that there were things Father wanted you to be able to tell me . . . was that just about the College of Physicians? Or was there something else?'

He hesitated. For a moment I thought I saw his eyes flicker, as if there was something he wanted to hide. But then he smiled and shook his head. 'No. Nothing else,' he said firmly. 'Nothing for you to worry about.'

We huddled together, looking up at the house, knowing it was time to go back. I knew I should feel nothing but joy, but this snatched meeting was so unexpected, and so incomplete, that my pleasure in it was bittersweet too, and tinged with sadness. So what I found myself saying, as we turned back up the path, arm in arm, was, 'You know, I miss the innocence of before . . . the time when there was nothing more to worry about than putting on a play that made us laugh after supper . . . when there was nothing worse than a weasel in the garden . . . when Father did nothing more dangerous than hearing court cases about ordinary street crimes . . . and when everything he wrote was just a clever game, instead of a war of words . . .'

'My darling girl, I think what you're saying is that you miss Utopia,' John quipped, and I thought for a moment that he might be laughing at me. That was the title of Father's most famous book, written in the summer that John went away, in which a fictional version of my teacher – known in the book as 'my boy John Clement' – had been given a minor role. It was the story of a perfect world, as perfect in its way as our own contented past.

I didn't feel like laughing back. 'Well, I do miss it,' I said defiantly. 'Who wouldn't?'

But the wind had got into his cloak, and was tugging at his beard, and he was very busily fidgeting his accoutrements back into submission.

'Let's go,' he said, as if he hadn't heard, stepping ahead of me, 'before we get blown away.'

But he had heard, after all, because a few steps later he added, rather bleakly, over his shoulder: 'Nostalgia is dangerous. Never look back.'

Or perhaps I'd imagined the chill, because by the time we got up to the door and stopped to catch our breath, now we were out of the wind, he was smiling again, and his face was as softly radiant as I could have hoped. He smoothed down the hair escaping out of my cap, and touched a finger to my lips.

We might have lingered for longer on the threshold, glowing with wind and love. But suddenly the sound of two lutes in duet began drifting out into the late afternoon: invisible fingers plucking, hesitantly and very slowly, at a bittersweet popular air.

'Listen!' he said, with a music-lover's delight, pushing open the door to hear where the sound was coming from. I didn't need to rush. I knew exactly what a mangled lute duet signified in our house in Chelsea. Father was home.

4

The hall was crowded with new arrivals. But one head stood out among the rest – that great dark lion's head, with the square jaw and long nose and the piercing eyes that could see the secrets in your soul, the head of the man with the glorious glow about him that fixed every other pair of eyes on him wherever he went. When Father threw back his head and laughed – as he often did – he always transported whatever roomful of watchers he'd gathered around him into a quite unexpected state of pure, joyful merriment. He wasn't exactly laughing now, as I slipped into the room behind John Clement. He and Dame Alice were sitting on two high-backed chairs, surrounded by a standing crowd of soft-faced admirers with stars in their eyes, and the pair of them were struggling to make their disobedient lutes obey them (he's always been tone deaf, but he loves the idea of playing duets with his wife). But there was a smile playing on his wide mouth as he tried to force his fingers to be nimble on their strings. He knew his limitations. He was ready to see the lute duets, like so much else, as the beginning of a joke about human frailty.

His magic worked as powerfully on me as it did on

everyone else. Glancing around past all the usual family faces and the stolid features of Master Hans, I saw he'd brought the Rastells and the Heywoods home with him, and John Harris, his bow-backed confidential clerk, and Henry Pattinson, his fool, fat and shambling behind them, and in the shadows John a Wood, his personal servant, who was probably tutting adoringly in his corner over the state of the master's muddy old shoes, sticking out beneath his robe, and plotting one of the sartorial improvements that Father loves to resist. The sight of Father emptied my mind of all my rebellious thoughts. With him here, the household was complete. The dusky room was lit up with more than candles. The warmth came from more than just the fire blazing in the grate. Like everyone else, I was ready to forget everything and just revel in the effortless happiness that came from enjoying watching him enjoying himself.

Until, that is, I sensed a shiver run down the back of the man in front of me. From where I was standing, I couldn't see John's expression. But, with sudden protective anxiety, I became aware of Father glancing up from the frets under his left hand and, for the first time, taking in the bearded face of his uninvited guest.

Father didn't miss a beat. With his hand still moving on the fingerboard, he held John's gaze for a moment, inclined his head in the merest sketch of a courtly bow, and murmured, in his softest voice, 'John.' The smile stayed on his lips.

Then he turned his eyes down, back to his difficult music.

It had been no more than a greeting. But I felt John flinch as if it had been a whiplash. He was shifting uneasily on his feet now, glancing back at the door, clearly longing to be off.

After the music finally dissolved into applause, Father

got up with the lute still in his hand. I was certain he was about to make his way towards us. I stepped aside, stealing a glance up at John's face and reading the pale signs of guilt on it.

Yet Father didn't part the crowd of acolytes to approach John. He had too much of a sense of occasion. He was turning now to the delighted Master Hans, and apologising for the poor musical entertainment – 'But I assure you something better will follow,' he was saying, and John Rastell, my uncle the printer, and his son-in-law John Heywood, were visibly quivering with secret knowledge of what that would be – and within minutes we were being organised into the impromptu performance of a play, and transported back into the carefree atmosphere of a family evening in the old days.

'Let's do *The Play called the four PP!*' young John More, excited and puppyish, was calling out. John Heywood's play, written long after John Clement went away, had been a family favourite for years – a satire on the trade in false relics by mendacious travelling monks. Young John was waving his goblet of Canary wine, and his grin was almost splitting the child's face, which now seemed far too small for his ever-growing body. 'We could use this as the wedding cup of Adam and Eve! . . . And this', he picked up a trinket box, loving the joke, 'as the great toe of the Trinity!' But the older Johns shushed him. They'd clearly agreed in advance what we'd be acting – and opted for no religion – because it was only a matter of moments before everyone was dressing up instead for *The Twelve Merry Jests of Widow Edith*, with Dame Alice assigned, with her usual good-tempered resignation, to play the starring role of the bawdy old fraud who debauches our family servants. 'If this is a punishment for all my shrewishness,' she said, and twinkled, 'I should learn to keep quiet in future,'; then, twinkling even harder and tapping Father on the shoulder in the middle of his mock-henpecked look: 'Just my little joke, husband.'

It was only when the shuffling and scene-setting was in full swing, and all the other Johns were fully occupied elsewhere, that Father finally approached my John. Who was still standing, looking ill at ease, while everyone else bumped busily past him.

'John,' Father said, opening his arms, dazzling the taller man with his smile. 'What a surprise to see you here. Welcome to our poor new home,' and he embraced his bewildered protégé before slowly moving back, patting him gently on the back, to include me in his smile.

'John Clement,' he said to me, with a hint of mockery in his voice as he pronounced that name, 'has always been a man of surprises. Ever since the time we first met. Do you remember our first meeting, John?'

And a current of something I couldn't define ran between them – what seemed a sense of threat masked by smiles – though perhaps I imagined it. John was smiling back, but I sensed he was hanging intently on Father's every word. So was I. I knew so little about John's past that any new light Father could shed on who my enigmatic intended had been before he came to live with us would be well worth having.

'It was in Archbishop Morton's house, Meg, when I was just a boy – maybe twelve years old. You've heard all about Archbishop Morton, I know: my first master, and one of the greatest men it's ever been my privilege to serve. A man whose great experience of the world made him both politic and wise. God rest his soul.' I was being drawn closer, into the magic circle. His voice – the mellifluous tool of his lawyer's trade – was dropping now, drawing us into his story.

Father, a pageboy in hose and fur-trimmed doublet, turning back the sheets and fluffing up the pillows late at night for the Archbishop, who'd also been Lord Chancellor to the old King, in his sanctum in the redbrick western tower of Lambeth Palace. Father was a boy tired after the daytime rituals of the house school, and the evening rituals of serving at table in the great hall, and already longing to join the other pageboys snuffling on their straw mattresses in the dormitory. But he was mindful too of the lessons of the books of courtesy and nurture, so he was also remembering not to lean against the wall, or cough, or spit, and to bow when he was spoken to, and to answer softly and cheerfully. (The boy More was so naturally skilled at all these arts of gentility that he'd become a favourite with his canny master, who'd taken to boasting publicly at table that 'This boy waiting on you now, whoever shall live to see it, will prove a marvellous man.') So when the Archbishop told him to take the tray of wine and meat and bread he'd brought up from the kitchens into the audience chamber next door – a public room of polished oak, never used at this hour – he stifled his fatigue and obeyed with the best grace he could.

And there in the audience room were two young men – coltish youths only slightly older than young More, with long limbs and travel-stained clothes, and swords propped against their boxes, drooping tiredly on the polished benches. With something watchful about the way they looked at him as he entered with the tray. And something angry about the way they looked at each other.

Try as he might, young More couldn't imagine who these surprise guests were. He'd never seen them at the school. He'd never seen them among the pages serving in the great hall. Besides, they were too old to be pageboys. They already had the close-cropped hair of adulthood. And former pageboys didn't suddenly show up to pay their respects in the middle of the night. In any case, their manners seemed too high-handed to have been learned in the Archbishop's courtly home. 'Wine,' the older youth, who must have been seventeen or eighteen, said imperiously. Young More bowed and poured out the wine. 'Wine,' said the younger boy, who was black-haired with fierce eyes, clearly annoyed that there was only one goblet and pointing towards his own feet as though young More were a dog to be brought to heel.

But the boy More was not afraid of these headstrong youths. He just laughed politely.

'Two drinkers, but only one vessel,' he said, keeping his countenance as the books taught. 'A problem I can quickly solve by running back to the kitchens for another goblet.'

And then an interruption – a great gale of laughter from the candlelit doorway, where they'd all forgotten that Morton, in his long linen nightshirt, was still watching them.

'Bravo, young Thomas,' he said richly. 'Your poise puts everyone else here to shame. This one,' and he pointed at the younger youth, who was now looking ashamed at being caught out in the uncouth business of bullying a child, 'has clearly forgotten to live up to his name.'

And the black-haired wild boy stared awkwardly at his feet.

'Tell the child your name, John,' Morton said. 'Let him in on the joke.'

'Johannes,' the youth said. He hesitated, in the manner of someone who might not really speak Latin. 'Johannes Clemens.'

Johnny the Kind. Archbishop Morton catching young More's eye, giving him permission to laugh. The small More joining in his master's unkind mirth at the difference between the tall black-haired boy's lovely name and unlovely behaviour. The older youth also beginning to guffaw. And, finally, John Clement himself – somewhat to More's surprise – losing his sullen look, clapping the young More on the back, and, with more grace than the pageboy would have expected, joining in the laughter at his own expense.

'. . . I liked that in him. We've been the best of friends since,' Father ended, superbly relaxed. He was talking to me rather than to John, but I felt John also gradually relax as the story drew to its close, in a way that made me wonder if he'd perhaps been dreading a different ending – one that might discredit him in some way. 'But I see you're still a man of impulse, John. Turning up without warning.' Father winked affably at me, encouraging me to laugh a little at the embarrassed figure between us. 'Still reserving your right to surprise.'

'So where had you come from that night?' I asked the mute John, curious to see further into this glimpse of his past. 'And where were you going?'

'Oh,' Father said smoothly, answering for John. 'Well, that was so soon after the wars that things everywhere were still in confusion. John and his brother had been brought up by family friends after their own father died. But it was time for John to go to university. So he was stopping in London on his way abroad, to Louvain, where he was about to become the man of learning – the kindhearted man of learning' – he chuckled again – 'that everyone in our family has always loved so dearly.'

And now Elizabeth was joining our circle, breaking the conversation. 'Won't you play one of the servants, John?' she was asking sweetly, and, before the pink-faced John could answer, wrapping him gently in a rough servant's cloak and shepherding him away to join in the revels. He looked back at Father, as if asking a question; and Father, as if answering, nodded what might be permission for him to stay and play.

Left alone with me, Father turned a kindly gaze on my

face. 'You see how it is, Meg,' he said. 'I made a promise to the Archbishop long ago to keep an eye on John Clement. And I always will. I may always need to. He's someone who's endured a lot of losses in his life; and sometimes suffering leaves its mark on a man's soul. With a man like that you have to take things slowly and carefully – and make sure there are no hidden depths you haven't plumbed. But you're a wise young woman. I'm sure you understand that . . .'

He held my gaze a moment longer than necessary. I didn't know exactly what he meant, though the gentleness on his face now reminded me of the gentleness with which he'd treated Will Roper's heresy. But I thought Father might be giving me a warning.

'We had a good talk this afternoon,' I said, masking my resentment behind a diplomatic smile of my own. Father was a fine one to talk about hidden depths, if he'd been secretly negotiating with John Clement for years about the conditions under which John might marry me, without ever giving me a hint of what was on his mind. 'I was glad to see him after so long. I was glad to find out everything he told me.'

And I was pleased to see Father look more closely still at me, carefully now, with what seemed to be a question in his eyes. I held his gaze. It was he who turned his eyes away. 'Good,' he said, but without certainty; and he moved off into the crowd to attend to his guests.

And so the rest of the entertainment, with all its applause and rumbustious punch lines and flamboyance and laughter, was reduced for me to a watchfulness of eyes. John Clement's eyes, avoiding mine and Elizabeth's and Father's alike. Elizabeth's eyes, searching my face and John Clement's with something I couldn't read in her expression. Father's eyes, coming thoughtfully to rest every now and then on John Clement. And, of course, Master Hans's eyes, giving us all the same long, careful, considering looks I'd seen him direct John Clement's way over dinner. A gaze that mapped the line of the back and the line of the heart at the same time. Which made me uncomfortable when I caught him staring for a slow moment at my hands moving in my lap. But which I then realised, with relief, probably signified nothing more than his artist's preoccupation with how best to paint us.

John Clement didn't stay late. I saw him slip up to Father as soon as the play was over, while the costumes were still going back into their chests and the servants were setting out the supper, ready to make his excuses and go. I moved closer, wanting to hear but not to interrupt. But Father gestured me into the circle.

'John tells me he has to leave now,' Father said, with equal measures of warmth and splendid finality. 'It's been a joy that he's found the time to let us welcome him here so soon after his return to London. And we'll look forward to seeing him again here very soon, won't we, Meg?' He paused, and gave John another glance I didn't understand, before adding: 'As soon as he has had time to find his feet again in this country, after so long away. As soon as he wins election to the College of Physicians.'

I took John out to the doorway to help him into his cloak. Out in the half-darkness, with none of the other eyes on us any more, was the first time I dared look up and meet his eyes at last. And he looked straight back at me for the first time in what seemed like hours, with all the sweetness and love on his face that I could have hoped for, and with a hint of what looked like relief too.

'You see, Meg,' he said reassuringly, with one hand on the doorknob. 'It's as I said. We just have to wait a while. Doctor Butts promises that I'll be put up for election this spring – it seems a long time, but it won't be forever – and then everything will come right for us.' And I felt his other arm move round my waist in farewell. 'I'll write,' he murmured, opening the door and letting in the night wind. 'I'll be back. Soon. I promise you.'

And then he was nothing but a black figure on the black of the garden, flapping away down the path towards the water, leaving me confused but as hopeful as the silliest of serving girls that I was about to live happily ever after.

Elizabeth sidled up and looked sideways at me as soon as I slipped back in.

'Master Hans has been making sheep's eyes at you all evening,' she said, with one of her brittle little laughs. 'I think you've made a conquest.'

I might have been embarrassed. It was just the kind of needling observation Elizabeth was too good at for anyone else's comfort. But luckily Master Hans wasn't making sheep's eyes at me now. He was sitting at the table, glowing in the warmth of Father's undivided attention, which, as it always did with everyone, was making him feel confident and expansive. He had a miniature copy of the portrait of Erasmus that he had taken to Archbishop Warham propped on the table, and a sketch of the answering portrait of the Archbishop's cavernous old features that he was planning to take back to Erasmus in Basel – he'd clearly struck lucky in his first two weeks in England to have got that commission (but then Warham, one of Father's bishop friends, had always been a kindly old soul, and even if he hadn't been it was fast becoming *de rigueur* to repay the gift of one of Erasmus' portraits in kind). Now he was talking enthusiastically in his accented English about how to do our family painting. I could see Holbein was a good salesman. There was already talk of two separate pictures – a portrait of Father by himself, to send to the other humanists around Europe, as well as the group picture for our hall that the German had originally been asked to make – and he was showing Father a completed picture too, a noli-me-tangere with a virtuous Christ shying away from a voluptuous Mary Magdalene, which I could see had struck a chord with Father and was about to bring the painter another easy sale. I sat quietly down near them to listen.

'There was a fresco I saw at Mantua,' Holbein was saying, so carried away by his idea that he was beginning to move saltcellars and knives around on the table to illustrate it. 'I can't get it out of my head . . . The Duke and his dearest love, his wife, facing each other sideways-on near the middle of the canvas . . . the family all around . . . someone leaning forward from the left for instructions . . .' He paused gleefully, visibly expecting to be praised for his cleverness. 'And, right at the centre, looking straight out of the picture,' he said, then burst out laughing at his own joke, 'the Duke's dwarf!'

It was a slightly shocking idea. There was a moment's silence when we all looked at Father, waiting to see how he would react. He paused for a second too. Then his face opened in helpless laughter – the kind of generous approval that made people everywhere love him. 'The fool at the heart of the family! That's a marvellous idea!' he snorted; and, without having been aware before of any tensions in his face, we could see all the worries of the court being wiped from it now, and we all began laughing too, in relief and sympathy and soft, adoring love.

'Let's see how it would look,' Father said, still grinning mischievously, and with his mind full of the idea. 'Henry!' And he beckoned out the fat simpleton from the corner. 'We have our own king of fools here, as you see,' he told Master Hans, and in a flash of enlightenment I saw in Henry Pattinson, the ginger fool whom Father so loved, a grotesque parody of the big features of golden King Henry himself, and wondered if that was why Father kept him; and wondered, if that were so, at the daring in Father's apparently disingenuous remark (and whether Master Hans had had it in mind all along to put our Henry the Fool at the heart of our family).

Before we knew it, we were in position, with Master Hans, masterful now, walking us to the places he'd given us in his mind's eye. Henry Pattinson staring, blank and baffled as ever, straight towards the artist. Father and his daughter Margaret Roper facing each other slantways (I was impressed at Master Hans's quick understanding of who Father's great love was). Me next to Elizabeth, and leaning over Grandfather to whisper into his deaf ear. Everyone else either arranged around us or watching and clapping us on.

And then, in the middle of the hubbub, Elizabeth whispered, 'Where's John Clement?'

'Gone,' I whispered back.

'What, without even saying goodbye?' she said, louder, and she turned her head so sharply round to look at me that she broke the composition of the group. Master Hans looked up, warning us with his eyes not to step out of line.

'He had to leave,' I muttered, frozen in my artificial position, looking down at Grandfather's velvet-wrapped old knees.

'Stay still,' Master Hans called to us.

She looked back at him. 'I'm sorry, Master Hans,' she said, in a small voice. 'I'm afraid I'm not feeling very well. I think I'll have to go to my room.'

And she detached herself from the group and left the room, followed, after a moment's indecision, by the bobbing Adam's apple of her husband. She did look pale.

We might have stopped then. But Father quickly filled the gap. He was too fascinated by the painter's imagining to countenance the group breaking up. The two men were revelling in the speed with which they'd come to an intellectual understanding, laughing together and catching each other's eyes as they saw the picture take shape. 'John,' Father called with a smile (knowing there were enough Johns in the room to stand in for multiple defectors), 'will you take Elizabeth's place?' And so the actors didn't disperse until after Holbein, who had magicked a scrap of chalk and a slate out of the old leather bag he kept with him, had finished a lightning sketch of how we would stand in our picture – a representation of the perfect humanist family that would be new in itself, as playful and forward-looking as any of the new learning, a far cry from the stiff old depictions of pious artists' patrons as saints with which rich men still liked to fill their chapels. And the party carried on until late in the evening, when, a moment after Father excused himself to write business letters and slipped away to the New Building, the light suddenly seemed to go out of the room, and all the guests remembered how tired they were and went to bed.

It was only late at night, when I was lying in bed (unable to sleep with excitement, my heart bursting at the memory of all that had happened that day and with all the plans I was making for my future with John), that I heard Elizabeth retching behind the closed door of her room, and the scrape of a chamber pot, and William's nasal whispering. I couldn't hear his words, but his tone was the mix of reassuring and nervous you'd expect from any father-to-be. It began to dawn on me what the reason for her sudden discomfort might have been.

5

'Elizabeth,' I whispered. 'Elizabeth. Are you all right?'

It was still dark. Just before four in the morning, long before first light, but long after I'd heard Father's footsteps tiptoeing down the corridor to begin his early shift of work and prayer in the New Building. In a few minutes the household would begin to stir.

It was hours since I'd sprung awake again and lain warm under the counterpane up to my frosty nose, waking up to joy and quietly loving the cold, creaking silence in which I could hug my secret to myself. But the miserable sounds coming from Elizabeth's room hadn't stopped. They were still going on now.

So I put a shawl over my shoulders and slipped out to the corridor, to pat at her door and see if I could help. I was the one with the medicine chest and the knowledge.

She wouldn't answer.

I shivered. I could hear the fires being laid downstairs.

Eventually footsteps did pad up to the other side of the door. I breathed out in relief.

But it wasn't Elizabeth's head that poked out. It was William's – tousled, drawn and more pink-eyed than ever from lack of sleep.

'Meg,' he said, with well-bred restraint but no great gratitude. 'What can I do for you?'

'I thought . . .' I began. 'I thought I heard someone being sick. I thought Elizabeth might need some help.'

He smiled. Perhaps it was just the way his features were arranged, but I couldn't help thinking his expression patronising. 'Everything's quite all right,' he said with visible patience. 'There's nothing for you to worry about. So run back to bed . . .'

I could almost hear the unspoken 'like a good girl' on his supercilious lips.

'Oh,' I said, feeling crestfallen, looking for information on his face and finding nothing he wanted to tell me. 'Well, if you need anything . . . I have a chestful of remedies in my room . . .'

'Thank you,' he said, with finality. 'We'll be sure to come to you if we need anything. Don't get cold out here.'

And, very gently, he closed the door on me.

Elizabeth didn't come downstairs for breakfast. William was one of the party that walked through the darkness to the village for Mass at seven – but his wife wasn't. He offered no explanations. Father, in a surplice, was acting as altar-server this morning, following the priest to the altar step as the Office and Kyries and censing and Gloria in Excelsis began. That gave me the freedom to sneak a look at William while we stood in the family chapel (whose twin pillars were still covered with the scaffolding that would soon be used to carve Father's symbols on the stone). His hair was slicked neatly back and, bar a little extra pinkness about the eyes, he was as expressionless as ever. Even when the bells rang out, and the candles and torches were lit in the heavy scented air, and the priest lifted the sacrament above his head – displaying the wafer that the common people believe to be a magical talisman which can heal sickness and cure blindness, as well as a holy sign, Christ's body and blood returned to earth – and everyone else's faces filled with joyful adoration, William only had his usual slight smirk as he knelt. He was a cold fish, I thought, taking less trouble than usual to pretend I didn't dislike him. He seemed a good match on paper. His father was a senior official in the royal treasury. But his conversation always seemed so limited, and his personality so stultifying and self-satisfied, that I knew I'd never enjoy his company. Not for the first time, I found myself wondering what pretty, witty Elizabeth could possibly have seen in him (apart from a way of pleasing Father by marrying a colleague's son). Bubbling as I was with my own happiness, I surprised myself by feeling a stab of pity for her.

She was alone when I sneaked into her room after Mass. She'd tidied herself up a bit and was flopping back in a chair by the fire. But her face seemed drained of blood and she barely acknowledged my presence. The rank chamber pot was still beside her, covered with a flecked cloth.

I could see she didn't want me there. But she was too weak to resist when I felt her pulse and temperature (clammy but cool). And gradually the expertise in my hands took the edge off her reluctance to speak. She relaxed, at least enough to say: 'It must have been something I ate.'

I nodded. It was up to her how she explained her sickness.

'Let me bring you some ginger tea,' I suggested. 'It will soothe you. And do you think you could keep any food down yet?'

She grimaced. A hand crept to her stomach. She shook her head.

'I'm going to bring my medicine chest in here and brew up your tea for you in front of the fire,' I said brightly. 'And keep you company while you drink it.'

My chest contained everything. Remedies against fever and ague, chills and chilblains, toothache and heartache. Jars full of memories of Bucklersbury. Knives and pans, and a pestle and mortar, and John Clement's balance to weigh out the powders I made. And a single ginger root, withering in its jar: expensive, but a more potent relief for nausea than anything else I knew, even slippery elm or chamomile leaves. I began scraping slivers into my little pan, loving the calmness of this quiet ritual and the sureness of my hand on the exotic spice from a faraway land, aware of both myself and my sister being lulled by it as much as by the rushes of sparks and slowly collapsing logs in front of us.

Grateful that she was too sick to mention John Clement, and enjoying the quiet warmth between us, I began softly telling her about the medicinal properties of ginger: that it makes the human body sweat, that the King himself has recommended it as a remedy against plague, that a compress of it applied to the face or chest will clear an excess of phlegm, and, most important, that it's a guaranteed cure for griping.

As I set the pan full of water on the hook above the fire, Elizabeth began to stir and sit up straighter and look into my treasure-trove. 'You have so many jars in there,' she said faintly. 'However do you remember what's in them all? Don't you ever muddle up, say . . .' she pulled out two jars at random, 'this one, and this one?'

I shook my head, sure of my mastery of the subject. 'Never. Too dangerous,' I said, and then I saw she'd picked up black haw and pennyroyal, and laughed. 'Especially with the two you've picked,' I added, taking advantage of the chance she was flatteringly giving me to show off a little. 'The one in your left hand is to ward off miscarriages. But the other one brings on women's bleeding. It's what village women use to wish away unwanted pregnancies. Pennyroyal oil. Not a mistake you'd want to make.'

She put the jars back in the chest with a little show of horror. But she smiled too.

'Ugh. And what else do you have . . . love potions?' she asked, trying to be light.

I shook my head again. 'You have to ask the village witch for those,' I said, just as lightly, then looked more closely at her. Beyond her sickness, there was something unusual in her eyes. If I didn't know her so well, I'd have said it was something like the desperation of a trapped animal. 'You don't need a love potion, anyway,' I added, with as much comforting warmth in my voice as I could muster, 'you're a newlywed bride with a brilliant young husband.'

The trapped-animal look was there again, stronger than ever – a hot dark shock of fear behind her eyes.

'. . . Yes . . . though sometimes,' she hesitantly began to frame a thought she'd clearly not imagined putting into words before, 'I wonder about William . . . what kind of husband he will be. What kind of father. We know so little about the people we marry, after all . . .'

Then she stopped. Took control of herself. Shut the trapped animal back in its cage and smiled at me in the coquettish social way I normally expected from her. 'Look, Meg,' she said. 'The water's boiling.'

She was right. And suddenly the air was filled not just with regrets and untold secrets but with the spicy smell of hot ginger.

Ginger was in the air all morning. It was a day for medicine.

When I slipped downstairs an hour later, after covering the sleeping Elizabeth with a quilt, I found Margaret Roper sitting alone in the parlour, looking out of the

78

window. There was a viol and a sheet of music on the table beside her. But I hadn't heard her playing.

'I smelled ginger tea,' she said as gently as ever. She'd always been my favourite of the sisters – the nearest to my own age, and the one I'd most often shared rooms and beds with; the quiet good girl who'd always been sensitive with other people's feelings and who was now, despite all that quietness, gaining a reputation (enthusiastically fostered by Father) as England's most learned woman. 'I guessed you were looking after Elizabeth. How is she feeling?'

'A bit queasy,' I said noncommittally. It was for Elizabeth to explain her sickness. 'But she's sleeping now.'

Margaret's eyes were shining. 'Will you make me some ginger tea too, Meg?' She smiled and paused, picking her words carefully before tremulously taking me into her confidence: 'For the same reason?'

Her dark bony face was so radiant that I couldn't stop my own face breaking out into a grin. 'Margaret! You're going to have a baby!' I cried, and held out my arms.

We were still brewing up the second pan of ginger tea, murmuring excitedly together, when Cecily put her head around the door, sniffing. 'That smells wonderful,' she said into our sudden silence, and I was already beginning to recognise the soft, knowing smile in her eyes. 'I've been so sick this morning . . . is there enough for me too?'

All three young matrons excused themselves from dinner at midday. But everyone in the house knew that Margaret and Cecily had announced themselves pregnant. Father, back from a long session closeted with Master Hans, being sketched and sitting perfectly still, was the last to hear. Looking as radiantly happy as they had, he offered a special thanksgiving prayer for them and their unborn children – his first grandchildren. He even broke with his usual water-only rule and drank a little wine with his pleased, pink-faced sons-in-law Will and Giles. Only William Dauncey was not there to join the toast. He was upstairs, like a dutiful husband, with his sick wife.

I waited for him to come downstairs before checking on Elizabeth again in the afternoon. She was lying on top of the bed, awake now, with some colour back in her face. But sad.

'I've been making ginger tea all day,' I said brightly. 'Have you heard? Margaret and Cecily are both pregnant. They're feeling so sick they won't touch anything else.'

She looked up, straight into my eyes.

'So you know,' she said flatly. 'So am I.'

'We'll have three October babies then!' I said, trying to pretend surprise.

'Yes,' she said. Even more flatly. Then she shook herself. 'I do feel ill,' she said piteously. 'Will you make me more tea?'

I pulled the counterpane up to her chin and tucked it round her.

'You stay warm,' I said. 'It won't take a minute.'

She was quiet while I grated and boiled my infusion. I thought she might be dropping off. So I was surprised to hear her tired voice mumble, even more piteously, from behind my back: 'Was it you John Clement came to see yesterday?'

I paused, considering how best to reply. But, by the time I finally turned round, with the steaming drink ready to take to her bedside and a soothingly fact-free answer ready on my lips, she'd fallen asleep.

6

'So it will be a fruitful family portrait,' opined Master Holbein, as he led me into the little parlour that had been turned into his studio. It had a friendly, cluttered air. There was an easel (with the first sketches for Father's solo portrait, made yesterday, still on it) and piles of cloths and props. At a table under the window he had the makings of his colours: almost as many jars and powders and oils and pestles and mortars and pans as I kept in my medicine chest. I felt instantly at ease.

I laughed. 'Yes . . . So many babies! You'll have to paint us quickly, before the house turns into a nursery.' And then I blushed, almost before I'd had time to catch my mind, or perhaps my body, flashing off into its private dream of my own belly rounding beneath me, and the pride I could imagine in the familiar, elegant man's hands touching the swelling and feeling proprietorially for the kicks and somersaults of a life to come. I touched my cheeks, trying to will the mental picture away, but not quite able to bring a self-possessed chill back to my expression.

He grunted. Looking at me without quite seeing me, reducing me to lines and blocks of colour in his head, ignoring my flaming cheeks, arranging me in his mind in a way that still disconcerted me. Gesturing me to the chair.

'Oh,' I asked, full of curiosity, 'but may I see Father's picture before I sit?'

His face closed. He shook his head and moved his body against the stretched frame behind him, covered with a cloth, as if to protect it from me. 'Not yet,' he said. 'It's not ready.'

'But when you start to paint?' I persisted.

A little surprised, he looked differently at me. Suddenly focusing on my face. Then he nodded and shook his head, both at the same time. 'Yes,' he said simply. 'Later. This is only a first sketch. I want to get it right first. I hope this will be an important picture for my future. You understand.'

I did. And I didn't mind his frankness. He'd only had a day to capture Father's likeness. Father had already gone back to court. Master Hans would have more time for the rest of us, since we weren't going anywhere. But it was getting Father's face right that would bring in commissions for him.

I sat, sometimes aching with stillness and tormented by tiny itches and sometimes lulled by my own inactivity, but always with a tiny, yearning part of me imagining that the footsteps approaching the door might be not those of whichever servant or sibling happened to be passing on whatever mundane errand, but those of John Clement, come back, long before time, to announce to everyone in the house that he was claiming me as his bride. Master Hans talked. Stolidly; perhaps to calm me and keep me still. Catching my eye every now and then – interrupting the train of thought in which Margaret Roper rushed merrily into my arms to congratulate both me and John, and Cecily laughed at the sight of my uncharacteristically girlish confusion, and young John More looked as surprised as he was by everything – but usually staring at the paper or at some part of me in his odd, impersonal craftsman's way. And I listened from my pink cloud of happiness, from very high up and far away.

He was talking about fathers first: platitudes about how much they teach you and how they love you. Then, matter-of-factly, he also told me about his own father's death: how relieved his wife had been not to have to send money out of their tiny budget to keep the old man afloat any more; how hard it had been to get his father's painting materials out of the Antonite brothers at Issenheim who'd been the old journeyman's last employer. 'I had to write to the burgomaster for two years before it was settled,' he said; 'Elsbeth would never have let it drop.'

He told me about the sketch he'd spent yesterday making. He'd already pierced the main outlines of Father's sketched face and neck with tiny pinpricks, two or three to an inch. Next, when he'd done with me for the day, he would prepare the surface he would do the final painting on; then pin up the sketch on it – a map of Father's face, a ghost of the reality he'd seen so briefly. He'd blow and smear charcoal dust through the tiny holes in the paper. That would give him the perfectly drawn outline of a face on his final canvas. That was when he'd show me.

And then he went quiet, and forgot me, and started to concentrate.

Sitting in silence left me all the time in the world to mull over the disquieting conversation I'd had yesterday with Dame Alice, when, as I hunted in her kitchen kingdom for more pipkins for the brewing of ginger tea, she'd mat-erialised out of a pantry with a mess of capons' brains for the next dinner in her big raw hands, encased in a grey-white pastry coffin ready for cooking. She had her usual entourage of boy servants behind her, loaded down with two headless capon corpses, bags of sugar, baskets of oranges, and jars of cloves, mace and cinnamon, and she was about to supervise the business of collecting knives and pots for the scaldings and boilings and stewings that would give us another celebration meal. Having guests, especially one as appreciative of a hearty meat dish as Master Hans, gave her the opportunity she was always looking for to show off her culinary skills. She was always saying Father didn't properly enjoy her cooking: he only ever took a little from whatever dish was nearest to him (though we all knew he had a furtive taste for her mess of eggs and cream). She was clearly planning to cook up a storm for Master Hans, and looking forward to her afternoon. But when she saw me near the spit, hesitating over two of the little copper pipkins hanging up around the fire that she had so carefully scoured with sand before Master Hans's arrival (not that she'd expected him to go near the kitchen – it had just been an excuse to use up some of her vast resources of practical energy), she sent the boys off to the storeroom again for nutmeg. For all her lack of Latin and frank scorn of book-learning, she had an innate sensitivity to other people's moods, and she must have seen the yearning for a moment's privacy on my face. So even though she looked curious to see me in the kitchen, she asked no prying questions, just said kindly, 'Take the smaller one if you want to make one of your potions. I use the big one for cream.' And waited.

I was embarrassed for a moment. Naturally I didn't want to tell her I was making ginger tea for all three of her More stepdaughters, which would have been as good as telling her straight out that they were all expecting. That was for them to tell. But something about the good-humoured way she was looking at me – with the same twinkle in her small eyes that I'd warmed to when I first arrived at the house in Bucklersbury, the same take-it-or-leave-it offer of low-key friendliness – made me think I could, perhaps, sound her out, as I had John, about my worries about Father. Perhaps she, too, would laugh away my fears, I thought hopefully. Now that I sensed happiness was possible, and probably not far away, it made sense to learn how to reach out and try to grab it.

I wanted to be brave. But I didn't like to come straight out with a question about why she thought Father would be holding a man prisoner in our gatehouse. I had no idea whether she even knew the man was there. Still, I came as close as I dared. 'Are you cooking for our guest?' I asked, smiling innocently back. 'I like watching him wolf down your food. And it's good to see Father so taken up with the idea of the picture.' I was feeling for words. 'It's been a long time since he thought of anything except the King's business. Sometimes I worry . . .' I drew in a deep breath and plunged ahead. 'Do you ever think Father's got – well, harder – since we came to Chelsea?'

'Harder?' she said, but lightly, as if I'd asked something that made her feel cheerful. The invitation to confide that I thought I'd seen in her eyes wasn't there any more; a different thought had clearly come into her mind. Her smile broadened and her hands settled on her hips, and there was a housewife's satisfaction in the look she gave her big, efficient new kitchen. 'Well, if he has, it was about time too. I don't mind having the odd good honest craftsman staying here, with some sensible skill to sell, like Master Hans, but it was high time your father put all those other wasters out of the door and got on with his career. And that's been much easier since we moved away from town, where any Tom, Dick or Harry could come calling and then move in for months on end. And did. No, I can't say I miss all that London foolishness at all.'

I sighed. That wasn't the answer I'd wanted. She wasn't talking about Father's deepening fascination with heretic-hunting at all. She was off on her old hobby-horse instead:

the fecklessness of our former guests, the foreign human-ists, talking in that comical way she so often slipped into, playing the grumpy, shrewish wife to the hilt.

'Erasmus and the rest of them,' she said, as if I hadn't realised; nodding as if I and everyone else must naturally think of them as nuisances, beginning to laugh mockingly to herself at the memory of them. 'All those clever-clever ex-priests. Too clever for their own good. Messing about with words, puffed up with pride, letting the devil in through the back door without even noticing half the time, no doubt, and bone idle, the lot of them.'

She took the two nutmegs that the boy was now holding out to her, nodded her thanks without looking at him, and put them down on the wooden table, carrying straight on, on her tide of well-rehearsed indignation.

'Now, the ones your father first got to know when he was a young man – the English ones, Linacre and Dean Colet – well, clearly they had their hearts in the right place,' she was saying, obviously choosing to take my silence for sympathy and warming to her theme. 'I've only heard good things about them. Setting up schools for poor boys, healing the sick. John Clement too: a decent, kind man.'

She paused. Although my gaze was suddenly fixed to the floor, I thought I felt her shrewd eyes on my face. All I could do was pray that I showed no trace of the wave of secret happiness sweeping through my heart at the sound of his name – a feeling made up of fragments of memo-ries that could not be shared with a stepmother, however kindly, of lips and tongues and the roughness of his jaw against my cheek and the strength his long arms had as they pulled me against him, and the man-smells of leather and sandalwood that lingered on his skin. But if she noticed any tell-tale signs of love on my face, she made no sign of it. She simply drew breath and swept on: 'I'm all for people who do some good in the world. But I never had any time for those others. The foreigners. The big talkers. Eating me out of house and home without even noticing what they'd had put in front of them. Sitting at my table chattering away in Greek without so much as a please or thank you. And keeping my husband up all night waffling on about nothing – philosophy, translating poetry, putting the Church to rights – without ever doing one sensible thing to make a single person's life better.'

She narrowed her eyes in comic exasperation, so that I began to laugh along with her. I knew the stories as well as she did, but she had a gift of timing that forced you to laugh in the right places. 'Ohhh, how my fingers used to itch to box that Erasmus' ears sometimes when he started teasing your father about being a "total courtier",' she said, raising her hands in the air as if she was about to box those vanished ears now. 'Your father was the cleverest lawyer in London long before they all moved in with us. It was quite right for him to go on thinking about advancing his career, not just sitting around with a bunch of blabbermouths, wafting himself away on a cloud of hot air. The last thing I wanted was that dried-up Dutchman putting him off.

'He was the worst, but I couldn't be doing with any of them, to be honest,' she added more seriously. 'Prate prate prate about reforming one thing and fiddling with another, changing this and improving that. They took themselves far too seriously for my liking. Nothing was ever quite good enough for them. My motto is, take life as you find it. Go to Mass. Give alms to the poor. Do your business. Advance yourself as God wills. And enjoy what He brings. Have your babies, love your family, look after your old folk. Have your play-acting evenings if you will; play the lute if you must. But don't get so carried away with your foolish ideas that you put others off living their lives.'

87

I moved a step forward, raising my hand, hoping I could get her to pay proper attention to a franker version of my question now her familiar flow of words had reached its natural end. 'That's just what I mean. Don't you think Father's more carried away by ideas now than he ever was when Erasmus lived with us?' I said quickly. 'With all this business of hunting down heretics? He's always away, and even when he is here with us he always seems to be cooped up in the New Building writing some angry denunciation or other. And I don't remember him being angry before. I never thought of anger as being his nature. The ideas he used to have with Erasmus always made him laugh. Doesn't that worry you?'

She didn't quite meet my eyes this time. Dame Alice would never actually lie, but it now occurred to me that this one small bodily sin of omission might indeed signal worry. Yet if she was anxious she wasn't about to share her fears with me, or perhaps even admit them to herself. I should have known that from the start. She was too much of a pragmatist to start wailing and beating her breast about anything she couldn't do something about. She liked looking on the bright side of life too much. Perhaps she'd even brought out her old rant about Erasmus to choke off my first question.

So I wasn't altogether surprised when, instead of answering, she picked up the nearest capon and the small cleaver that the second boy had laid by her hand before slipping away, theatrically measured the distance between bird and implement, and began rhythmically chopping off small legs and wings. 'Much better to be the King's man and the friend of bishops is what I say, and doing a sensible job of work,' she pronounced firmly. Chop went the blade in her hand. 'Archbishop Warham: a sensible, God-fearing man.' The cleaver rose again. 'John Fisher, Cuthbert Tunstall,' – chop – an approving look at the neat cut –

'good men too.' She placed the pieces carefully in the pot. 'Even Cardinal Wolsey,' she added, looking for an easy laugh to shift us back to the jocular kind of conversation she felt happier with. 'He might be greedy and devious, Wolsey, and too worldly for a good Churchman, but at least he appreciates good cooking,' she finished triumphantly. 'He had three helpings of my capon in orange sauce at Candlemas. And he's praised it to the heavens every time I've seen him since.'

With a determined smile, Dame Alice brought her cooking anecdote to its cheery close and swept off to the fireplace to harass the waiting kitchen boys to hook the pot up and start boiling the capons. She might like to be seen as straightforward, but Dame Alice could be as much a mistress of diplomatic half-truths and evasions as any courtier. She clearly didn't want to discuss any worries I might have about Father. I wasn't going to get a chance now to raise the matter of the prisoner in the gatehouse, either, because our talk was firmly over. She was off hustling a boy out to fetch more kindling and water. She still wasn't looking me in the eye. And, somewhere in her rush of words, the comfort I'd briefly taken from John Clement telling me Father could only be keeping a prisoner here for the man's own protection had been quietly swept away.

Hans Holbein looked at the glowing, fierce face of this tall, skinny, unworldly English girl, with her piercing eyes and angular movements, trying her best to stay still although some sort of worry kept furrowing her brow and making her very nearly fidget, and, for reasons he didn't understand, found himself remembering Magdalena. The softness of her: the ripeness of shoulders and breasts, the honey of her eyes, the vague scents of violets and roses. And the deceit. The soft mouth-shaped bruises on her neck. The confused look in her eyes when he asked where they came from; her silly explanation, murmured so gently that he was almost ready to believe they really could be gnat bites. The sheets on her bed, already rumpled and warm and sweaty on that last evening, when he'd tumbled her into it after a hard day at the printshop with Bonifacius and Myconius and Frobenius. More 'gnat bites' on her: on breasts and belly and buttocks. And the hot red imprint of his palm on her white cheek, and her hands both fluttering up to hold the place he'd hit her as he slammed the door and clattered off back down the stairs, practically howling with his own pain. His last memory of her: wounded eyes staring uncomprehendingly back at him.

Well, Magdalena was who she was. He shouldn't have asked more of her. She had her own way to make in the world, after all, and times were hard. There weren't many pickings for an artist's model any more. And so, when a few months later Master Mayer turned out to have taken her under his wing ('a young widow . . . angelically beautiful,' the old fool kept burbling), Hans made no bones about painting her face into Master Mayer's family chapel as the Virgin of Mercy protecting the old man and his various wives and children, dead and alive, from ill-fortune. Master Mayer could believe whatever nonsense he wanted in the privacy of his own home. Hans Holbein wasn't going to argue with such a good patron. But he knew he'd never look without scepticism at another religious picture after that. He probably wouldn't paint any more religious pictures, either. He'd had enough of dressing women of dubious virtue up in blue robes and pretending they were Madonnas. All that was just play-acting, children's stories. What he wanted now was to portray the real-life faces and personalities of the people God had put on this earth to enchant and torment each other, without costumes, without artifice. To get at the truth.

But he was a bear at home. Snarling at poor Elsbeth,

90

till her face turned as sour and rough as those hands sticking out from under her pushed-up sleeves, permanently reddened from tanning hides. Hating the stink of leather up his nostrils all the time, till even his food tasted of animal skins and poverty. Hating little Philip's endless whining; yelling at Elsbeth's scared-looking boy to take better care of the child. Even hating the long-winded abstract talk of his humanist friends, whom he usually admired. Part of him was now blaming them for his gloom – for starting the whole upheaval of these evil times with their clever-clever talk about the corruption of the clergy and their desire to purify the Church. Look where those ideas had landed everyone now. And look how panicked the humanists and even the most determined of the reformers were, at the violent enthusiasm of the mob for their elegantly formulated ideas – even Brother Luther, thundering 'strike, stab, slay' from his Wittenberg pulpit in a vain attempt to stop the thugs destroying civilisation.

Suddenly Hans Holbein hated the humanists' silly, clever faces; suddenly even the Latin names they chose to call themselves seemed pretentious. His brother Prosy, under their influence, had renamed himself Ambrosius; Hans wasn't so grand, and, in his current black mood, resented the Latinised name they insisted on calling him: Olpeius. If they had to be foolish enough to call him something classical, the only name he'd have liked was the one they were always giving Albrecht Dürer – the only real compliment a painter could desire – Apelles, the greatest painter of antiquity, the court artist to Philip of Macedon and a famous portraitist. So he sat knocking back tankard after tankard at the tavern with them, in thunderous silence, hating whey-faced Myconius's thin mockery: 'Poor love-struck Olpeius – drowning his sorrows in beer.'

And there was no work, or hardly any. With the hate-filled, frightening turn public life was taking – now that the peasants' revolts in the countryside had given way to mobs of image-breakers roaming the city streets and smashing windows and burning devotional pictures and hacking statues to bits – the rich weren't keen on displaying their wealth by having frescoes painted on their houses. And of course there was no new work to be had in churches that were being stripped down and whitewashed. Painters' studios were closing down on all sides. Woodcarvers and carpenters were fighting over the same menial tradesmen's work. And there was a limit to how hard you could fight for the few book-engraving jobs or tavern sign commissions that still came on the market.

It had been so exciting before. Before the year of doom three years ago, when all the planets coalesced in the constellation of the fish and brought chaos and destruction. In the days when Magdalena had always been there in his studio, ready to drape her naked form in whatever scrap of velvet or silk he could find to pose for him. When there had still been enough work to justify keeping a model. When he personally had more work than he could cope with, doing the pictures for both Adam Petri's and Thomas Wolff's versions of Luther's New Testament in German – and getting an extra payment from Tommi Wolff, as well as an extra dose of grinning thanks from the impish little blond man, Basel's biggest charmer, with his fangy teeth, sparkling eyes and that dark mole on his right cheek, for making his best best-seller even more of a success – a payment big enough to buy Magdalena a dress and give Elsbeth extra housekeeping money. Well, they were good pictures, after all.

He had read the New Testament properly for the first time (his Latin had never been up to much; it was one of the things that the humanist circle that met at Johannes Froben's publishing works laughed at him for). And he was painting at his peak – able, for the first time, to show the divine truth as he knew it really was in the Book; without recourse to a priest or a preacher to tell him how they read it. And he had felt enlightened. Purified. Transfigured by the truth.

Hans Holbein was all right for longer than most people, after things went wrong, because he had the Rathaus fresco commission. But then the burghers got scared of his daring design for the last wall – respectable if hypocritical Jews shrinking away from the presence of Jesus, in the parable of the woman taken in adultery; Christ warning the Jews, 'Let him who is without sin cast the first stone.' So the respectable if hypocritical burghers cut off his contract. They preferred looking at a blank wall to being reminded that their integrity might also be questioned. And the money stopped.

The last straw was his Dance of Death engravings. Forty-one of them, using every ounce of imagination and passion he possessed. He started them after his father died. They were the only way he had to show the truth about today as he saw it, through a theme he chose for himself without any interference from a patron. Two years' work: his and Hans Luetzelberger's blockmaking skill combined in merciless mockery of every one of the failings and offences of the age's corrupt priests, the powerful and pious and their bedazzled followers. All exposed as vanity-filled frauds at the moment they met Death. The Pope crowning an emperor, waving a Papal bull, full of hubris – and surrounded by devils. Death coming to the Judge, accepting a bribe from a wealthy litigant while a poor plaintiff looked disconsolately on. Death coming to the Monk, who, even though his calling meant he should have been prepared, was trying frantically to escape, clutching his money box. No one would publish the pictures. The Council was scared. Erasmus had told them not to publish inflammatory pamphlets, and – too late – they'd begun to heed his advice.

Then, last summer, Hans Luetzelberger died. Bankrupt. The creditors settled on his goods like scavengers. The Dance of Death blocks ended up being snapped up by a printer in Lyon and shut up in a storeroom. And Hans Holbein hadn't got a penny out of any of it.

'Go travelling,' Erasmus said phlegmatically. 'Take a *Wanderjahr.* Go to quiet places where all this trouble isn't happening. Learn something new; find new patrons; get your heartache out of your system.' Erasmus never stopped travelling. True, he had to stay on the move these days. He'd just come back to Basel – still a relatively civilised and free-thinking place – after three years in Louvain; Louvain had got too militantly Catholic for his taste, but he was already worried that Basel was going too far the other way. Still, Erasmus genuinely didn't mind taking to the road. He'd always travelled. Then again, he was a famous man; there were homes for him everywhere, and people begging him to endorse their religion or their political beliefs just by living among them. He had it easy.

So Hans Holbein cut the old Dutchman off in mid-flow, just as he was pronouncing his favourite maxim: 'Live every day as though it were your last; study as though you will live forever,' and asked, abruptly, 'How could I travel? And where to?'

Hans Holbein wasn't scared of moving. He and Prosy had managed to set themselves up in Basel when they were young men, after their father went bankrupt in Augsberg and even Uncle Sigmund started suing him for thirty-four miserable florins, the old skinflint. Hans had talked his way boldly into job after job – fresco painting and chapel decorating jobs he'd never actually done before, and certainly had no expertise in. But he'd coped. People trusted him. And he felt at ease with talking up his talents. No client of his would be disappointed in the results he produced. His kit packed up small and he was ready for anything. He'd been to Italy and France to look at the paintings of the south, and got back safely. He just needed practical advice.

'Go to Aegidius in Antwerp,' Erasmus said without a pause. 'He can introduce you to Quentin Massys, who painted both our portraits long ago. Quentin's a man of talent – he could help you. Or go to Morus in London. He can introduce you to people. England is full of rich men.'

Hans Holbein pocketed Erasmus' loan and went travelling, saying goodbye to Elsbeth and the children and the stink of the tannery without more than a moment's sadness. She was pregnant again, but she'd be all right. She had the business to keep her, and the money he was going to make on his travels would make it up to her later. He was beginning to feel ashamed of the passion he'd felt for a younger, lovelier woman. He didn't want to face up to the uncomfortable truth of how badly he'd behaved. He needed to get away from the resigned knowledge in Elsbeth's eyes. He went by cart and on foot and slowly. Pieter Gillis in Antwerp (Hans Holbein refused to call him Aegidius) hadn't been particularly helpful. But he'd got here in the end, had a quick stroke of luck with that easy commission from Archbishop Warham, and he could see straightaway that things would work out for him in London. It was just as Erasmus said. It might be cold and muddy in these streets, but it was quiet, and everyone was rich. And he hadn't thought of Magdalena for more than an instant in months.

So he was irritated to have his senses invaded again by the cloying memory of her as he looked at this English girl who was so unlike her. This long-nosed girl, Meg Giggs, whose dark blue eyes were snapping with intelligence in her pale face; who was leaning forward in her chair, ready to engage him in sprightly conversation, visibly trying to think of simple ways to talk to this foreigner whose grasp of her language was slow and whose grasp of Latin was almost non-existent.

'Do you think,' Meg was saying now, speaking slowly and carefully for his benefit, pushing back the messy wisps of black hair that were escaping from her headdress without really noticing them, and looking earnest (she didn't make much of herself, though he could see she'd be pretty if she only tried a bit harder), 'that it's – vain – to have your portrait painted?'

Practically the first thing Nicholas Kratzer, the astronomer here, had told him in German, in a whisper of warning during dinner, was 'They'll all try and get you to talk philosophy with them. But don't, for God's sake, talk about anything serious until the two of us have had a proper talk and I've explained how things here are – because nothing is quite the way it seems. And loose talk could get you into trouble.' Which sounded worrying. But Hans Holbein was so disarmed by the gravity in Meg Giggs's face and voice as she asked her un-girlish question that he stopped worrying. He just burst out laughing.

'I meant it seriously,' she said, looking nettled, though with a flush coming into her cheeks that she probably didn't realise softened her face into prettiness. 'It wasn't a silly question.' She was talking faster, going pinker, and getting cleverer by the second. 'It's what Thomas à Kempis wrote, isn't it – that you should renounce the world and not be proud of your beauty or accomplishments?' And then she began quoting: '"*Let this be thy whole endeavour, this thy prayer, this thy desire: that thou mayest be stripped of all selfishness, and with entire simplicity follow Jesus only; mayest die to thyself, and live eternally to me. Then shalt thou be rid of all vain fancies, causeless perturbations and superfluous cares.*" . . . That's what I mean. If you think that way, then you'd think a portrait was a vanity bordering on blasphemy, wouldn't you?'

She stopped, a bit breathless, and looked provocatively at him. Hans Holbein had never seen a woman looking provocative in this completely unflirtatious way, any more than he'd ever come across a woman who had read the *Imitation of Christ*. She was challenging his mind instead of his body. But Erasmus had told him about More's family school. This must be what happened to women when you taught them Latin and Greek and the skills of argument. He'd stopped laughing a while back; now he put down his silverpoint pencil, and nodded more respectfully. But there was still a smile on his lips. 'You look like an elegant young gentlewoman,' he said, liking the challenge, feeling as though he was home again and about to get caught up in one of the involved conversations at Froben's print house that he now missed so much; 'but I see you have the mind of a theologian.'

She tossed her head, more impatiently than in acknowledgement of his compliment. 'But what do you think?' she insisted.

Surprised by himself, Hans Holbein paused to think. He was remembering the hundreds of sketches of faces and bodies he and Prosy had done in their father's studio; not a money-making venture, just a technical exercise, back in the days when capturing a likeness was still considered not as an art form in itself but just a lowly artisan's trick. And he was remembering glamorous Uncle Hans, coming back from his years in Venice full of the new humanist learning and new ideas about painting faces so realistically that you saw the inner truth in them – God in every human feature. Uncle Hans brought the southern ways home and made his fortune making portraits of the great and good from the Pope to Jakob Fugger, Ausburg's richest merchant. He'd been the young Hans Holbein's biggest hero. But the younger artist was also remembering the new reasons for denouncing painting. He was remembering how Prosy had stopped painting altogether a few years back, because – as he liked to say, in his irritatingly dogmatic way, thumping his fist on the tavern table – he wouldn't provide any more 'idolatrous' images of the saints' faces for the churches. What tipped Prosy over the edge was being jailed after he'd publicly abused the clergy for mass superstition, and being forced to apologise to them. Prosy wasn't the only one to react so violently and self-destructively; artists everywhere were giving up their paintbrushes to purify the Church. That was what they kept telling people, anyway. But Hans had no time for this sort of thinking. Prosy shouldn't have gone out on the rampage after too many hours in the tavern. He certainly shouldn't have gone yelling at priests with his red face and his uncouth voice and his unemployed layabout friends. Prosy, who didn't quite have the talent to get the commissions, who'd always struggled with money, and who'd always resented their father for pushing him, as the smarter younger brother, was just the type to fall back on the 'art is idolatry' argument now. In Hans's opinion, all those ex-artists now denouncing art in the name of religious purity were just losers who couldn't get commissions any more and needed excuses to explain their failure.

'I think,' he said slowly, searching for words, becoming fully serious as he engaged with the odd English girl's question. 'I think that Erasmus was right to start having his portraits painted, and engraved, and sold. I felt honoured to make likenesses of him. I don't believe it is right to renounce the world when God has put us in it and our presence here is part of His holy design. You can see God in a human face. And, if God delights in His creation, and in the beauty and talents of the people He put on this earth, why shouldn't we?'

He was a little embarrassed by his own unexpected eloquence. But he was strangely pleased, too, to see it rewarded when she nodded, slowly and approvingly, and thought over what he said. So he told her about getting to know Erasmus while painting his portrait. Three times in the last ten years. 'If I look that good perhaps I should take a wife,' Erasmus said mockingly when he saw the sycophantic first picture; but he went on commissioning more. Then she grinned and threw back her head, and he liked the spark in her eye. It made Hans Holbein think she might even understand something of how becoming so engrossed in form and colour that he didn't notice time passing or hunger in his belly was his passion, his act of worship.

All she said, in a gentler voice, was, 'I'd love to see more of your work one day.'

That was enough to send him rushing awkwardly to the side of the room, where his sketchbooks and copies of the printed books illustrated by his engravings were piled up, to bring her the drawings and copies he kept of the work he was most proud of. He was surprised to find his hands shaking slightly as he reached for them.

Somehow his copies of the three pictures of Magdalena came to the top of the pile. Not just the Madonna that Jakob Mayer had ordered, but also the very first picture, from the early days, when she was Venus, soft-eyed, smiling gently and gesturing alluringly out of the page; and even his revenge portrait, painted in the evenings of those bitter days when he was working on the Madonna painting. Also smiling – but with a flintier tinge to her expression – and holding out her hand again, but this time as if for money. It was the first time he'd looked at this work without being catapulted back into all the emotions of the past. Now he just felt exposed, and anxious about how Meg Giggs would react. But if she noticed any of the feelings he'd filled the three pictures with, she had the restraint not to comment. It was the Virgin of Mercy picture that she stopped at.

'How beautifully you've painted her,' she said neutrally; but it was Hans Holbein's daring innovation in design – the humanist conceit that the Baby Jesus, rather than the Virgin, was blessing and protecting the family with his pudgy, outstretched arm – that caught her attention. 'I like that composition,' she added, with assurance. She admired the rich scarlets and crimsons of sashes and legs. And she praised the background which Uncle Hans had taught his nephew to paint in the Italian style, glowing with earthly life: a luminous sky-blue colour, broken by sunlit branches and oak leaves.

It was only when she reached for the next picture – his tiny copy of the mural of Christ in his tomb – that he began to feel uneasy for more down-to-earth reasons. As she looked with a mixture of fascination and horror at his depiction of a putrefying corpse in a claustrophobic box of a coffin, with its face and the spear wound in its side going blue and its dead eyes staring open, Hans Holbein suddenly remembered Kratzer's warning about not letting himself be drawn into philosophical conversations with these people or revealing his less conventional beliefs. If anything spoke of the reformist belief that religion must be stripped back to nothing but the private relationship between Christ and man – forgetting the whole edifice of the Church which had come between them for so long – this picture, which had shocked even some of the free-thinking humanists, was it. It was so clearly that of a man, not a manifestation of God. Hastily, he put a hand on the portfolio cover, ready to shut it. But her hand was already there, holding it open. Lost in contemplation, she didn't even notice his hand appearing next to hers. But he did, and was so startled by his own effrontery at having so nearly touched her that he pulled his own hand back as if he'd been burned.

She turned her gaze back up at him, unaware of his confusion.

'You are a wonderful painter, Master Hans,' she said warmly. 'I didn't expect you to be such a master.'

If she noticed his dampness and quickness of breath now, she would probably think it just a reaction to her compliment. He smiled awkwardly, and, noticing that her hand had moved, reached for the portfolio cover. He was almost sweating with worry, with more and more memories of what he kept in this folder stabbing back into his mind. The next work down was one of the Dance of Death engravings. And somewhere in the pile was his engraving of the front page of Luther's New Testament (Eleutherius, the Free Man, as Brother Martin had been called while he'd still been part of the humanist brotherhood). It would most definitely be dangerous for the Mores to have any inkling that he'd had anything to do with that.

Reaching over her arm – and noticing, even in the middle of his panic attack, how long her slim fingers were, and finding that only made his heart beat faster still – he finally snapped the cover shut.

'Oh – but can't I see the rest?' she asked, and dimpled up at him.

'Another time,' he said, forcing a genial smile back on his face and gesturing as firmly as he could towards his easel. 'But first we must work.'

He was surprised when they were called for the midday meal. The morning had flashed by, and he'd hardly put more than a few lines of a sketch together. Hans Holbein was ushering Meg Giggs out of the door and towards the great hall when he saw Nicholas Kratzer standing in the shadows, watching him, with a sardonic grin on his bony face.

As Meg took off up the stairs with long, tomboyish strides ('I must tidy myself up!' she said, flashing a backwards smile), Kratzer caught up with him.

'You're smitten,' Kratzer challenged.

Hans Holbein shook his head and looked down at his feet. He liked Kratzer, and thought they would almost certainly become friends while they were both living in this house. But there were things he wasn't willing to share. There was something absurd about an artisan who'd painted house fronts having his heart turned over by a young lady so impossibly out of his reach. He didn't want to look a fool. He didn't want to feel a fool.

'No,' he said stolidly, not meeting Kratzer's eye. 'Just doing my job.'

I tidied out my medicine chest that night.

I couldn't see where I'd put the pennyroyal oil.

It was the excuse I'd been waiting for to write my first letter to John Clement: asking for him to shop for a replacement in Bucklersbury Street, for old times' sake. He'd surely send a reply with the gift. I spent a while wondering whether to mention Dame Alice's evasiveness when I'd tried to ask her about Father, and finally decided not to. I didn't want him to think I was doubting his faith in Father. And then I lost myself, spreading the handwritten sheets over the table, making my writing as elegant as I knew how, in a long account of the portrait-painting and of some, though not all, of Master Hans's previous paintings, and his stories about his father, and his nerves about painting my father, and the endless brewing of ginger tea in recent days, and the three pregnancies, and the walk I'd gone on by myself to the river when I'd finished with Master Hans that morning, to look at the brisk waves on the shingle with young John and Anne Cresacre (whom I'd been more used to taking out walking back in the days when they'd spent their hours of freedom innocently climbing trees and playing tag on the lawns), trying not to notice the way their arms crept so hungrily around each other's waist whenever my gaze was politely averted. (My willingness to avert my gaze so politely, so often, had made me their favourite chaperone in recent days.) Though I didn't write this but hugged myself indulgently in the knowledge of it as I sealed the letter, I'd found it easy enough to look away. Encouraged by their breathlessness and flushed cheeks and sparkling eyes locked on each other, I'd felt myself becoming almost as much of a happy child as my companions. However hard I tried, I hadn't been able to stop myself from seeing, in every boat coming towards us from London, a host of imaginary John Clements, with long legs and elegant backs hunched against the wind, each of them with sky-blue eyes fastened longingly on me as the water brought us closer and closer together.

But even while I was losing myself happily in the rose-petal commonplaces that every lover thinks are unique, I did go on wondering where the little jar of pennyroyal had gone. And, as the house settled into night, that took the edge off my joy. Gradually all the other worries that buzzed round my head like gnats, but which I'd briefly stopped noticing, became louder and more insistent too, and my vision of John Clement's eyes, looking at me with love, faded into uneasy recollections of the man in the garden, Father writing in the New Building, and Master Hans's artwork.

One way or another, I couldn't sleep. My mind was racing. My body was full of unspent energy. I needed to do something. So I went downstairs. I waited till Master Nicholas had shut himself and Master Hans inside his room, and listened outside the door until I heard them unstopper the bottle Master Hans had brought. Once they began to clink glasses and laugh, I tiptoed back downstairs towards the studio. I couldn't get the Christ corpse out of my head. I wanted to see the pictures he hadn't wanted to show me.

It didn't take more than a peep to show what a simpleton

the man was. An engraving of the Pope – surrounded by devils, waving a Papal bull – leapt to my eyes. And right under it was an engraved frontispiece for the New Testament in German. I didn't know the German words, but anyone could understand what '*Das Neuw Testametrecht*' must mean. And the date was 1523, so it must be Luther's work. The discovery was so explosive that it took me a while to notice that Master Hans's drawings of St Peter and St Paul, on either side of the text, were extraordinarily beautiful and finely executed. They didn't look any more the work of the devil than Will Roper had sounded during his flirtation with heresy. But that didn't mean that Father – if he was becoming the persecutor I feared – would hold back if he found out what kind of work his painter had been doing before he appeared in Chelsea. Part of me wished that Hans Holbein and I could talk freely about what kind of God he believed in. I'd never knowingly talked to one of the new men (Will Roper in his Lutheran phase didn't count – he was just a sweet, silly boy having a rebellion) and I wanted to hear for myself what God looked like if you believed whatever it was that the heretics believed. But another part of me was grateful that neither he nor I had tried. It was too frightening. I shut the portfolio cover as hastily as Master Hans had earlier on in the day.

After all the punishment the German merchants at the Steelyard had taken for smuggling their heretical books into London, Master Hans was playing with fire. Literally. It was obvious to me that he'd brought his past work only to show potential clients in the hope of attracting new commissions. But that proved he had no idea of the danger he would face if anyone saw these pictures. If our jolly, open-faced painter was to survive here in these watchful times, he was going to need saving from himself.

Without quite knowing why I was taking it on myself to help – except that I liked his bluff ways – I pushed the portfolio under a table and piled his sketchbooks on top of it to make it harder for anyone else to have an unauthorised snoop. I found a skull and put it on top of the heap. I draped the table with one of Master Hans's scraps of cloth so nothing was visible. Then, wishing I could see my way upstairs without my candle, which marked me out to any observer who might want to come and ask what I was doing, I vanished upstairs.

It was only when I'd reached the solitude of my room, with my heart beating faster than usual, that I wished I'd sneaked a look at Master Hans's portrait of Father so I could tell John about it in my letter. But it was too late now. Knowing what I knew, I wasn't about to go back downstairs.

'I was surprised you didn't come out of your room last night. So much noise,' Master Hans said. His eyes, slightly puffy after what must have been a late night with Master Nicholas, were fixed on his drawing of me. He didn't appear to have noticed that his pictures had been stowed under the table.

'Noise?' I asked.

'Your sister falling down the stairs,' he said, and I could feel him watching me. 'Perhaps she had too much drink. That is not good, with a baby on the way.'

'I didn't hear anything,' I said, feeling a new kind of unease. I must have been too wrapped up in my letter-writing, or asleep. 'Do you mean Elizabeth?' She hadn't come to breakfast.

Master Hans nodded. And suddenly I had a nasty idea about where the pennyroyal might have gone. I needed to get it back. What I hadn't told Elizabeth was that pennyroyal didn't just bring on abortion; it was a dangerous poison that could cause internal bleeding and would kill a mother as easily as an unborn child.

105

The painter must have seen a hint of my alarm and tried to offer reassurance. 'She hurt her ankle, but I helped her up to her room. She fell as I came out of Kratzer's room – right from the top step. But I think she will be all right.'

'Poor Elizabeth,' I said, trying to sound light and natural. 'I didn't hear a thing. I must have been fast asleep. Will you excuse me for a few minutes, Master Hans? I think I'll just run up now and check to see if she's all right.'

She was asleep, sprawled on her bed. She was breathing as lightly and naturally as I'd been trying to sound. I didn't try and wake her. But I did fish around under her bed. The bottle was hidden there. She must have stolen it. I breathed out in relief when I saw it was still full. I put it back in my medicine chest, locked it carefully, and took the key back downstairs with me.

'She's fine, Master Hans,' I said, as I settled myself back into my pose.

He furrowed his brow. He wasn't ready to drop the subject. 'I think she is worried, to be going up and down corridors in the night and falling down stairs,' he said a little dogmatically. 'So, I know she is married and happy to be a mother. But this is an accident that often happens to a woman who is unhappy to find she will have a child.'

For someone who was so blissfully unaware of danger to himself, I thought with new respect, he was acute enough at observing other people's feelings.

'Sometimes it is difficult for sisters to talk to sisters, brothers to brothers,' he went on. Then he did his big belly laugh. 'Now, my brother is impossible to talk reason to! But perhaps you will talk and make sure she is all right.'

'I'll definitely have a chat with her when she wakes up,' I said, impressed by the kindness of his heart. 'But she's happy. You don't need to worry.'

I only wished I believed it.

*   *   *

Mary, the cook, was back from market. Two serving boys were unpacking packages and baskets and scurrying off with them towards the kitchen. I noticed her through the glass when Master Hans and I came out of the studio; and I saw Elizabeth, coming out to take the weak sunshine, called to her side. Mary delved into the big bag she had propped on the seat beside her and pulled out two letters and a bottle. Her big raw arms pushed both of them under Elizabeth's nose. I saw Elizabeth take both and look at them. Then I saw her pick up the bottle and give it a long stare. Then she put it back down, and, with very visible composure, took just one of the letters and walked slowly back inside. She was shielding her eyes against the sun, but she saw me as she pushed the outside door quietly shut.

'Mary has something for you from town,' she said, looking down.

And she continued her slow path towards the stairs.

Only when her back was turned to me, and I was already stepping blinking into the daylight to collect my letter, did it cross my mind that the last sound that had come from Elizabeth might have been a stifled sob.

'Love letter for you, too, Miss Meg,' Mary said hoarsely as soon as she saw me. She had a ribald sense of humour: all letters were love letters to her. 'And a love potion to go with it, I don't doubt.' She cackled.

It was a jar of pennyroyal oil. Forgetting everything else, I reached for the letter that went with it and, just managing to restrain myself for long enough to put a few paces between myself and Mary as I turned towards the garden's main avenue, tore it open. '*My darling Meg,*' began the short note, in the spiky writing I remembered so well:

*I can hardly convey my happiness: first at the joy
of our meeting, with all its promise for the future,
then the pleasure of receiving your note. Here is
the gift you were asking for. You will see from the
speed of my reply that I went straight to
Bucklersbury to buy it. The first person I saw there
was Mad Davy – still alive, though with precious
few teeth these days, and a lot more wrinkles. As
soon as he knew I was shopping for you, he sent
his fondest respects and tried to sell me a piece of
unicorn's horn to bring you eternal youth. I told
him you were looking enchantingly beautiful, and
were the picture of youth, and he'd do better to
keep it for himself. He insisted he'd only lost his
teeth because he got into a brawl. I didn't like to
ask how he'd mislaid his hair.*

I laughed out loud, with sunshine pouring into my soul,
and turned a corner as I turned over the page, so no one's
prying eyes could see my blushes and probably foolish
smiles.

It was a while before I came in, with the letter carefully
tucked inside my dress. While I was still dazzled in the
house's darkness, I hid it in my room, in my medicine
chest, locked away with the new jar of pennyroyal. I could
hear voices in Elizabeth's room: at least one voice, hers,
raised in the querulous tones that were becoming characteristic of her.

I didn't like to interfere. I still felt uncomfortable when
I remembered William's barely polite refusal of my first
attempt to help. But he wasn't there; he was in London;
and, when I looked in the corridor, I saw her door was
open. So I plucked up my courage and put my head inside.
Slightly to my surprise, it was Master Hans who was with
her. Sitting at a chair by the bed where she was reclining;

with a little posy of snowdrops from near the front door beginning to wilt from the heat of his forgetful bear-hands. He must have picked a few flowers and trotted straight off after her. He was leaning forward and murmuring something comforting. Her eyes were red-rimmed; but she was already composed enough to smile at me with dignity.

'Oh Meg,' she said brightly. 'Could you possibly find a little vase? Look what Master Hans has brought me. Aren't they lovely?'

'I am telling Mistress Elizabeth,' he said, with a touch of embarrassment on his broad features, as he brazened out my gaze, 'how to have a baby is the most beautiful thing anyone can ever hope for. A miracle in everyday life. And how lucky she is to have this joy ahead.'

He blushed slightly. Surprised at his forceful enthusiasm, I asked: 'I didn't know you had a family, Master Hans?' A little unwillingly, as if he didn't want to discuss this with me, he nodded. 'In Basel?' I went on, and he looked down and nodded again.

'Tell me again – tell Meg – what it was like when you first looked at little Philip,' Elizabeth interrupted, and even if she didn't really want to look at me there was a hint of pretty pink back in her cheeks, and her eyes were fixing his and drawing him back into the conversation I'd interrupted. 'When the midwife held him out to you . . .'

'She said he was the spitting image of his father . . . and I couldn't believe that this tiny bundle of white could be a person at all. And then I looked into his eyes, and he was staring at me so curiously, from big blue eyes, wide open and watching everything, and blowing kisses and bubbles out of his tiny mouth. And I saw his little hands were the same shape as my big German bear's paws, ha ha!' said Master Hans, warming up to his theme again. His eyes were sparkling with memory. 'That's when I knew what love was.'

'That's beautiful,' Elizabeth whispered. 'And what about your wife – did she feel the same way?'

And they were off on a long conversation about childbirth, and prayer, and the shortness of pain, and what happens to women's hearts after they see the child they've carried for so many months for the first time. They didn't need me, and I couldn't join in – I didn't know the feelings they were talking about. But I was pleased to see Elizabeth beginning to look reassured. Perhaps she'd just been scared, in these last days, of the heaviness of pregnancy or the pain of childbirth, or fearful of leaving her own childhood behind. Whatever it was, Master Hans must have guessed. It was unorthodox to come visiting her in her room; but he was clearly doing her good.

Quietly, I took the sagging snowdrops out of his hand. I arranged them in a little glass by Elizabeth's bed. And I moved the letter on her bedside table to make way for the glass. As I did so, I recognised the spiky writing I'd loved for so long. John's writing. Stifling my sudden indrawn breath, I folded it into my hand.

Murmuring an excuse, I left the room. I needn't have bothered excusing myself. Master Hans's head followed me for a moment, but Elizabeth hardly noticed me go, so deep was she in this earthy new kind of talk.

I had no qualms about opening the letter. There was too much I didn't know about John Clement to pass up any opportunity of knowing more. There was no doubt in my mind, no morality, just crystal clarity of purpose. But this note was short and formal. Shorter than the one he'd written me. '*My dear Elizabeth,*' it said:

I write to congratulate you. I hear that you and William are to have a child in the autumn. You will remember from the classroom that my favourite advice has always been: look forward, not back. Your

husband is a good man with an excellent career
ahead of him; I wish you both every happiness in
your family life.

By the time I'd got this far, my conscience had caught up with my hands. I didn't usually think twice about inspecting any correspondence that might relate to me; life is too uncertain not to look after yourself any way you can. But this was a harmless expression of formal good wishes, a private matter not intended for me. Feeling awkward at the contrast between my own cold-hearted prying and the warmth being shown by Master Hans, a stranger in our midst, I slipped back in, plumped up Elizabeth's pillows, rearranged her quilt, and contrived to drop the letter back on the floor by her bed. She'd think it had simply fallen down; she'd never guess I'd looked it over. Then I went away properly, secretly relieved to leave the two of them to their conversation, which had turned to full-blooded midwives' anecdotes about waters breaking and forceps that I didn't much like the sound of – but which the usually fastidious Elizabeth seemed to be finding fascinating. If I'd been a different person – less self-contained, less able to reason – I might even have felt a little jealous that she was so effectively managing to monopolise the attention of my new friend the painter. But I'd never been the jealous type. I was pleased she was finding comfort in his gory stories, even if I didn't really want to stay and listen.

So I went back out to the garden to find a patch of sunlight far from the gatehouse where I could close my mind to everything but the warmth on my back and the drifting clouds of blossom all around, and sit and murmur 'he loves me not, he loves me' as I pulled the petals off daisies, like a lovelorn milkmaid, and read my own letter over and over again until I knew it by heart.

*   *   *

Hans Holbein felt almost unbearably sorry for the pitiful little scrap of femininity huddled up in the bed, hating her life. He hadn't completely understood all the words in her wounded outpouring: 'It was me who found John Clement and brought him here – and he as good as ignored me when he got here, and just talked to Meg, and went away without so much as a word. They all do that: talk philosophy to clever Meg Giggs and Greek to intellectual Margaret Roper. No one here has time to waste on an ordinary girl – someone with nothing better to recommend her than a pretty face. And now he's sent the kind of pompous little note a stranger might write. As if he hardly knows me. As if I'm nothing to him . . .' But Hans Holbein had understood the sense of what she was saying; he knew she was feeling something like the howling pain he'd felt with Magdalena. And when she bit her lip, and tears started out of her eyes, and she began to furtively dash them away, he wanted to give her a big comforting hug and tell her any sensible man should love her for her lovely eyes and her heart-shaped face. But he couldn't tell her that. Who was he to tell a client's daughter things like that? It was her husband's job. But it wasn't difficult to see Elizabeth was in love with the wrong man. And who should rightly comfort a married woman crying because a man not her husband was being too distant with her (and not distant enough with her witty, bookish sister) – even Hans Holbein, with his respect for truth, couldn't tell. He was too fascinated himself by Meg Giggs's awkward movements, blazing eyes and odd ideas to fail to understand if other men also fell under her spell.

Personally, he couldn't see the attraction of John Clement. The older man he'd shared a wherry with down the river might have chiselled, fine, noble features and a handsome athlete's body. He might speak Greek and know medicine. But his pale, kind eyes didn't have any of the fierce glitter of intelligence that you could see in More's eyes, or Erasmus', or, for that matter, young Meg's. You could see at once that his mind wasn't of the same calibre as those of the people around him. He gave the impression, too, that he'd fought hard battles in his past and learned what failure was. If Hans Holbein had been feeling more objective, he'd have admitted more easily to a grudging respect for a man who he also felt had probably learned to accept his defeats gracefully and find a different kind of victory in adapting to new circumstances. But Holbein had taken against the other man, with a rivalrous male prickle of muscle and brawn. He wasn't about to give John Clement the benefit of any doubt. The man was a loser, he'd decided; it would be better for both women if they could see it too.

But it wouldn't help Elizabeth to tell her his opinion of John Clement. The one thing about women that he knew for sure was the fierce, devoted way they fell in love with their babies. The kindest thing he could do for Elizabeth was to hold out that hope to her – that a happiness she couldn't yet imagine was waiting around the corner. Over the next few days, he made it his business to walk in the garden every afternoon with Elizabeth. He found her birds' eggs and pretty pebbles. He sketched her little newborn cherubs. And – stifling his guilt about Elsbeth alone in Basel with two children to feed and his baby growing in her belly – he talked about the joys of bringing life into the world.

It was a relief to do this small good deed every day, because Hans Holbein was worrying about his work. His picture of Sir Thomas wasn't coming out the way he'd imagined when Erasmus had first talked to him about the man who was the witty, humble, perfect model of humanist friendship. Hans Holbein was beginning to wish he hadn't got drunk two nights in a row with Nicholas Kratzer, and heard from him the frightened stories the Germans of the Steelyard had been telling about his employer ever since he'd smashed his way into their London enclave at the head of a troop of men at arms. The merchants were sitting innocently down to dinner in their hall at Cousin Lane, next to their river mooring with its wooden crane, hungry after offloading all the day's import of grain and wax and linen safely into their storehouses, when a scowling Thomas More, with dark shadows about the chin and surrounded by a bristle of swords, burst in on them, hunting for heretics. 'I have been sent by the Cardinal. Partly because one of you has been clipping coins; but also because we have reliable news that many of you possess books by Martin Luther. You are known to be importing these books. You are known to be causing grave error in the Christian faith among His Majesty's subjects.' He arrested three of the merchants and had his men drag them off into the night. He had a list of the rest drawn up by dawn. The next morning he was back, watching, narrow-eyed, thin-lipped, as his heavies searched rooms and slashed into boxes. Eight more Germans were forced off to Cardinal Wolsey that day to be rebuked.

It was a mistake to know about that. It was even more of a mistake to know that Kratzer, whose wit and humour had earned him not only Sir Thomas's patronage here but even that of Cardinal Wolsey, might rely on having powerful English admirers promoting his work, and also freely admitted to enjoying Sir Thomas's company and the sharpness of his mind when they talked, but at the same time secretly considered himself among the freest of freethinkers. The astronomer boasted (true, only in a whisper, and in the safety of German; a patron respected all over Christendom was a patron worth keeping, even if he hadn't been so confusingly likeable as More was from the safety of his own household) of having written to Hans Holbein's hero, Albrecht Dürer, to congratulate him on Nuremberg turning 'all evangelical' and to wish him God's grace to persevere in the reformed belief. Because all that secret knowledge – and the open knowledge that Sir Thomas suspected the German merchants skulking uneasily around the Steelyard of being the main conduit for the smuggling of heresy into England – was coming out in his picture. And the face looking back at him from the easel now was the face of the persecutor: with red-rimmed eyes, a narrow mouth and grasping hands.

Even the composition wouldn't come right. He'd meant to put a *memento mori* in the corner. But his usual prop – the skull he often used for the purpose of warning his sitters and viewers against worldly vanity – had somehow gone missing in his mess. Someone must have tidied it away somewhere, or he'd buried it under an avalanche of books or boots. He'd never been good at keeping track of things. He had no idea where in London to go to lay hands on a human skull – except to the Steelyard, where at least he could understand what was said to him without difficulty. But he also knew it would be worse than impolitic to go near the Steelyard.

He couldn't shake off the worry. It nagged at him while Meg sat for him every morning. He fretted secretly during his afternoon walks. He obsessed through the evenings over the painting that wouldn't come right.

And when he wasn't worrying about More's picture, he was worrying over what Meg Giggs felt about Clement. Meg glowed with secretive radiance. And he'd noticed that she had started slipping outside to the cart to see the cook every morning, to ask for messages from town. If he only knew her better, he'd be better able to tell whether her sparkling eyes meant she was in love. But he couldn't see into her heart; she was as unreadable as a dazzle of sun on water.

He didn't dare ask directly. He was afraid of the anger

that any forwardness might spark in Meg's eyes. He sensed that she wasn't someone who would take well to being interrogated. But, as her portrait began to take shape, Hans Holbein found himself fishing cautiously for information.

'Do you know,' he said, with his back to her, mixing paint, 'that I published John Clement's likeness more than ten years ago, back in Basel?'

'You said something about it once,' she replied, ready to be engaged; with a sinking heart he noted her quickening interest as soon as Clement's name came up.

'Well, it wasn't really his likeness, as it turns out,' he said awkwardly. 'Your father has explained everything to me now. But I thought it was at the time. You see, I drew the frontispiece for a Basel edition of *Utopia*.'

Now he had her attention.

Holbein had spent his first day in Chelsea wondering whether this (old) John Clement had anything to do with the (young) John Clement whose picture he'd drawn, on Erasmus' instruction, ten years before, when *Utopia* had just come out. More's book had sold so well that Johannes Froben wanted some of the action; Erasmus had arranged for a new edition and got More's permission to republish. The mischievous story was ironically framed by an account of how a sailor with a liking for tall tales described Utopia – the perfect society – to More himself, his real-life friend Pieter Gillis of Antwerp and the character whom the author called '*puer meus*': John Clement.

'So naturally I drew a boy. With long hair. Fifteen years old at most. I've got it here somewhere,' Hans Holbein said now, gesturing helplessly around the worsening chaos of paints and pictures and props behind him, wondering for a moment at Meg Giggs's sudden, secretive flash of a grin. 'And then I got here and saw the real John Clement. And he's not so young – he could be my father! So I was embarrassed. I realised I'd done a bad job. And I thought your father would sack me on the spot for being a bad painter, ha ha!'

Meg was smiling more gently now, seeing and hearing his professional discomfiture. 'But Master Hans,' she said softly, 'it was only a turn of phrase. Father just meant that John Clement was his protégé – not that he was really a young boy. John Clement was working as his secretary on a mission to the Low Countries while Father wrote *Utopia*. But you weren't to know that. You were quite right to illustrate the words "*puer meus*" with a picture of a boy. No one would fault you for that.'

It was a kindly meant answer, and he felt warmly towards her for it, even if it didn't answer his unspoken question about what she thought of John Clement.

'Yes,' he said, persisting a little more, 'that is what your father told me when I asked. He was very kind. But I still felt uncomfortable. I was so sure that Erasmus had told me to draw a boy . . .'

But she didn't respond in a way Hans Holbein could understand. She just settled deeper into her chair, perfectly still in her pose, and began to dream of something private with a blissful smile on her face.

'You're glowing, Meg,' Margaret Roper said. 'It must be all those walks you've been going on. You've caught the sun. You look radiant.'

Margaret looked to Cecily, next to her on the bed, for confirmation, but Cecily only laughed weakly. 'It's probably just that you've spent the past week looking at me in this bed all day and I'm still all sick and green. Anyone would look radiant by comparison,' she said to Margaret.

I was perched on the side of the bed. I was giving them another dose of ginger tea. It had become a habit. Then Cecily began to look curiously at me. She wasn't as quick-witted as Margaret, or as kind, but now the idea had been suggested to her she was letting her imagination get to work.

'It's true, though,' she said mischievously. 'She's right. You've lost that tight-lipped look you've had all winter. And now I come to think of it you haven't flared your nostrils at me once in days either . . .' She twinkled.

I stared. 'What do you mean, flared my nostrils?' I said with a hint of sharpness, suspecting mockery.

They looked at each other and began to giggle helplessly, two little dark heads lying on the bed like puppies and shaking with mirth.

'. . . but you're doing it again now,' Cecily said. 'Look.' And she pulled a haughty face, with her nose in the air and her lips pursed together and her nostrils flared so wide that the tip of her nose went white. 'You always do it when you're cross,' she said, relaxing her face back into a giggle. 'Didn't you know?'

'You did it every time we tried to introduce you to anyone at any of the wedding parties,' Margaret confirmed. 'One handsome young potential husband after another, frozen by your deadly looks. Don't you remember?'

I was shaking my head in amazement. I recognised the expression Cecily was imitating as my own, all right, but I'd had no idea it looked so angry and so forbidding from the outside. And all I remembered of the endless winter parties was being fobbed off with one dull young man after another – the wallflowers no one in their right mind would want to talk to – and politely making my excuses to avoid spending more time than necessary with the spottiest, most unpreposessing stopgaps. It had never occurred to me that Margaret and Cecily were trying to find me a husband from among their new cousins-in-law. It took a pained moment or two of struggling with my pride before I could bring myself to react. But then I found myself grinning and screwing my face up in rueful acknowledgement. 'Do I really do that all the time? And did I really scare off all the husbands?' I asked, joining in their giggles. 'Oh dear.'

'We were in despair,' Margaret said, and her laughter was tinged with relief.

'Ready to give up on you.'

'You were so fierce . . .'

'. . . that Giles started calling you the Ice Queen . . .'

'. . . till Will stopped him.'

'. . . But then you bit Will's head off for introducing you to his cousin Thomas . . .'

'. . . so he stopped sticking up for you . . .'

I'd slipped down onto the bed with them now. I was holding my sides. We were groaning and snorting with laughter.

Then Cecily rolled onto her tummy and took some deep breaths. 'Ooh, I must stop,' she said, between bursts of giggles, 'all this laughing is making me feel sick again.' She breathed herself back into seriousness again and propped her head onto her hands and gave me an inquisitive look. 'So what's changed?' she asked. 'You can tell us, Meg. What's put you in a good mood again?' She paused before adding, melodramatically: 'Perhaps you are . . . In Love?'

It was such an innocent, relaxed moment that I almost let down my guard and blurted out a serious 'yes'. For the first time, perhaps ever, I could imagine confiding in my nearly sisters. But they were still in the grip of the giggles, and Cecily's question had been too much for them. Before I got a chance to say anything, they'd both subsided back against the pillows, and were rocking each other again in helpless, painful glee. I wasn't sure whether I was pleased or not that I'd been saved from the indiscretion I'd been about to commit.

*   *   *

119

'How's Father's picture coming along?' Meg asked, at the end of her fourth sitting. 'Will you show it to me soon?'

It was an overcast morning. The light was softer than usual. With a soft light in her eyes, she'd been telling Hans Holbein a long-ago story about Sir Thomas's wit: about how he'd met a fraud of a Franciscan monk in Coventry who'd told him that getting to Heaven was easy if you only relied on the Virgin Mary. All you had to do was say the rosary every day (and pop a penny into the Franciscan's purse every time you recited the *psalterium beatae virginis*). '*Ridiculum*,' Sir Thomas said matter-of-factly, even after the monk brought out all his books 'proving' that Mary's intervention had worked miracles on many occasions. Finally, with a lawyer's respect for logical argument, he silenced the monk with the reasonable argument that it was unlikely that Heaven would come so cheap.

Hans Holbein had roared with appreciative laughter. 'That sounds the kind of thing a friend of Erasmus' would say,' he chortled. It was also the kind of thing that he might say, or Kratzer, if either of them had the presence of mind to get the phrases off their lips with More's panache. But he also noted her nostalgic look, and the fleeting sadness on her face as she quietly said 'yes'. They both knew that this wasn't how the Sir Thomas of today, the defender of the Church at all costs, would behave.

He didn't understand why, but something about the complicity of that moment meant that he instinctively nodded assent when she next asked to see the picture.

'I am not usually shy about my work. But this one I am having problems with,' he said, dancing a little jig of unease in front of the covered picture. 'I have seen your father, and talked to him, and I know he is an intelligent, good, gentle man who loves to laugh. Only the other day I was laughing to hear his judgement in court when your Dame Alice adopted a street dog, and a beggar woman took her to court saying the dog was hers; and Sir Thomas ruled that Dame Alice must buy the dog; and everyone was happy, the kind of justice I can understand, ha ha! But my picture is too serious. And nothing I do will put laughter into the face of the man I'm drawing.'

She'd got up from her chair and was standing beside him, waiting for him to tweak aside the cloth. He could see the pale skin on the nape of her neck. Reluctantly, he stepped aside. But he couldn't bring himself to raise his arm so close that he would maybe brush against her to show her the picture. Instead, he stepped back. 'Look for yourself,' he said, almost closing his eyes.

He stared out of the window, not daring to look at her expression, making a futile effort to hear what her breathing said about her reaction to his picture. But there was nothing to be learned from listening to that soft, rhythmic in-and-out.

Eventually, he turned and sneaked a look at her. She was standing thoughtfully in front of the picture, with the cloth in her hand, not moving her body but nodding her head very slowly up and down. He thought she recognised her father in the face before her, with its black cap and black furred cloak and gold chain of office against the simple backdrop of a green curtain; and he thought she looked resigned at seeing that this harsh version of Sir Thomas, staring into the shadows, was a true likeness.

'You have a gift for the truth, Master Hans,' was all she said as she became aware of him looking at her. And her voice was definitely sad now. 'Father does a hard job. It's changed him. It shows on his face, doesn't it?'

Their eyes met, and something in hers told him she knew at least some of the crueller rumours circulating now about Sir Thomas whipping heretics tied to trees in the garden, or taking gloating personal charge of physical interrogation sessions in the Tower. He looked away.

She sat down again. Heavily. Looking at the floor. Looking up at him again; then, softening with sudden trust, she said, almost in a whisper: 'People say ugly things about Father these days, don't they? I expect you've heard some of them.'

He realised she was sounding him out, but he didn't know how to reply. He spread his hands helplessly. He had no idea how the witty, charming man who sat for him could be the same person as the anti-hero of the Steelyard rumours. Personally he liked More; liked the way his mind sparked like fire and his eyes blazed with ideas. That was the paradox. 'Ach, there are always slanders,' he stammered. 'If you really want to know the truth about someone, the only honest way is to tell them the slanders against them to their face. And if you trust them enough to ask for the truth, you must believe the answer they give. Then you can forget the slanders.'

She didn't answer directly. She looked at her hands for so long that he wondered whether she was thinking of something completely different. Then she said, with a sombre air: 'Well, you've certainly painted truth in his face – he won't deny that. You shouldn't change your picture.' And suddenly she lightened. 'But I've just thought of something you could put in too that would make him laugh.'

She got up, suddenly almost floating with the idea she'd had, and skipped out of the room. 'Don't go away!' she whispered.

Astonished, indulgent, hopeful, baffled, rejoicing at the laugh in her look, he waited.

She came back with two heavy pieces of red velvet, grinning all over her face.

'What are these?' he asked, getting more bewildered by the moment.

'Sleeves, of course,' she answered briskly. 'Look.'

And she pulled them up over Hans Holbein's own workmanlike linen shirtsleeves. Sleeves they were – big, sensuous, crimson velvet things, with a puff of splendour at the upper arm richly gathered at the elbow, and a long, soft, floppy forearm cuff. At the top there was a row of buttons, as if to attach them to a gown. But there was no gown. He'd never seen anything like them.

He looked down helplessly, watching the top of Meg's head moving busily under his as she tied the buttons on each side to the laces of his shirt. He didn't want to start imagining her undressing him, or worse, but there was something so suggestive about her bobbing head below that he felt beads of sweat break out on his forehead. He turned his head hastily to stare out of the window.

'There!' She stood back. Relieved, he also took a step away. He looked down at himself. From wrist to shoulder he was a grandee. Maybe one-eighth of his body was covered in Italy's finest clothwork. The rest of him was the same rough artisan he'd been born, in humble wool and leather.

She laughed at the look on his face. 'It's a family joke,' she said happily, transported back to easier days. 'You know Father still does bits of *pro bono publico* legal work for the London guilds, for old times' sake? Well, when the Emperor Charles V came to London a few years ago, before the war with France, they chose Father to give a speech praising the friendship between the two kings, and they gave him a ten-pound grant towards the cost of a new velvet suit as a reward. But of course that wasn't enough to pay for a whole set of clothes – and I don't know if you noticed, but Father hates dressing up. So he ordered just sleeves. Ten pounds' worth. He loves them. He puts them on over some ordinary old gown, and wears them to court. His manservant hates it – poor old John a Wood, he thinks Father's making a mockery of public office. But Father thinks it's hilarious – a remedy against vanity. So do I.'

There was a hint of defiance in her voice; the defiance

of someone who knows that the person she loves is a mass of contradictions and is daring the inquirer to mock. But he didn't want to mock. He was looking down at his red velvet arms, turning the idea over in his head, beginning to get excited about it.

'So – just red velvet sleeves – sticking out of his cloak?' he asked. He could already see it. It was almost perfect. Now there was just one more problem. 'Yes . . . yes . . . that would help. And I need to find the skull, too . . .' he said, thinking aloud. 'I want to put a *memento mori* in a corner. But I can't think where it is. My fault; my big disorder. I can never find anything I want.'

Half-heartedly he began ruffling through the top layer of his mess. He was disconcerted to see her put a hand to her mouth and start laughing behind it.

'Master Hans, haven't you noticed?' she was saying. 'I put your skull away for you days ago. It's under the table, on top of a pile of your pictures. I covered it all with a cloth to discourage people from snooping. You shouldn't leave things like that lying about. Your pictures, I mean, not the skull. You could get into trouble.'

He was rooted to the spot. He felt his face go hot and cold. She'd seen his pictures.

Then, in the middle of his terror, he noticed that she was smiling – almost conspiratorially – at him. He breathed for the first time in what seemed an eternity. She was still talking.

'And while we're on the subject, if Master Nicholas takes you to London, you shouldn't go to the Steelyard,' she was saying. Rushing her words; lowering her voice. A warning. 'Father doesn't like what goes on there; especially after he nearly lost Will Roper to the heretics. You must be very careful.'

He nodded, meeting her eyes again and seeing for certain now that she knew every dark thing he'd been finding out.

'Don't make the mistake of thinking Father is always the scholar and gentleman you see in this house,' she said. 'Flirting with Lutheran ideas can get people into serious trouble. You shouldn't take risks.'

He nodded, even more dumbly.

'And if you doubt what I'm saying, just take a look in the far gatehouse next time you go for a walk,' she added. Then she stopped, as if she'd gone too far, and bit her lip. 'Isn't it nearly dinner time?' she said, in a quite different voice. Hans Holbein nodded, now slavishly ready to obey her every word, and began to follow her out of the room. Then he realised he was still wearing the flamboyant red sleeves, and he fell behind for a rueful few minutes of solitary pulling and teasing at buttons and strings with his big sausages of fingers, which, for a variety of reasons, were trembling.

I should have kept my mouth shut. I knew it almost at once. But I got carried away by the moment. Master Hans seemed such an innocent that I wanted to make quite sure he understood that his behaviour could put him in danger.

There was uproar the next morning in the servants' quarters when it emerged that the prisoner in the gatehouse had escaped during the night. The stocks were broken, swinging loose on their hinges. The rope that had tied his arms was frayed loose. The door was open. Mary, the cook, and Nan, our maid, were full of the news – which was odd, considering that none of us would have admitted to knowing the man was there at all until he'd got away. How had the door come to be left unlocked, they chattered: would the gardener be sacked?

I went to see the scene of the crime for myself before my last sitting began. It was a relief not to see those thin shoulders inside, heaving with their prayers for death; secretly I hoped the man would have the sense not to go

125

straight home to Fleet Street and instant re-arrest but would lie low for a while. I tidied away the rope into a bag, and pulled the door shut. As I walked back, I noticed something glinting in a bush not far from the gatehouse. It was a palette knife with one sharpened edge. I put that in the bag too.

It was Friday, and Father had come home. He was sitting by the fire, looking into its depths, still in his cloak and dirty boots. He looked tired but calm. The first thing he'd done after getting off the boat had been to speak to the gardener, but we knew he'd let the man off with a reprimand. I wondered whether I would ever dare to follow Master Hans's advice to tackle rumours head on, and ask Father to his face who the man was, what the charge against him was, and why he'd been kept at our home in the first place. The thought made my heart thud crazily against my ribs. But my courage failed me. It was Will Roper – sweet-natured Will, now the world's most passionate Catholic and Father's devoted slave – who was bravest. But when he timidly expressed distress over the escape of a miscreant in Father's charge, and we all nodded and murmured assent, Father only laughed as if the loss of his prisoner was a matter of no importance. 'How could I possibly object to someone who has been sitting so uncomfortably for so long taking his chance to move around at his ease?' he said lightly. Discountenanced, Will smiled uneasily back. We all dispersed to begin the day's business.

The first thing I did was to give the palette knife back to Master Hans.

I didn't say a word. He blushed to his gingery roots and put it clumsily down.

'Do you remember our conversation yesterday?' I said, by way of warning.

He nodded and stared at his tree-trunk legs. I could see he was truly terrified of his own carelessness.

'About the *memento mori*,' I went on, less coldly, thinking I'd scared him enough now. 'I've thought of a different idea. Something a bit more sophisticated than a skull.' And I pulled out the rope from the bag, with a flourish worthy of a unicorn-horn salesman on Bucklersbury. 'The Latin for rope is *funis*,' I said; 'and the Latin for deathly is *funus*. You could make the rope your *memento mori*. They'd be impressed by your grasp of Latin' – I paused – 'and it might teach you to be less forgetful.'

His face was a study in bewilderment again. Mouth gaping like a fish. Chest heaving in and out. He was a sweaty, straightforward sort of person; too prone to melt into a puddle of damp when shocked to have a hope of succeeding at diplomacy or deceit. Then he picked up the rope, and looked from it to me several times. Once it dawned on him that he could trust me, which took some time, he began shaking his head with appreciation and the beginning of a twinkle in his eye. And then the laugh began to well up out of deep inside him. '*Funus*,' he chuckled, '*funis*. It might just work.'

It was a fortnight later, and the solo portrait of Father was nearly finished, while the group portrait, a more complex affair, was still in its early stages. Master Hans had followed all my suggestions in portraying Father. He'd painted the rope dangling loosely down the side of the green curtain, behind Father's shadowed chin and scowling face. Red velvet sleeves had made an appearance on Father's painted arms. And somehow all the different jokes worked together. I felt almost as proud when I looked at the picture as I could see he did.

I was sitting in the window reading when I heard him and Elizabeth come in from their after-dinner turn round the garden. She was beginning to look bigger already, but she was calmer and sweeter too, in the soft, accepting way of pregnant women – even with me. And she was touchingly grateful to Master Hans (as I was) for his devoted kindness to her.

'If my baby is a son,' I could hear her saying now, scraping her boots as he took her cloak from her shoulders, 'I've a good mind to call him after you, Master Hans.'

I laughed silently to myself. So she hadn't completely lost her old taste for empty compliments, then. I couldn't imagine haughty William Dauncey taking kindly to a son with the workmanlike foreign name of Hans, I was thinking, and I was beginning to have a quiet chuckle to myself at the absurdness of the idea when I heard the rest of what she had to say.

'Johannes,' her thin little voice was piping, sounding unexpectedly cheerful. 'Well, that's what it would be in Latin, anyway. But of course my child will be English, won't he? So what I'd actually call him would be John.'

7

No sooner had I got used to the new, livelier rhythm being established at Chelsea – the sittings with Master Hans each morning, first for Father, then me, then all the true More children, Elizabeth, Margaret, Cecily and young John, and his fiancée Anne Cresacre, then old Sir John, then, as it was to be, Dame Alice, one by one – when it stopped, as suddenly as it had started.

One Thursday evening at the beginning of February – a dark, wet winter's night in which the swollen river raged past the garden and the wind beat at the trees – Father came back from court soaked to the skin but with an idea glimmering in his eyes. The idea was still lighting him up even after he'd removed every other trace of his journey: changed his clothes and warmed up at the fire and joined us at supper. It was almost bursting out of him as he watched Nicholas Kratzer being teased by Dame Alice at table. 'I swear, Master Nicholas, you've been long enough in this country not to speak such terrible English,' she was saying, with her usual twinkle. She was fond of Master Nicholas and Master Hans, with their down-to-earth ways, solid bodies and general willingness to fetch things down for her from tall cupboards; they were nothing like the fey, penny-pinching, Latin-speaking humanists she'd loved to hate before, she now often said; they were real men. And they liked her robust humour too. 'Ach, I have only English been learning for twenty years or whatsoever,' Master Nicholas was laughing back, exaggerating his foreignness, enjoying the cut and thrust, 'and how can anyone speak this terrible language properly in so little time?' That exchange made Master Hans, who until then had been sitting quietly slurping up his food with his usual gargantuan appetite, suddenly hoot with laughter – he knew his own English could do with some improvement – and Master Hans's laughter was so infectious that it made everyone else start gurgling and slapping their sides with mirth. Father smiled approvingly, and after supper he took Kratzer and Holbein away to talk to them.

It was Friday the next day, and Father was locked away in the New Building praying and fasting from long before dawn, with the rain still lashing down outside, so it fell to Master Hans to tell me what had been decided.

When I went into his studio at the end of the morning to call him for dinner, there was no sign of Cecily, who was supposed to have been sitting for him. At first I assumed he'd told her to go because the light wasn't good enough to paint by. We had candles everywhere in the great hall, even at midday. But he was packing paints into his leather bags. He was wrapping each jar in one of his rags, carefully, before stacking it inside. The easel and silverpoint pencils were already rolled up into a bundle. He was beaming all over his snub-nosed face and the short beard on his stubby chin was practically curling with delight. Even the damp smell of boiled carp wafting from the kitchen, a fish he'd told me he didn't like, couldn't take the grin off his features.

'What's happening?' I asked, bewildered.

'We're going to court!' he answered, a bit too loud, a

bit too happily. Then he looked embarrassed at his own puppyish excitement, looked down and composed himself. 'Kratzer and I. Your father has a job for us there. A court job!' He was bubbling with joy again.

'But,' I stammered, surprised at the little stab of selfish, childish disappointment I was feeling. 'What about unveiling Father's portrait? And finishing ours?'

'Later,' he answered, suddenly looking curiously into my eyes as if trying to see the answer to a question of his own there. More gently, he added: 'It is only for a month or two. We will come back. I will finish the family picture by the end of the summer, and it will be beautiful. Your likeness,' he paused, 'will be beautiful.' He hesitated again, almost as if there was something more he was thinking of saying.

I smiled, remembering to be pleased for him. 'Well, it will be much duller here without you around, Master Hans,' I said lightly. 'What will your court job be?'

It was to do with the peace treaty that Father and Cardinal Wolsey were supposed to start negotiating with the French ambassadors. So confident was Father of the successful outcome of the talks for the English side – and so confident too that Master Hans shared his impish sense of humour and would be able to weave some anti-French jokes into his artwork – that he was getting him and Master Nicholas involved early on in designing the artwork for the celebrations that would result from his achievement: an astronomical design for the ceiling of the pavilion at Greenwich Palace in which, at some future point, the signing of the treaty would be celebrated. (William Dauncey had been talking about the preparations at dinner one day: talking half-mockingly, half-full of admiration, about the King's lavishness, in what must have been an echo of his own father's mixed feelings as he tried to balance the royal household's books.)

The pavilion itself had yet to be built for a peace that had yet to be made. But hundreds of craftsmen of every sort – from leatherworkers to ironworkers to casters of lead to gilders to carvers to carpenters to painters – were already being hired. Having a brilliant display of memorable pictures and decorations would cement Father's diplomatic victory. So it was in his own interest to ensure that the best possible talents were working on the display as soon as possible; it was worth waiting for the completion of the paintings his own family would later enjoy if that public point could be made first. And it was a big opportunity for Master Hans, something the painter should be grateful to Father for forever. I'd seen the polite note Father had written to Erasmus after Master Hans got here, agreeing that he was a wonderful artist though doubting he'd make his fortune here – but I hadn't realised he'd try so hard to help the painter get on his feet quite so soon.

I could have wished he'd make the same effort to launch John's medical career, but I stifled any resentment that thought might arouse. Like Master Hans, I had a sense, now, that life was beginning to go my way. Father might not have confided to me his intentions for my marriage, but I felt that John was determined enough to win me, that he'd find a way to meet Father's condition, and get elected to the College of Physicians. 'Doctor Butts has become something like to a friend,' John had written in the letter I'd received that morning:

I think you'll like him. He's an innocent; long, grey beard, very serious, passionate about his studies, rather disorganised at everything else, no conversation to speak of, but very kind, worries endlessly about his protégés and the scrapes they get themselves into. And there are plenty of scrapes, so he has plenty to worry about. It seems the College of Physicians is a hotbed of religious radicalism. He doesn't tell me everything, but I've heard that when Doctor Butts unaccountably goes missing for a day, he's off paying calls on anyone he thinks might be able to help get one of his students off a heresy charge. He came in last night looking very downcast. He'd been away on one of his mystery errands for two days. I took him for a good dinner at the Cock Tavern to cheer him up, and didn't ask any awkward questions, and I got the impression he was grateful for both things. He hugged me very warmly when we got up to go. And he said I could go to him and go through what we'll talk about formally, later, at the College of Physicians, so he can help me present it in the best way to his colleagues. So you see – he's a good man. And a remarkable man. He seems the opposite of your father in many ways. But I think his passion and compassion give him something of Sir Thomas's magnetism, even if his concerns and the ways he addresses them are so very different. And I think he genuinely likes me too – maybe just because my calm is something that all these excitable men of genius are drawn to. They all want someone to bounce their ideas off, someone who will listen intelligently. So he's being very friendly. And I really think I've got a chance of being elected with his help.

I thought John's election was a foregone conclusion (though I crossed fingers and spat over my left shoulder to ward off evil spirits whenever I found myself thinking it). Very soon, it wouldn't matter to me any more whether or not Father treated me as affectionately as he did his real children, and whether, out in the cold on the edge of the family, I'd stumbled on the darkness in Father's soul. I wouldn't care any more once the man I loved came to claim me. Father wouldn't stand in John's way. I woke every morning now with hope in my heart; it was only a question of time.

'*And* he says I will probably be asked to paint a big fresco of a battle scene,' Master Hans was rattling on, lost in his triumph again, '*and* who knows what else will come up on such a big project that I might be able to help with too? *And* Kratzer and I will be paid four shillings a day. *Four shillings a day!* Six or seven times more than I've ever got before. Four . . . shillings . . . a . . . day.' His eyes were glittering greedily. For the first time, I noticed that his breeches and shirt had been patched, many times, in tiny, careful stitching.

At dinner, ignoring the sombre weather and the spartan Friday food, Master Nicholas was even more euphoric than Master Hans. They sat next to each other at the bottom of the table, and grinned and wolfed down carp, and whispered excitedly in German, trying Dame Alice's patience even if she did her best not to show it.

By Sunday evening – 7 February, Father's fiftieth birthday, which we'd once been supposed to celebrate with the unveiling of at least one of the portraits, but which, since both were unfinished and most of the assembled diners were leaving, we just marked with a morning prayer for the success of the French talks – they'd gone. Master Hans must have stowed his pictures away under his bed, or in Master Nicholas's room. The painter's studio was as empty (except for the skull he'd forgotten under the table) as the house now felt. Father was away at Greenwich, closeted with the French ambassadors and Cardinal Wolsey, his big, proud, cunning, devious, greedy, intelligent master, who wrapped his portly body in the crimson robes of his office, wore a sable scarf and a scarlet

134

hat on his head, and liked to poke his nose into an orange pomander full of vinegar and herbs to ward off the infections in the air and the smell and infestations of the populace. Will Roper was mostly with Father, working as an extra secretary. Even William Dauncey was off at Greenwich. The young wives had left to visit their new families (their in-laws having all, as one, developed a passionate new interest in them now they were expecting).

It was going to be quiet, with only Dame Alice and the servants in the house, though it wouldn't be unpleasant to be left alone with my peaceful, expectant thoughts now I could see events shaping up more positively. I could stop worrying about what I'd find in the western gatehouse. I could stop sneaking into the New Building. I was happy to read and embroider and take solitary spring walks whenever the rain let up. But I thought I would miss Master Hans.

So there were only two women in the house (and young John and Anne Cresacre, who didn't count, in the schoolroom) when, after a wet spring, the first cases of sweating sickness began to be reported as the burning summer began.

I'd had first-hand experience of the sweating sickness the last time it had ravaged London. When I was fourteen and John Clement had still been my teacher, it had struck our house on Bucklersbury. It was a lightning strike of an illness. Andrew Ammonius had lasted twenty hours, raving in his darkened attic as we rushed doctors and cool drinks and poultices in and out. But the disease killed most people on the first day, sometimes within an hour, dissolving them into heat and profuse sweat, raging thirst and delirium. Then they fell asleep and died.

It was just me and John Clement, Ammonius's friend, in the sickroom when his moment came. The stink was unforgettable. All the talk I'd heard about the sweating sickness until that moment was forgotten, though the words came back later: John Clement telling me about the very first time it appeared, in 1485, at the uncertain start of old King Henry's reign – a sign he would rule by the sweat of his brow, people said then, in trouble forever; and the second outbreak in 1517, which came while we were at Bucklersbury, in the year of Martin Luther's declaration of war on the Church, and which, according to Father, was the fault of the heretics who'd started to poison the body politic anew.

Ammonius had been yelling, 'Liars, liars, liars!' and we didn't know who he was talking to. We were exhausted from restraining him, and the room was full of wet cloths and buckets and doctor's instruments, and it was dark, and it was dangerous for us to be there with him. But none of that mattered; the point was that his tormented, quivering frame was still full of life. Until he started drooping. 'I'm tired,' was all he said, and suddenly he was so heavy that even with one of us on each side of him, with his arms draped over our shoulders, we couldn't hoist him up. 'Stay awake,' I murmured, and there were tears on my cheeks. 'Please.'

John was crying too. 'You mustn't go to sleep!' he said, as persuasively as he knew how, 'Listen to me!', but this time the Italian was in no state to listen. His eyes were closing and there was nothing we could do to shake him awake. We both knew his eyes would not open again.

I never felt so helpless as in that moment: gasping for breath myself; laying the suddenly heavy form down; pulling the sheet up over the dying man as though there were any chance he were still going to live; watching the tears on my teacher's face; listening to the weird rhythms of our two wild exhausted sets of breath and the other mouth that had just stopped inhaling. John had told me since that this was when he resolved to become a doctor; it was certainly what strengthened my own interest in treating the sick. But at that moment all I could think of was the smell of defeat: dark and absolute. What Father called the smell of heresy.

So when I heard now that people were running from London to get away from a new outbreak – and camping in the village – I went out to help. I couldn't see the point of cosseting myself at home. There was no danger in Chelsea yet, just a lot of hungry people who needed a roof over their heads. I felt invincible, anyway, floating on a bubble of anticipation and happiness. I didn't tell John Clement in my daily letters that I was going out to take the new arrivals food, and that Dame Alice and I were arranging with Father's farm manager to turn over the second barn behind the great field to putting them up and providing more regular supplies of food. It was the month of his election to the College. I'd told him not to even answer my letters until his entrance was secured, so I left anything that might worry him. He had other things to think about. I wanted him to focus every effort on impressing the College, not on worrying about me.

When Father returned to Chelsea, immediately after the conclusion of the peace treaty – and before any of the young people, who lingered on in the country, or, in Will and Margaret Roper's case, in town, staying at Bucklersbury to my great envy – Dame Alice told him to stop me going to visit the refugees every day.

'You should be more careful of yourself, Meg,' Father said gently to me, the first time he saw me with my basket heading into Chelsea. But he didn't put a hand on my shoulder to stop me – the kind of simple gesture of paternal familiarity and concern I'd spent so many years hoping for, and feeling excluded when it never came, especially when he was constantly embracing the grown-up children

137

he'd raised from birth – and he didn't try very hard to dissuade me. So I carried on. Perhaps, even though the French negotiations had been successful, he had too much on his own mind. The King had asked him personally to intercede in the matter of getting the royal marriage annulled. He hadn't directly said no, but people outside the family said his ardour for heresy hunting had re-doubled. One of the ragged men in the barn told me in a whisper one day that the word was that Father had gone to search the house of Humphrey Monmouth, one of the patrons of the heretic William Tyndale, and found every grate in the house burning merrily with papers he'd been unable to pull out in time. 'God help him stop the heretics,' the man muttered, giving me a cagey look. 'Look at the trouble they're bringing down on our heads. Death, disease, the curse of the Lord. God speed him.' It was what he thought I wanted to hear, but I thought the man sounded so insincere that I wondered what God he prayed to himself. There were arrests of Lollards in London and Christian Brethren in Colchester. Still, there were no more prisoners in the gatehouse (I checked from time to time, but the floor was empty and swept clean; Father must have learned from that last experience). And what happened away from Chelsea was coming to seem remote again – a different world, a game which people played by different rules, with little connection to our daily experience; a world as remote as Father's behaviour. If he noticed me at all these days, it was just to chat as politely as if I were a stranger; he was so preoccupied with the letters that I assumed contained arrest lists and death lists that kept arriving for him that his eyes had become glassy with fatigue. And yet I was oddly cheered by him being here. The very sight of him in the house most of the time, sitting at the table, or going down the path to his private office early in the morning and at all hours of the night in his endearingly shabby gowns, rather than going away to do business I didn't understand in unfamiliar, stiff court clothes, was an odd kind of comfort in itself. If you chose to be encouraged by it, his presence, his eyes glowing as we talked at dinner, his manservant tutting over his unshaven jaw and nagging him into a weekly shave and something like respectable dressing, made our household seem more complete, less full of shadows and empty spaces, more like the days before he was at court. I was so full of hope for John's success that I felt detached from Father's detachment. I was even almost able to shut out the nag of unease about what actions Father might be taking to stem the tide of heresy.

There was talk of sweating sickness – and plague, as if one blow from on high wasn't enough – all over London. Preoccupied as he was, there was a distinctly un-Christian note of hopefulness in Father's voice on the day he read out a letter to Dame Alice and me over breakfast, informing him that Anne Boleyn herself had gone down with sweating sickness. (I found that oddly endearing, as was the disappointment I saw in his eyes the next day at the dispatch that she had survived the crisis.) And I was touched when he said he was writing begging Margaret and Cecily and Elizabeth and their husbands to return to Chelsea; and he was pleased when Master Hans wrote saying he was cutting short the triumphal tour of portrait appointments that had followed his appointment at Greenwich to come back to the safety of our village and finish our picture. I liked him wanting to gather his family and friends around him; I liked the idea of that warmth still burning deep inside him, even if it only seemed to flicker coldly when it came to his behaviour towards me.

We all wanted them back. We needed what cheer we could get. Even in the early days of what was going to be a hot, desperate spring, the crops in the Chelsea fields lining the lane were failing. The first shoots shrivelled. The plants that came up afterwards were stunted and deformed in earth so dry it cracked. The cattle were thin and gave scarcely any milk and their cries sounded like cries of pain. Even the leaves on the apple trees were scabbed and grey with mildew. The price of corn doubled in a single week in April. 'He says,' Dame Alice hissed, 'that the lack of corn and cattle is a sore punishment from God for the spread of heresy.' She rolled her eyes as if mocking the idea; but I thought she was half-convinced or she wouldn't be repeating it. She hadn't ever had much time for big talk about God's punishments, but now everyone was giving way to superstition. We had more than one hundred people being fed in the barn at the farm by then. I went every day to watch their coarse, desperate faces turn down into their bread and bowls of broth, and ask if there'd been any reports of sickness.

And that was where I next saw John Clement.

I was watching a butterfly. It was fluttering gently in a waft of breeze that was cutting through the smell of the bodies clamouring round the cauldron. Two children had retreated with their hunks of bread and bowls to a rough patch of cow parsley and were sitting in the dappled sunlight watching it too – a moment of peace in the cracking, waving heat.

Then one of them saw me. 'Miss,' he began calling, in his dry little voice. 'Eh, Miss.' He waved frantically with his bread hand. He must have been looking out for me, and now he was tormented by the choice facing him. I could see he didn't want to lose me and he didn't want to lose his dinner. His little legs were scrabbling for the ground, trying to stay steady as he slurped down another faceful of broth and eased himself up all at the same time. I hurried over. 'My sister's not well,' he said, finishing the bowl and putting it back in his bag without wiping it, still clinging on to his bit of bread. 'My mother said to ask, will you come and see her?'

There hadn't been any sweating sickness yet here. It was just a fear. We hurried over the rough ground, tripping on clods of earth that hadn't yet dried up to dust that would get in our eyes. The boy's mother was part of the encampment in the back of the barn, but she'd taken her little girl out that morning and made a rough blanket shelter for her away from their friends and family, near the hot, buzzing stink of the trench. The child might have been five or six, a ragged blonde moppet with red eyes, and when I drew the blanket away I saw that her breathing was rough.

'She woke up with a nightmare,' said the skinny, toothless mother hovering over her – who was maybe my age, but was so wizened and gnarled she could as easily have been my mother. 'She was screaming blue murder. Said her neck hurt. And she got the shivers. So we brought her out here and wrapped her up warm in the sunshine. She can hardly move.'

I felt her forehead. The cold spell at the onset of disease was passing – it was raging hot now. I left my hand there for a moment. I could feel her pulse speeding up under my palm. 'But it can't be the sweat, right – because she's cold, not hot?' the mother was saying, in a nasal, hopeful whine. 'You got something in there you can give her, Miss?' And I could see her eyes fasten on my basket, with its strips of clean cloth and innocent herbal remedies – nothing that would save anyone from sweating sickness. Nothing could.

I drew back my hand and showed it to the mother. My palm was wet with rancid sweat. The child was beginning to drip with it now, and groan. The mother looked closely at my hand for a few moments before she understood the significance of the sweat glistening on it. Then she pushed it away with a stifled howl, flung herself down next to her little girl, covered the child with clumsy arms, and lay there, rocking her against her breast in her own agony of love, murmuring, 'Janey, Janey, don't worry, love, Janey, we'll get you well, Janey . . .' and ignoring me.

For a moment, I panicked. I didn't know what to do. 'Go and fill up every bowl you can find with drinking water, and bring them back here,' I told the scared, embarrassed boy standing mutely at my side watching his mother and sister rock on the ground. It was a way of filling up the empty moment; a way of putting off acknowledging my inability to treat this patient. 'She's going to get thirsty soon.'

He ran off, barefoot and light with panic. The footsteps that returned, just seconds later, before he could possibly have found water, were heavier – the sound of boots. The shadow falling over me from behind was big, even in the shrivelling late-morning sun. When I looked up, over my shoulder, it was straight into the sun. I couldn't see the man's eyes. But I'd have known that silhouette anywhere – the long legs, the back tenderly stooped towards me, the beak, the black hair.

'Meg,' John Clement said. Just one measured word.

I put a hand over my eyes against the sun and squinted up at him from its shadow. A part of me wanted to know what luck he'd had at the College of Physicians. But it wasn't the time to ask, and there was nothing to see in his expressionless face, turning now to the woman squatting beside her child. All I could find to focus on was the basket of medicine he was carrying.

'I've come to help,' he said into the buzzing silence. He wasn't talking to me. He was talking to the woman on the ground. She stopped her panicked crooning, looked at him in a startled way, then accepted what he was saying.

Very gently, she laid the child's head down on its blanket, disengaged herself and got to her feet. And she stood before him, as mutely accepting as I was of whatever he was going to say.

'What's your name?' he asked.

'Mary,' she stammered.

'Right, Mary, this is what we're going to do,' he said briskly. 'Janey is going to feel very hot for up to a day. But if she lives her temperature will have dropped by the morning. So you have to be as strong as you can until then. All right?'

She nodded.

'Your boy's coming back with water for her. That's important. She'll be thirsty. Keep her drinking – that's important too. And it will be hard for her to breathe. You have to prop her up so she's half-sitting; that will make it easier for her. But the most important thing is that you mustn't let her go to sleep. The time will come when she'll want to sleep, but it will kill her if you let her. So keep her awake. All right?'

She nodded again.

'Have you got a husband?'

She shook her head. 'Dead,' she mouthed. 'In Deptford last week.'

'God rest his soul,' John said. There'd been sweating sickness in Deptford for days. I didn't know there were runaways from there at our barn. I crossed myself.

'God rest his soul,' she mouthed back. Her hysterical fit was over. And there was a determined look to her slack mouth as she sat down again by the child and cradled the little head in her lap.

The round-eyed boy came back with two friends and three leather buckets of water.

'Right, boys,' John said firmly. 'Don't come back until morning. And keep everyone else away too. It's your job

143

to make sure people don't start crowding us out here. Your mother and the two of us will look after Janey. You're better off keeping the rest of them in the barn. Do you hear?'

They nodded, too. The mother pressed her son's hand. He was maybe eight. They had no words. But John was giving them hope. He was giving me hope.

I should have wanted to cry inside. But I didn't. Everything was too blurred and confused for that at this deathbed scene in the brilliant spring sunshine, with butterflies.

'Meg,' he said, in the same brisk tones. 'How long can you stay?'

I nodded, drinking in the beauty of his taut, tense body, limbs poised for action, obscurely comforted by his presence. We both knew I meant 'as long as I need to'. He nodded too.

'And what have you got there?' He gestured at my bag.

'Cloths. Soap. Nothing much.' I had willow bark, too, which the old wives said soothed fevers. But he'd think that superstitious. I didn't want to tell him.

'I have leeches. If the crisis comes soon I can bleed her,' he said.

I was silent for a moment. If her blood was infected, any doctor would agree that bleeding her would restore its purity and the balance of her humours. And John had had the best training any doctor could have; there was no one who could know more. He had the whole majesty of the Siena medical school behind him. Still, bleeding wasn't a treatment I'd have favoured, especially not in these filthy surroundings, with the stink of the trench so close and the dust getting into our faces and hair – a miasma of infection. I put a hand over my nose.

'We'll see,' he said quietly, perhaps registering my reservation, 'how it goes.' And he looked at me for a moment longer, a long look so exactly like the looks I'd spent this lonely spring imagining him giving me that now I saw it, it pierced my heart, and added: 'I want us to talk when this is over.'

I nodded again. My heart was beating fast. My face was as impassive as his. But the racing in my temples was reminding me that I felt more alive than I had for months.

I swabbed the child's scrawny body through a soaking shift. I was sweating under the blanket roof. It was the middle of the afternoon. The mother was rocking her rhythmically, and singing under her breath. She'd stopped noticing me long ago. She was too taken up with willing her daughter well. But I could see the whites of little Janey's eyes flickering in panic. I could hear her choking breath, the gurgles in her chest sounding like a person drowning. On the out breaths, she muttered 'no . . . no . . . no!' on a rising tide of terror. She couldn't drink any more. The stench was terrible, and getting worse. It was the smell of rotten meat, of blackened blood.

I heard footsteps. I peered out from under the blanket.

'Turn her over and slit the back of her shift. We'll bleed her now,' he said.

I didn't question his decision.

'Mary,' his voice said. 'Turn Janey over and hug her tight in your lap. We're going to bleed her.'

The woman did as he said. She didn't stop her dirge-like singing for a moment, or her rocking. The child clung to her with the last shred of her strength.

I peeled back the shift and wiped at the bony little back. New drops of sweat glistened on it at once. It was hopeless.

'Move over,' John said, coming in under the blanket with his bag. He gave me the box of leeches to hold and drop, one by one, into the glass cups. And he began to place the filled cups in rows across the child's back.

Several of the leeches refused to attach themselves to

the child's skin, but he tapped at them patiently with the knife until they bit. And when he ran out of leeches he began very tenderly making more small incisions on different parts of her skin. There was no room to move or breathe. I thought I'd pass out if it got any hotter. Finally, the child's head slumped forward on her mother's chest. The woman began crying, 'She's fainted, she's fainted . . . what's happening?' but John shushed her.

'It's all right,' he said calmly, and he began to prise free the blood-soaked leeches and bind up the wounds with my clean cloths. 'Don't worry. Just keep singing to her. She can hear you.'

We cleaned her as best we could and turned her on her back again, with her mother propping her up and cradling her and a blanket over her nakedness. She was breathing better now – still noisily, but without panic – though she was still wringing wet and deadly pale.

'Meg,' John said. 'Come out. Take a rest. Stretch your legs. Save your strength.'

I scrambled out, drenched myself and streaked with dirt and blood. It was almost surprising to see the familiar sight of the barn and the cauldron and the people cowering in the doorway. I hadn't thought of any of them for so many hours. 'We'll bleed her again at sundown,' he said calmly. He looked hopeful.

'I'm out of cloths,' I said. I couldn't think beyond detail.

He put an arm under mine. He had courage enough for two of us. I felt some of his practical strength surging back into me.

'Don't worry. I've sent a woman to the stream to wash the first lot out. They'll be dry in no time in this sun.'

I walked up the lane in a daze. I'd already turned to come back, feeling the afternoon air freshen my mind, when I heard the wailing begin – the desperate, animal sound that meant Janey was dead.

I ran back. They were still in the same position – the child cradled in her mother's arms. But now it was the mother shrieking 'no . . . no . . . no!' as if the air was being sucked out of her lungs, and shaking the motionless little body as if to will life back into it. And John was sitting behind the mother, embracing her in the same way she was embracing the dead girl. I made as if to join them; but it was him she'd warmed to and obeyed from the start, not me. He shook his head at me. 'Find the boy,' he mouthed.

I nodded. I went towards the crowd at the barn door, realising exhaustedly that I didn't even know his name.

I didn't have to. He was waiting, empty-eyed, standing alone. The other boys were scared to go near him. Falteringly, he stepped towards me. I had some idea of what he was about to feel.

'Your mother needs you,' I said, as gently as I knew how. 'I'm sorry.'

We walked towards the house together in the last light. There were men behind us digging at the edge of the churchyard. I ached with fatigue and failure, though not enough to weaken my confused sense of wonder at being alive so close to death or my admiration for John's valiant efforts to save that small stranger's life. I was too tired to turn my attention to the specific reason that had brought John back. I was just glad he was there – an instinct, an animal's mute comfort when its mate is slinking through the woods beside it in a time of need.

'There was nothing else we could have done,' I said, trying to comfort him.

He shook his head.

'However much I've learned since Ammonius died, it wasn't enough,' he said. 'It's never enough, what we know. Half of those people could be dead in days.'

147

His voice was so bitter that I turned to stare. He was angry with himself for not saving that child. I'd never seen him angry before. But he was deep in his own thoughts. He didn't notice.

'And the rest of them will be calling it the curse of the Tudors. The hand of God, punishing the usurpers. As usual,' he said, perhaps to himself, much further up the lane. His voice was bitterly contemptuous. 'The same old superstitious rubbish. If only they remembered how much worse things were before.'

'Father's calling it an Act of God too,' I said, panting slightly as I half-trotted along beside him, trying to keep pace with his furious stride. 'But he says it's a divine punishment for heresy.'

'I doubt that poor girl was to blame for either thing,' he snapped, and relapsed into angry silence. Feeling his defeat.

It was many more steps before I found breath to speak again.

'Are you coming to the house with me?' The thought seemed surprising. There'd been no prior agreement. We'd just both started walking that way. It felt the natural thing to do. But my question jogged him back into the here and now.

'Yes,' he said, and he turned his face towards me with the surprised memory of a smile. 'Your father invited me. The court is leaving Greenwich. London is so full of disease that the King is frightened. Your father thought I could be useful here, since Chelsea is getting so full of displaced people. He thought it would be helpful to have one of the elect of the College of Physicians on the spot.'

The phrase was no sooner off his lips than he began to scowl again. 'Though it didn't do that child much good to be treated by one of the elect,' he said, and redoubled his speed, as if to punish himself further.

But I pulled at his arm until he stopped, and stared until he was forced to meet my astonished gaze. 'You've done it?' I mouthed, feeling the world spin around. 'You've actually got in? And he's said you can come to us?'

He stopped scowling. Suddenly he smiled with almost unbearable sweetness and the sky came back into his eyes and he looked straight at me. 'Yes. I have. I set out here this morning so proud,' he said, in a softer voice. 'I couldn't wait to tell you what a great doctor I'd become – truly worthy of you.' He grimaced and shrugged, but his rage had passed; there was just wistfulness on his face now. 'Well, it seems I'm not such a great doctor as all that after all. But yes, I've passed the test your father set.'

And he put two trembling arms on my shoulders and his face softened into something like love. 'So if you still want me, Meg, I'm yours.'

There were so many ways I'd imagined responding to this news. But there was no place on this day, when the disease had touched us, for excesses of joy. I nodded my head, still filthy and aware of the stigmata of death on us both, but comforted by his seriousness. 'Yes,' I said quietly. 'I want you. Let's go home.'

'Ah – a new arrival,' Father said calmly, when John walked through the door behind me, as if there were nothing odd about the sudden appearance of this virtual stranger at the house. He didn't seem to have noticed our sweaty, dusty clothes either. 'Welcome back, John.'

I stared at him, wondering at the complex thought process that must lie behind that calm welcome, wondering whether he guessed that I knew the deal he'd struck with John, wondering whether he'd think it necessary to mention it to me, and if so when, but he was too busy embracing his visitor to meet my eye. I stared at Dame Alice, too, who was bustling around in the background, supervising a pair of maids carrying a bundle of linen upstairs and not really concentrating on us. 'You'll need more things for the east bedroom now too,' she was saying to them, very matter-of-factly. 'And put a bowl of water in there too.' She didn't have time to look at me either, but she wasn't the same quality of blank-faced diplomat as Father, and I guessed from the quietly pleased look in her eye that John's arrival wasn't as much of a surprise to her as it had been to me.

'There will be supper in about an hour,' she said, 'or are you hungry now, John? I could get something cold brought out to you if you're famished from your journey?'

John shook his head, unable to think of food after what we'd spent the afternoon doing. 'Are there other guests?' I asked, wondering why the maids were carrying around so much linen and water. She smiled more broadly, waving the maids away. 'Master Hans has sent word he'll be here within a day, and Will has just arrived with Margaret from London,' she told me happily.

'We've been at the barn,' John was saying to Father, not paying attention to our domestic chit-chat. 'I met Meg there. And I'm afraid there's bad news.'

Dame Alice stopped talking. I saw her take in my dusty, stained appearance for the first time. Father and she both stepped closer.

'A child died this afternoon,' John went on. 'Suddenly.'

'A runaway from Deptford,' I added. 'A girl of five or six.'

Even now there was no real surprise. But I saw dread etch its acid lines on both parents' watching faces. There was a long silence, while they considered what it might mean for us that the disease laying waste to London had reached this quiet country place. Then they both spoke at once, with the kind of simplicity that made you forget every trick they'd ever played with your heart, and love them.

'God rest her soul,' Father said. 'Was it the sweat?' But he knew the answer.

'Are they burying her straightaway?' asked Dame Alice – the practical question of someone worrying about the spread of disease. 'Are there others with her?'

At a hushed supper, at which we all felt as close as friends, a gentle, engaged Father offered prayers for deliverance and we echoed his thoughts with amens. There is no safety but God's will, he said. John and Will had nothing good to tell us about how things were in the city – the streets half-deserted, the shops and taverns boarded up, the apothecaries' market full of desperate people. And Father prayed for Elizabeth and William and Cecily and Giles, all still far away in their new homes. 'How I want everyone to be safe; I wanted you all to be safe here with us,' he said. 'But there's no point any more in begging them to come here. All we can do is commend them to God and pray for everyone to be spared. We are helpless before God.'

'You must stay for as long as you want to and need to,' Father added, in a more everyday voice, and his gesture included John, who had sat firmly down next to me, on the other side of Margaret, and was paying equal amounts of quiet attention to listening to Father's every word and filling my platter and looking at me. Quiet, long looks, drinking me in like a thirsty man emptying a tankard of water. And I was looking back at him in the same way, and whenever I passed him dishes of this or that – Dame Alice's lark pie, I noticed, catching sight of one from what seemed very far away – our hands found themselves brushing against each other.

'John,' Father went on. 'I'm glad you're here. You'll be needed. And I'm glad you'll have Meg to help you.'

John caught my eye again now, and held my gaze for a second longer than necessary. Modestly, blushing at the nakedness of his look, I lowered my face.

We walked in the garden after supper. It was hot and there was no wind. The night sky was dizzy with stars and the air was full of the sticky scent of the first red roses and we could hear the rush of the river in front. It was drunkenly, impossibly beautiful. Behind us, though, we knew there'd be the distant fires of the village if we turned to look. And, invisible now, the small grave of the small girl; and the weeping of the mother; and the terror of the young boy; and the hostility of the others in the barn, with the cloud of disease on them.

None of it stopped the fire inside me; the slow melting, the agonisingly private memories of pain all muddled up with the possibilities of pleasure, the way I felt the strong arm around my waist with every inch of my being.

'We shouldn't be out here so late,' I said, trying to sound firm.

He sighed. I couldn't see his face, so high above mine, so close – just the angle of a firm chin, just the tightening of fingers against my waist and the instinctive knowledge that he was as near as I was to nudging my mouth against his and losing himself in a kiss under the swimming stars.

'You're right,' he said. 'We need to be back there early in the morning. We should get some sleep.'

He stepped back. I shivered. But I had only a fraction of a second in which to feel that sadness of his body leaving mine, before he'd taken me back into his arms, unresisting, with the quietest of laughs that even wrapped up inside that embrace I could only guess at having heard.

'Well, in a minute, maybe,' he whispered, and I could just see the way one side of his mouth was curling up in half a smile. 'I can't leave just yet.' And he bent his head another inch towards me and covered my lips with his as my hands crept unbidden into his hair and hugged his head closer still.

*   *   *

The gravediggers were at work again on the edge of the churchyard. Four of them, two in the pit, three or four feet down, with piles of fresh earth thrown up by its sides. They were sweating already from the rhythm of their work, although the air was still fresh, and they had kerchiefs knotted on their heads against the morning sun. The hole they were digging was bigger this time.

John stopped by them, with a mute question on his face.

Their leader shook his head.

'Just in case,' he said, and crossed himself.

We walked faster.

The barn was empty. Boys were dragging logs down to the other end of the five-acre field, where the fire and the cauldron had been moved. The hungry were sitting down there, in the shade of the hedgerow. Even from the barn we could hear their buzzing, as angry as swarming bees.

Outside the barn, by the stinking trench with its insect buzzing, the only people left were the mother from Deptford and her boy. He must have brought more water up from the stream by himself. Two leather buckets nearly as big as he was caught the sun in flashes. He was as pale as ever, standing helplessly to one side with his thin little arms trembling in the light. He looked as though he might have been standing there all night. But she was red-eyed and wild-haired, with horror on her face, squatting on the ground underneath her blanket roof, wrapping herself in scraps of blankets then pulling them off, half-mad with grief and fear. She saw us and her eyes lit up as she flung herself towards us. 'You got to help my boy,' she implored. 'Those bloody bastards won't let him near. They gone down there. They took his bowl off him. How's he going to eat?'

'Calm down,' John said, and lay her down under the

biggest blanket and began to wipe at her with one of my cloths. It wasn't just grief and fear that were driving her mad. The sweat was beginning to come. 'We'll see to it.'

I left him, and the boy, and the woman. I walked down to the cauldron, with its greasy bubble of vegetables and a pigeon carcass bobbing around on top. I was aware of my feet treading heavily on nettle and burdock and cow-parsley and buttercup. I was aware of the hiss of hostile looks. Roger the miller stepped forward from behind the cauldron when I reached the little knot of people.

'Give me a bowl of soup, Roger,' I said evenly.

'Send 'em away, Miss,' he answered, showing his last two black teeth. 'They've brought death with them. We want them out of here.'

'The soup,' I said. 'Now.'

He shook his head. His big meaty hands were playing a strangling game with the rope knotted round his waist.

'She's sick already,' I said. 'She's in no state to be moved.'

He crossed himself. But he shook his head again.

I stepped forward and took the bowl I'd seen on the ground by him.

'Don't question the will of God,' I said angrily. He looked unsettled.

I filled the bowl from the cauldron myself. He didn't stop me.

'I'll take the boy with me when I leave,' I added, and turned my back on him. I didn't think the mother would live.

The boy never ate the soup. His mother was already in the throes of the sweat by the time I got back. I put the bowl down on the ground. John was cutting her shift away. I nearly said, 'Don't bleed her,' but I stopped myself: what was my basic schooling in herbal remedies, after all, compared to his years of study and his confidence with his patients? She didn't complain. Didn't cry out. Didn't shy away from the blade that was taking the black blood out of her. Fainted, as she was supposed to. But she didn't come round either. Mary from Deptford was dead within half an hour of our arrival. The boy went on standing there, not moving, looking down in bewilderment at the brown-stained blankets as John and I got up with the stink of finality on us. He only came up to my waist.

I left John to arrange for the woman to be buried. It wouldn't take long since they'd already dug the grave before she got sick. They'd be glad to tip her in and cover her up. They'd feel safer now she was gone.

I didn't discuss what would come next with John either. I just took the boy's hand and began to lead him back up the lane. I didn't know what to do with him. I couldn't bring him to the house. I couldn't turn him loose. Scarcely aware myself of where I was going, I found myself standing by the river with the unresisting child, then opening the door of the western gatehouse. The irons had gone, but there was still a scrap of blanket on the floor.

'You can lie down on that,' I said, hearing my voice sound more rough than kind. He stood, staring. 'You'll be safe here,' I added, rummaging in my bag. There wasn't much in it: the clean rags I'd brought out for today, the bottle of willow-bark infusion I always carried, and a piece of bread. 'I'm going to get you some water,' I said. 'There's bread for you here. And I'm going to give you some medicine.'

I fetched in the gardener's pail of water, sweating myself from the heat. The child's stare was unnerving. 'Sit down,' I said. 'Drink this.' And I held out the bottle. He didn't want to take it at first, but I put his hands on it and guided it to his mouth. And he drank it down. 'Now lie down,' I said. 'Cover yourself with this blanket, and keep as still as you can. I'll come back this evening.'

He was still staring blankly as I pushed the door shut. Outside, I arranged the chain over the door so it looked locked. And I strode off, not wanting to berate myself for not knowing enough to save the sick, but full of an angry vigour that I put down to pity, back towards the house.

I couldn't eat. But I went in for the midday meal anyway. It was time. It was a kind of relief to do what was expected of you in civilised society – an antidote against the void that had opened up beneath my feet during the day. Margaret saw me first. 'Where's John?' she asked. I shook my head, beyond words. She understood without needing to be told that something bad had happened; she put an arm around my shoulders. 'Meg,' she said gently. 'You're doing so much good, but you look exhausted. Please take care of yourself.'

I nodded.

'Master Hans is here,' she added, trying to cheer me up. 'Looking very prosperous, with a full set of new clothes. And he's got a bit fat.'

I nodded again. I couldn't find space to think about Master Hans's climb up the greasy pole now; there was too much else on my mind. I needed to wash and change. I needed to boil up more willow-bark tea. I needed to make sure there were more clean cloths. I needed to know whether John had noticed any fresh signs of sickness (or rebellion) in the crowd at the barn.

But when the painter bounded up, full of gingery–blond cheer, and chortled, 'Mistress Meg!' at me, I was charmed despite myself. He'd just sat down, and had already speared a vast amount of beef and deposited it on his platter. He forgot it when he saw me, and stood, almost dancing up and down on his broad legs, with stories bursting out of him about Norfolk, where he'd been painting all the local gentry (which, I knew, meant he'd made friends with the

Boleyn set's relatives while he was at court, but I didn't want to ask too much about that; it was his business).

'Did you know, Master Hans, that I was born in Norfolk?' I said, briefly distracted from my worries despite myself, and surprising myself by sharing this confidence with him. It was years since I'd thought of my birthplace. 'Near Burnham. I know it well.'

'Burnham!' he said with delight. 'But I went to Burnham! If I'd known, I'd have drawn you a sketch of your house! Norfolk was beautiful, and now I know everyone who is anyone there, and I have painted their pictures!'

His English was better than I remembered. He'd learned some new phrases.

'It's an ill wind that blows nobody any good,' he said, proudly moving his tongue round the phrase, looking delightedly round at the group. 'It is bad to come together at a time of disease. But it is a great pleasure to see you again, and a great opportunity for me to go back to the work I came here to begin. I have been forgetful, ha ha! I feel I've come home.'

And his eyes came to rest on me, in a way that made me remember Elizabeth's long-ago taunt that Master Hans had spent his first evening with us making sheep's eyes at me.

I lowered my eyes, embarrassed. But not so fast that I didn't spot the look of intense dismay on Master Hans's face as John came quietly into the room and walked straight up to me.

Ignoring Master Hans – or, if the truth be told, perhaps partly pleased to be able to demonstrate my love directly – I looked into John's eyes for news.

He looked tired too, but calm. 'Nothing more,' he said. 'I'll go back and check later. But it's all quietened down for now.'

He took my hands. I didn't look away, but I was aware of Master Hans quietly slipping out of the room.

By that afternoon there was more bad news. But it didn't come from the encampment by the barn. In the middle of the afternoon, while I boiled up more willow-bark infusion in my room, Margaret began to feel unnaturally cold. By the time I reached her bedroom, hurrying ahead of the maid who'd called me, Margaret was sweating.

I sent Will downstairs, out of the way.

I sent others out for water and towels.

I stood in front of her bed, alone, watching her toss and turn under her blanket, and I prayed for a moment.

I called a servant boy so I could send him to the village to find John. Half an hour there; half an hour back. John would most likely be with us before the crisis hit Margaret.

Then I thought – about Mary from Deptford and her daughter, and the agonised way they'd died fainting and bleeding under the knife. And I thought about John's superior medical knowledge, and what he'd told me about his admiration for Galen the Greek doctor, who'd made his reputation in Rome by dissecting living pigs in front of admiring audiences, and proving that understanding and treating pain was within the ability of man, and saving an entire civilisation from the terror of the Gods that had paralysed them for centuries by turning medicine into a rational and natural art. And I thought about John's respect for the dramatic Galenic cures of bleeding and leeching the sick, so that the impurities in their bodies would drain out with their diseased blood.

It was pure instinct, but suddenly I knew that I didn't want Margaret to go under the knife. Before the boy's head came round the door, I found myself doubting whether I'd send for John after all. I remembered how I'd cured Father's mysterious fever once without any

Galenic heroic doctoring – just by giving him my simple willow-bark remedy. I thought of how Father's head had dropped gently into sleep and how he'd woken rested and cool. I thought of how I'd given the boy from Deptford, hiding in the western gatehouse, a dose of the same willow-bark potion that morning.

In the end I sent the servant boy away without any order to fetch John. Instead, I ran downstairs to Master Hans, who was unpacking his easel in what was about to be his studio again. He was the only person I could send on this errand and trust his silence. He talked too much, but he was a quick thinker. He'd obey without question. He looked surprised to see me – as if he wanted to talk. 'Don't ask questions,' I hissed fiercely. 'There's no time. Just run to the western gatehouse, and come and tell me what you see. And don't tell a soul. Quickly.'

I got back to Margaret's room before Father came rushing upstairs. He was paler than I'd ever seen him, snuffling with tears: a stranger, a victim, a distraught relative of the damned, a person I'd never seen before. He flung himself down on his knees by her bed and hugged her soaking head. She was lost to us; delirious; muttering fearful half-thoughts and half-prayers.

I pulled him gently aside. My arms were aching to sit with him and comfort him; but there was no time. I sat at the bed-head with my pail of water, dipping cloths in it and wiping the sweat from her, dropping the used cloths into a pile behind me.

On his knees, Father wept and prayed. He got up. He stared at me. He stared at her. She was getting hotter. He paced up and down the room. There were tears streaming down his face. I'd never seen him in this state. It was so much part of his personality to laugh, and to talk of laughter, and to show a smiling public face to the world. But now he was as hysterical as a woman in grief; almost more delirious with his fear than she was with her sickness. 'Oh Margaret,' he howled. 'Don't go. Oh God, spare her. If she dies I'll never meddle in worldly matters again. Oh God, spare her.'

'Father,' I said, and he looked around, bewildered. I said, with the best confidence I could muster: 'Father, don't worry so. It's God's will. We're going to try to save her.' And I was relieved that he gave me another long, half-comprehending stare, before he began sobbing again.

There was a knock at the door. It was Master Hans. He stayed outside, looking frightened at the howls of pain coming from inside. I could see he recognised Father's voice. 'I didn't realise,' he stammered. 'I'm sorry . . .'

'It's not him. It's Margaret. But never mind that,' I snapped. 'What did you see?'

He looked even more frightened, as if I'd gone mad.

'Why . . . nothing,' he stuttered. 'A blanket. A bottle. A bucket of water.'

Which meant the boy had gone. Which meant he hadn't caught the sickness. Which might mean the willow-bark medicine had helped.

Which meant I was going to trust my own remedy to save Margaret, more than I was going to trust John Clement's knowledge.

'Master Hans,' I said, 'thank you.' And I leaned impulsively forward and kissed his cheek, before leaving him looking astonished in the corridor and darting off to my room to where the willow-bark tea, cool now, was waiting.

Margaret drank it down. Half of it went down her chin, but the other half went into her slack mouth. I breathed a prayer of my own and went back to my mopping and swabbing.

There came a point where only Father's prayers could be heard. There came a point where only his anxious breathing could be heard. There came a point where even that seemed to stop.

'Meg,' he said, in a voice so normal it was shocking. 'Is she dead?'

'No,' I said, shocking myself by the answering normality of my voice. 'She's fallen asleep. But I think it's normal sleep.'

The bed was still soaking with sweat. The room still stank of death. And she was still flushed. But she was breathing as quietly and innocently as a baby.

Father looked down at her properly for the first time in hours, and the terror left his face. Then he looked at me, and I saw a reflection of the love he felt for his first child in his shining eyes. For a second I thought he would embrace me. But he just whispered, 'She's alive,' and stepped away to the window, and crossed himself, and went back to staring at me from a distance. 'It's a miracle. No, you're a miracle. You've saved her.'

Since there was something so unexpectedly like love in the soft way he was looking at me, and since we were both so tired from what had happened and what we'd done and felt in that darkened room, around Margaret's prone form, for those few strange, panicked hours, I felt my own gaze shine softly, lovingly back on him.

And then I shook myself and came back to reality. Father's loving look was an expression of shock more than love, my rational self told me. He would look away in a moment and forget everything. And there was something important I had to do right now. So I looked away; down to the dresser, feeling for the bell. I rang for a servant. And only then, feeling deceitful and ashamed (but secretly sure I'd done the right thing), did I finally send for John. By the time he rushed in nearly an hour later, with his bag on his shoulder and the panicked, purple-faced boy behind him, I was clearing away the rags and bucket. By the time Margaret woke up, early the next morning, she was better.

'A life restored,' Father said as he began our prayers over supper. There was awe in his voice still. 'A life restored, by the grace of God. Let us give thanks.' His voice was weak still and his reddened eyes shone as they caressed me in the candlelight.

Margaret was still asleep. But she would wake up, and she and the baby would (God willing) live. Will Roper's eyes were fastened as gratefully and uncomprehendingly on me as Father's. No one was exactly saying that I'd saved Margaret (though I was still glowing from Father having said that, in his confusion, in the sickroom), but just by having been the one on the spot to mop her brow I'd gained a kind of credit for helping her through her crisis. And Master Hans, who had asked for no explanations but who knew the errand I'd sent him on had something to do with Margaret's deliverance, was staring at me with almost religious awe. Only John, at my side, was quiet; glad though he was to find Margaret alive, I sensed he felt he'd failed the family by arriving too late to treat her. I felt guilty to have deceived him by failing to call him; but I was pleased, too, that I'd trusted my own judgement. Margaret might not have lived through a blood-letting. Under the table, I squeezed his hand comfortingly; and I was relieved to feel an answering pressure from his fingers. I could have shown compassion to anyone that night. It was pure vainglory, of course, but my mood was as sweet as the song of the nightingale outside the window.

No one quite knew what to say next. We ate in silence. It was Master Hans who broke it. With his fingers and mouth still sticky and glistening from the beef and pigeon – no one else had much appetite, but he was tucking in with as much enthusiasm as ever – he cleared his throat, sniffed the honeysuckle, and said, a little awkwardly, 'Sometimes it is beautiful to remember family. My picture of your family is finished except for a few details. When you have finished eating I would like to invite you to come and see.'

Master Hans fussed over the lighting for several minutes when he'd got us all in the studio. It was a small room, and a tight fit for six adults fidgeting against the window. His pictures were messed up on the table again. I closed his portfolio and put the skull back on it. He flashed me a grateful smile, and went back to fiddling with candles and moving his easel.

The picture was propped up against the wall with its back to us. When he'd got the easel fixed up to his liking at last, he moved the canvas to the easel, still covered with its rough cloth. Then, with a little flourish, he pulled the cover away.

It was a revelation – like no picture I'd ever seen. No religion in it, except that Dame Alice was kneeling at one side of the composition, but it was God in a breath of ordinary life. There we all were, in miniature, in the great hall, with our faces, our expressions, the way we held our heads, all perfectly reproduced on the easel: Margaret and Cecily in the foreground, near Dame Alice, whose hair was swept back off her noble forehead and who had a hint of a smile on her face; Elizabeth standing to one side, looking pretty but distant; me next to her, leaning forward over a glassy-eyed Grandfather and studiously pointing something out to him; and, in the centre, flanked by Grandfather and young John and in front of Anne, Father himself, looking solemn but without the torturer's grimness that had been such a feature of his solo portrait; and, in the very centre, staring mockingly out at us from above his ginger beard, was Henry Pattinson, the fool.

I drew in a sharp breath, and I wasn't the only one. The idea of the composition had been a joke one evening long ago. But now it was a vision of lives restored – an invitation to nostalgia. It was almost like seeing our family reunited, with every personality full of remembered beauty, depicted with love. Father fixed his gaze on Margaret's prayerful little head. But I found myself drinking in the sight of the absent Cecily, with her neat profile and her kindly face, and then, less easily, turning my eyes to Elizabeth. How watchful her beautiful eyes were, above her perfectly straight nose. How unsmiling her lovely lips. She looked unhappy, I thought, with a shock of realisation; as if she didn't fit into our circle and was withdrawing to the edge. For the first time, it occurred to me that Thomas More's true daughter might have felt as ill at ease in the More family as I sometimes did – though for different reasons, in her case: because she was better at pretty repartee than rhetoric, and more skilled at the galliard than at her Greek. And, unusually for me, I found myself longing to see her as much as Cecily, their babies and their husbands. I wanted to talk to Elizabeth in a different way, to be more straightforward with her, to admit that I'd sometimes felt more than a twinge of jealousy for her prettiness, to try and bring to life something a little warmer between us.

When I looked around, I could see everyone in the room had been thrown into a reverie by the sudden reappearance of our family, reunited. I didn't want to interrupt all their separate trains of thought.

I was no painter, but the picture looked finished to me, with a cluster of objects at the back of the painted room and our heads in a semicircle at the front. But I suppose pictures are only really finished when the most important clients are satisfied. I looked to see what Father and the Dame were making of it.

Like two sides of the same coin, they were both looking awkward and uncertain. 'You should,' Alice said, breaking the spell and making me half jump out of my skin, 'put some lutes on the shelf at the back of the hall.' Her voice was challenging. I thought the feelings the painting had stirred up in all of us might be embarrassing her. She was trying to break the transcendent mood that had suffused us all and bring us back to earth. She didn't like being carried away by emotions. Like Father, perhaps, she was scared of their messiness. 'Do Sir Thomas's musical gifts justice.' She laughed jarringly.

Father looked at her. Then he took his cue from her and burst out laughing too, trying as hard as she had to make light of the magic of the emotion that we'd been feeling. 'If you're going to put musical instruments in,' he added jocularly, 'why not put Dame Alice on a chair? She complained about her knees aching all the time she was posing for you.'

We all laughed along. 'I'll change everything so it's just how you want it,' Master Hans said expansively. I supposed he just might draw in some lutes later, or put the Dame on a chair, but I didn't think anyone seriously meant him to change anything. The picture was perfect as it was. Father was just feeling vulnerable. We quickly fell silent again and went back to looking. I wanted to catch Master Hans's eye. Yet even he was in his own triumphant dream. He was looking from one lost, thoughtful, haunted face to another, and gently nodding his head. He could see us all remembering love, or wanting to create it. He knew his picture had had the effect he'd wanted.

When Father made his usual apologies and slipped away towards the New Building a little later, I slipped away after him, leaving John in the parlour with the rest of the family

165

without a backward glance. I was suddenly full of courage. Of all nights, I thought, tonight was one time Father couldn't be too busy to speak to me alone.

'Father . . .' I called softly from behind.

He turned in the dusk, in a cloud of cow parsley, surprised to be followed. 'Meg?' he said, equally hushed, but accepting; waiting for me to catch him up.

There were so many searching questions I'd wanted to ask him for so long, but not dared. I'd imagined dozens of private talks between us: interrogations about the man in the gatehouse and the question of heresy; discussions about politics, Cardinal Wolsey, or the King and his loves, or frank talks about John. But in the end, now we were walking together through the tender gnats and stars, what we talked about – walking a little further apart than we might need, too far to make it possible to link arms, but cautiously feeling a way towards something approaching intimacy – was genius.

'How lucky we are to be alive, and to have Margaret with us still,' he said reverently, almost in a whisper, as if he were praying. 'How lucky we are to have your gift for healing.'

'And John Clement's,' I murmured back, happily embarrassed by the implied praise and hoping to deflect him onto the subject I wanted to talk about most, but he didn't seem to hear.

A few shadowy paces further on, I tried again. A little uncertainly: 'So many of your circle have extraordinary gifts. Didn't you find Master Hans's painting astonishing . . .'

But he only sighed at that, as if I'd uncovered the secret discontent in his heart. 'I'll be frank with you, Meg: of course I love excellence, like any gift from God, but I find some of these modern gifts and geniuses disturbing,' he said confidingly, 'when they produce work that you feel is assaulting your senses, like a great shout in your ear.

Like Hans Holbein's painting tonight. I looked at it and wondered: is he sharing his vision of the world with his friends – or is he thrusting it down their throats?'

He wasn't looking at me, but at the hot, dry ground opening up before him. I kept my steps steady. I didn't want to appear startled. I hadn't expected him to feel so threatened by a picture which he'd commissioned himself and which, to me, looked so like an act of worship anyway. The secret part of me that distrusted Father and suspected him of hiding a growing taste for cruelty felt a twinge of alarm – a protective sort of unease on behalf of that great German innocent in the parlour, who'd looked so radiantly happy that his picture had touched us as deeply as it had. But the man at my side was speaking so trustingly, as any affectionate father might to a child he loved, that I stifled my worry, and only nodded, and made a little noise to encourage him to go on speaking his mind.

And he did. 'The ideas I enjoy are those that everyone has a share in; the work that's accomplished together,' he said, almost to himself. 'The cathedral whose loveliness is the work of hundreds of artists whose individual names we don't need to know; the choral singing whose beauty is that no single voice dominates; the riches brought by a prosperous guild for the benefit of every master and journeyman.'

And he sighed again, a little sadly, like rain melting into a sunny garden.

'But Father, you're famous for welcoming men of genius. Every man of learning in Europe comes to you. And they don't come to show off. They come to bring their gifts to you. They come because you're one of them, and you can appreciate them intelligently. They come to be near your genius,' I said cautiously.

'Oh no,' he said, with a modest wave of the hand, a denial of vanity. 'There's no genius in me. I'm just a humble lawyer, a public administrator. And, more and more often now, I feel I'm a man of the past, too. I can't help feeling nostalgic for when people all worked together, when the world was held together by people doing God's bidding together at God's direction.'

He turned his face towards me now, for the first time, and I could see it shining with sincerity. 'What's a good way to explain it to you, Meg? When I was a boy, there were wars in the land and we should have felt more uncertain in every way, every day, than we do in this time of peace and plenty,' he said. 'But we didn't. When I walked to school at St Anthony's in the morning, with a candle in my hand, London looked like a map of the face of God. Monasteries, nunneries, guilds, churches; it used to be a city where everyone – every man, woman and child – knew his place and his role. Life was an act of worship and a dance. We knew the weight of a loaf of bread and the bride-price of a silk-woman in the Mercery and the fee for a Mass for our dead and the length of service of an apprentice in the rope-makers' guild and the words of the Holy Bible and the proper respect to show to our fathers and our monarchs and the princes of the Church; that was all part of what made up our lives, the whole that God had created for us. Even if there was war, we lived at peace with God.'

We were at the door of the New Building now, and he was fiddling at his belt for the key. And I was still nodding and murmuring encouragingly, honoured that he'd reveal his mind to me, doing whatever I could to spin this rare moment out, and he was saying: 'But now the world seems so full of loud discordant voices, each crying out "listen to me!", "no, me!", "no, me!", that it sometimes feels like anarchy.

'Some of them are genuinely evil – like the pretenders who've tried so often to take the throne from our kings, or the renegade priests who want to tear the Holy Church apart. Luther, Tyndale: the men of darkness. But others aren't evil at all. They're just young people, brought up with all the choices of our times and not enough reverence for God's holy order, who think they can ignore it and scream for attention for themselves. Like young Holbein. But in some ways it's those people – the Holbeins – that make me feel uneasiest of all. Because if you see it as your life's work to bring back the harmony that's been lost from the world, to draw men back together into that virtuous bond with each other and God and banish the darkness, it's easy enough to condemn a man who openly spits anathema at all that – a Luther, say. But what do you do with a Holbein?'

'Oh Father,' I said helplessly. I could understood a little of why he'd find Hans Holbein's boisterous individuality to be part of the same path that led, at its most dangerous, to Martin Luther or William Tyndale. His own instincts, his upbringing, were so different. With sudden tenderness I found myself recalling all his public acts of respect and obedience to Grandfather, even today. The family authoritarian, a tough judge and a man of the old school who favoured beatings and hunger and the hard school of life, was always seated first at church and at table. His every barked opinion and desire was deferred to even now he was wrinkled and infirm. And even the twitch of Grandfather's stick in his constantly irritated hand had Father looking deferentially his father's way to bring the old man whatever comfort he might need. I knew Father hadn't been brought up in the soft way we had. He'd been left to the mercies of a nurse even before his mother died. There'd been no suckets and marchpane for him if his lessons were learned well – just the fear of beatings if they weren't, that would never have been with the peacock feathers he'd waved so laughingly at us, but with real sticks. The fact that he'd made our childhood so different from his own, rewarding us so lavishly for developing unexpected gifts and talents, suggested that a part of him had rejected that constricting old order. But he must have had more respect than I'd previously understood beaten into him for the old ways – for things being the same, generation in, generation out, because that was God's will. And that hidden part of him probably did fear the very fearlessness with which someone like Master Hans loved experimenting with his art.

My glimmer of understanding wasn't enough to make me agree, though. My hands tightened on the stuff of my skirt, crimping little pleats into it. 'But Master Hans is a good, kind man, Father,' I said, in a kind of weak protest, 'and surely he's using his gift as God intended. You can't see anything ungodly in that.'

He laughed, but gently, and I felt myself beginning to relax. 'Oh, I don't think he's ungodly; I'm not saying that; you know I'm a man of moderation, Meg,' he acquiesced.

And when I peeped sideways at his face, and saw not harshness but a soft, almost pleading expression on it, a wave of tenderness for him swept through me. I whispered: 'I know.'

'I know Holbein's a good man as well as a wonderful artist,' Father went on warmly. 'I like him. All I mean is that he makes me realise how life has changed since I was young. That sometimes I find his vision too overwhelmingly, selfishly, his own. That Holbein feels life as a freedom that makes me dizzy; the kind of freedom which I fear threatens to destroy the ties that bind us and send us all toppling together into the abyss.'

He unlocked the door and began lighting the candles inside. Behind him I could see Master Hans's noli-me-tangere picture, sold to Father when he first reached our house, with its ethereal Christ shying away from Mary

170

Magdalene's fleshy curves, glowing in the dim light. 'I don't worry about all his work,' Father added reassuringly, catching my glance at the religious picture and turning to look up at it himself. 'In *this* picture, for instance, it's easy to see a painter who recognises his gift is God-given. I love it for its humbleness, for being a work in which the man has harnessed his genius to giving thanks to God. It's pictures like this that make me recognise Master Hans as a kindred spirit . . .'

I felt confident enough by now to try to argue. 'But Father,' I said, holding his gaze, 'our family portrait was never going to be a religious picture, and even if you don't like the way it's come out you can't hold Master Hans solely responsible. Don't you remember? It was you who encouraged him to paint it the way he did. You spent most of an evening plotting it out with him. You made us all rehearse our positions in the hall; you roared with laughter at the thought of putting a fool at the heart of the family. It was your idea as much as his.'

There was a small silence. He looked down. Then he sighed again, put a weary hand to his forehead, smoothed away what might have been a pain under the lined olive skin, and looked back at me, meeting the challenge in my eyes with a nod of recognition.

'You go straight to the heart of things, Meg,' he said ruefully. 'And you're more right than you know. I'm to blame for more than I like to recognise. I *have* encouraged free thinking and experiment in my time – perhaps too much. Change for its own sake seemed so exciting in the golden years, when we were young and everything looked fresh and innocent. And now, when I hear these innocent shouts of "Me! Me!" – let alone when I see the destruction being perpetrated by those who are really doing the Devil's work – I often wonder how far I'm to blame in the eyes of God for having enjoyed all that tinkering and altering. How far my own idle curiosity has been responsible for opening Pandora's box and letting so much evil fly out into the world . . .'

His eyes were full of anguish now, so much so that I felt mine filling with compassionate tears too. I couldn't find the words to banish his cares, but I did find the courage I had never had before to put a hand out and touch his fingers – an inarticulate gesture of comfort, but one I hoped he would understand.

His skin was dry and cool. He didn't draw his hand away from mine, didn't take his eyes away from mine, and I was heartened to see some of the pain in his dark gaze fade away. 'The world changes, that's all,' I found myself muttering. 'Not through any one man's fault . . . Not because of any one man's actions. You can't turn back time . . . don't blame yourself. Nothing is your fault.'

He went on looking at my face, and slowly the blurry look of pain left him and something of the familiar quizzical amusement with which he usually met the world came back into his expression.

'I see you're a child of the new world too, Meg,' he said in a more everyday voice. 'And I know,' he lifted a hand to stop me pointing out the obvious, 'it's the education I've given you that has made you that way. I can see you think I'm just an old man being old-fashioned. And perhaps I am. Perhaps I am.'

He gave the beginning of a hesitant smile. And I was suddenly, radiantly certain of something else. It would be impossible for this man to commit any kind of cruel act. John must be right; I'd leaped hastily to what must have been the wrong conclusions and needlessly tormented myself for months with the fear that darkness had crept into Father's soul, simply because I didn't know his reasons for bringing a prisoner home to our gatehouse. But now that we were talking from the heart, just the two of us, it seemed blindingly obvious to me that Father was simply too reasonable to turn fanatic. I was struck dumb by the force of the relief that the revelation brought.

How long had we been standing like this? I wondered – on the edges of the same pool of candlelight, with the figures from the devotional picture looking down at us, gazing at each other almost like lovers.

'Will you pray with me, Meg?' he asked, very gently, detaching his arm from my hand. 'Give thanks for Margaret's salvation?'

There was a lump in my throat. I nodded and we shambled awkwardly to our knees. Keeping my eyes turned away from the scourge hanging behind the door, I prayed, like him, that we could all believe the same things and be at peace with one another and God. As my mouth formed the Latin words that believers like us had spoken for a thousand years and more, I let my mind dwell nostalgically on Father's childhood London: a city that was still a prayer in stone and wood to God's goodness, in which even walking the tracery of lanes leading out from St Paul's, with their holy names, *Ave Maria* and *Paternoster*, had been an act of worship. I couldn't help but believe Master Hans's family portrait was also God's work, worship in a new shape, worship for our richer times. But I was honoured to have been invited to share Father's private vision of God – his search for the lost innocence of childhood. It felt like one more proof that my God was smiling on me and making my life come right. Even if this encounter between the two of us wasn't quite the embrace I used to dream of, it was the closest my adopted father had ever let me come to him.

'What would Father say?' I whispered, watching almost drunkenly in the dapples of sunlight as John stretched my arm out straight and traced a line down it, very slowly,

173

with a single finger. I shivered with pleasure and half-closed my eyes, following the touch as it moved towards wrist and palm.

'He knows,' John murmured back, as his finger reached the end of its journey and he raised my hand to his lips. Gently he kissed the little mound of flesh between thumb and forefinger, pushing it slowly open with his tongue and nipping softly at the thin web of skin under it with his teeth. Then he stopped, and glimmered with laughter. 'Of course. And you know he knows, Meg.'

The funny thing was that I did. Everything had become so simple when we'd woken up the next morning. In the midday heat on the way home from the village, where no one new had fallen sick, in the shady copse he'd led me into and where I'd unquestioningly followed, sleepily enjoying the sound of insects buzzing tipsily and the sight of sun glittering on the golden river water, it was getting simpler all the time. I nodded as if I understood. I felt I did.

John covered my hand, still tingling from being kissed, with his, and guided it down to rest on his hip. I felt his other hand slide around my waist and move down. As if we were dancing, as if our bodies knew the steps to take next, I found we were turning towards each other and my body was leaning back against a tree trunk while his pressed up against me so close that I could feel his heartbeat, very fast, as fast as mine under my rumpled cloak. From very close, I could see his eyes on mine and the little half-smile on his lips as he whispered, between breaths, 'He might horsewhip me if he saw me now . . . true. But this is the point. He married off everyone else. But he saved you for me. And he knows why I'm here now. To claim you.'

His words were part of it – the relief of the idea that I hadn't been forgotten by my family as Father arranged marriage after marriage; that there had been a quiet purpose to it all. The heat of the sun on my arms was part of it too. But if I found myself turned to a trickling sweetness of honey it was also because of the feel of him against my skin, all hard muscle and flesh surging forward, kissing my neck.

I had no idea, I thought hours afterwards, drawing the crumpled clothes around my sticky nakedness with a sense of wonderment. No idea. I snuggled closer inside his heavy, sleepy arms, full of memories that were all sensation and no words, just happiness. There were rough black hairs on his chest and a line of black hair leading down his flat torso. He had pale skin and more dark hair on the big bones and lean muscle of his arms and legs. He stirred and half-opened his eyes to look at me, lifted a hand to raise my chin and smiled as he put his lips to mine. Then he ran his hand down my body, following it with his eye, circled my breast with it and laughed very softly, with the same wonderment I was feeling. 'Beautiful,' he said sleepily. 'Mine.' And his arms enfolded me again.

I woke to find him raised on one elbow, looking at me, and the happiness inside me welled up at the tenderness of his smile.

'So ours will be a marriage of doctors,' he said. He seemed not to be aware that he was still naked; not to feel the light breeze ruffling his hair. Suddenly self-conscious, I looked down and started fumbling for my shift. I didn't just feel naked; I realised I'd been dishonest not to have told him about the way I'd tended to Margaret, yet I was still embarrassed to mention willow-bark tea to someone of his high learning and have him laugh off my remedy as an old wives' tale, and I also thought I might, in his place, feel discountenanced that an untrained girl had saved a life which his science might not have rescued. Which was unfair; the disease took some and spared others; it was the will of God and not necessarily anything to do with the simple tea I'd made Margaret. And no one could have been braver than John in risking his own life and health to treat the diseased strangers from the Deptford slums. Rushing awkwardly into my linen, getting lost in sleeves, buttons and laces, I was wondering what to do, when I heard his voice say:

'So tell me, what did you give her?'

And there was nothing in it but interest.

'Your father said you gave her a draught . . .' he went on, and now I looked up and saw kindness in his eyes – the look I remembered from the schoolroom, when he wanted to draw some discovery from me. 'I'm listening,' he said, and I knew he truly was. And suddenly I also knew he wouldn't laugh at me.

I answered, still a little awkwardly, 'Well . . . while I was waiting for you to get word . . . I gave her willow bark. Something one of the women on Bucklersbury told me about long ago. It's supposed to cool the blood. It's worked before for me, and I was desperate. I thought it might help . . . But I think we were just lucky.' My voice trailed away.

He smiled, but without mockery. He was genuinely intrigued by the idea, and I thought he looked impressed. There was so little selfish pride in John, I thought, in a happy muddle of love for his simplicity and relief that he didn't seem to feel threatened by my having tried a remedy he hadn't thought of and which had, miraculously, worked. I thought his modesty might have come from being of an age to have grown up in the aftermath of the wars; he'd probably been shaped by the suffering of back then in ways that we prosperous children of peacetime couldn't even imagine. 'Willow bark, eh,' he murmured. 'Well, you have healing hands and good instincts. I wonder if that's something I should talk to Doctor Butts about, now I'm

176

going to be working with him. We could try using it more; start trying to understand how it helps. Would you mind, Meg?'

I shook my head. I was blushing, but with pleasure now and not just out of shame at my nakedness. I'd be so proud if my homespun remedies could somehow help his medical career. More bravely, I said, 'I was relieved she survived her crisis before you needed to cut her. I'm scared of bleeding people.'

And instead of frowning at my small medical heresy, he nodded thoughtfully. 'Yes,' he said. 'I sometimes wonder about whether these things work, too.'

He noticed my bashfulness now. I think to put me at ease, he also began to stretch for a shirt and shake it out before putting arms into sleeves. But he went on looking happy and comfortable.

'John,' I said, taking courage from the easy intimacy of the moment to ask the question I'd never dared ask. 'If we're going to marry now, shouldn't you tell me about your family? I don't know anything about where you're from and who your people are. You sprang up from nowhere as our tutor . . . fully formed . . .'

Not that it really mattered, I supposed. So many people that we knew were men from nowhere, rising in the ruins of wars that had wiped out half the aristocracy, destroyed fortunes, and caused chaos throughout the land. Cardinal Wolsey was the son of a butcher; his secretary Thomas Cromwell the son of an ale-house keeper. Father's grand-father had been a baker. John had always been part of our circle, and that had been enough; but if we were to be united before God, surely I should know something about whatever sisters and brothers, parents and shires, he'd hailed from?

He looked vaguely round, with the shirt flapping over on his taut chest. I could smell him on me; I breathed in and savoured the memory of our closeness as he began to tie up the ribbons. 'I'll have a lifetime to tell you my stories, so I won't rush them all out now,' he said, and I could see him choosing his words. 'I lost my family young. You know that my father died. And then I had a good stepfather, but I lost him suddenly too.

'After that I went to live with my aunt, in Burgundy, until she died,' he went on, with a faraway look in his eye. 'That's when I studied at the university at Louvain. And then I travelled. I went everywhere when I was young, looking for a way to –' he paused '– find part of my family again. Looking for people who remembered me after the wars. You don't know the half of it. It wasn't just the Low Countries. I've been up and down the kingdom in my time, and beyond. I've been to Ireland. I've been to Scotland. But nothing came of it. The only kin I have left is a brother, and we didn't ever get on well . . .' There was wistfulness on his face now. 'He's in London, oddly enough. One of the things I wanted to do when I came back was to renew our relationship. But coldnesses creep in. Gaps develop that can never be bridged.'

I thought I might have begun to understand that. When I looked at the expression on his face now, I was half-seeing Elizabeth, and a part of me was quietly resolving to make things better between us when we next saw each other. 'So that's how it happened,' John was saying, stockings already on his feet, putting a hand out to feel around for breeches.

'Then Erasmus told me – and your father – that I'd find a new family in the fellowship of learning.' He stood up, easing on his clothes. And he passed me my skirts, and handed me into them as expertly as a lady's maid. 'That felt like a homecoming. So I started a new life. It's irrelevant now, of course – now I have you.' He laughed, ending the conversation. I realised, a little disconsolately, that I scarcely knew any more now than I had before. Perhaps he'd always be an enigma. 'We'll be a real family for each other now,' he said, kissing away the bewildered frown on my forehead. 'That's enough for me.'

He turned me around, and bent his head in suddenly businesslike fashion towards my laces. 'Breathe in,' he said briskly, tucking a visible flap of shift under the bodice.

I wasn't ready for that. Slightly taken aback by how much he understood about the way women's clothing was put together, I said, more tartly than I meant to, 'You could be a lady's maid, Master John.'

He laughed, and pulled at the laces as if I were a doll. He wasn't ashamed of this knowledge, I realised, nor of knowing the secret ways of the crochet lace of my modest collar, which he attached next. He almost seemed proud of it all. He picked up my bonnet, too, and slipped it onto my head, adjusting it with deft fingers to cover my hair. I thought he might be showing me something.

'Well,' he laughed, finally catching my inquiring eye, still full of his own lightness of spirit. 'In the name of truth, then, Meg, you must know that I haven't always been faithful to the idea of you.'

I nodded reluctantly, not wanting to know this but not wanting to appear naïve either, feeling a little of my own happiness leak away. 'Italy . . .' I said, trying not to sound disconsolate.

Apparently not aware of my uncertain tone, he charged on. 'No – I actually led a monkish sort of life in Italy – I mean back here at court. It's a lascivious place, King Henry's court. They talk about it all over Europe: the stamping-ground of the new rich – show-offs and self-made men grabbing everything they can. When I came back I found that everything they say is true. Every entertainment ended the same way: a lot of drink, a lot of wild talk, and a lot of wild behaviour. And there's nothing wilder than the respectable married ladies who flirt with you so demurely from behind their masks early in the evening. By the small hours, when they've drunk their way through half a barrel of wine, they're only too ready to let you take them off into the draperies – or the rose garden by the light of the full moon – and take whatever liberties your own wine-fuelled fancy tells you to. So I let myself be led astray once or twice,' and I could see private memories flit across his face. Then he took in my shocked face and, looking repentant, he went on, pulling my chin up so I had, reluctantly, to meet his eye. 'Oh Meg, don't look so disappointed in me . . . because it was one of those encounters that finally brought me to my senses. Someone who reminded me of you. And suddenly I realised it was time to put all that behind me, and come and find the grown-up Mistress Meg and try and win her hand.'

He kissed my nose again and looked deep into my eyes. 'I've offended you,' he said, sounding stricken. 'I should have held my tongue. Too much truth is always difficult.'

I broke away and picked up my cloak, still feeling and, it seemed, against my will, looking unsettled, suddenly wretchedly vulnerable at the memory of having given myself to this man in this wood, at my recall of the ripping of maidenhood and the red kiss marks on breasts and neck and the stains on clothes; suddenly fearful of the heart-stopping possibility that he might talk about me, one day, to some other woman in the same way: *She reminded me of you.*

'It's the past, Meg,' he said persuasively, keeping his distance, not foolhardy enough to risk trying to touch me until the hurt passed but clearly guessing what was going through my mind. 'Never look back. It was never anything serious; you know I'll never notice another woman again. I've found you.'

I put my cloak around my shoulders. He was still standing in stockinged feet. His boots and cloak were forgotten in the nest of crumpled grass and leaves we'd made. He looked like a giant stork, or a raven, standing there so tall and black and suddenly anxious. And just as suddenly I wanted to forgive him.

'Isn't it time for us to go?' I said, and found a smile for him, and enjoyed his visible relief as he scrambled for boots and hopped, comically, on one foot and then on the other doing them up.

'And,' I went on, before he'd had time to compose himself, wanting to be able to forget feeling vulnerable and alone forever, 'isn't it time for you to tell Father I've accepted you and ask for permission to marry me – tonight?'

'Tonight.' He had his cloak on now and was arranging it over his shoulder. Then his jaw hardened into decision, and he grinned at me and held out a hand to start guiding me back out of the wood. 'You're right, wife,' he said firmly. 'You have good instincts. Tonight it is.'

We parted at the gate. He went towards the New Building to find Father. I went alone to my room with my feet hardly touching the ground.

I took off my clothes. I looked at myself in the glass. There were scratches on my back and buttocks, twigs in my hair, red marks on my breasts and a small, sharp, invisible ache between my legs. But my lips looked full and red, my eyes were shining, and even when they brought me water, I almost didn't want to get into it because I wanted to go on smelling his smell on me. After I'd scrubbed myself till my skin was pink and my teeth chattering from the coldness of the water, I dried every inch of skin carefully, rubbed salve on myself and prepared for a new life without any need for secret hopes and fears. I

181

dressed festively in the yellow dress I'd worn on the January day he'd reappeared. I found the pearl choker Father had given me when I came of age, which I'd had hardly any occasion to wear. (Full of my new contentment, I suddenly remembered pouting Anne Cresacre and the string of peas Father had given her in place of pearls, and realised I'd been luckier than her with my present.) I reddened my bruised lips and flushed cheeks. Far from my usual businesslike way before the glass, I pirouetted and smiled at myself, enjoying the feel of the silk under my hands and the way it flared out as I turned. I wanted to look my best for Father's announcement at the table.

I didn't want to have to talk to anyone before my news became public, so I sat down on my bed to wait for suppertime. I couldn't concentrate on needlework or reading. Time dragged. I could hear Margaret, still in her bed down the corridor, singing with happiness; a maid beating at something in a closet nearby; Dame Alice murdering a lute tune downstairs. I stood at the window and looked into the garden and saw Master Hans and Master Nicholas taking a turn just outside; I ducked away in case they saw me and invited me to join them. From a step further back, I watched two squirrels jerk playfully across the lawn and up and down the nearest tree. I sat down again. The sun was still high in the sky. There wasn't even the sound of pots clattering that might have meant the afternoon was nearly over.

Finally I couldn't stand the quiet any more. I tiptoed downstairs and out into the garden and stood basking in the sun and drinking in the oily sweetness of the roses and the singing of birds. Everything my senses were aware of reminded me, with a secret thrill, of the smooth movement of body on body in the woods that morning; even the starling looking inquisitively down at me from a spray of greenery, whose black beady eye reminded me of John.

182

When I saw Father, walking slowly down a path towards the New Building with a letter in his hand, I almost danced towards him over the daisies and buttercups, so lightly that he didn't seem to have heard my footsteps on the lawn behind. When I put a soft hand on his shoulder, and said questioningly, 'Father . . . ?' he jumped. He turned. I thought I'd see excitement and pleasure on my behalf on his face; I thought I'd see a blessing for our future forming on his lips; but I didn't. He was unshaven and set-faced and full of cares. 'Father, have you . . .' I faltered, stopping at the savage gloom in his eyes without even reaching the words '. . . spoken to John?'

Of course he hadn't, I realised, kicking myself for my foolishness. John was waiting for him in the New Building, and he was only just heading off to it now.

There was something that might have been pity in Father's dark face. 'I know you've talked seriously with John,' he said sombrely – not the answer I expected. It was as if he hadn't heard my question. 'But I'm afraid I have bad news.' He waved the letter. 'Edward Guildford is dead.'

I was baffled. What was he talking about? I didn't even know who Edward Guildford was. Father was getting letters every day telling him who had gone down with the sweating sickness. Why was he suddenly so worried about this stranger's death? What could it possibly have to do with me and the important question I was asking?

But I could, at least, see that he thought I should have understood better. When he saw my blank stare, he shook his head angrily. 'You don't even know who he is, do you?' he snapped. Less certain of my happiness than a moment ago, I shook my head. My mouth began to form the innocent word, 'Who?', but he saw it and shook his head again, even more angrily. 'Not now, Meg,' he said brusquely. I'd never seen Father less than courteous. But now, without another word, he turned on his heel and stumped on towards the New Building.

Bewildered, I stood where I was and watched him go.

As he reached the door, I saw a figure disengage from the shadows behind the New Building and come loping towards him. *John*. My heart lifted again, especially when John followed Father in through the door and shut it.

I walked to the river, full of anxious feelings I couldn't name. I watched the fishing boats come in. When Master Hans came to stand beside me, grinning all over his big face, I said without ceremony: 'Who is Edward Guildford?' He'd just spent two months at court scoping out everyone who might give him a commission. I knew he'd know.

I wasn't disappointed. He didn't ask why I was asking, just looked pleased at getting a chance to display his knowledge, and answered: '*Sir* Edward Guildford, you mean. One of the most influential men at court. He ran the celebrations at Greenwich. A big man. Black-haired.' He wriggled in delighted self-importance. 'I met him many times.'

'Thanks,' I said, and nodded to him. I still didn't understand.

I left Master Hans at the water's edge and walked back, past the New Building. I peered inside. I could hear voices in the dusk inside, but speaking too quietly to make out what they were saying. I fidgeted around for a few minutes, but there was no sound of chairs scraping or keys.

I walked back towards the house and stood by the back door, watching the sun sink towards the horizon and the shadows lengthen. I was too restless to stand still; too restless to go inside. When I finally saw the two little figures come out of the New Building door, and Father stop and fiddle with the lock while John came striding up the path towards me, I ran to meet him.

When I got close I saw he wasn't going to stop. His

eyes were red and swollen and there were wet streaks on his cheeks. But whoever he'd been crying over, it wasn't me. He looked at me with an empty face and kept walking. 'John . . . ?' I began, feeling the beginning of fear, turning to trot along behind him. 'Not now, Meg,' he said, as brusquely as Father had earlier. And, with what sounded like a sob, he quickened his pace, lengthened the distance between us and escaped into the house.

One look at Father's face turned the mood at table to ice. I had the impression that no one knew any better than I did what the matter was. Master Hans wiggled an eyebrow at me to express his secret puzzlement but stopped when I ignored him. John was not in the room. It seemed unreal; a waking nightmare intruding into my dream come true. I tried not to move too much to avoid drawing attention to myself decked out in my yellow dress and choker. I kept my eyes lowered and tried not to think of the sharp little nag of pain – sin remembered – between my legs. We ate in a deathly hush.

'We will go to chapel tonight,' Father said, pushing aside a platter of untouched food, 'for a funeral. Sir Edward Guildford, who has died of the sweating sickness, will be buried among us. God rest his soul.'

Eyes rose, furtive signals passed from one bewildered diner to another. I saw Will Roper and Margaret (up, but still with a sickbed shawl around her thin shoulders) raise eyebrows at each other. Was this an explanation? Even they, who clearly knew who Sir Edward Guildford was, had no idea why he would be buried in our family chapel. It was unheard of. Father offered no further information. The two foreigners gave up any pretence of politeness and stared in frank curiosity from one pinched face to the next. Dame Alice kept her nose firmly down and stared at her food.

185

We put on black cloaks over the clothes we were wearing, and walked by torchlight to the village. Margaret went, despite her weakness, with Will holding her arm. Dame Alice walked with Master Nicholas. Fifty yards ahead, Father led the way with John, who'd slipped out of the house to join us when we set off but was so wrapped in his outer garment that you could hardly guess at his face. He'd walked straight past me. He hadn't spoken to a soul. His shoulders were shaking.

And that left me, slipping as far back as I could to avoid the humiliation of even seeing those shoulders, bringing up the rear with Master Hans. 'I don't understand anything,' he whispered plaintively. 'What is this funeral?'

I shook my head to indicate that I didn't understand either, but kept my eyes ahead. I felt, by turns, numb, hot with a monstrous embarrassment, and sick as though I'd eaten splinters of glass and was slowly shredding inside. I was having too much trouble controlling my own emotions to have anything to say to anyone else. I didn't want him to insist on talking to me.

'Is the funeral why you are unhappy?' he persisted with his usual embarrassing frankness, still whispering but at larger-than-life volume.

I shook my head again. Despite myself, I was touched by his concern. But the last thing I wanted was to have to answer an interrogation whispered at full pitch just behind the rest of my family. If I spoke, I'd weep; and I would do anything to avoid the humiliation of weeping.

'No one understands about the funeral,' I whispered back through set lips.

The event became still more numbingly unreal when we reached the chapel. Not just our priest, robed in black; not just the coffin of a stranger ringed by candles to greet us; not just the door of the family vault Father had had prepared for us, open to take in someone none of us had known in a mist of frankincense and damp. But people already kneeling in prayer by the time we walked in. All men. All tall. All in black cloaks. And all strangers. They'd come from the city, clearly, because there were horses outside, stamping and blowing and dusty from the London road. Pages with brightly coloured legs and wrists sticking out under the muffle of cloaks – which meant boys in livery – murmuring at them. And an armed escort in the shadows beyond, quiet, but unable to avoid clinking or stop light falling on the polished metal they were wearing about themselves.

One by one, seeing Father and John, the strangers got up and approached them through the fog of scented candle-light. One by one they huddled together. Heads leaned forward to whisper. Black-clad arms touched John's shoulders. His head bowed lower.

It was only after the heavy footsteps of the procession, and after the priest had begun to declaim, '*De profundis* . . .' (Out of the depths I have cried to thee, O Lord: Lord, hear my prayer) that I felt another tweak at my arm.

'Look,' hissed Master Hans, eyes staring so wide open that they looked as though they might pop out of his square face. His arm hadn't moved, but he'd raised the first finger of his right hand. It was poking with priapic insistence forward towards the strangers.

One of the black hoods had fallen back. For a moment, before a hand pulled it forward again, the face of the man inside it – the man standing next to John – was revealed. A big slab of a face, reddish and lardy, with tiny sharp eyes; and hair and a beard the hot stinking ginger of a fox. I knew that face from the day last winter when he'd come to Chelsea to walk in the garden with Father, his 'old friend', and discuss the vexed question of his marriage. I would never forget the sight of Father's set, threatened expression at that meaty arm weighing down his shoulders and periodically clapping him on the back. 'Did you see?' Master Hans whispered now, and even his whisper was hushed by the sheer shock of recognition. 'Isn't that the King?'

He was sharper than I expected. But, however little I understood of what was happening, I suspected he shouldn't know if the King was here. Tapping reserves of family loyalty I didn't guess I had, I summoned up the strength to give him a deceptively reassuring smile and shake my head with all the certainty I could muster. 'But,' he whispered again, 'I'm sure it is. I saw him at Greenwich. No one else looks like that.' I ignored him.

I escaped Master Hans as soon as the service was over. I was preparing to get away from him before the priest intoned his last Latin words, '*If thou, Lord, wilt keep record of our iniquities, Master, who has strength to bear it?*' And I was already flitting down the path while, in the vestry, the priest and his servers were still chanting *Kyrie eleison* as they disrobed; before the troop of horsemen cantering off back to London with their torches were out of sight.

John must have rushed off alone, lost in his private grief. The only black figure ahead of me in the darkness, carrying a torch, was Father. The rest of them, hesitant, murmuring among themselves, were streaming out of the chapel behind us.

I rushed forward to catch Father, tripping over pebbles and roots in my urgency, feeling brambles and branches whip against me in the darkness, with the tears I wouldn't shed rising dangerously inside me. I caught his arm again; nearly clawed at it. 'Meg, sweetheart,' he said gently; but was it the deadly gentleness of a man who has forbidden a suitor to marry his daughter? I hardly dared to ask, but I couldn't not.

'You must tell me,' I panted, trying but failing to keep my voice steady. 'I must know. I've waited all my life. I don't understand . . .' I saw his face tighten against me. 'He told me he'd ask you,' I rushed on. 'Today. This afternoon. But then . . . all this . . .' To my horror, I found myself gulping wetly. He began to walk faster. 'I must know, Father – are you going to let me marry John?'

It was out. I half-expected Father to shake me off and walk off into the darkness, leaving me without an answer. The thought brought the shameful tears out onto my face.

But he didn't. He was astonished by my question. So astonished that he stopped dead and moved the torch closer to my face. He peered at me for a long moment and wiped the wetness gently off one cheek with his free hand, and looked at the tears on his finger as if doubting his senses. Then he put the hand to his own forehead, as if nursing a splitting headache.

When he finally spoke, his reply didn't make anything any clearer.

'He's asked you to marry him now – now, of all times?' Father said numbly. He seemed to be talking as much to himself as to me. 'Without even telling you about Guildford?' And he suddenly looked angrier than I'd ever seen him. His face darkened into the kind of cold, set fury I could imagine a heretic seeing in the torture chamber. And he took me roughly by the hand and dragged me toward the New Building without saying another word.

The door was open. A candle was lit inside. John Clement was hunched in the chair, with his cloak ruffled around him and arms wrapped around his chest and head, as lost to the outside world as a sleeping bird. He must have heard our two pairs of hurried footsteps but he didn't even look up when Father tugged me inside. It was only Father's voice that roused him, with the cold clarity of a knife at the throat. It was only when he started speaking that I realised it was John who Father was angry with, and not me.

'John,' Father snapped. 'Meg tells me you've proposed marriage. But I told her you could only do so after you'd told her the whole truth – and you haven't told her anything. There are some confidences you have to share. If nothing else you have to tell her about Guildford. I'll be back when you've had time to talk.'

Then he walked out. At the sound of the latch clicking, John Clement finally raised red, haunted eyes and stared dully back at me.

PART TWO

Lady with a Squirrel
and a Starling

8

Sometimes flesh-and-blood reality is less persuasive than shadows. John Clement blinked, but for a while he scarcely recognised the scared face of the young woman standing before him, with her deathly pallor, panicky eyes and the muscle twitching in the corner of her jaw. He was in another time; a child again, playing knucklebones with his brother Edward, two boys squatting on skinny haunches in the draught.

Listening to the grown-ups quarrelling on the other side of the door.

Different voices over the years. His father: bellows of rage, followed by the banging of fists on tables or the rumble of furniture overturned or the slash of knife on cloth. His mother: the cold whipping tones, the hot screams of anger. And the uncles. Uncle Richard, with the cautiousness of the runt of the litter, dark and dour, always biting at knuckle or lip: and between the relentless tearing of his own skin, a relentless exposition in flat northern tones of unpleasant necessities or unpalatable facts. Uncle George, with the fading prettiness of a wilful boy gone monstrously wrong: his every attempt at menace, intimidation, bribery and double-cross discovered, his treachery unmasked, and only his temper left intact. More howls of fury. And the grand-mothers: one with a voice like grating metal; the other's a honeyed, manipulative whine, at least until she was crossed and turned venomous as a snake.

And the quiet look in Edward's eyes matching the expression he knew would be on his own smooth young face: the resigned dread of children with no control over the adults running their lives. Running amok in their lives.

There was no use thinking of the names of the places they'd listened to the grown-ups quarrelling on the other side of the door. They were always somewhere different, though in essence it was always the same place. Always on the retreat, or the attack; always coming to terms with the allegations of betrayal by one treacherous ex-friend or ally or family member; with the children always struggling to catch up with the latest bitter account of wrong-doing by whoever had last flounced tempestuously off, threatening apocalyptic revenge, and so was no longer there to defend his good name; drawing what conclusions they could from the accounts of the latest battles. Not as to who was right or wrong. They knew, with the darkness and certainty of rational beings, that all the adults were almost entirely wrong all of the time. There was no point in apportioning blame or accepting any of their tortuous, furious self-justifications. What the children needed to deduce was simpler: how their own lives would next be turned upside down as a result of whatever the latest raging battle was, and what new corridor they'd find themselves in a week hence.

They lived the same lives of uncertainty and fear. But their degree of knowledge was different. He was three years younger; and that meant three years too young to inspire confidence. It was Edward who was told things (though only the wrong things). 'You'll be the head of this family of no-goods one day, much good may it do you,' his father would slur, when he was drunk enough to be maudlin – but only ever at Edward. And the man would start pouring out his heart to the boy, who would wince and nod. Edward didn't want to be the head of his family of no-goods. He didn't want to know who his father was pursuing, or wanted to kill or make war on, or why yesterday's dearest friend had turned into a bitter enemy today. He didn't want to sit at table with this terrifying blond tornado, watching him crunch the bones of birds between his big teeth or knock back wine by the barrel. He was a quiet child, small and thin for his age. He wanted a quiet life.

John Clement remembered feeling envy as well as relief at not hearing all the stories. He remembered his boyhood self longing to be the one clamped in those needy paternal embraces and whispered to before the big figure slumped into oblivion. Not that he'd actually wanted to know the one time he had stumbled by himself into one of his father's secrets: wandering down a corridor, pushing open doors, eight years old, aimless and unsettled after Anne's funeral, whistling under his breath. He'd looked into an anteroom and seen a writhing shape under the window on the other side. Cloth and movement. He'd looked longer and the shape turned out to be his father, lying face down, squirming and gasping. Then he'd seen an arm and a leg belonging to someone underneath. And a head of long, dark woman's hair turned away. He'd walked quietly out and on down the corridor, still whistling, to his own rooms – but not before he'd sensed his father's eyes turn towards him. In his own rooms he went to the window and began to play with the dagger he'd just been given; silver, with his insignia chased on the hilt. Pulling it out of its holder, enjoying the satisfying swoosh of metal on metal; pushing it back in; over and over again. Not thinking. So that he was surprised when his father rushed in, looking dishevelled, still picking at bits of clothing as if he wasn't sure they were in place. Looking anxiously at the boy sitting in the window seat. Saying, 'I think you saw something.' Everyone knew he went with every woman he could find; everyone turned a blind eye; but he was still always scared of being found out by his wife.

'No,' John Clement remembered his boyhood self saying, raising blank, deliberately uncomprehending eyes to that handsome, reddened face. Coldly, so there could be no more talk. Curling up with embarrassment inside at the idea of the conversation that might follow. 'No. I don't know what you mean.' And the relief he'd felt when the big man nodded, slowly accepting what he said, and shut the door.

He still couldn't say whether it was a blessing or a curse to be the younger son; to stay innocent for that much longer of more of the worst excesses adults can indulge in. But he'd never meant for the bitterness to creep into his feeling for Edward, who'd been with him through it all. Or for them to grow up, after the men of their father's generation self-destructed, to shout and bang fists and wave weapons at each other in their turn, like yet more murderous fools – as if all the rage that they'd endured for all their years together had been a poisonous inheritance they couldn't but submit to and accept. For the silence of what he'd thought would be a brief journey to the Continent to turn into a lifetime of unspeaking resentment, a chasm that couldn't be bridged even when, years later, he admitted that Edward might have had the right idea all along, and that it was worth making sacrifices for a quiet life.

The bitter irony was that Edward had wanted to bury the past and start a quiet new life. John Clement remembered with self-loathing that he himself – who now, as an adult, had learned enough to do anything to avoid conflict – had been the hothead then. He'd been the one who was hot for justice, vengeance, retribution. He'd been the one who thought Edward a coward for giving in – and, unforgivably, told him so. The quarrel had been all of his own making.

And now Edward was dead, and there would be no unpicking of the hatred. No last chance to make something more positive of his family legacy than the murderous man-trap he'd grown up in. And no one to remember it with. Just a memory of a room at Lambeth Palace, after Archbishop Morton had gone to bed in the room next door, and the hurt in Edward's eyes as he'd turned his back to go to sleep; and his own last word, in the arrogant tones he'd favoured in those young days, echoing between the beds: 'Coward.' When he'd woken up in the morning, Edward had gone. And now he was here, drowning in the blackness of it, and he was alone.

She was staring at him, the young girl with the black hair under the white bonnet, in the candlelight. And there was such fear on her face that he felt an answering flicker of pity. Enough, anyway, to try and focus on the present. To remember that he was a man well-advanced in age, and that in the long life he'd lived since he and his brother played knucklebones in every draughty castle in England she'd been part of his dreams for years.

'Meg,' he said, struggling with words, surprised at first to hear how easily her name came to his lips, then leaning on it for support as he came lurching back into a present in which he loved this woman. 'He was my brother.'

He saw her draw breath. Saw her eyebrows come together as she puzzled over what he'd said. Then she relaxed. He could see her begin to believe that she understood. The fear went out of her. He could see her confidence return.

She stepped quickly forward and stretched down to

where he was sitting. For a split second he saw her face transfigured by an almost maternal tenderness. Then she took him in her arms, and hugged him like a child. He let himself relax into the comfort of her embrace, trying not to allow his mind to take him even a few minutes forward in time, dreading what was to follow. On the edge of his mind was a recent memory of the yielding of buttocks in his hands and the fierceness of her dark blue gaze as he pinned her under him in the woods. But he couldn't bear to linger on that moment, when all his present hopes had seemed finally to have triumphed over all his past despair. The surge in his heart was cut off almost instantly by the darkness closing back in on him. A part of his mind knew what was causing this fear, though it couldn't control the great dirty flesh-shrivelling tide of sadness. He had to tell her everything now. Sir Thomas had given him the order. But if he told her everything, she'd know. And if she knew, she might go. It took his breath away.

'I'm sorry,' she was murmuring, stroking his head. 'I'm sorry. Your brother.' He wished he could see her face, but it was above him and he didn't dare look up. He could hear the secret relief she was trying to keep out of her compassionate voice, and feel her sense that she'd penetrated a mystery and could hope after all for happiness for herself; and he didn't want to jolt her out of that moment of certainty. 'That's the brother you were talking about, isn't it? The one you couldn't mend your quarrel with,' she added softly, with her hand coming to rest on his head. He nodded. 'You did everything you could . . . Don't reproach yourself . . . I know it wasn't your fault.'

Then she remembered. Shook herself. He felt her pull back a fraction. 'But,' she said, puzzled again, 'is that what Father was insisting you tell me?'

He couldn't speak. She took his answer for assent. 'Well,

you haven't done anything wrong,' she went on, and now he heard the beginning of indignation on his behalf. 'What was he so angry about?'

He pulled away. Shook himself. Took control. He stood up, towering over her, put an arm around her shoulders and drew her very gently towards him so they were both half-leaning, half-sitting on the table top. 'I don't know how to tell you,' he whispered.

She looked at him with unbearable trust. 'We don't need to have any secrets from each other any more, do we?' she said – a murmur – and there was the ghost of a smile on her face.

I so want to have no secrets from you, he implored silently; but my life has been so long compared to yours and there are so many layers of old secrets to be explained. I don't want you to think I have feet of clay.

She put a hand on his on the table and interlaced her fingers with his. She was still looking at him. Her gaze was becoming uncomfortable. He shifted his eyes sideways. Then he looked down at her white hand and took a deep breath.

'Your father is right. There is one more thing I have to tell you,' he said, louder, through the deafening beats of his heart. 'If I'm to be truly honest.

'But I don't want it to make any difference to us,' he added, feeling the words come now – the eloquence of despair, a gift that silvered his tongue. 'He wants me to tell you about my past. But I want to say first that what unites you and me is that we've chosen what to make of our lives. It's our present and our future that matter, together, not what each of us has left behind in the past. We both had dark beginnings.'

She nodded. Embarrassed, but still trusting. Still almost smiling. 'Are you going to tell me about women you've loved?' she asked. 'I won't mind.'

No. He shook his head. 'Look,' he began. 'Do you remember the game I made you play when you were children . . . with the princes in the Tower? The beginning of your father's book?'

'The princes who were killed by Richard.' She took up the familiar schoolroom theme, trying to make him smile with the same nostalgia she felt for the game. 'Wrathful, forward Richard. Kissing when he thought to kill.'

No; that wasn't the right way. He didn't know how to start. It had been too long since he'd had to explain himself. Hardly anyone still alive knew; and those who did didn't need telling. Perhaps he should start somewhere else.

'My brother's name was Edward,' he said dully.

'Yes,' she said, with a mystified expression. 'I know. Sir Edward Guildford.'

'Did you wonder why he didn't have the same family name as me?' he added. Blearily aware that he'd got going, and that everything would take its course now, and that he could perhaps save the situation if he explained it right.

She shrugged. She didn't see why he was asking her. 'Because your mother married twice?' she said, with a touch of impatience.

'No,' he replied, going faster now, looking down. 'It wasn't his name. It wasn't the family name he grew up with.'

He could feel her look sharpen. 'So was he Edward Clement?' she asked, as if trying to establish a clear diagnosis.

'No,' he said, and he shut his eyes and pushed out the words. 'Plantagenet. He was Edward Plantagenet.'

Everything stopped except the blood drumming in his ears. The room was still and close. He could feel beads of sweat break out on his brow, but she hardly seemed to be drawing breath.

When he finally raised his eyes to hers in the candle-light she was staring back at him with her mouth open.

'The prince in the Tower?' she mouthed.

Miserably, he nodded.

'Then who were you?' she gaped; her voice had vanished.

'Richard,' he said. 'When I was a boy they called me the Duke of York.'

I thought he'd gone mad – that grief had unhinged his mind. Or I thought it was a wild story dreamed up on the spur of the moment to save him from telling me something worse. Or perhaps I thought a little of both things. Or perhaps I just didn't know what to think at all. My head was spinning.

But one thing I could see straightaway was that saying those names had relieved him in some way. He got up from his perch on the edge of the table and turned to face me. He was standing taller than usual, as if he'd shed a burden. And the eyes fixed on my face were almost defiant – with a 'believe what you choose' look mixed up with the imploring 'believe me'.

'But they disappeared,' I stammered. My body had gone completely still, like a rabbit frozen in a dog's mouth. But my voice was beginning to come back; and it was coming back shrill and accusing. 'They were killed forty years ago. It was the game. It was our rhetoric lessons. That's what you taught us.'

Through the window I could hear night creatures rustling in the dark garden; far away, the unearthly scream of a vixen. My head was full of classroom memories; of his voice, calling us to our books, opening up the world to us. If the game was a lie, then everything else in the calm landscape of learning where I'd found meaning might also be full of treachery and traps. If the game was a lie, then the man standing in front of me, without the anxious stoop that made my heart melt with tenderness, with his muscles taut with tension, was a stranger.

The new John nodded his head. 'Yes, the game,' he said, regretful but not really sorry, as if the game were nothing more than a necessary deceit; a tactic for survival. A detail, perhaps even an amusing detail, in a much bigger story. Which perhaps it was for him. 'I thought you might ask about that. That was your father's idea when I came back to England and he took me in – a way of protecting me. He worked out the outline of the story and told me to teach it to the children at St Paul's. When I came to your house, I taught it to all of you too. It was supposed to be a way to spread the story that Edward and I were dead; a way to make sure I'd thought out and talked over every detail of it, rehearsed it forwards and backwards, filled in any gaps. So that all you clever children – and the clever boys at St Paul's – knew it from childhood and thought of it as history. So it would go down the generations and become history. But it went further than we expected, and faster. He's a clever man, your father, but even he never realised you children would make such a good story of it.'

He laughed mirthlessly. 'He's always been proud of his children's accomplishments. But never more so than of the aplomb with which they – you – killed off two little princes.'

I could imagine that. I could imagine the quiet smile on Father's face as one of his games became reality. The secret satisfaction he would have got as we trustingly repeated and embroidered what we were learning as the truth. But I couldn't join in John's bark of laughter; couldn't appreciate the cleverness of the idea. I couldn't breathe. The idea that I might have been so manipulated in one of those games for almost all my life, by the people I loved most, was growing in my chest, like a pig-bladder ball inflating and crushing every organ in my body. If that was a lie, how many other lies might I unwittingly have accepted? My hands were clenched tight on the table top. I opened my mouth and sucked in a long gasp of air.

'That's not the end of your father's wit,' John Clement added, sounding almost proud. 'Once we'd "killed off" Richard of York with the game, he finished the job of turning me into a new person by writing Utopia. Do you remember? It was the summer he took me abroad. He put me into it – "my boy John Clement" – standing in the square in Antwerp and listening with him and Pieter Gillis to Raphael Hythlodaeus tell his tall tales. We've all read it; we all know it's full of jokes. Utopia: no-place; on the banks of the No-water river; run by Governor No-People. But the best joke was what it did for me. Did you ever wonder why he called me "my boy" in it? It was far more than a turn of phrase. It was salvation. It wouldn't fool anyone who actually met me; no one who looks at the grey in my hair could think I'm a boy, or even that I could have been one thirteen years ago when it came out. But until I came back to England last year I led a quiet life; I hardly knew anyone outside the universities; I didn't give many people a chance to see my real age. While the book was a best-seller all over Europe. Thousands of people have read it. "John Clement" is only a mention in the book. No one who reads it notices my name particularly. But if they hear it somewhere else later, the memory it triggers is that I'm far younger than I really am – and far too young to be Richard of York. Especially if they read one of the European editions, which even have a picture of me as a long-haired fifteen-year-old. Utopia was a stroke of genius. It made me safe as No-Prince.'

Now I remembered Master Hans's question in the studio. That must be the picture he'd drawn. The boy Clement. I pulled my mind back from my memory of that conversation – Master Hans's innocent puzzlement, my innocent certainty – to the John Clement standing in front of me, with that pleading look that was inviting me to admire Father's subtle mind.

'If this is true . . .' I began, summoning up all the self-control I possessed to unclamp my hands. Seeing they were blue-white and cold despite the heat of the night. 'If you really were Prince Richard.' Seeing him nod, anxiously. Feeling my arms, as if full of a life of their own, slowly wrap themselves round my bursting chest and hug my shoulders; feeling my chin fall till my crossed arms supported it and I was curled in on myself like a baby, hugging myself to try and maintain contact with reality, drawing deep breaths. 'Then what really happened?'

He paused, gathering his thoughts. He couldn't remember proper sequences of events; just threat and fear. It was all threat and fear back in those days. No one had expected his father to die so suddenly. It brought out the schemer and the hater in every one of them. It was Uncle Richard against his mother and her tribe of scheming relatives. And the first game was to control Edward.

Uncle Richard was away in the north on 9 April, when everything changed. Uncle Richard, the Duke of Gloucester, governed the north from his home in Middleham. Edward had been sent back to Ludlow Castle after Christmas with his mother's sharp-eyed brother Anthony. Earl Rivers. His mother had always been determined to make sure her family were involved in the bringing up of her royal heir – to push them in the faces of the reluctant nobility and make sure they had positions of influence. The rest of the children, his ten-year-old self included, were still with their mother in London. So all he knew of what followed was what his mother told them. With her eyes scarily open;

her eyebrows working; her breath coming fast. Gathering the children to her breast; then showily holding them away so her anxiety could be better displayed; raising her eyebrows and lowering them, breathing fast then slow, as if lost in her own all-important feelings.

Two days after their father's death, when the funeral preparations were only just beginning, the town criers in London proclaimed Edward king. Edward V. There were so many funerals in their childhood that he was used to wearing black into church and hearing the chant of '*de profundis clamavi ad te, Domine, Domine*'. His eldest sister Mary had died a year before; Anne, the little girl he'd been married to at four so his father could get his hands on her dead father's estates, a year before that. But his mother said there were worse things than death. He was lucky, she said tartly, to have escaped the terrifying memories that she and his sisters had, of the time just before he was born, when his father had been usurped by Neville's armies, with Uncle George waiting hopefully in the wings in case he got to marry Neville's daughter and be made king; when his father had run away to Flanders, and she'd had to take her little girls into sanctuary at Westminster and give birth to Edward there. 'Alone,' she added melodramatically; as if none of the people with her had counted.

Like chess pieces, the rival family members now moved on London. The old hatred between his father's family and his mother's surfaced: the rage the Yorks felt against his mother, the nobody woman with the heart-shaped face and the willowy body who'd interrupted their strategic plan to marry Edward to a French princess with her own secret royal marriage. The woman who'd moved her hordes of relatives into power with her and displaced England's true leaders.

Two weeks after their father's death, Rivers armed two

thousand men and set off with the new king from Ludlow. 'Thank God, thank God,' the new king's mother said, melting down into near tears when she received the message. 'He'll be safe with Anthony.'

He wasn't. One week after that, Uncle Richard and his friend Henry Stafford, the Duke of Buckingham, headed Edward and his entourage off and arrested Rivers. His mother wept and paced and wrung her hands. He remembered trying to comfort her; half-frightened, half-bored; putting a small hand in hers and saying, timid as a child, 'Don't cry, Mother; don't cry.'

And he remembered her beautiful eyes raised slowly, dramatically, tragically towards him, glittering above her black weeds, and the splendidness of her embrace as she gathered him in her arms. 'A mother's love knows no bounds,' she said; a declamation. 'I can't help but worry.' Little Richard stifled the thought that Uncle Richard was only doing the job his father had asked him to – becoming Lord Protector of the realm while Edward was still a child – by taking the new king out of the Woodville family's hands. Voicing that thought would have done no good. He held his peace.

It was another four days before the royal entourage arrived in London, escorted by the dukes. His mother hadn't waited; the funeral had already been held at Windsor. But the whole city was ready for the new king. The Mayor, the aldermen and five hundred citizens in velvet went out to meet Edward on 4 May. There was a banquet for him at Hornsby Park. He stayed with Uncle Richard at Crosby's Place for a few days. Then they put him in the royal apartments in the Tower.

The boy Richard didn't see any of this. His mother snatched them up and moved them into sanctuary at Westminster – a tactic that had worked before – and railed against fate from that safety. 'That any child of mine should fall into the hands of that scheming fiend is a tragedy,' she wept. Little Richard felt his older sister Elizabeth stiffen as she listened. He nearly laughed. Round-faced, implacable Elizabeth had been in love with dour old Uncle Richard, with his hatchet face and his dull administrator's manners, since before he could remember; her life was devoted to imagining that her uncle's wife would die and he would choose her as his next spouse.

But a few days later his mother called her to him, with a letter in her hand, an earnest expression, and secret hope in her eyes. 'My darling,' she said, 'you are to go and join Edward in the royal apartments.' She must have surprised a look of astonishment on his face.

'I've heard from Edward and from Richard,' she said, with a look that implied her suggestion should not be gainsaid. 'Edward is lonely. And, as Richard says, you both need tutoring; you should be together.'

He couldn't remind her of what she'd been saying so recently about Uncle Richard. It would only have enraged her. So he stifled his misgivings and his fears and let himself be sent off through the city. He was ten.

It was true that Edward was lonely. His face lit up at the sight of his brother walking into the big, echoing apartment. He looked six inches taller than at Christmas, and much thinner. But they were children who didn't wear their hearts on their sleeves. All Edward said, through his huge smile, was: 'Knucklebones?'

And then they played, and waited, and played, and waited, and heard nothing more. Later he found out that all Edward's most prominent supporters were being arrested: Thomas Stanley; Thomas Rotherham, the Bishop of York; John Morton, the Bishop of Ely; Oliver King, their father's old secretary, who had started working for Edward but now abruptly stopped; and even Jane Shore.

But at the time all he noticed was the day it went quiet.

There was a fitting for the coronation clothes, so it must have been before 22 June. When they finished with the pins and tweakings, the guards wouldn't meet their eyes. Their mother sent a note through their tutor, the tubby Italian man who came into the Tower every morning for Mass and lessons, which he slipped them as they came out of the chapel. It was a scrawl. '*A rumour is being spread – a groundless, damaging rumour – about your birth. Believe nothing you hear. It's lies, all lies. Trust no one,*' the note said.

They read it together. They exchanged meaningful looks and raised jokey eyebrows at each other. Children's bravado. Edward put the note gently down on the table, without comment, and opened his books. But, after their Latin lesson, he went to help the Italian who was struggling into his cloak. 'Doctor Gigli,' he said quietly, with the dignity that was coming to him with his new height and role, 'what is the rumour my mother's letter talks about?'

The usually garrulous and gossipy Giovanni Gigli winced as if in agony and looked longingly at the door. But he told. He hadn't got to be Archdeacon of London by failing to humour the whims of princes. He always told everything. The Bishop of Bath and Wells was saying that their father had entered an earlier secret marriage before his secret marriage to their mother. His story was that, in front of him twenty-one years ago, their father had sworn a legally binding marriage contract with a pretty young widow called Lady Eleanor Butler. He hadn't bothered to actually get the marriage blessed in church after sleeping with her; instead of banns and a Papal bull blessing a royal wedding, she got an austere cell in a nunnery until she died. Robert Stillington's silence had been bought until now by his appointment to a bishopric and a salary of £365 a year. But now the bishop's royal protector was

208

dead and his conscience was apparently suddenly troubling him. No one on the streets or at the court would have believed the story, as Dr Gigli said, 'except that your father . . .' and his English failed him, and he raised plump shoulders in a shrug, then wiggled his fingers suggestively as if there was a female body between his arms. If he'd been talking to someone else, Richard thought, the podgy teacher might have sniggered.

Dr Gigli waddled hastily off before this difficult conversation could go further, with a regretful wave of his hand and none of his usual eagerness to talk. But the boys didn't need the rest explained. If this story was true, they were the offspring of a bigamous marriage. They were illegitimate.

'Don't worry,' Richard said, more bravely than he felt. 'Remember Mother's letter. It's just a rumour.' But there were no more knucklebones. Edward prayed in muttering silence through the afternoon and took confession the next morning. Richard lay on his bed and rattled the bones.

Uncle Richard joined them for midday Mass, looking sombre. Neither boy knew what to say to him. He looked carefully at Edward and said, 'I see you've already heard. We won't speak ill of the dead. But I'm sorry. Pray with me.' Afterwards, just as dour, he told them: 'The Bishop will tell his story to Parliament. There'll be a full hearing. But there will be turmoil while it's going on. I'm going to send you out of London until it calms down.'

Edward, in his muted way, seemed almost relieved. But young Richard saw the look in his uncle's eyes. And what he saw was that for all the older man's sanctimoniously pursed lips and the downturned corners of his mouth, he was secretly delighted. Young Richard could see there would never be a full hearing into Bishop Stillington's allegations. It also crossed his mind that a part of his sister Elizabeth would be pleased, with her crush on Uncle

Richard and her endless hope that his wife would die (she was a shoot off their father's tree all right). Now she could dream of being Richard's queen.

The Bishop of Ely, fresh out of jail, joined the three of them in their rooms; narrow-eyed and quick-tongued and decisive (but secretly almost breathless, the young Richard saw, at the scale of the events he was participating in). He stumbled over whether to call the boys' mother the Dowager Queen or just the Lady Elizabeth, but he'd talked to her; they'd worked out a plan.

It took a while to put it into practice. The boys stayed in the Tower when, four days after Edward's coronation would have been, Uncle Richard was crowned Richard III. They stayed through a sweltering summer in which, as he found out afterwards, Uncle Richard had taken off the heads of Hastings, Buckingham, Rivers, Grey and Vaughan. They stayed long enough for the young Richard, primed by the talkative Dr Gigli who brought the gossip of the streets of London to them, to be fully convinced that the Bishop's story had been nothing more than a smoke screen to help his uncle grab the throne. And in October they were taken away.

That was what Meg would want to hear now, all these years later, John Clement realised: where they went next.

He couldn't dwell too much on logistics. On the to-ings and fro-ings of messengers; on his mother's later decision to turn his sisters over to Uncle Richard's care too; on the contradictory whispers that she was negotiating with Henry Tudor, the Lancastrian pretender planning his invasion from France, to marry Elizabeth off to him. His memories were flashes: like the memory of his silent fury when the undistinguished horses on which they'd mounted him and Edward, wearing rough dark cloaks, ambled past Crosby's Place as their anonymous cavalcade made its way out of London – Crosby's Place, where Uncle Richard was living now – his acid determination to come back and pay his uncle out and take back the throne.

But the older boy, Edward, didn't want to plot revenge. Unlike young Richard, Edward believed their uncle to be telling the truth. Edward had given in.

What tormented John Clement now was remembering himself nagging at Edward over the months and years that followed to assert himself; to bide his time but start to plan ways to take back his throne; to turn his mind to justice and revenge. The young Richard had been always angry, always insistent; furious at being the younger brother who had no right to avenge the wrongs done against Edward. 'It's against God,' he'd hiss. But Edward's whispered response, between prayers, was always: 'Richard, let it be. We can't know what's right. Let God's will be done.'

John Clement cleared his throat. Looked at Meg's tight face in the light of the one candle left burning; realised from the birdsong that dawn would soon be coming. He spoke in the contemplative monotone of someone reciting a difficult past – with the emotion taken out. 'A family friend took us in. We'd known him all our lives. We'd played with his children when we were smaller. He rode down from York and took us to where his family lived: Gipping, in Suffolk. The servants called us Lord Edward and Lord Richard and asked no questions. It was strangely easy. We stayed on with him until long after Uncle Richard was killed two years later. His name was Sir James Tyrrell.'

Her gaze burned him. 'Sir James Tyrrell killed you,' she said accusingly. 'Miles Forrest and John Dighton held the pillows over your heads, but Tyrrell paid them.'

He said, 'No, no, no, that was just the story. Tyrrell was a good man. One of the best.'

And she said, 'If it was a story you made up, why did you repay a man who'd done you service by giving him such an infamous part?'

211

And his eyes shifted down to his feet, and he scuffed them as he considered his response.

'Look,' he said anxiously, after a long pause, not wanting to remember Tyrrell's big hands clapping him on the back and his hearty voice instructing the boys at sword-play. 'I didn't choose the story. It arose out of need. By the time your father came into this – when the need arose – Sir James Tyrrell was dead and gone. It couldn't hurt him. But I never felt good about it.'

She nodded reluctantly. He could see now that she believed him, however hostile she seemed. It gave him fresh strength.

'When Henry Tudor came to power he married my sister Elizabeth. It was a way of signalling publicly that Lancastrians and Yorkists had ended their war. But first he had to make her legitimate again. It was the only way for the marriage to have its proper symbolic value: a true York princess marrying the conqueror from the house of Lancaster. But you see Henry's dilemma: as soon as he repealed *Titulus Regius*, the statute by which Richard had declared all my father's children illegitimate and taken the throne, then my brother Edward would become the rightful king. And although there were plenty of rumours by then that we'd been killed, Edward was alive.'

'Any king from my family would have killed us without a second thought if it suited them. The Yorks were always short on scruples. But Henry was a different sort. Calculating and greedy and mean-spirited, as people always said, but cautious too. Not a really evil bone in his body. And he was scared of the women: his mother; my mother. They saved us. My mother got the Bishop of Ely back on the job to talk to his mother. John Morton had been made Archbishop of Canterbury by then, and he was practically running the country; but he still remem-bered he'd been a Yorkist in the old days; my father's man. The deal he worked out was that Henry could marry Elizabeth; but we had to be kept safe and given new lives, appropriate for men of noble birth. So he changed our names and took us into his household.

'It wasn't that risky. We looked different by then; we'd gone away as little boys in wartime and we came back as young men with beards after half the young men of good birth in the land had been slaughtered. It was a new world. And it was a new household; he was just building his palace at Lambeth; new people were coming together. The Guildford family was happy for Edward to be counted as one of their sons; Archbishop Morton couldn't find me a new family who'd give me their name – Tyrrell baulked at that – so he just made my name up. Morton laughed about it; his view was that even if someone who didn't know our blood did notice that we looked like Plantagenets, they wouldn't make anything of it – there were so many royal bastards, after all. Our immediate family knew, but no one would talk; they were happy with the power they'd managed to hang on to through Elizabeth's marriage. Sir James Tyrrell was made Constable of Guisnes and moved to France. My mother wasn't a discreet woman, but after a year or two she fell out with Henry and shut herself up in the Abbey at Bermondsey. So I imagine all those nuns from noble families at places like Bermondsey and the Minories knew a lot about us. But no one living in the world wanted to remember the past. People wanted different things after the war was over: what they wanted to talk about was trade and diplomatic alliances and the new learning. It was as if England became another country once the rulers of the land had stopped devouring each other. No one wanted to go back to the war.' He stopped wistfully. 'So we spent half the year with Morton, showing our new faces to the world; and the rest at Gipping. We started again . . .'

There was light through the window now, and he could hear footsteps on the path.

'I met your father at Lambeth Palace, through John Morton,' he said, listening to them coming closer. 'After we got away from London, Edward only ever wanted to bury himself in the country: to hunt and pray and hide. But I wanted to see the world. The truth was that I hadn't given up the idea that we could somehow take back the throne – even if Edward didn't want to. But I couldn't tell them that. So I told them I wanted to learn the new learning and find a different kind of future, and when I was sixteen or so Morton let me leave England for the university at Louvain. My aunt Margaret was the Duchess of Burgundy; we knew I'd be safe near her (and I thought she might help me take back the throne – she always hated the Tudors). I stayed at Lambeth Palace for a couple of days before I took ship. Your father was there. He was just a clever pageboy in those days, but Morton kept saying he was marked out for greatness. He was an astute man, Morton. "When I'm gone," he always said, "I hope you'll be guided by young More."'

The footsteps stopped outside the door. 'And I always have been,' John Clement said, loudly enough for More to hear as he pushed it open and stepped inside.

Sir Thomas was blue-jawed, with black smudges under his eyes and yesterday's linen – in the rumpled physical disarray he so often scarcely noticed when he was away from the display of public life. But the threatening expression of the night had gone. Now he had the composure of a man who'd been in prayer for hours. His first words to John Clement took up the words he'd left the chapel on. But now his voice was measured and calm.

'So have you told her?' More said sternly. 'I'm sorry if I was abrupt last night; but you must understand how important this is for us all.'

214

John Clement found he'd stood up straight, moving away from the table and away from Meg without even noticing. He was nodding with his usual almost reverential respect. 'About Edward. Yes,' he said.

His eyes were on More. But, as More turned to his adopted daughter, he also became aware of Meg's head rising and falling in an automaton's nod.

More strode over to Meg, who was still perched on the table top, hunching into it like a bird that has fluffed itself up on its branch ready to sleep, holding on tight with her hands. 'Do you understand, Meg?' he said, very kindly, and Meg swayed towards him as if hoping for a comforting arm around her shoulders. But More perched beside her instead, side by side, taking John Clement's place. 'Do you understand the life you'd be choosing by making this marriage?'

She moved her head, but so indistinctly now that John Clement couldn't tell whether she intended the movement to signify yes or no. Her eyes were as wide as saucers. There was no expression in them.

John Clement could see the love More felt for her in the comforting way he was stroking one of his own hands with the other; but he also knew Meg, so close beside her father, was unaware of that movement. He looked away, trying not to see this small sign of his patron's difficulty in communicating love. It wasn't his place to criticise; he was devoted to this man.

'The problem wouldn't just be the secret in his past; always living a fragile version of the truth, and always living with the risk of discovery,' Sir Thomas was saying to Meg, in the softest, tenderest voice imaginable. 'Difficult though that's been at times, we've managed. And the situation's been stable for years – peace and security; Edward in the countryside; John a remote younger brother.'

'But it's not stable now. There's new danger on all sides.

215

There's sickness spreading through the land, and the curse of heresy, and people whispering in the streets about God's retribution on the Tudor dynasty. Calling them usurpers; picking at old wounds. And the King so desperate to end his marriage to the Queen, with or without the Pope's permission, that I fear he could easily be corrupted by the heretics gathering around the Lady Anne. If he is – if he does turn towards heresy,' he paused for dramatic emphasis, a public speaker's trick, looking deep into Meg's eyes, 'then every Catholic king in Christendom will be looking for the man who could unseat him. The Tudor kings have brought with them a peace and prosperity that England has never known before; it's been my duty and my pleasure to help preserve their reign in whatever modest ways I can. But they rule by right of conquest, not blood. If England divided along religious lines and the existence of a legitimate Plantagenet prince became known, Catholics from all over Europe would flock to support him against Henry Tudor. Until yesterday that would not have concerned you directly – it would have been Edward who interested them. But now poor Edward is dead,' and he crossed himself. 'God rest his soul. And the last Plantagenet prince left is John.'

John stepped forward, making inarticulate protesting noises in his throat. Sir Thomas waved him superbly aside. 'I know, I know, John; it's the last thing you'd want. Your one aim is to avoid being pulled into statecraft and the intrigues of kings; I know.

'But secrets get told. However lucky we've been all these years, enough people still know this secret that it might yet come out. And, if it did, you'd have more than the Catholic kings of Europe to worry about. There'd be the King of England too. Henry isn't the timid man his father was. I always say that if my head could win him a castle, it would be off my shoulders tomorrow. But if

216

he thought you represented a threat to his throne, yours would be off tonight.'

John stepped back, nodding his head miserably at the undeniable truth of what Sir Thomas was saying. The statesman hardly saw; he was still looking searchingly at the girl beside him; and she was still looking away. Her hands were still clamped to the table top, but two fingers had been plucking at a fold of her skirt so hard that she'd made a stiff pleat in the yellow material.

'Do you understand, Meg?' Sir Thomas said, his voice dropping to just above a whisper. 'I've wanted this from the start. This is the match I'd always have chosen for you. That's why I brought John to the house all those years ago. I couldn't have been happier when I first saw the friendship between you deepen. But the time wasn't yet right for it back then. I knew he'd been an impetuous hothead when he was young, always spoiling for a fight. I wasn't sure, even once he came to us, that he'd settle down permanently into the new life I'd sketched out for him. And I didn't want to marry you to a man who might go back someday to jockeying for political power, especially with so many religious troubles suddenly threatening to pull Christendom apart. I wouldn't have wanted to put you in that danger. Anyway, if he were a prince of England, his high degree would rule him out as a husband for you – his blood would be too exalted for city people like us. He'd been John Clement since before you were born; and he'd been the teacher of my children for a good four or five years. But I still wasn't sure of him. However sober he seemed to have become most of the time, there'd still be flashes of something else every now and then. Something dangerous. And before I could let you marry, I needed to be sure he'd want to go on being plain John Clement forever.'

Sir Thomas paused. 'And then there was the night after

Ammonius died,' he said. Very quietly. Very neutrally. Looking down. But the measured words still brought a sweat to the watching John Clement's brow, and made his guts churn hot with shame. 'Only John could really tell you what happened that night, if he remembers. All I know is that he was dragged before me by the night constables after starting a brawl in a tavern on Cheapside. They'd recognised him as the tutor to our house; and anyway, I was the magistrate; they'd naturally have brought him to me. He was dead drunk. They said he'd attacked two men. Tipped their jug of Spanish red over their heads, so their clothes looked as though they were drenched in blood; then followed up that assault by bashing their heads together. And then drawn a knife on them. It took half a dozen men to wrestle him to his knees and disarm him, and they all looked as though they'd been dipped in a barrel of wine by the time they'd done it.

'When I asked him why, he wouldn't say. Just snarled something about having been insulted. "If I'd had my sword," he said – slurred – "I'd have run those bastards through." And that's what the constables said he'd been yelling in the tavern too.'

More paused to see if Meg responded. 'Which was obviously a dangerous thing for a tutor to a London lawyer's house to be yelling in a tavern,' he went on calmly, when she didn't. 'Because it's one thing for a man in a tavern to pull out a knife, but it's quite another for him to be raving about carrying a nobleman's sword.'

John Clement was still shaking his head, as if denying the story; but the voice went pitilessly on.

'That's why I took him away abroad with me that summer,' More was saying. 'And that's why I wouldn't let him come back to you until he'd been properly tested by time. He wasn't safe. I was always frightened that there'd be another of those moments of violent rage, and that it might destroy him. Or you.

'But I think he's passed the test now. And with a doctorate and his place at the College of Physicians – and the steadiness of his wish to marry you through all these years – I truly believe he's become the man he wanted to be. They're kind enough to talk of me as a writer and lawyer and statesman – but my greatest creation, the one I'm most proud of, is John Clement, the civilised man of learning you see before you. This is the outcome I most wanted from the task I've cared about most in my life. This is what I've hoped for.'

Meg was still looking down at the pleat between her fingers. She wasn't moving. Only her stillness showed she was listening.

If she'd looked up for an instant, she'd have seen something else flash between More and John Clement – a questioning glance from More; a shake of the head and an imploring answering look from Clement. More sighed gently, and went mellifluously on, turning his gaze back down to Meg.

'If you choose him, you have to accept that you're choosing a man who's grown used to living with secrets. He may be unwilling to share everything from his past with you. But now that you know about this, I'm prepared to swear that I'm aware of nothing else in his life that could be an impediment to your marriage.'

She raised her eyes finally and looked at her father. John Clement, watching, couldn't read what was in her motionless gaze. Yet he was obscurely comforted that Sir Thomas seemed encouraged by it.

'You had to know the risks,' More went on, undaunted by her silence. 'But you're a grown woman. You know your mind. I'm not going to stand in your way if, knowing what you now know, you tell me that this marriage is still what you want.'

He stopped. His eyes and his daughter's were still locked

together. John Clement waited, scarcely drawing breath. Meg said nothing; didn't move.

'Is it, Meg?' More went on, gently, implacably. 'Do you want to marry this John Clement?'

Silence. A long silence, long enough for John Clement to be aware of birdsong and the dust motes dancing in the first rays of sun to penetrate the window. Then the fierce, blank gaze turned to him for another long moment. Then back to her father.

Then Meg put her hands up to her eyes and covered her face. Thinking she was about to cry, John Clement steeled himself to step forward and comfort her.

But before he could move she brought her hands down again. Lifted herself off the table. Stared wildly at both of them, cried out, 'I don't know! I don't know! I don't know who he is!' and fled sobbing out of the door into the shocking green of the garden.

9

Hans Holbein, sitting under a mulberry tree, shaded his eyes to squint after Kratzer's departing back. Then he sighed, picked up his pencil and went back to his sketch.

Kratzer's original purpose in coming out to talk to him before breakfast had been to discuss the astronomical treatise he wanted to write as a gift for the King. He wanted Holbein to illustrate it. But on the way into the garden he'd met his friend, the groom with the Lutheran sympathies. So by the time he'd found Holbein, pensive in the green shade, he was full of raw-boned indignation.

'They've caught the Rickmansworth villagers,' the astronomer said hotly, jutting his jaw. 'They're in prison. They're going to be hanged.'

The Rickmansworth villagers came from near one of the country retreats of Cardinal Wolsey. In Kratzer's mind, Cardinal Wolsey, the Lord Chancellor – with his fleshy face, greed for earthly power and pomander stuck perpetually under his nose to keep the stink of the people out of his nostrils – was the embodiment of everything that was wrong in Church and state. (In Holbein's mind too; Holbein liked to laugh and attribute to his friend the hottest anger against the rapacious corruption of clerics, their hunger for the last bit of bread from a peasant's mouth and every last crumb of earthly power when they were supposed to have renounced the material world, but in his heart of hearts he felt the same way.) The villagers shared that antipathy – but acted on it. All London had been whispering about them for days. They'd gone into their local church, wrapped tarred rags around the rood and set fire to it.

Holbein only shrugged when he heard what Kratzer had to say. Whatever his opinion of the cardinal, he had no time for suicidal fools like the Rickmansworth villagers either. It had always been obvious what price they'd have to pay for their pointless act of desecration. Why die when there was life to be lived? He began shading his sketch. He was only half listening to his emotional friend's voice. Holbein had been loitering round the house for the past day and a half, unable to concentrate on anything.

He'd finished the last few details of the family portrait. He hadn't, after all, had to make the revisions Sir Thomas had said he'd wanted when he first saw the picture the night before last. More had come up to him the following morning, out here in the garden where he was hiding from the enervating heat, and given him the sweet look of a friend, and said, 'I've been looking again at your work, Master Hans.' Holbein had nodded, warily. However proud he was of the picture, and the effect it had had on almost every member of the family when they'd seen themselves through his eyes, it hadn't escaped his notice that it had made Sir Thomas and Dame Alice feel uncomfortable. But More went on, in his gentlest voice, 'Meg has been praising your talent – she says you have the gift of showing God in a humble human face – and I've spent an hour in front of your picture this morning, and I must say I agree. You've made us a masterpiece that we can treasure forever.'

And Holbein suddenly felt warmed again by the glow of the older man's personality; warmed and cherished; until, that is, he realised that if More accepted the painting as it was, there would be nothing more to keep him here in Chelsea. 'But,' he stammered, 'don't you want me to paint in your lutes and viols on the back shelf any more? Or give Dame Alice a chair?' He could see now that More was holding a bulging purse in one hand – his fee, already counted out – but he wanted to delay taking it and accepting that it was time for him to move on. 'I've already done the sketch of how the changes should be,' he said hastily, playing for time; looking in his sketchbook, finding the sheet, pulling it out to present to his patron. But More only smiled and shook his head. 'Your painting is beautiful as it is, Master Hans,' he said. 'It would be graceless of me to demand alterations now. And yet,' there was the glimmer of mischief in the smile now, 'one never likes to think a fruitful partnership is ending altogether. I've enjoyed our conversations; and I've enjoyed seeing your work develop more than you might realise. I'd like to think you might come back some day soon to visit us and – who knows? – perhaps, if we haven't thought of something better to occupy you, you'll paint us some more lutes then. So perhaps you'll leave me the sketch?'

It was better than polite. It was a warm and gracious conversation with a generous patron. But it was a final one. And it meant there was nothing left for Holbein to do here but frame the picture, get his things together and go: a couple of days' work at most. He just didn't have the energy to begin. Perhaps it was the heat. Or perhaps it was Meg's face, glowing with happiness, hardly bothering to do more than sketch a smile at him as she passed, rushing about her new work tending the sick with all the vitality he would like to be feeling. He had an uncomfortable feeling that John Clement – that schoolmaster

223

with the irritatingly handsome profile, whom he disliked more every day, and whom he darkly suspected of toying with all the girls' affections in general, and of having encouraged Meg's sister to fall in love with him in particular – might finally be about to take her away. It was enough to try the patience of a saint.

'So are you saying we should announce our sympathy for the villagers and leave London, eh, Kratzer?' he said now, not especially pleasantly. 'I've got a wife waiting at home and a child I've never seen. My leave of absence from Basel is about to run out. You can't stay here forever either. And all the stories you hear in London these days are as crazy as the stuff we left home to get away from. Bloody fools and bigots at each other's throats over the meaning of God. Nothing but ugliness whichever way you look, and us sitting in this house pretending we believe a whole lot of things we don't. I'd say it would be more honest just to go.'

He laughed at the baffled, cross look appearing on Kratzer's face. 'But we won't, will we?' he pursued, lashing out at his friend for being unprincipled because – as he really knew – he was disgruntled with himself for having been such a fool as to fall in love. 'We like to tell ourselves it's because we can't help admiring Thomas More when we're with him, however ugly he might look when he's burning our Bibles. But deep down we both know the truth. We just never have the courage to say it. The real reason we're here is because he's doing us a power of professional good. Our careers are going far too well to think of leaving.'

It was only after Kratzer started stumping back up the path, looking hurt, after raising his arms helplessly and saying, 'I can't talk to you when you're like this. You sound . . . cynical. I don't know what's got into you recently,' that he began to feel sorry. Kratzer was a good man. He hadn't deserved to be snapped at.

He was drawing her face again. From memory. Lingering over each stroke of the pencil as if it were a caress (his studio was full of images of her now). Enjoying the melancholy green of the shade he was sitting in. Wondering idly what to do; knowing there was nothing he could do; adding another touch to her eyes.

When suddenly there was a rush of footsteps over the grass, and the kind of short snuffling breaths that almost certainly meant tears, and she was there with him in person. The pale face above the skinny girl's body; the long nose; those eyes. Flinging herself into the green shade, almost knocking him over in her eagerness to hide. Then stopping dead at the sight of someone else in what she must have thought would be a private place.

'Mistress Meg,' he said, so happy to see her that it took him a while to make sense of the appalled answering look on her tear-streaked face.

'Oh.' She began edging back, poised for flight, not wanting to talk. 'I . . .' and she began to turn away.

But now that he'd seen the state she was in, he wasn't going to let her go so easily. He lunged forward, dropping his sketchbook, and grabbed her by both upper arms. 'You're upset. What's happened? What's the matter?'

There was no fight left in her. She was drooping in his grasp. He had the feeling she might fall over if he let her go. She looked up at him with eyes full of some nightmare. Her teeth were clenched as if to stop them chattering. It wasn't horror at the sight of him, Holbein realised with relief. 'Tell me,' he said, almost shaking her in his urgency.

She sniffed. Tried to compose herself. Failed, and let more helpless tears course down her cheeks. 'Oh . . . it's nothing,' she snuffled, making a watery attempt at a smile as she cried. 'Nothing important,' she gulped, 'I had a shock . . . I've found out a secret . . . but I'll be fine in a minute.'

Elizabeth, Holbein thought as soon as he heard the word 'secret'. She's realised Elizabeth is in love with John Clement. And maybe she's found out more. 'So you know,' he said, softening his voice for her, but already imagining himself walking up to the double-dealing physician and punching him as hard as he could in the teeth. He liked the idea.

'Know what?' she whispered back, with a twist in her face – so suspicious suddenly that Holbein began to realise dimly that he must have made a mistake. Not in time to stop him plunging ahead anyway, though. He'd suspected it for so long he'd come to feel sure it was true. He couldn't resist probing.

'Nothing, nothing,' he said hastily. 'I didn't mean anything. Just my bad English, ha ha! But . . . for a moment . . . I thought you might be going to tell me something about Elizabeth . . . ?'

'Elizabeth?' she echoed vaguely, losing interest, gazing vacantly around her. His suspicion had meant nothing to her, Holbein saw, and he felt his face go red with embarrassment at having blurted it out so crassly. 'Why Elizabeth?' she whispered wonderingly, but she didn't expect an answer. She was just marking time, trying to fight back more tears.

'The villagers, then?' he queried hopelessly, but he saw in the glassiness of her answering look that she had no idea what he was talking about now. 'Your father and the Rickmansworth men . . .' he tried to explain, but felt his voice trail away when he saw an unexpected coldness creep into her expression. She'd guessed he was referring to some religious crime; she didn't understand what but her old alert interest in hints about the religious strife being waged around London seemed to have vanished.

'My father's a good man, Master Hans,' she said faintly but firmly, closing her eyes. 'I don't know what rumours you've heard, but he hasn't done anything wrong.' Then she was taken over again by whatever was troubling her. She drew in her breath in a gulp that was almost a hiccup, and closed her eyes.

'I'll be fine,' she said weakly, glancing up at him, pulling feebly away. 'Honestly, Master Hans. Just give me a few minutes.'

But Holbein wasn't listening – or at least he wasn't obeying. A glimmering of a much bigger idea had just come to him; a flicker of wild hope that maybe, just possibly, John Clement might have rejected Meg altogether. The idea was so intoxicating that, instead of letting go of her arms, he found himself pulling her closer to him.

Until she was crushed against his chest, and he could hear the rush of her heart and feel her breasts pushing up against him and the warmth of her back under his arms. Until he felt her face rise slowly towards his, like a bubble escaping out of water, and his mouth lower itself onto hers. Until the tongue he began sliding through her lips met an answering tongue. Until . . .

It took me longer than I like to remember to pull away.

But somewhere in the swoony mess of breath and teeth and arms and heartbeats that we'd so unexpectedly become, with his great warm hands massaging me into his big fleshy body, I began to separate.

In my head at first; when I put a shivery hand on the head so close to mine, and was shocked to feel coarse, wiry waves of hair under my palm instead of the fine dark mane that it seemed should be there. But it was when he half-stepped back to put one hand on my shoulder and another under my chin, so he could peer into my eyes – and I looked at those big fingers on my dress, with ginger hairs coming off them and broken nails blackened with charcoal, and knew they weren't the hands that should ever touch me – that I finally came to my senses. Suddenly I knew that the only hands I wanted to feel on my body were thin and long-fingered and elegant. And that they were John's.

I stood there for a moment longer, with those wrong hands still on me, letting my private realisation sink in. A peace that I'd probably never known before was stealing into my heart. Nothing I'd heard in the night mattered, I suddenly saw. John's story was shocking; there were risks in his future. But there was nothing worse. However emotionally I'd reacted when I found that one of my dearest childhood memories was based on falsehood, there was no malice in the creation of that falsehood. He'd done nothing that wasn't dictated by need. He'd deceived but never acted in bad faith. He loved me. Now, irrationally, insanely, even while I stood there in the arms of a man I didn't love, I felt my heart soar with joy that I'd at last understood what I felt; with a kind of ecstatic nostalgia for the feel of John's body on mine, the sense of profound rightness in the world that I'd briefly thought I'd lost. Now I knew I would experience it again.

Poor Hans Holbein felt me retreat. His grin faded. The corners of his mouth began to droop. He dropped his hand from my shoulder. He was a gentleman after his own fashion.

'No?' he whispered, and then he answered his own question with a lugubrious sigh and a shake of the head. 'No. I see. I'm sorry.' And he took a couple more stumbling steps back, until we were standing staring at each other across a space the width of a grave. He was blushing furiously.

'I'm so sorry,' I said, meaning it. I didn't know a kinder, more likeable man; one whose feelings I'd less like to hurt, even though that moment of proximity was now making me resent him too. 'I didn't mean . . . I don't know what I meant . . . I should have . . .' I shook my head. 'I mean, I shouldn't have.'

I took a deep breath. 'What I mean is, I have something to tell you,' I said, trying to make my expression convey gentleness as well as honesty. I wanted to get out of this embarrassing situation as fast as possible, but I knew I had to put things right first with Master Hans. 'My secret. I'm going to marry John Clement.'

He nodded his head. Gloomy but not surprised. I was probably more surprised at what I'd said than he was.

He went on nodding, rhythmically, and making little 'tk-tk-tk' noises with his tongue against his teeth. He was thinking his own thoughts. He folded his arms across his chest.

'Yes,' he said simply in the end. 'I see. You love him.'

'Yes,' I said. Feeling the green sunlight in my hair; sunlight in my heart. Seeing him look a little sardonically at my teary face; thinking it wouldn't be beyond him to ask why I was crying at the good news. 'Tears of happiness,' I said hastily, wiping at my face. 'It was a shock. I didn't expect it to happen the way it did.' Then I fell silent, feeling I'd said too much.

But he just went on nodding. 'I have a secret too,' he said sombrely, after a few more tk-tks, with his arms still tightly crossed. 'I've been thinking of going back to Basel for some time.'

I had no idea; and since his career, moribund there, was going so well here, and he had half the gentry of England waiting for him to paint their portraits, it struck me as an odd decision. I nodded without questioning it though; forming my lips into a politely disappointed 'oh' – a minimum response. The encounter between us had robbed me of all spontaneity with him; but not of

229

all questions in the privacy of my own mind. Perhaps he missed his family. Or perhaps there was another embarrassing personal reason for this announcement, connected with me; something I'd do anything to avoid him telling me.

Did he look disappointed by my failure to expostulate, to try and persuade him to stay? I couldn't tell. And not because of any subtlety of expression flitting across his face, either, but just because he'd turned and started ferreting through the big leather poacher's bag he kept sketching materials in. Head down, arms flying, back muscles rippling: full of energy. I laughed to myself, relieved; he'd already got some new idea in his head; he wasn't the type to let confusion over trying to kiss me ruin his life.

He grunted with satisfaction and began pulling a paper out of the bag. 'I've got something for you,' he announced, raising his head, with a forlorn smile on his face. 'I've been working on it for a while.'

He held it out.

A little jewel of a painting; bright colours on paper. Me in my white fur cap and a simple black dress. Behind, the blue of the summer sky and a few green leaves in sunlight. The painted me was looking very seriously out of the side of the picture, apparently lost in thought. From a perch on one of the twigs, a starling was sitting, looking beadily over my shoulder as if about to hop onto it, trying to get my attention. It took me a few moments to see that there was a second animal in the picture: a red squirrel, not noticing the chain that linked him to my hand, happily sitting in my lap and eating a nut.

Somehow he'd given the starling the intent, questioning look of John. I stared at it, entranced; moved. 'Oh Master Hans, it's beautiful,' I whispered.

'It's a goodbye present,' he said firmly. 'There's nothing

to keep me here any more. I could take the afternoon boat into London. Time to break my chain.'

And I blushed, hotly realising who the squirrel represented, astonished and ashamed that he could have been making that picture in these past days, thinking of me and putting such care into portraying my hands and throat and skin tone when I'd scarcely noticed his existence. 'Remember me,' he added.

I nodded; nearly ready to cry again now, with a soft lump in my throat. 'I'll miss you, Master Hans,' I said, realising, now it was too late, how true that was; trying to find some way of conveying the real affection and respect I'd come to feel for him. 'Write to me from Basel if you ever get a moment. Tell me how you are . . .'

It sounded weak. He nodded, but sadly; I could see him thinking he never would. It wasn't likely, I realised; I'd never seen him pick up a pen if he could avoid it.

We bowed our farewells at each other from our distance, awkward now about touching. I muttered, 'Thank you again' (nods from him) and 'I'll see you in the house later' (which elicited a dour look that I interpreted as meaning 'Not if I see you first').

I knew how our last seconds together should go. Dignity was important. I should set off gently back across the lawn with the picture in my hand. There was no need to hurry now I knew my mind. I could enjoy the sunlight. I should feel Hans Holbein's eyes on my back, watching as I made my way to the New Building to find my father and my husband-to-be. But I shouldn't let that spoil the pleasure of the decision I'd made.

It didn't turn out quite like that, though. It was Hans Holbein who got in first with the final word; who said, in a tight little voice, 'Well, goodbye,' and who began to walk away across the lawn, towards the house, without looking back. Never look back, John liked to say. And it was me, clasping his picture to my breast, who was left staring at those solid shoulders moving out of my life with a disconcerting sense of loss that I didn't fully understand.

PART THREE

Noli-Me-Tangere

10

That confused dawn in the garden was the end of my suspicious, lonely girlhood, from the moment when I walked back into the New Building, with my head held as high as I knew how, and moved towards the tall, still figure standing with his back to me in the shadows looking up at Master Hans's noli-me-tangere picture, and realised I didn't know what to call him.

'. . . Richard?' I whispered hesitantly.

He didn't move, but I thought there was a more alert quality in his stillness. He waited until I was almost touching him before turning a ravaged face down to me. His long eyes searched mine; but he must have seen something reassuring in my face. He closed his eyes and wrapped me in his arms. 'That's not my name,' he murmured in my ear. 'My name is John Clement. It has been since before you were born. You've always known me,' and from deep in the folds of the cloak still draped over his racing heart I guessed the beginning of a smile was coming back to his lips.

When, gaining courage, I whispered, 'I will marry you,' he sighed back, 'Thank God,' then 'thank you.' But he wouldn't say any more about what we'd talked about in the night. I tried. 'Do you believe people might really come and try to find you?' I asked, still timidly; 'people who would want you to be king?' He shook his head, but more to stop any further conversation about that than to answer my question. 'That's all over,' he said, so firmly that I felt he might be trying to convince himself as much as me that this was the truth; 'long ago. Dead and buried like Edward. It won't make any difference to our lives. We don't need to think about it, whatever your father says.' I nodded. Even if he didn't quite believe what he was saying himself, anything else seemed too fanciful to live with. 'Forget it all, Meg,' he added, and his voice was getting stronger and more confident. 'I have. It would drive anyone mad to spend their days going over the past, and I'm no exception. I want an ordinary life, and ordinary happiness. Perhaps it was wrong of me not to tell you about this before, but I didn't want you to start worrying over it. No one else's life should be poisoned by what happened years ago. It means nothing to me now. I never look back, never think about it. And you shouldn't either.' And he shut his mouth tight. Now that my resolve had come flowing back, and I'd realised that I still only wanted one thing in life, and that was to marry John, there was so much more I wanted to know. It was on the tip of my tongue, for instance, to ask, 'was that really the King in the chapel?' – but I stopped myself before those particular girlish words came out. I didn't want to seem as unsophisticated as Master Hans. I knew he wanted to cut off my questions and drag me back to the present; I guessed I wouldn't get many chances to ask them in future. So I tried just one more. 'Don't you wonder,' I asked, feeling breathless at the strangeness of the idea and blushing at my own boldness in mentioning it, 'whether – if you . . . we . . . have a son – you'll one day look at his face and think "this boy should have been the king of England?"'

He only sighed. He waited for a moment and I thought I could see a thousand thoughts chase across the face of a man who might himself, perhaps, if fate had turned out differently, have been a king, living a life I couldn't share. But when he did finally answer his face had none of the shadow of wistfulness I thought I might have detected; just a slight smile. 'No,' he said firmly. 'I'll be happy to think: "This boy is Meg's and mine; and Thomas More's grandson."' And he kissed me on the lips, as if to stop me saying any more.

He quietly put aside the sorrow he must still have felt for his brother, too, although for a few days he would sometimes appear with red eyes. But that morning he retreated to his room, saying he wanted to sleep and pray a little, but blowing me a kiss as he walked away down the path. ('We have the rest of our lives; shall we observe the proprieties for the next few weeks?' he murmured, and there was a ghost of the old laughter in his eyes as he said the words.)

I stayed a few more minutes in the sunshine, feeling the welcome heat on my shoulders cleansing away all the terrors of the night. When I walked into the shadow of the house, with my eyes still full of dazzle, it took me a moment to make out the waiting shape of Father looming up before me. 'I said yes,' I said, with as much of the lawyerly restraint I'd always known he expected of those close to him as I could muster. Nothing prepared me for what followed: the rush of air from his mouth; arms wrapping me close to his chest in an unfamiliar hug; bristles on my cheek; tears on his. 'I'm so happy for you . . . for him,' Father was whispering, 'for all of us.' I tightened my own arms around him by way of reply, almost more overwhelmed by this unheard-of gesture than by being promised in marriage. I couldn't remember Father ever hugging me before.

In the warmth of that embrace, I was briefly ashamed. How could I have been so suspicious? Everything seemed suddenly clear now: Father was a good man and I could trust him and trust John's trust in him. It was almost as though I'd recovered from a sickness I hadn't known I was suffering from: an excess of melancholy that had unsettled my mind, making me as 'solitary, fearful, envious, covetous and dark of colour' as the medical books said, or a bout of hysteria, the rising of the womb that makes women mad. What else could have stopped me seeing from the start that Father's scourge and hair shirt were nothing more sinister than proofs of an austere form of devotion? The furious, filth-spattered writings whose dark energy had so frightened me were, just as John said, no more than an official point of view, written under a pen name because they didn't show Father's own mind. And the cobbler who'd been beaten so brutally back into the ways of God had, must have, simply fallen victim to a violent jailer before Father took him away to contemplate the error of his ways in the peace and solitude of our garden. My mind shied away from the stocks and the ropes that were also part of my memory of that little prison in the gatehouse. I couldn't quite explain them, any more than I could quite forget them. But they hadn't been as constraining as I'd imagined. After all, the man had escaped, hadn't he?

So my doubts became part of my past. From then on, I only knew tranquillity; a sunlit state in which it was impossible to believe I had ever been the tormented young spinster who could have kissed a painter under a mulberry tree at dawn. Without knowing how it had happened, I now found myself inhabiting a place where happiness could be expected. Everyone we met seemed to be pleased for us and to enjoy helping us. The tears that I'd always felt somewhere inside, waiting to burst out through guarded, dry, watchful eyes, drained away.

'I always wanted this for you,' Dame Alice said over the ruins of supper, her face transformed by her smile, and she folded me into a capacious embrace. I saw her wink merrily at Father over my shoulder. (Father, with his arm round John's back, dwarfed by my future husband, looked different too; his face showing no signs of the night's powerful emotions, yet softer somehow, as though his efforts to look as lightly amused as ever weren't quite working. But perhaps it was just the candlelight.) Dame Alice didn't appear to notice John's bemused air behind his quiet smile, his dark clothes, or the black rings under my eyes. She was off, romping back to the practical side of life which gave her pleasure. 'There's going to be a lot of organising,' she added affectionately. 'Linens. Cooking pots. Cutlery. A housekeeper. Maids. And tapestries. Yes, we'll have to do something about tapestries. It's a freezing old barn after all; completely impractical, as I always said; you'll spend all your days worrying about how to stop up all the draughts.'

'Where?' I said, stupid with happiness.

She peered at me, then at Father, looking at his feet now, with the small smile of a magician who's performed a good trick on his face. 'Husband,' she said in mock-indignation. 'You amaze me. Can you really not have told them?'

She turned back to me, shaking her head. 'The Old Barge, of course,' she said, as if it had been obvious all along. 'Your father thought that's where you'd want to live once you were married. It's your wedding gift.'

And when John and I both turned on Father, with a mixture of joy and disbelief, he had nothing to say, for once. Instead he folded us both into another of the clumsy new embraces that seemed to signify we'd all entered the happy-ever-after phase of our lives.

*   *   *

We married quietly, on a September morning with golden late-summer light pouring over us, exchanging rings at the door of Chelsea church. The Ropers and Herons and Rastells were there as well as Father and Dame Alice, three of the More girls and their husbands, young John More and Anne Cresacre (now betrothed themselves), and old Sir John, using a stick but propping himself as fiercely upright as ever, kissing us as we stepped away from the church and wishing us well for the future with his usual fierce stare. Elizabeth was unwell; she sent her regrets. I hardly noticed. We took the boat into town for the wedding meal afterwards in John's and my home to be, organised by Mary and Dame Alice. I watched the wild Surrey shore recede with each fall of the oar, and rejoiced at the river water fouling up as we got closer to the landing-stage and the jagged city skyline opened up to embrace us, and almost laughed as we picked our way over cobbles to where we'd spend our first night in our new house.

I was a little dizzy from the importance of the day, the heat, the tightness of my lacing, the lack of food, and the journey. John squeezed my shoulder and we exchanged glances before gazing up at the rambling stone façades on the corner of Bucklersbury and Walbrook, full of joy at the sight of that familiar alignment of tall windows and red-and-ochre bricks and high chimneys opposite the church with the ancient scars of tidemarks on its walls, the home of almost all our shared memories.

It was afternoon by then, and to Londoners who lived there every day the street must have seemed quiet. But our newly countrified ears could still hear the hubbub of the river from one direction and Cheapside from the other. To London eyes the people hurrying by in drab worsteds or brightly coloured leggings and liveries would probably have seemed just the dregs of a busy morning's marketing;

but to my eyes they seemed a crowd. And when Mad Davy, who it seemed was still selling nonsense remedies made of newt's eye to the gullible but might possibly believe that they worked, popped out from the alleyway beside St Stephen's Walbrook and yelled, drunk and half-mocking, 'It's little Miss Meg back again! Welcome back, missis! Well done, Master Johnny!' and doffed his cap to me – before John stepped forward with a dark warning on his face and Father gave him a look stern enough to send the old fraud dashing back into his smelly hole, still yelling from behind the alley walls, 'God bless!' – I felt as though the city itself had acknowledged my return with a knowing, cheery wink. Father and John were still chuckling together over Mad Davy's outburst – '"Master Johnny" indeed!' Father laughed, shaking his head – as we clustered in the ewery to wash the traces of river grime from our hands before beginning the feast Dame Alice had set out for us in the hall. And I still had Mad Davy's cries ringing in my ears as John began spearing slices of swan and pork and chitterlings and slivers of apple and quince puddings to lay before me, and the toasting got going. That cracked voice seemed more real than this dream-like feast surrounded by people wishing me and the love of my life an eternity of happiness together.

Yet it was all real, I began to see in the months that followed, just as it was real that whenever John half-closed his pale, unreadable eyes and ran a finger down my arm or back, making me shiver with desire and turn my face up to him to be kissed, we could lock the bedroom door and melt into each other's bodies and know that the only outsider who would notice would be the secretly smiling maid in the morning. I could still hardly believe it as I gathered in the sweet apples from the garden and watched the leaves go gold and hung the parlour with a copy of Father's portrait which Dame Alice had given us, and the map of the world that the Ropers had had made for us, and, with some doubt, the picture of me in the garden that Master Hans had worked on so quietly before leaving England (I needn't have worried: 'That's beautiful,' was all John said innocently when he saw it, 'Master Hans is a talented man.'). The parlour became home, too, for our measuring pans for medicine and the three hundred books that John had amassed over the years. I set up a loom and made ribbons; I ground corn in the kitchen and picked at the lute and embroidered baby smocks. We'd become a part of the world. It seemed too good to be true.

John's work at the College and with Dr Butts, the King's chief physician, gave our days and nights their perfect, regular shape. His days were spent away with the learned men of medicine, talking, reading, experimenting, treating the illnesses of the greatest men in the land. He'd become as devoted to Dr Butts – an absent-minded old thing, who dribbled food down his front, scarcely noticed anything he couldn't cut up or push medicine into, and spent his nights sitting up reading treatises by candlelight – as he'd ever been to Father. I thought he found Dr Butts's very lack of sophistication reassuring. As he said, the one thing he'd learned from his past was that he didn't need to strive to live in the King's smile – or risk being lost in the King's frown. And there was no danger this doctor would ever attract the King's close friendship, causing the kind of unnerving changes in our lives that the More household had experienced when royal recognition came Father's way. Dr Butts could never be a courtier.

Compared with the men of the mind who'd always gathered around Father, Dr Butts just struck me as eccentric and woolly-minded and a bit of a show-off. But I suspended my disbelief because there was so much about medicine I didn't know, and because John, whose medical knowledge was so complete after all those years of foreign universities, told me he admired Dr Butts's mind. 'There's nothing great about my mind, Meg,' he told me modestly. 'I'm never going to have an idea so startlingly original that it will set men talking for years. I know my limitations: I'm a follower, not a leader. Still, I love working with these mighty intellects. Your father. Dr Butts. It's like warming yourself at a fire bigger than you could ever build for yourself.'

I thought he was being too modest. And I felt proud when I heard that he and Dr Butts had begun corresponding with Andreas Vesalius, a Flemish student at Padua, and with Berengario da Carpi, the author of a commentary on human anatomy that they'd just read together, to explore the shortcomings of Galenic medicine. 'It was your success in treating Margaret's sweating sickness without draining off the bad humours in her that gave me the idea of writing to them,' John said generously. 'It fascinated Butts. If you were a man, you'd probably be a far better doctor than I'll ever be. You've got a real nose for truth. The fact that you're a woman is probably a great loss to science. But,' he buried his face in my hair, 'I don't think I mind. Do you?'

He walked out of the house every morning in his dark cloak, after Matins and a browse through his books and breakfast, kissing me on the lips and – if he timed it so that the maid had left the breakfast table and no one was looking – sometimes also down over throat and breasts or squatting down to run his mouth reverentially up over foot, ankle, calf and the beginning of thigh, surprising me, laughing gently at my parted lips and flushed cheeks, and whispering teasingly, 'Till tonight, my darling – wait for me,' and slipping away into the freshness of another day. All our talking was at night, in the quiet, by firelight or candlelight, with the ruins of laundered linen around us and bodies languid with satisfied love.

He was more quietly irreverent than I'd expected; readier to tell stories that had a note of mockery in them that made me smile. When I asked him about how Father was faring at court, he grinned and told me about the astronomy lessons Father had recently been inveigled into giving the eager King. 'He sits up half the night on the roof at the moment, showing Henry how to find Mars and Venus. If you ask him about it, he likes to look modest and suggest that it's all a bit of a chore. But you can see how pleased he is, secretly, that the King has noticed Thomas More offering a far higher class of assistance than Cardinal Wolsey. He's taking to scheming for favour as if he'd been born to it. My diagnosis: court sickness. However independent they seem, they all get it in the end.'

Not that our talking was much about anything but our quiet togetherness. He'd gone back to meeting any questions I asked about the past with eyes that suddenly went distant, the smiling phrase, 'Never look back, Mistress Clement,' and a finger placed gently on my lips. And I was so lost in the contentment of those months that I didn't try too hard to probe.

His reticence didn't change even on the night he came home in the frosty dark at Candlemas to find me in the parlour looking at Master Hans's stern portrait of Father in red sleeves, with a handkerchief twisted in my hands and tears on my face. 'What is it?' he said from the doorway, before I'd even heard him, with the kind of alarm in his voice that twisted my heart; and he rushed to wrap me in his arms. 'What is it, Meg?' and he pushed my face back to look into his eyes.

'I think we're going to have a baby,' I snivelled, surprised myself by the sadness that had come on me, like a memory, at the same time as swollen breasts and fatigue and the strange hungry sickness that had had me retching all day at the smell of food but longing to eat to settle my stomach too. He hugged me tighter, but not so tight that I couldn't see his face lit up, as full of burning spring as St Stephen's doorway, through the window, was full of candles.

'I'm so happy,' he began, and I could hear the joy in his voice.

'But I can't even imagine what it will look like,' I wailed, interrupting whatever he'd been going to say, full of my own woeful fancy. 'I don't remember what my own family looked like, I never knew yours, and when it's born,' I crossed myself to ward off ill fortune, 'if all goes well . . . I won't even know who it looks like.'

'Shhh,' he murmured. Patted my stomach proudly. 'Calm down,' he muttered, and I could see him thinking, Shh.

He made me ginger tea from the root at the bottom of the medicine chest, shaving it himself, pouring hot water on it and letting it infuse in a pewter mug. I was still sniffling but I took it, moved at the humility of his gesture, dabbing at my eyes again. He took away the handkerchief and kissed away the tears from under my eyes himself. 'Now stop that,' he said, very kindly, when he'd made me laugh a little despite myself. 'No more tears. I'm going to tell you who our baby might take after.'

He lowered himself to the Turkey rug and sat leaning gently against my knee. He looked up at me, as encouraging as if he were sweet-talking a beloved child out of a tantrum, and raised one finger.

'Our baby will be dark . . . and blue-eyed, like both of us,' he said. 'He'll have your pretty straight nose,' and the raised finger traced a line down the bridge of my nose. 'And your creamy skin,' and he touched my cheek. 'And your rosy lips,' and he touched my mouth.

'And he'll have my long legs . . . and quick reflexes . . . and instinct for finding happiness with a good woman,' he whispered, twinkling up at me as he added, 'But he won't ask as many awkward questions as his mother. He'll be handsome and good and wise and happy, and it'll be no thanks to anyone but you and me.' He tipped my face down towards his. 'Remember?' he whispered, and laughed, and this time I laughed back, reassured, wanting to let my lonely fearfulness pass and share his mood. 'It's tomorrow that counts. Yesterday's gone. Don't fret about it.'

So we didn't. I stopped trying to find out more. And all through that spring and summer we lived apart from reality in our own joy. We paid no attention the day the poor devout Queen went on her knees in the divorce court and swore, in her Spanish-accented voice, that she had come to the King's bed a virgin all those years before, or to the stories of the look of disgust on the King's face as he publicly pushed her away. We took no notice when the proceedings petered out because of the Papal envoy's excuses. We didn't turn a hair when a mob of market women marched off to the riverside house in London where Anne Boleyn was staying, hoping to do the 'bloody French whore' some serious mischief, marching straight past our window to their encounter with the constables. We were hardly aware of the stories of priests emptying their own churches of religious images to pre-empt the heretical vandals who might otherwise be doing it for them, or of parishioners mockingly sticking pins in statues they'd once revered to see if the statues would bleed, or of the parishes of All Hallows Honey Lane, St Benet Gracechurch, St Leonard Milkchurch and St Magnus taking their priests to the Star Chamber for illegally charging too much for holy offices. We just slept and woke and laughed and made love and felt the baby grow and kick inside me until it seemed that our perfect happiness might really last forever. It was only after he was born that I got the first inkling that, after all, it might not.

It was a luminous autumn afternoon, with laughter in the small, brisk, pale grey clouds chasing across the skies outside. I'd had a fire lit in my bedroom. I could hear people talking on the street outside but they were vague and muffled; I didn't have the energy to focus on whatever they might be shouting at each other. I was sitting half up in my bed, hardly aware of the aches all through me, propped on one elbow, watching the tiny smooth face wrapped in white strain inside the curve of my arm and somehow ease himself closer to me without appearing to move, until he was snugly, miraculously, snuggling up against my breast and stomach. We'd spent a night and a day like this, little Tommy and I, sleeping curled up together and waking and staring at each other in the blankness of wonder. When he opened his eyes they were huge and dark blue and full of intensity. When I saw his miniature fingers wrapping round my huge thumb, or his tiny head with its smooth dark fluff nudging against my breast, I felt my eyes open just as dark blue and intense. He had my eyes, the midwife said. He had John's nose, though she politely forbore to mention that – a tiny, perfect, aquiline hook; John's great beak in elegant miniature. It looked beautiful on his tiny face: incongruous, but proud. It took my breath away to see it. And he had his father's generous mouth, darkish skin and long, rangy limbs. 'Oh, he'll be a handsome boy, this one,' the midwife said, winking at me with the shared joy of a successful birth.

The whole household was happy. I'd heard snatches of song from the kitchens that morning; and now, with the clank of water being heated for my bath in preparation to receive my husband, I could hear bursts of whispers

247

so cheerful that they sounded as if everyone around me was on holiday.

There were tiptoes and giggles on the stairs outside. 'Shh,' whispered a familiar female voice downstairs, trying to stifle love and sound stern, 'don't, Tommy'; and an alarmed burst of birdsong from the great cage in the parlour, and a clear, piping toddler's voice crying, 'Tweet tweet! Birdies! Tweet tweet!' When the two maids opened the door softly, to see whether I was awake before pulling the empty bath to its place by the fire, Margaret Roper peeped her head round too. She had little Alice in her arms and her Tommy at her ankles, small and thunderous, as if he'd been dragged away from a great pleasure downstairs, and she was laughing. 'Your chaffinches are in mortal danger,' she said merrily, ruffling her son's hair, then came quietly to the bed and sat down beside me to stare at the baby. He looked like a doll compared to Alice, who had seemed a miniature until today but whose black curls framed what now looked like a giant face.

The baby blew bubbles and clutched at the finger Margaret put to his hand. 'Look, Tommy,' she said peacefully to her little boy, who'd come to the bedside behind her and was staring at the newcomer with as much fascination as if a toy had moved. 'It's your new cousin. Another Tommy. Look, darling. Say hello.' And, as big Tommy reached forward to hold little Tommy's hand and looked surprised at the baby's grip, she dimpled at him in pleasure, then slid her one free arm around me in a sideways embrace and kissed me. 'You look well,' she said gently. 'Cheeks full of roses. Have you slept? How do you feel?'

I grimaced, half-joking. 'They say it was an easy birth,' I laughed weakly, trying to make light of it, knowing from my first rough attempts to arrange myself when they brought me water and a glass and put fresh sheets on the bed that I had dark bruises under my eyes and must still be a sight that would frighten children. No one seemed to mind, though. There were only bright eyes and acceptance wherever I looked. 'So who am I to argue?'

She nodded knowingly. 'Thank God it wasn't worse,' she said, and I had a sudden shock of understanding about what the agonising two- and three-day labours her tiny thin frame had endured with both her children might have felt like. I hugged her back, fiercely. 'Thank you,' I whispered, full of half-disbelieving gratitude at so much unconditional love coming my way.

She held the baby while I washed. By the time John brought Father back from Mass, I was clean and smelling of roses and milk in the new white-embroidered nightgown she'd made for me.

John sat on the bed with his arms around me; Margaret pulled a stool up for Father beside us. Every head turned towards the baby, murmuring and marvelling. And I lay back against my husband's arm, feeling the baby's body lying against my breast and glowing at the simplicity of a life where everyone who mattered most to me could be enclosed in a single room, where I could have weeks more lying here with little Tommy before I'd need to walk across the street and be churched and go back to normal life.

It was Margaret who broke the spell. 'Listen!' she said suddenly, and went to the window with a look of great surprise on her face. We all looked up, a little startled to hear her talk above her usual soft semi-whisper. She pulled at the window.

'Don't,' John said sharply, 'no cold breezes.'

But she took no notice. 'What are they saying?' she said, just as sharply. 'Did you hear?' and she turned back from our uncomprehending faces and struggled with the catch until the urgency on her face infected John too and he got up and opened it for her, just a few inches, to keep the harshness of outside at bay.

And then his face changed too as he listened to the hubbub coming in with the chilly air. As I hugged little Tommy closer to me to keep him warm, I saw astonishment dawn on John's dark, even features – astonishment mixed with consternation. And Father leapt up to pace towards the window, so I couldn't see his face, just his dark head in its velvet cap. He was listening intently. I saw his body go tight.

I must have been the last to distinguish the words coming up from the street outside, though I could hear from the start that they weren't the usual come-and-buy cries of the apothecaries' market. 'Yes of course it's true!' I made out in Mad Davy's cracked falsetto, 'The scarlet carbuncle's been burst!'

Hubbub; cheers mixed with jeers. I thought I heard the strange words 'Wolf-see' caterwauled in the background. 'I swear to Almighty God!'

John leaned down and boomed: 'Davy! Keep it down! You're disturbing the peace! What's this nonsense you're howling?'

More noise from the street; footsteps edging back from our window. I could imagine the half-circle of faces looking uneasily up. But Mad Davy wasn't embarrassed. I could hear him hawk in disgust at the stupidity of those around him; I could almost see the demented look of triumph in his eye that he had a respectable witness now.

'It's not nonsense, Doctor John!' I heard him bellow back, and this time there couldn't be any doubt about the words. 'I just heard it at St Paul's Cross! Everyone on Cheapside's talking about it! Go listen for yourself if you don't believe me!' He paused for effect.

'What, then?' John yelled back impatiently. 'Come on, spit it out, man.'

'Cardinal Wolsey's under arrest!' the voice yodelled triumphantly back up. And this time there were more cheers than jeers behind him. There was no more unpopular man in London than the grasping, paunchy Lord Chancellor – the alehouse-keeper's son, and the only royal servant closer than Father to the King. Even Father, for all his forbearance, didn't respect the Cardinal much. You could see it in the lift of his eyebrow, and his sideways smile. John felt in his purse, dropped a coin into the street and closed the window without another word.

Even with the window shut, the room felt suddenly cold. We all stared at Father, who looked expressionlessly back at us.

Margaret broke the silence. 'Is it true, Father?' she asked timidly, putting a little white hand on his arm.

He softened a little as he looked down at her face, framed in her modest bonnet. Then he nodded.

'It appears the king is making his disappointment in his servant plain,' he said, raising a quizzical eyebrow, Erasmus fashion. 'For all his fraudulent juggling, the Cardinal hasn't been able to juggle the matter of the royal marriage to the King's satisfaction.'

He stopped. He had no more to say on the subject.

'So who,' Margaret persisted bravely, 'will the King make Lord Chancellor instead?'

'Margaret,' Father said in gentle reproof, 'you know I don't have an answer for you. All I know is that I'm summoned to see the King tonight. I may know more afterwards.'

He would never admit to wanting the job himself. 'But I tell you this,' he said as he got up to go. 'I'd happily be bagged up and drowned in the Thames if it would make three things come true in Christendom. If all the princes who make war would make peace . . . If all the errors and heresies afflicting the Church would melt away and leave

251

us in perfect uniformity of religion . . . And if the question of the King's marriage were brought to a good conclusion.'

He bowed. I didn't think that his idea of a good conclusion for the question of the King's marriage could possibly coincide with the King's idea of the best outcome, but no one commented on what he'd said. We hardly heard his footsteps on the stairs. When he wanted to, Father could move as quietly as a cat in the night.

Afterwards, clucking her children into place around her as she got ready to take them to bed, Margaret said, 'It will be him, won't it?' and she had hope in her voice.

But it was the way John said, 'It will be him, won't it?' when we were alone in the room again that I remembered afterwards. His voice was harsh. 'The cleverest men can be the biggest fools. He doesn't realise himself how much of a court man he's become. But I can tell: he's interested enough in the exercise of power now that he won't be able to resist taking the job. He'll find himself conveniently forgetting that the only thing the King really wants of his next Chancellor is to make Anne Boleyn his Queen. He may even find himself thinking he can use his new powers to persuade the King to change his mind.'

I remember not really taking in the seriousness of John's tone as he spoke. I was kissing the top of Tommy's head, thinking sleepily that the smell of his tiny scalp was the smell of happiness, feeling the sharp aches around my body but not minding them.

Yet I did look up at John's next words, spoken with utter certainty: 'Nothing's going to stop this king marrying that woman. You only have to look at his face to know that. Sensuality is in his blood. A wise man would keep prudently away from the mess that Henry's going to make.' He was staring into the fire, and maybe it was the red flickering light from below that lent his features their brooding otherworldly aspect, or maybe just the darkness of what he was thinking. 'I worry that your father's about to fly too close to the sun,' he added. He prodded at the embers of one half-burned log with his boot. With a rush of flame and ash, it fell forward into the grate, as John added, 'and crash.'

11

'So write to her, dear boy,' the old man murmured. He was leaning across the table, over the ruins of a dinner he'd only pecked at (though Holbein had made more serious inroads into it), and his face in the candlelight was more alive than those of most men a third of his age, and shining with persuasive charm. 'You could, for instance, tell her how much I admired your picture.'

Holbein couldn't resist sneaking a sideways look at the small copy of the painting of the Mores, propped up against a jug on the table on top of its cloth wrapping. He'd been quietly saying goodbye to it all day. But then he turned his eyes down towards his tankard again and wriggled the feet he couldn't see under the table. Mulishly, he shook his head. 'You know me,' he muttered. 'I'm no writer.'

It was the first time he'd seen Erasmus since his return to Basel. The old man, appalled by what was happening to the cheerfully freethinking city he'd made his home for eight years; at the damage the evangelical hotheads had done to the physical fabric of the city and to its mood with their rampages and violent demands for change, had wrapped his thin body in his furs and left Basel for placid

Freiburg, a short ride downriver, right after the rioters had succeeded in getting new religious laws put through in April. 'There was no one who didn't fear for himself when those dregs of the people covered the whole market-place with arms and cannons,' he'd been telling the younger man earlier this evening. Holbein could see that he'd never forgive the uncouthness of that mob, smashing the cathedral, whacking the great alabaster altar with clubs and hurling statues through stained glass. No wonder people had started calling the evangelicals Protestants. 'Such a mockery was made of the images of the saints, and even of the crucifixion, that you'd have thought some miracle must have happened,' Erasmus added waspishly, with all the disdain that a man who always seemed a little surprised that his mind was attached to a flesh-and-blood body would naturally feel for the kind of people coarse enough to revel in their muscle and brawn and ability to intimidate with hot breath and roars of rage and clenched fists. He had the smell of the ashes of the bonfires of the vanities in the square still in his nostrils; he was never going to accept praying in a whitewashed church.

The old man's absence had been one of the things Holbein had found to mourn in the pious new Basel of the *Reformationsordnung*. There were plenty of others. Prosy had been killed in a tavern fight. Old Johannes Froben, the publisher, was dead. Bonifacius Amerbach had absented himself, though he hadn't formally left; he could usually be found in Freiburg too. Holbein's two best patrons, Jakob Meyer and Hans Oberreid, had openly refused to declare for the reformed faith and so had lost their positions in the Council. The university had been closed since the riots. The printers were under strict censorship. The spirit had gone out of the rest of the crowd he'd expected to find discussing the state of the world over a tankard of ale at the taverns and printshops. Now that everything they'd all dreamed about and discussed endlessly in their late-night conversations long ago was actually coming to pass, Basel didn't feel quite like home any more. The newly reformed authorities were watching public morality too zealously for comfort. That wasn't why the centre had gone out of Holbein's world; but it was a good enough lie to try and fool himself with for now. And whenever he found his head turning hopefully after a dark female head of hair, or his heart lightening at a tall girl's body tripping awkwardly down the street, he always muttered to himself, in that dreary moment afterwards when she would turn out not to be English Meg after all, 'the bloody bigots', as if somehow the authorities were to blame for the gnawing wretchedness that had been consuming him all these months.

He looked at the picture that was meant for Erasmus all the time – a small copy of the More family portrait, a present from Thomas More to his old friend, with Meg's head leaning forward to point out a line in a book to old Sir John. He kept it in his bag. He took it out in the safety of the tavern several times a day and stared at it with a pain he couldn't name mixed up with his pride in its execution, and drank too much beer to take away the darkness inside. In one burst of guilt at the bad-tempered failure of a family man he'd become, he painted Elsbeth and the children. It was meant to be a love gift. But it came out as he felt, a picture of gloom: a worn old *hausfrau* and whining children, all looking hopelessly out of the frame and away from a father who loved someone else and hated himself for it.

Still, for months Holbein resisted the notes that came to him from Freiburg. He recognised the spidery writing straightaway. He told himself he didn't want to go gallivanting off down the Rhine just to sit around moaning with the Freiburg exiles about how hard times were. He was going to make a go of it in Basel, where, however hard the times were for painters as the churches were whitewashed, he was still somehow finding scraps of printshop work here and there to keep money flowing in. Deep down, he knew there was a better reason why he was avoiding visiting his first patron. He hadn't yet worked out what he could tell the sharp-eyed philosopher about his time in England without betraying himself as a broken-hearted fool. Anyway, he didn't want to give away the picture just yet. So he stuffed the notes under the half-tanned hides in the smelly downstairs room at St Johannes Vorstadt. After little Catherine, scooting round the floor with apparently endless energy, found them and began tearing them up for a game and scattering the scraps, he took to crumpling them into balls and pushing them down the mouth of the big jug that never seemed to get moved from the top shelf in the kitchen. It was Elsbeth this time. She didn't say anything. Just put the three notes she'd found, with their crumples smoothed out, in a heap beside him at dinner one day, and fixed him with her usual tired, red-rimmed, reproachful stare. He couldn't stand the guilt. Why did she always have to look like that? He'd bought them a new house with his London money, hadn't he? She had a new brown dress, bought with the proceeds from the sale of his velvet jacket, didn't she? He stuffed the letters angrily in his pocket without a word and swung himself off out, past Froben's book depository and into town, stomping down the riverbank without eating the stew she'd made for him. Then he got hungry and stopped for a meat pie at a cookshop. With the reassuring smells of beer and pork all around him, lulled by the restrained hubbub of the other men in drab clothes escaping their wives, he calmed down. He pulled out the notes and read them. They were as full of easygoing friendliness as Erasmus always was, with none of the grandeur you'd expect from someone of his fame: longing to know about London, eager for news of More and his family, and especially, all the papers said, hopeful of hearing how Holbein himself was faring. 'Bonifacius and the others ask after you,' one note added. Holbein felt his heart softening.

He was no writer. He could only put his own thoughts to paper with a clumsiness that embarrassed him. There was nothing for it but to go to Freiburg. He went home, pulled Elsbeth into the rough half-shrug, half-embrace that he so often let pass for an apology after he'd got irritated with her, registered the reluctant half-smile on her face that usually passed for acknowledgement, if not quite forgiveness, and got her to put together a bag for him. Then he got on the river transport.

So he was here, and full of food and drink in the comfortable house that the city fathers had put at their star guest's disposal, and Amerbach had been at dinner, and he'd shown him the copy of the family picture he'd brought from More to Erasmus, and the two others had praised it to the heavens, and he'd gone at a brisk trot through his tales of London, careful to spend more time describing the glitter of the court and his successes at getting commissions and all the sights of that huge, stinking, lively city than the family, and everything was all right. While he'd been talking about London, he'd felt the city spring to life in his mind, and his dreamlike sense that Meg too was just a boat ride or a walk through the garden away hadn't yet dissipated into the wretchedness of reality. The exiles hadn't even complained much. All Erasmus had said about the troubles, as he looked thoughtfully up and down the river during their pre-dinner stroll, was: 'Strasbourg, Zurich, Berne, Constance, St Gallen, and now even Basel: all gone the way of the bigots. It's hard to find a place these days where you can think your own thoughts. But it's not bad here.' So Holbein hadn't had to make a decision about whether to be disloyal to the city he'd returned to; and that was a relief. And now it was a hot night in the middle of August, but Erasmus had a fire. And Holbein was mellow enough now to be enjoying the sweaty warmth of the fire and the renewed friendship, and feeling affectionate at the sight of Erasmus wrapping himself all the time in that furry robe that was always falling open – the old man felt the cold, even when it wasn't cold; those skinny limbs with no real flesh on them, Holbein thought with benevolent contempt, complacently aware of the power in his own big powerful frame – and he'd relaxed right back into his bench long before Amerbach left for the night. For the first time since leaving England, he was feeling truly at home.

'Tell me more, dear Olpeius,' Erasmus said, with his bright eyes glittering, settling back into his seat after saying goodbye to his guest. 'More about More.' Erasmus liked his puns, Holbein remembered fuzzily; his best-selling book all those years ago, *Moriae Encomium*, meant 'In Praise of Folly'. But the title, which had been written at More's house and was prefaced by lavish compliments to his host that had made More famous all over Europe, could also read, 'In Praise of More', whom Erasmus had praised as the best friend and wisest scholar in Europe. Erasmus laughed his small, dry, inviting laugh at his own little sally, and fixed his eyes on Holbein's flushed face, and waited.

Holbein was too relaxed now to care if Erasmus guessed his secret. He settled his hands comfortably on the table, and began to talk – about the Mores, Erasmus' old friends, with an enthusiasm he'd tried to forget he felt; about the beauty of the house and the garden at Chelsea; about the earthy humour of Dame Alice; about the vibrancy of More's mind and the pleasure of discussing any subject under the sun with him; about the lute duets; and about the esteem in which the lawyer was held at court.

'Of course the Steelyard men didn't like him breaking up the trade in religious books,' he recalled, too, in the interests of fair-mindedness, 'and Kratzer and I spent more time than I like to remember puzzling over how hard he was on the people who read them.' He stopped to see how Erasmus reacted to that before venturing further.

Erasmus nodded sympathetically, not seeming to mind a hint of criticism of his friend. 'Yessss. What he writes about religion these days often puzzles me, too,' he said in his thin, precise voice, leaning encouragingly forward.

He looked so receptive that Holbein wondered whether he could tell the story of the prisoner in the gatehouse. In the end he decided not to. Frankness was one thing, but he wasn't a gossip. And he couldn't be sure himself what the truth of that episode was, any more than he could be sure how far he sympathised with the wretched Rickmansworth villagers: he couldn't believe that a man of More's integrity could have had anything but a worthy motive for keeping a man with his face beaten to a pulp in a shed; he just couldn't think what the worthy motive could be. So he changed the subject.

'Well, I don't know,' he answered, with a bark of laughter, 'but I tell you what. For all I spent so many evenings sitting with Kratzer criticising More for being a brute with the new men, now that I've seen what a mess our new men are making of governing Basel I'm beginning to think More might not have been so wrong after all!'

Erasmus snuffled with laughter at that, and Holbein retreated quickly to safer territory. 'And More's still famous for charm,' he said, with an easier chuckle. 'They love him for that. They even teach schoolchildren Latin by getting them to translate sentences like, "More is a man of singular learning and angels' wit".'

'Ah, my old friend; I do hope it will be granted me to

see him again before I die,' Erasmus sighed, sounding nostalgic. 'And his children. How well I remember those little dark-haired girls . . .'

'All grown up and married now,' Holbein said, suddenly wistful. 'All probably with children of their own, too.'

'Margaret and Cecily . . . little Lizzie . . .' Erasmus sighed. 'Even little Johnny. How well my old friend More chose the wards he adopted; what good spouses they've all turned out to make for his children. Good inheritances on them from their parents; a good education from him; an eminently sensible arrangement. Even little . . .' he paused, giving Holbein his bright, birdlike stare from the side. 'Little . . .'

'Meg,' Holbein said flatly, bitterly resenting the thumping of his treacherous heart. 'Meg Giggs.'

'Yeeess,' Erasmus drawled. 'Meg Giggs. A lovely child. Clever, too. She came late to the household, I remember . . .' He looked thoughtfully at Holbein's burning cheeks. 'I call them little, but of course purely from force of habit. Foolish of me, when I can see from your portrait that they're all taller and more graceful these days than either you or me!' and he cackled encouragingly at the painter.

'She's in her twenties now,' Holbein said. Thunderously. To his secret horror, he felt tears pricking at the inside of his eyes. He wiped furiously at his nose. 'Summer cold,' he excused himself, indistinctly. 'She got engaged just before I left. That was more than a year ago now. She'll be long married.'

'To John Clement . . .' Erasmus prompted again, with one eyebrow going up that quizzical quarter-inch.

Holbein nodded, only half-surprised to find Erasmus already knew. He had admirers from all over Europe writing to him, after all. 'We were friends,' he added, continuing to wipe at his face with his big striped scarf. 'Meg and I, that is. Clement, well, I didn't understand . . .' and he stopped, suddenly aware of his voice drunkenly beginning to blurt out his secret.

Erasmus nodded kindly. The little half-smile on his delicate old face, with its crumpled-paper skin, always seemed to suggest he understood far more than was being said. The eyebrow went up an extra fraction. 'A good husband for Meg, do you think?'

Holbein nodded glumly. 'I suppose so,' he said lugubriously. 'She said she was in love with him, anyway.' He stopped. He shouldn't be talking about this.

'Have you kept in touch with her?' Erasmus went gently on. 'Your friend Meg? Where's she living with her new husband? How is she finding married life?'

Holbein began to feel uneasily that there might be a point behind these questions. 'No,' he mumbled, looking away. 'I haven't. I wouldn't know what to say.'

Erasmus laughed again, with the slightest note of mockery. 'Dear Olpeius,' he said. 'You must get over your fear of the written word. You're an intelligent man. And what's the point of travel if you don't let it broaden your world and make you new friends to keep from a distance?'

The probing went on for a few more minutes. If Erasmus had been Elsbeth, Holbein thought, he'd have called it nagging. And he went on bashfully shaking his head.

'Well, it's a pity you feel that way,' Erasmus finally said, graceful in defeat, and turning for the jug to pour the younger man another drink. 'I used to know John Clement myself when he was a younger man. I thought you might be in a position to help me renew my old acquaintance. Still . . .' he concentrated on pouring straight. His brown-spotted hands shook these days, Holbein noticed.

'Never mind that, anyway. I want to ask you a favour,' Erasmus said, suddenly seeming serious. 'I'd like you to come back and paint my portrait again.' He stopped and coughed. 'When you have time, that is,' he added politely. 'I appreciate you're a busy man.'

Holbein's heart raced. Paint Erasmus again? Have his work displayed all over Europe by the great man's many noteworthy admirers? Get proper payment, get weeks off his joyless grubbing round the printshops for scraps of work that in London he'd have sneered at, especially the job he'd just been offered fixing the town clock? Get out of Basel and out of the house and away from the family? He'd do it tomorrow. It was almost enough to chase away all those tormented dreams in which dark heads slipped away from him in remote gardens. He nodded, trying not to look too eager. 'I'll come back in the next couple of months,' he said, then thought he'd sounded graceless and added hastily, 'of course. I'd be honoured. I'll come as soon as I can.'

'You must be tired, and I should go to bed soon too,' the old man added, watching one of the three surviving candles sputter out and stifling a yawn. 'But if you'll sit here and finish your drink with me, I've another favour to ask. I'll just write a brief note to the Mores myself to thank them for the picture. Then perhaps you'll be kind enough to arrange for it to be sent on your way home tomorrow?'

Holbein nodded. The old scholar nodded back, got up lightly from his bench, and took one of the last two candles over to the stand-up writing table in the corner, where his inks and papers and feather pens were laid out for him. He still stood very upright and his veiny hand moved fast over the paper. Holbein watched the way the light fell on his face from below, creating a circle of sombre colour in the dusk and showing the hollows of the old man's cheeks and eyes and temples, and marvelled at the speed with which Erasmus covered paper without even pausing for thought. 'There,' the old man said, flattening

263

the page into his tray of sand and turning to fix Holbein with another encouraging birdlike stare, 'that wasn't so difficult, was it? I'm delighted you're coming back to make another likeness of me. And there's just one more thing.'

Holbein nodded eagerly. If he couldn't have love in the dreary new Protestant world he'd wanted to see created, he'd do a lot to have the companionship of geniuses again. It was only this evening, after more than a year back, that he'd remembered he could feel alive again.

'If you do find, before your next visit, that you have time to contact that dear girl Meg Giggs . . . Clement . . .' and Erasmus fixed that beady look on the painter again, 'I'd love to know how she is getting on.

'Naturally,' he said, 'you're delighted to be home again, with your family and friends. But you never know, do you, when you might begin to feel a little, mmm, bogged down in Basel.'

He gave Holbein another of those bright, considering glances, and it showed the painter more clearly than any words that his secret was exposed and that the wish he'd hidden even from himself to return to London and beg, plead, shout or do violence to make Meg change her mind had been noted.

'Now that her father's been made Lord Chancellor of England,' (Erasmus rolled his tongue luxuriantly over the words, reminding the painter how valuable a connection like that could be) 'the Mores could be in a better position than ever to advance your international career. Or, who knows? It may be the other way round. These are troubled times in England as well as in Basel. Meg and her husband may soon need real friends more than ever. Either way, my advice to you, dear boy, is keep the door open. Write. Tuck a little note of your own in when you send mine. There's really nothing to it.'

Holbein nodded, looking more reluctant than he was

beginning to feel. He couldn't go on saying no now, not if he wanted the portrait commission. And writing at Erasmus' request would at least give him an excuse to approach Meg again. Not that he understood what bee Erasmus had got in his bonnet; but it didn't matter. This was clearly a command, only thinly disguised as a request. So he'd just have to do it well – force himself to be eloquent and persuasive enough on paper to impress her. 'Well, I'm no scribe,' he said, tucking the parchment into his bag. 'But you know that, so perhaps it doesn't matter. Perhaps I should. Try.' And without really wanting to know why, he felt his heart lighten.

It was only when he was already in the boat the next day, with the parchment safely wrapped in his bag next to the bread and cheese and beer that Erasmus insisted on providing him for the journey, watching the herons dip and dive over the fish in the shallows, that the fresh river breeze chased last night's fug out of his brain enough for him to remember that he'd been meaning to ask Erasmus all the time he was in London about how, and when, the scholar had first met John Clement anyway.

12

They were hardly aware of me there, on a cushion in the corner of the parlour, under the window, in the fading light, with my embroidery. John, at his desk, was listening, enthralled, to Dr Butts, on the bench, expounding his theories on the causes and treatment of plague in his reedy, high-pitched voice. I hadn't minded at all that Dr Butts couldn't talk about anything except his knowledge of the human body. I'd hoped to learn so much from hearing England's greatest physician discuss the science of medicine with my learned husband. But if I were honest, my first few experiences of listening to their professional conversations were proving a disappointment.

Perhaps my own education had been too much based on scepticism; on marrying the findings of learned men and books with commonsense. Perhaps my own ideas about medicine had been too much influenced by the simple wise women of the street. What had fascinated me in medicine was the examination of disease – the intellectual challenge of painstakingly assessing symptoms – and the gentle application of whatever minimal herbal remedies tradition suggested might calm and cure the patient, from *aqua vitae* to cleanse a wound or relieve the pain of an aching tooth, to herbal lotions and grease for smallpox and measles scabs. Of course, those were simple skills; perhaps not sophisticated enough for the treatment of the kings and courtiers Dr Butts dealt with. But some of the great theories that were taught at medical schools and occupied the minds of serious physicians of his stature, which I was now hearing for the first time, seemed uncannily like the superstitions of the odder salesmen on the street outside. They featured astrology, magic, and even, at times, the application of the unicorn horn sold by the likes of Mad Davy. I couldn't take them seriously.

I stabbed a needle into the heart of a silk flower, puzzling over what was making me doubt all Dr Butts's knowledge. I didn't have the experience to know whether the human pulse really beat in dactyls in infants and in iambs in the old, which he'd just told us had been the learned Pietro d'Abano's contribution to medical knowledge, or whether there could be, as he said, nine simple varieties and twenty-seven complex varieties of musical rhythms in our pulses that made up part of the *musica humana* of our bodies, which could be described in terms of comparison with animals as, among other things, ant-like, goat-like, or worm-like, and which changed as we aged. Yet, even if I didn't know what caused plague, I couldn't credit what Dr Butts had just been saying about it either: that the particularities of one person's horoscope, or the balance of the four bodily fluids within his body, contained the secret of whether or not he personally would get sick during an epidemic of plague, when other people all around were dying.

'It's too dark for me to sew any more,' I murmured. 'If you'll excuse me . . .' and I slipped away. Perhaps it was because they were so entranced with their ideas that they hardly noticed me go. 'Goodnight, my dear,' Dr Butts said absently as I reached the door, but John was still gazing at him with that disciple's look of hushed devotion and didn't even turn round. (He looked like that at me most of the time, too, I thought, suddenly critical; but did he always look so foolish when he did?)

I put the embroidery down on a table and climbed the stairs as quietly as I could, with the memory of that conversation still hot on me. It took me a long while, as I prepared myself for bed, to reason myself back to a kind of understanding. Of course John had to follow every turn of his new master's mind. It was only right for him to do so with respect; and natural, too, since John, an orphan like me, had always sought out the kindly guidance of older men. Equally, I told myself firmly, it was only right for Dr Butts to re-examine every kind of old folk remedy in the light of the university men's new thinking. Yet I still thought some of Dr Butts's ideas for treatment were frivolous and silly at best; at worst they were cruel and thoughtless.

When John stumbled into the darkened room an hour or so later, and got into the bed beside me, I found I couldn't look into his eyes. So I shut mine and pretended to be asleep. I didn't want to look into his face and see the reverent stupidity I thought I'd glimpsed downstairs – a look which, for a moment, had stripped his features of the beauty I usually saw in them. That wasn't a look I'd seen much of in the men who surrounded Father, whose minds were always as sharp as sword blades, whose eyes sparkled with lively, sceptical questions. It was our first night together without making love.

Margaret only laughed when I asked her.

'Heavens, no,' she said cosily, settling her hands on her belly, which was already round with another baby. 'To tell you the truth, Meg, I'm actually relieved to be out of the hothouse atmosphere Father creates around himself. All that obsessiveness. I don't miss it a bit.'

'And you don't miss the way Father's friends go to the very heart of the ideas they're discussing?' I persisted, disconcerted. 'You don't feel we've settled for second best by marrying husbands who don't have it in them to do that?'

She grinned, almost impishly. She'd stopped behaving like England's most learned woman since she left Chelsea for Will's home at Esher. She looked better for it too. She was glowing with happiness. She shook her head.

'I love Will just the shambling way he is!' she said with no doubt in her voice, and no offence at the question. 'Of course I love Father too, but he's impossible,' she said, seeing me still looking unconvinced. 'Always in the grip of an idea . . . doesn't come to meals . . . sits up half the night in the New Building writing . . . and fills the house with priests and protégés who end up staying on for years. I know it drives Alice half-mad with frustration, however well she hides it. She never has her husband or her house to herself. It's no life for a wife.'

'If you really want to know, Meg, I only wish Will would do what John's done and find some nice sensible new master to adore. Preferably someone abroad, who he'd have to write to rather than go and see. Will spends far too much time hanging round Father, doting on him. And I'd like him to be with us at Eltham, so I didn't have to traipse up to London or Chelsea so much with the children.'

'What I want to do more than anything is plant a really beautiful new garden at Well Hall,' she said, and her eyes sparkled at the idea, 'somewhere the children will be happy playing. My dream is to have Will in it too, not lurking around here, getting all worked up about Father's latest ideas.'

She laughed sweetly. She meant it. I wished I had her gift for contentment.

*　　*　　*

They brought the man to the church door before they called me over. It was December by then, with the kind of snowless, loveless cold that turns earth to iron and freezes birds off bare trees. I was shivering even under the cloak I'd thrown on by the time I'd walked the ten paces across the flagstones.

There were two of them: respectable-looking women in anonymous shrouds of grey wool. One, judging by her weight and gait, maybe my age; the other could have been her mother, but both now turned into ageless, spectral, sister hags by pain. It was still dark; too early for crowds. I think they'd been waiting for a while. I think Mad Davy, hunched over at their side, wanted to make sure Father and John were out of the house before knocking at my door. For once he wasn't grinning. He just jerked a thumb at the two women and trotted away. 'He says you're good with herbs,' the younger one quavered. 'Can you do anything, missis?' and she pointed at the human-sized pile of rags on a plank in the doorway. She was heaving, breathless, hiding her hands in her blanket, and her eyes, puffy and bruised with past tears, had an agony of hope in them. The older woman didn't speak. She was breathing in great gulps of air and holding her sides; I didn't know whether it was fear or exertion that had turned her face purple even in that cold and got her tongue. I had a feeling they'd been carrying the man themselves.

He was as good as dead, of course. I should have known from their faces. I had him brought into the quiet dry room by the stables where I saw the simple people who sometimes came asking for treatment. (There'd be someone most weeks, some desperate-looking soul who'd heard that I'd gone out to look after the poor during the sweating sickness and believed I might know a poultice for their ailments or a binding for their wounds.) When the servants had gone, puffing and blowing, I pulled away the blanket.

The man underneath had injuries I'd never seen or even imagined possible. For a nauseous moment, I couldn't do anything except stare. The wounds looked methodical. The body below the lolling head was crushed; arms broken straight across just above the wrist and elbow; legs broken straight across just above ankle and knee; and the surface in between a mangled stew of imploded ribs and twisted back and great dark bubbles of blue and red. There was blood coming from his anus. There was blood coming from his ears. He wasn't quite dead; there were little whimpering noises coming from the smashed mouth, under a blancmange of swellings and caked blood where eyes and nose could only be guessed at.

'I can clean him,' I whispered at the women, hushed by a brutality I could only guess at. My expression had already extinguished the last flicker of hope in their eyes. 'I can make him comfortable . . . give him poppy oil. But shouldn't we call the priest?'

They flurried. Looked around, looked at each other. Looked trapped. Shook their heads. Moved protectively towards each other, then towards him. Stood shielding him from me as though I'd suddenly become part of their problem.

'I'll clean him up a bit, then,' I whispered, into the harshness of their breathing, trying to give them relief. And I fetched a pail of horse's drinking water myself from the nearest stable. Its bay head turned my way over the stall; gentle curiosity in his soft eyes, breath coming in white clouds, like mine. By the time I came back in with the bucket, slopping puddles on the floor, the women were at their man's side, their backs shutting me out again, muttering at him. They shied away from me as I approached and went silent. But I heard the last word. 'Amen.'

My hands were shaking as I approached that ruined,

gargling body. I didn't want to make things worse; I was frankly scared to touch these injuries. But before I could touch the corner of my cloth to his face, his mouth and slits of eyes opened. A word or two came out – or at least a sound or two that might have been words if his mouth hadn't been so bashed about. The women startled back towards him; we all stared; and he shivered into stillness, with bubbles of sticky blood coming from ears and mouth. The white puffs that had been rising into the air from his face stopped.

'He's gone, then,' the younger woman said. A flat voice, unexpectedly loud, out of white lips; an anticlimax of a voice. She looked round, vaguely threatening, defying me to silence or contradict her. And when I nodded agreement, she stepped awkwardly towards him, then stretched her hand forward to touch his bloody forehead. Her palm was almost as torn and blistered and bleeding from the weight she'd been carrying as the dead man's face. She touched at the puffed-up eye slits as if she could somehow shut them properly and dignify the face into a semblance of sleep. The older woman went to the body too and leaned down to kiss his forehead. 'My Mark,' she said, then straightened up. No tears. She was probably his mother.

'Do you know . . .' I whispered, chilled to the bone by this death and the suppressed anger in these women's grief, '. . . what happened?'

The younger woman looked back at me with something like pity on her face, or maybe contempt. 'Don't you?' she said. 'Don't you, missis?' I shook my head but I could see she was suspicious of my answer. 'You should come round where we live then,' she went on, as loudly and brutally as she dared. 'We get a lot of it our way.' Then she looked harder at me; something changed in her. She laughed – more of a bark. 'You really don't know, do you?' she said. 'He met the Scavenger's Daughter, didn't he?' When I still didn't respond, except with bewilderment, she shrugged, turned away and muttered: 'Ask your father. He knows.'

Her tone made me prickle; but I thought perhaps she was blaming me for not being able to save her brother's life. So I put a hand on the mother's shoulder instead, and felt it shivering. 'We could have him buried here?' I asked, and the older woman shook her head, unable to speak, clearly trying to choke down her grief for now, but dead against the notion of burial at St Stephen's. 'I could pay?' Another shake of the head. 'Or I could have him brought back to your home today?' She nodded for a second, then shook her head. Then put raw hands over her dry eyes and stood still, thinking. They hadn't wanted a priest, I remembered. No last rites, so they wouldn't want a Catholic burial either. Their story was slowly coming together in my mind. They must be heretics. He must have been tortured and thrown out on the street. He might have been tortured into betraying his family. It probably wasn't safe for them to be home. The mother didn't know where to go.

'We'll take him with us,' she said at last, squaring up to the burden with a determined straightening of the shoulders.

There was no point in arguing with her. She knew the risks she was facing. There was just one thing I could do. 'You need your hands bound up before you try,' I said firmly. 'You can't carry anything with your hands like that.'

And before they could protest I was off, half-running across the courtyard, sliding over the kitchen flagstones, hardly seeing the nurse peacefully rocking little Tommy by the fire, trying not to imagine the blackness in my gut if someone brought him back to my door in that state;

rushing into the larder to saw off two hunks of cheese, grabbing at two small loaves and stuffing the cheese inside, finding cloth to wrap them, a bottle of small beer, and more cleanly laundered cloths to tend their wounds. I hardly had enough hand space free by the time I got to the medicine room to pick up the soothing ointment I used for wounds. I was scared the women would just go.

But they were waiting, staring at their lost son, or brother, or whatever he was to them, with those same ghostlike faces, wrapping the blankets around him again in a shroud, as if he needed warmth where he'd gone. They let me bathe their hands and rub ointment in and tie the wounds up with strips of cloth until their sores disappeared under clean warm strips of white. They watched as I tied the food bundle up with a knotted handle that would go over a shoulder. The older woman even looked me in the eye. 'He said you were a good-hearted woman,' she muttered. 'He said it would be all right to come to you. Even the way things are. Didn't he, Nan?'

The younger one didn't answer, or look at me, but just went to the dead man's head and lifted the plank under-neath, testing the strength in her bandaged hands. 'Come on, Mother,' she said. The older woman took the bundle of food from me, turned her back on the corpse and her daughter, and picked up her end of the plank. I didn't think she'd have the strength to go far. Yet she nodded at me before she strained it up into the air and they trudged out of the door, wincing and banging against the frame. 'God bless,' she puffed. Or did I imagine it?

The red and gold and savoury smells of the kitchen were still there when I got back inside, as if the chilly episode outside had never happened. But it was the warm calm that now seemed unreal. Trying to banish the memory of those two women staggering away to find a quiet place to bury their man, I took Tommy from the nurse and held him very tight, touching his nose to mine, watching his sleeping face change as he dreamed, and running through all the prayers I knew to keep him safe.

'Oh Meg,' John cried out. 'Oh Meg.' And he slipped off my body, and kissed my nose in the same reverent way I'd kissed Tommy's in the kitchen, and cupped my face in his hands.

I'd forgotten that moment of distance I'd felt from him. I'd missed him for the entire two days he'd been away with Dr Butts; longed to get him back to tell him about what had happened here. 'Essex,' was all he'd said when he'd ridden into the courtyard, muddy and alone, and I'd asked where they'd been. He'd been quieter than usual, lost in his own thoughts. He didn't even say whom they'd been treating. And I was so preoccupied with how to raise the question of the dead man and his family that I didn't pursue the subject.

For a second now I lost myself in the beauty of his eyes crinkling in pleasure as the pale blue of them glinted out at me in that deep contented smile. I moved my hands up from his buttocks and along his back, rejoicing in the strong, lean muscles of arms and shoulders I felt under my palm, so I could stroke the elegant line of eyebrow and cheekbone and jaw.

But the shadow wouldn't leave me. I had to ask. I pulled myself up on one elbow.

'John,' I began.

'Mmm?' I heard back, a noise tinged with the hope of laughter. He thought I was about to tell him something charming Tommy had done; then perhaps he'd tell me something Dr Butts had said at the College and then we'd chuckle together. 'I'm listening,' he encouraged.

'What's the Scavenger's Daughter?' I said, almost fearfully.

There was a different quality to his attention now. He lifted himself up on an elbow, too, and although the second arm was draped over my waist, hugging me to him, his gaze had sharpened. 'Whatever put that into your mind?' he asked back – he often answered a question with a question – and his voice was light, but without laughter.

'Oh,' I paused. 'Just something I heard on the street.'

He looked harder at me, and shook his head. 'Meg,' he chided, and I felt as though I were back in the school-room, 'no secrets.'

So I told him the whole story. When I'd finished, he crossed himself. 'I wish that hadn't happened to you,' he said, with an edge in his voice. 'I want to keep you innocent of all these horrors. If it comes to that, I don't much want to know about them myself.' He shivered.

'So what is the Scavenger's Daughter?' I persisted.

'A device made for Leonard Skeffington, at the Tower.' He stopped again. 'For interrogations.'

I waited. He didn't want to go on. His eyes had the haunted look I'd only seen on the one night he talked about his secret past; since then he'd been John Clement again, laughing off all my attempts to find out about his past.

'You know, Meg, I find this incredibly difficult to talk about,' he said tightly. 'The very idea of torture sickens me.'

'But I need to know; I saw the man's body,' I insisted. Hearing myself sound shrill and urgent; disliking my voice, but still determined to understand.

He sighed reluctantly, not looking at me. 'All right then. It's a metal frame with holes for arms and legs. If you tighten the screws in the frame when someone is locked into it, it compresses their limbs and chest. Eventually the bones break.' His voice had become clipped and scientific; I could hear his mind skid away from the reality of smashing bones and crumpling chest and blood.

'For heretics?' I said, equally clipped. They'd been dragging them in from everywhere in the past few weeks, doing their best to destroy the literary underground, and burning every copy they could get their hands on of the new heresies by Simon Fish and William Tyndale. No one believed the King was the prime mover in the latest clampdown. There was a different story doing the rounds about him. People were saying he'd read Tyndale's latest banned book, which Anne Boleyn had given him, and begun to see the point of the rogue priest's thinking. Henry might not have time for Tyndale's belief that the Church of Rome was evil and should be dismantled, but the word was that he'd warmed, at least, to the man's notion that the clergy should have no place in politics. I didn't know the truth of that. But it was unnerving hearing the rumours. It was unnerving being confronted by the prisoners too. The one I'd seen had been riding facing his horse's tail, with the texts he'd been caught with pinned to his jerkin as if he were a living book of heresy, trying feebly to raise bound hands to protect his head from the dungballs and rotten fruit the Cheapside street boys were throwing at him as his horse was led to St Paul's Cross. The street was full of ash and stories of arrests.

'Mostly.' He was looking away still. 'Are you tired?' he asked. 'Shall we sleep?' And without waiting for an answer he snuffed out the candle.

In the comfort of the darkness, though, he put his arms around me and hugged me close into his chest. I could hear how fast his heart was beating.

I stroked his arm as if he were a horse needing gentling; and he murmured, 'Promise me something, Meg.'

'Anything,' I whispered back, lulled again by the smell and feel of love. 'Of course.'

'Don't go looking for trouble,' his voice said. Then he gained speed and intensity. 'I've been thinking a lot about this in the past couple of days because I found myself looking for trouble too. You don't know where I've been, do you? Well, I have to tell you. Dr Butts was called to Cardinal Wolsey in Essex, and he wanted me to go with him. He's grateful to Wolsey; Butts has a lot of friends among the new men, and he says Wolsey was always more moderate with them than your father's likely to be in future. I felt I couldn't say no. I owed it to him. And poor old Wolsey is dying, you know; I can't see that he'll even make it to London to stand trial. But it didn't take long for me to realise it had been a mistake for me to go. I owe as much loyalty to More as to Butts, and I don't want to make an enemy of your father. All the way there and back I was thinking how mad it was to run the risk of being there just to avoid offending Butts. I've been kicking myself for being so foolhardy. I've got you and Tommy to think of now. I'm not some impetuous boy any more. All I want is to keep out of trouble and enjoy my family. You should be doing that too. Leave life's ugliness at the door. Let's choose to be happy inside. Please. Don't court danger.'

I murmured what might be taken for a yes, and went on stroking him till his breathing eased into sleep. I was momentarily distracted from my troubles by his story – surprised to feel a twinge of respect for Dr Butts for having followed his heart and visited his old patron even though the Cardinal had fallen from favour; touched too by the workings of John's conscience. But I didn't know whether I would do as he said if anyone else came knocking at my door. I didn't know whether I would be able to turn away someone who needed help.

I couldn't sleep. For some reason the most obvious thing of all had only occurred to me once John was tossing and turning under the blankets: that the woman had said, 'Ask your father. He knows.'

Father and John Stokesley, the new Bishop of London, were leading the new anti-heresy campaign. He was spending his days rushing very publicly through the backlog of legal cases Wolsey had left for the Star Chamber and Chancery, and his evenings grumbling wryly over supper at home in Chelsea or with us in London about the mess he'd found the legal affairs of the land in. That was the man we saw: the smiling charmer; the Lord Chancellor impressing the King with his speed and grasp of his duties. But he was doing something else, too, now that he had all the power of the Lord Chancellorship in his hands (something that might or might not also impress the King, depending on how far you believed the talk that the King was reading Tyndale and enjoying it): he was pushing as hard as he could to shut down the banned book trade once and for all.

I'd got so complacent in my domesticity that I'd failed to put together all the stray bits of information I'd accrued going about my humdrum daily business. But now they were falling ominously into place, reminding me unpleasantly of my old worries about Father's outpourings of furious pamphlets against his religious enemies, of his willingness to go home after a long day's work and spend his nights writing frenzied denunciations of heresy signed with other men's names. I'd chosen to believe that Father had been doing no more then than carrying out the King's wishes; that the hatred in his writing had been a diplomatic position. But had I been naïve? It was Father who'd written the new index of banned books that meant instant jail; he'd ordered all those in a position of responsibility to turn in anyone suspicious; the agents out in the docks and drinking dens, listening, were his. It might – it must – be his own fury being translated into the breaking of young men's bones. I lay very still, feeling the peace of the warm darkness all around me being corroded by the black bile seeping back into my gut. The woman was blaming Father, and she was right. Whether or not he was personally breaking men's bodies wasn't the point any more. The point was that he, or one of his subordinates, must have ordered the man I'd seen die that morning to be tortured. Whoever's hand had turned the screw, he was still responsible. Wolsey had gone. The King was wavering. It was Father who was giving the orders.

There was a whimper from the corner of the room. I felt my way towards Tommy, picked him up and sat down with him at the chair by the fire. For a moment there was nothing in my mind but the innocence of his hands kneading my breast, and his little body squirming with concentration as he rhythmically drew milk from inside me. When my thoughts came back, they were calmer too. Mixed up with the darkness were memories like flickers of light: Father sitting in this chair laughing as the hungry baby sucked at the braiding on his jacket; Father tiptoeing in with a bunch of violets on the last day of my lying-in; Father hugging me and the baby; Father sitting by the bed after he'd stopped for a drink at St Botolph's Wharf, chuckling over the mouth on the alewife who he swore could talk without ever drawing breath. And with the memories came hope. That man, whose gentleness I'd come to know so much better since my marriage, just couldn't know irrational fury. There wasn't a malicious bone in his body. He couldn't have ordered a man shut up in a metal embrace that tightened around him until his bones broke unless there was a compelling reason. What I had to do was find out what the reason was.

The old me – the person who hadn't believed trust or happiness were possible – would have been down in the parlour we'd given Father by now, snooping silently through the papers he left on the desk, looking for evidence. I considered that idea for a second, but banished it before I lay Tommy back down in his crib, full and sleepy with milk dribbling out of his happy mouth. I got back into bed, and snuggled myself into John's heavy arms, ready to sleep as well now I'd decided what to do. I was going to choose happiness, as John wanted. But not the way he wanted me to, by choosing ignorance. My new happiness wasn't something to be preserved by being cowardly. I was going to have the courage to ask Father the truth, and the trust to believe the answer he gave me.

I took Tommy to Chelsea in the morning, just the two of us.

Mad Davy was waiting for me in the street, ignoring the iron in the wind. He pulled himself away from the wall where he was lolling staring at passers-by as soon as he caught sight of me, with a great idiot's smile plastered all over his rough face, as if yesterday had never happened. He was a short, stout man with bandy legs, no teeth and greasy mousy hair going grey, who lived with his white-haired widow mother in some thieves' alley nearby. There was no reason for him to have attached himself to the apothecaries rather than any other market. I'd never seen anyone actually buy the murky-coloured bottles and powders stinking of rotten egg that he arranged on bits of wall and windowsills. But he was always around, and it was impossible not to enjoy his half-crazed gossip and opinions, one outrageous indiscretion after another belted out into the crowd. He always knew the street talk first. The herbalists liked the old bigmouth. Even if he scared me a little, so did I.

When he got up to me now, the fool's smile left his face. 'You did what you could,' he murmured, for once not speaking at a volume that the whole street could hear. He nodded sagely. 'I told them you would. I knew you were a good woman.' He touched his orange cap to me, and I saw his hands, too, were blistered and bleeding.

I didn't know what to say. Part of me wanted to slide past and rush down to the river and the bustle of boats. If I had to talk to anyone about the women, it was Father and no one else would do. But another part of me wanted to know what Davy knew. I made an effort to breathe quietly. I was trying to work out what questions I could ask. But he pre-empted me – again in that quiet voice, not unfriendly, but with the play-acting left out.

'Things have been getting worse since they got rid of old Wolf-see,' he said, searching my face with his eyes. Then, without warning, he said: 'They say your father tortures people in his garden at Chelsea.'

'No,' I said hurriedly, feeling the blood drain from my face, trying not to remember the gatehouse. I didn't want this madman disturbing my composure. I had to ask Father myself before I could revisit those old doubts.

He nodded quietly, as if confirming something to himself that had nothing to do with my gabbled words. Then, moving so close that I could smell the egg and piss and beer on him, he hissed: 'They say there's going to be a burning.'

My mouth opened. How could I have expected that, when there had only been half a dozen burnings in a century? I stared back, lifting my shoulders helplessly and feeling Tommy shift in my arms. 'I don't know,' I said soundlessly. And I fled down the side of the street.

Father was in the great hall. It was his new experiment – transferring the court from Lincoln's Inn Hall to home so he could get through the cases faster. They said it amused the King to hear that Father had inherited a backlog of more than nine hundred legal matters from Wolsey's time, but had already cleared more than half of them. The great table was covered in green baize and piles of books and papers, with four chairs against the side nearest the wall in which three barristers in their striped uniform flanked Father. One was reading out a declaration to him. The room was full of strangers and whispers. It felt as though I was watching the cosily professional scene through a pane of glass. Father smiled as the stripy lawyer finished, and said something I didn't hear. But everyone close up laughed.

'I feed them in Master Hans's parlour,' Dame Alice said proudly at my elbow as I looked in from the doorway at the unfamiliar tableau. 'It's quite a to-do, I can tell you.' She took me into the smaller room so I could see the table under which I'd once hidden Master Hans's drawings set out with platters of beef and baskets of bread and tankards and bottles ready for midday. 'I just tell them to help themselves when they're through,' she said, rocking the baby in her arms with a grandmother's calm gestures. 'They're a hungry lot, lawyers. You wouldn't believe the amount of meat they get through in a day.' She caught my eye, then raised hers to the heavens in the kind of mock-exasperation that showed she was loving every minute of her new life.

Dame Alice hurried me on to her parlour. 'We'll eat in here today, though,' she said, 'a proper hot dinner. Your father's got a guest today. He's only just arrived. Sir James Bainham; do you remember him?'

I did, vaguely. A lawyer from Middle Temple with a daughter Margaret's and my age; we'd played together when we were very young, though I couldn't remember her name. I thought he'd retired; I remembered thin greying hair and a thin anxious laugh. He'd walked around Chelsea village once, with John, at the height of the sweating sickness, looking at the scale of the problem; trying to determine

283

what he could do to help. A good man (though I also remembered Father raising his eyebrows when word reached us last year that Bainham had remarried, mostly because his bride was the widow of the heretic Simon Fish, who'd become notorious after publishing a raging pamphlet claiming Purgatory did not exist and accusing the priests of lining their own pockets by taking money from the gullible to pray for the souls of the dead). But my heart sank at the thought of Bainham being here now. Even though I was surrounded by all the cheerful apparent normality of life at Father's house, I was almost sick with the urgency of my mission. If we were to pass Father's one free hour chatting politely to a guest, how could I ask the questions I needed answers to?

Sir James was standing next to the chair where Dame Alice did her tapestry – the frame was up, and the basket was open, and skeins of bright silks were arranged neatly on the small table she worked at. In this cosy, feminine retreat, he was the same anxious wraith I remembered, with a thin back bent over into an accommodating question mark. If anything, he looked still more ill at ease, with furrows across his forehead. I could have sworn there was a lurch of relief from fear on his face when he saw both of us walk in, cradling a baby. But perhaps rabbity twitches were just in his nature.

'A joy,' he said with bloodless courtesy, 'to have the opportunity to see you, Mistress Meg. Grown so beautiful. And blessed with a bonny baby already.'

He fell silent – he visibly didn't really want to talk to me any more than I wanted to talk to him today – and lowered his nervous head over Tommy. Tommy smiled delightedly back at him and stretched out a fat little arm to grab at the long, thin nose jerking so near his hands. Trying not to look alarmed, Sir James shuffled back. The man definitely had a tic. His hands were clasped together, almost as if he knew to make an effort to stop them moving, but he couldn't keep his face still.

I was just beginning to wonder in earnest what was the matter with him when I heard Father walk in behind me. I turned, hopeful despite all the turmoil of feelings inside me that his presence would lighten the room as it always did. But I was aware as I drank in Father's face – unusually sombre, but lightening up in a copy of delight at the sight of me – of Sir James just shuffling and tightening his face still further, as if to hide away his true feelings.

'Meg!' Father exclaimed, striding decisively forward. 'What an unexpected pleasure,' and he put one warm arm around me and Tommy.

He turned to Sir James, and I sensed something amiss in the look that passed between these two old colleagues. 'It's not often I get visits from my grandson out here in the sticks, Sir James,' Father went on. 'Perhaps you and I could do our business a little later?'

I was relieved that Father seemed to have read my mind and understood my wish for privacy. Sir James nodded hastily and bowed again. He was, I noticed, still half in his cloak; he looked almost as though he had half a mind to scuttle away for good. 'Dame Alice will take you to the room where we're serving a very humble dinner for the lawyers,' Father said, and smiled a smile that didn't reach his eyes. 'I hope it will be adequate.'

Dame Alice knew an order when she heard one, and led the awkward guest away.

Father turned his gaze back on me. I could see tired lines on his face, but his expression was so tender that I thought I must have mistaken the chill I imagined I'd seen in it while he was talking to poor Sir James.

'Meg, have dinner with me,' he said, stepping forward

and taking Tommy from my arms, with the new ease that had developed between us since my marriage. 'It would be good to see you properly, away from the crowd.'

'Yes,' I said, as nervous as Sir James now, feeling my face muscles tighten with tension under his hand. I hadn't thought out how to proceed. 'Father, I wanted to ask you . . .' I hesitated.

He nodded, all affectionate attention, rocking the baby. I ached with longing for him to find the words to banish my fears, so I could give him the same look back.

'A man was brought to my house yesterday for treatment,' I said, trying for a lawyer's calm, choosing my words as carefully as I could. 'We got him inside, but he died. I think he'd been tortured. When I asked why, the people who brought him said I should ask you.'

He only sighed and stepped back, still rocking.

'Meg, Meg,' he said, with a hint of reproach creeping into his face. 'These are ugly times we're living in, if a daughter can think it's right to question her father's actions.'

I felt cold inside. I must have misunderstood. Could he truly be admitting responsibility? 'First Will, then you,' he went sorrowfully on. 'Though he saw sense in the end. But I wondered then, and I wonder even more now: do you children have any idea at all what it is you're sympathising with?'

'Well, what?' I snapped, almost surprised by the sudden hot anger driving my mind and my mouth before my heart had accepted what I was hearing. 'And why shouldn't I question what I see, when we've always been so proud of the gentleness of your justice, and suddenly there's a man – a boy, almost – bleeding and dying under my hands, and they say you're to blame?'

He didn't respond to the hardness in my voice. His stayed reasonable. 'This isn't the same as sentencing some baker who's been cheating on his weights, or a pair of ruffians brought in for making a rumpus in a tavern,' he said, and I thought there was a pleading look in his eyes. 'Surely you must see that, Meg. It's one thing to be gentle with a crook who'll chip away at the rules a bit if you don't show him you're watching. But it's quite another to stand meekly by and let the kind of evil take hold that will sweep away all the rules and the laws we live by. I can't make little jokes with heretics and bind them over. They're not the pitiful boys you seem to be taking them for. They are the darkness. They want to snuff out the light we've always lived by. If we don't destroy them first, they'll destroy the Church we've lived in for fifteen hundred years. We have no choice.'

He paused. I think he wanted me to back down and agree with him, admit I'd been a foolish child. But I couldn't, however convincing his mellifluous voice seemed, however sincere he sounded. I couldn't apportion evil as neatly and completely in the camp of his enemies as he was doing. I'd seen the blood trickling out of that boy's body.

'Have you ordered a burning?' I asked dully. It still seemed impossible. It must just be Davy's raving. In the inexplicably cruel old days, members of a half-crazed sect called the Lollards had been burned at the stake for daring to translate the Bible into English. But surely that was just part of the savagery of the past?

He sighed, and shook his head, and for a last wonderful moment I thought he might yet say 'no'. But he went on shaking his head, in rhythm with the rocking motion of his arms, and gradually I understood that all he meant was a regretful 'yes'.

'It's none of my doing,' he said.

'So it's true,' I replied, and my cheeks stained red. He ignored my interruption.

'A priest,' he went on smoothly, still rocking, 'a man called Thomas Hitton. He was seized in the fields near Gravesend by some men who thought he might have stolen the linen that had gone missing from a hedge. They found hidden pockets in his coat full of letters to the heretics overseas. One of them was to William Tyndale.'

Tyndale was a shadow, a bogeyman: Father's worst enemy. A renegade priest who'd gone over to the other side. There were no pictures of him. He lived in hiding on the Continent, invisible to English spies and trouble-makers. But the Bibles and prayers he translated into English kept coming, hidden in butts and barrels and packages and parcels unloaded in quiet seaside coves or right under Father's nose at the Steelyard.

'The Archbishop of Canterbury interrogated Hitton,' Father went on, and the harshness Master Hans had once painted into an image of his face was etched deep into the real face before me now. 'He was handed over to the secular authorities at the beginning of the week. He'll be executed at Maidstone on 23 February. Hitton's only excuse was "the Mass should never be said". He's a priest, but he's an abomination of a priest.'

Father was smiling, though it was a smile that didn't reach his eyes, still visibly refusing to engage with my anger. 'I was not personally involved in this decision,' he said. 'But I'd have made the same judgement if I had been. Anyone who believes that peasants without a scrap of learning to their names should have the right to rage at the priests and impudently claim to be able to determine God's meaning for themselves is destroying the Church we live in. Not just the Christendom of today, but the sacred way that joins everyone alive now with every Christian from St Augustine onwards who has believed what we believe and worshipped as we worship. Take that away, defile the body of Christ on earth . . . lose the beauty of Latin, the common language that unifies all believers . . . and you're left with nothing but the ranting and babbling of lunatics. *Anarchos.*'

He was so persuasive. Against my will I found myself imagining Davy lolloping at the door of St Stephen's, waving his unicorn's horn and yelling his crazy street-man's sales talk. Did I really want to leave the company of genius and worship what I felt must be the confused God of lunatics like Davy? I turned away to hide my moment of weakness, feeling unwanted tears come to my eyes, trying to master myself by staring out of the window. But I wasn't ready to admit defeat. As soon as I could control my voice, I muttered: 'I thought you were a humanist. Not a torturer.'

My gibe made him angry at last. He followed me across the room and, with one hand, pulled me roughly round. From close up, his face was flushed. Words were pouring out of his mouth. 'Stop being a fool! Just think for a moment what we're talking about!' he shouted, as hotly as I had. 'Hitton's evil – the devil's stinking martyr!' There was disgust curling his lips. There were prickles of sweat breaking out on him. There were flecks of spit landing on my face. 'The man is so possessed by the spirit of lying that it's taking his wretched soul straight from the short fire to the fire everlasting! He deserves his damnation!'

He stopped. Looked at me as if he was only just remembering where he was. Breathed carefully out through whitened nostrils to calm himself. Wiped the moisture from his brow. He was beginning again to look like the kindly man I'd grown up with, but the image of the venomous stranger who'd been standing before me a moment earlier was seared on my mind. I caught him reading the half-scared, half-repelled expression on my face, understanding it, and taking a step towards me to comfort me. But I retreated again.

In the silence, Tommy began to whimper. He must have been jolted into wakefulness by the tension in Father's arms.

We both spoke at once.

'I didn't mean to shout,' he said.

'Give me my baby,' I said.

I stepped forward across the chasm that had opened between us, snatched Tommy from his arms, and withdrew to the window again, looking down so I couldn't see the stubble on his chin or meet his eyes. He didn't resist. I could feel Father hovering behind me, but it was beyond me to say any more.

'Tommy's very dear to me,' he said, hesitantly now, through the shrill crying. 'You all are.' But I kept my back turned.

'Meg,' he pleaded. I rocked Tommy faster, making little love faces at him, shutting Father out. But I couldn't stop his voice. 'What does being a humanist mean to you anyway?' I heard. 'What are you accusing me of? All I and the friends of my youth ever wanted to do was to reconcile the Church, as we found it, with the learning of the Classical scholars we were discovering. Our dream was to strip out the cobwebs that had gathered in the corners. Clean away the dross that had gathered over the centuries. One of the ways to do that was to stop the friars who got fat on other people's labour, and the priests who could hardly read the Bible, and the traders in false relics. Of course it was. There were abuses. But our aim was only ever to restore the Church to purity, so we could worship more intelligently. Not to destroy it.'

I didn't want to hear. He sounded as measured and moderate as ever. If I listened, I was in danger of being persuaded. But none of the words, which the obedient daughter in me wanted to believe, were part of the same world as the trickles of blood coming out of that boy's body. Nor did they fit with the look I'd surprised on his face just now, or the shouting, or the gloating words 'he deserves his damnation'. So I went on rocking Tommy, rhythmically, back and forth, so I didn't have to think – as much to comfort myself as him.

'Meg,' he said, trying to call me back into conversation. 'You and I have had the good fortune to be part of a unique circle of men of distinction, men who know how to explore ideas with subtlety and intelligence, but also with respect and humility. Men who know when to stop. That's not a freedom that can be vouchsafed to just anyone. You can't put God in the hands of the mob.'

I stopped rocking, though I kept my back turned. Tommy wasn't crying, just nuzzling against me. I stroked his head and murmured at him.

'He's a beautiful child,' Father's voice said. I sneaked a glance up at him from under my eyelashes. He was pressing his hands so tightly together that his knuckles had gone white. 'Do you ever think . . .' he began, then paused, marshalling another thought. 'Don't you ever think, Meg, of the danger all this might expose him to? Doesn't that make you hate the heretics, if nothing else does?'

I didn't mean to speak, and I did manage not to turn back to face him; but I found myself saying, 'What do you mean?' over my shoulder, and the voice I heard come out of my throat was hoarse and frightened.

'You must know the King is wavering. He's in such a fury with the Pope over the annulment that he's of a mind to read the books that woman gives him. What if he threw his lot in with the Lutherans?'

'Well, what?' I said, turning to face him. He was lowering his voice now, trying to make me draw closer, certain at last that he'd got my attention.

'What Catholic king in Europe could be happy about that?' he answered, holding my gaze hypnotically. 'It's taken long enough as it is for the Tudors to win acceptance abroad as the rightful rulers of England. It took this Henry, in his golden days, to stop a generation of talk that they were a family of usurpers, and to stop the endless upheaval of pretenders and invasions and threats from abroad. But his magic's worn off now he can't get an heir; every court in Europe is full of mischief-makers whispering that God's against him. If he turned Lutheran, the first thing his enemies would go looking for would be a Catholic king to replace him. We'd all go back to living in fear of what foreign fleets might be landing on a remote beach somewhere. And you'd have to live with something worse: the fear that some ambassador, sooner or later, would sniff John out of hiding; that if they hit on him as a Plantagenet survivor, Tommy could get caught up in the struggle too.'

He stopped. Looked at me. Found my face immobile. Pushed for a response. 'Don't you see?'

'Don't . . .' I said quietly, and he leaned forward, with the hope of reconciliation written all over his face. I saw it fade as I went on, grinding out the words one by cold, furious, determined one. 'Just – don't – ever – try – to – convince – me – that – you're – doing – all – this – for – me.'

He looked anguished. 'That's not what I meant,' he pleaded. 'Meg . . .'

But whatever he read on my face now, before I wrapped my body tighter around Tommy and said, into the baby's shawl, 'He's hungry,' was enough to make Father admit defeat.

I heard his footsteps move away towards the door. 'I'll leave you to feed him,' he said. 'I'll eat with the lawyers.'

*　　*　　*

My eyes were red and my cheeks blotchy by the time I let myself out of the parlour, cradling Tommy, who'd fallen blissfully asleep after his feed. I wanted to leave the house without speaking to anyone else, to creep away and be alone with my thoughts. When I saw John à Wood scurrying down the corridor I hid under the stairs for a moment until I heard his footsteps retreating above me. His arms were full of two of the grand new velvet robes Father had had sewn for his new office, spilling over the servant's brown-flecked hands like dark foam. Their weight bent his skinny old back right over – but his fingers were stroking at the lavish fur trimming with love, and his face was full of such pure joy at Father's new sartorial splendour that I was briefly, painfully, happy for him.

It was harder than I'd thought to slip away unobserved from a house now so full of the servants of a man of Father's new stature. Before I'd had a chance to dart out from under the stairs, another door opened, and a stream of lawyers in striped robes trooped back towards the great hall, only a few feet away, in a hubbub of chat. I drew back again, hugging the sweetly sleeping child to myself, feeling my heart race with dread at the possibility that I might come face to face with Father again.

I didn't, but from my shadowy hiding-place under the treads I heard his voice. It was as urbane as ever. 'I'll join you in ten minutes, gentlemen,' he was saying, from round the corner, and I heard the outside door shut quietly and two sets of footfalls fade into the gusty garden.

I waited a moment more until all the doors had shut and silence had fallen and my heartbeat had slowed to something like normal before I took my courage in my hands and tiptoed out, into the cold light, making for the door.

But I practically walked into the arms of Dame Alice. She'd gone on standing between the closed doors of the parlour and the hall after everyone else had gone to their appointed rooms, looking out of the window; an unusual moment of contemplation for someone so busy.

I saw her only as she heard my step and whisked round, a polite hostess's smile on her face – clearly ready to show some new lawyer to the ewery or the privies or find them a glass of something. It was too late to escape. But when I saw her look of concern, when she drew me into the window seat in a plump, capable embrace, I suddenly didn't want to escape anyway. I didn't even mind when I felt silent tears coursing down my cheeks again. Suddenly there was nothing I wanted more than to have a kindly adult take care of me.

'Hsssh, there, there,' she murmured, stroking my back. 'What's upset you so? Here, give me the baby. And dry your eyes on this . . .'

I hiccupped into her embroidered handkerchief. 'Is it the baby?' she was saying now, looking into my face, then his. But he was sleeping so angelically, and there were still dribbles of milk coming out of his mouth, proof that he was eating, that she shook her head in her own answer to her question and looked more searchingly at me. 'It's not like you to cry. What is it?'

'I've been trying to talk to Father,' I sniffled helplessly. 'But it all went wrong. We had a row . . .'

She was nodding, and patting my hand. I thought I glimpsed understanding on her face. 'And you've been getting on so well,' she said sympathetically. But she didn't ask what the row had been about. She'd never criticise Father to any of us behind his back, however much she cheerfully upbraided him in front of everyone. She believed in loyalty.

But I had to try one more time to discuss this with her. I didn't know what else to do. 'They've ordered a burning,' I blurted out, and saw her face tighten (though I knew as I watched her that my news wasn't news to her). 'And Father says it's right. He'd never have done that before, would he? There's something new in him, something cruel, coming out. You must think so?'

She began shaking her head, but perhaps that was more just puzzlement than anything else. Someone as common-sensical as the Dame wouldn't welcome ambiguity. 'Well,' she said eventually, and that pause before she answered reassured me that she was anxious too. 'I don't under-stand the rights and wrongs of it myself. I'm no statesman. I suppose people have to be punished if they do wrong. But it doesn't seem right; I can see why you're so upset. He had that new bishop here the other day, you know – Stokesley – and they couldn't talk about anything else all through dinner. Heretics, heretics, danger, danger. And every time Stokesley said "danger" he stabbed his lark pie again with his knife. By the time he came to eat it, it was cut to shreds on his plate. I can't say I liked the look of him much. Mean little eyes. Sunken cheeks. And I didn't like the way he shouted at the servants when one of them knocked something over on him either. The man's a bully. I could see he enjoyed other people's fear. And Ellen told me later that he actually boasts about the name they've given him in the taverns – *the hammer of heretics*. But you know how your father is with his friends. He won't hear a word said against the man. So what can I do?'

She lifted her shoulders helplessly, then patted my hand again. 'You're not the only one who's worried, you know,' she went on, looking out of the window again. 'William Dauncey's just turned up to see him too. I could see he was going to try and talk some sense into him as well.'

I looked up, startled. I wouldn't have thought Will Dauncey would ever criticise his patron. He was too prag-matic; too knowing about what sheltered him. But Alice didn't notice my surprise. In her own way, she was hunting for reasons to be cheerful. 'Still,' she added, trying to look as comfortable as usual, 'if your father's wrong about this, we can be sure it won't take him long to realise. He's not the man to do things without thinking them through carefully. You know that. And he's the one who has the King's ear, when it comes down to it. Not Stokesley.'

By the time she'd folded me into my cloak, wrapping it carefully around the baby, and embraced me more tenderly than usual, and waved me out of the door into the garden and down to the riverbank, I'd begun to feel, if not calm, at least less alone.

But any composure I might have gained was stripped away again when, crunching through the frosty grass on the way to the landing stage, I saw the two shapes standing, lost in conversation, just behind the mulberry tree.

The wind was blowing; I couldn't hear every word. But I could imagine the way Will Dauncey's pale boiled-gooseberry eyes would be fixed on Father when I heard the first snatch of his thin voice, with the exasperation carefully removed: '. . . all I'm saying is that this isn't necessarily what the King would want.' It was only then that I saw Father's face through the branches. It was as set and angry as it had been earlier, with his lips pursed tight, and they only pursed tighter as Will's voice went on through '. . . wants a Chancellor who does his bidding . . . not a crusader . . .' and '. . . he doesn't really care about theology except where it concerns himself . . .' and '. . . he's fond of you, of course, but a king's favour doesn't last forever . . .' and '. . . not lust, good state-craft; he needs an heir . . . England needs a prince,' and, finally, '. . . steady on'.

Father's eyes were staring into the distance. His wasn't the face of a man heeding advice. It wasn't the face of a man who believed his most important duty was to serve a king thinking more about how to get himself an heir than how to save the Church. I thought it was the face of a fanatic.

I watched the oars enter the water and the neat spray at the end of every stroke as they came out again. I stared at the bits of driftwood and the bobbing rubbish floating past us in the gloom.

My heart was colder than the City streets with their shiver of snow coming. My head was full of the cold, biting, angry things I'd said; and the cold, independent things I might now do to make sure I knew what was going on, and couldn't be taken for a fool any longer.

When Mad Davy popped out of the shadows, moving towards me with his eyes full of curiosity, I wanted to run. But I stayed. I met his eye. I nodded back at him, slowly, consideringly, the same way he was assessing me. We each knew things the other wanted to know, even if neither of us quite knew how to begin finding out.

'I'll come and find you tomorrow,' I said finally. I was aware of the alley he scuttled down, after he'd nodded briefly back at me, with his sackful of potions clinking behind him. And then I opened the service door of the Old Barge, locked out the darkness beyond with a single slam of oak and iron, and stepped, with relief, back into the warm light of my own inner courtyard where a brazier was burning. John's steaming horse, Moll, was being given a blanket and a bucket of water and stripped of her leather and iron harness and led back into her stable. I almost ran inside.

John found me in the parlour, alone, staring at the cruel eyes in Father's portrait. He was carrying the baby, rocking him back and forth as he walked. 'The nurse put him to bed, but no one heard him crying,' he said mildly.

'Father has ordered a burning,' I said.

There was a silence. 'There, there, my lovely,' John murmured into the quiet, but not to me, to the baby. He made him a nest of furs on the floor and laid him carefully down. The look of infinite happy trust that passed between them pained me. There was no place for happiness right now. I looked away.

'He's not hungry. He can't be. I fed him upstairs,' I said sullenly, with too much on my mind to be able to bear anyone making demands of my body too. 'John, did you hear what I said? I said, Father's ordered a burning!'

'I know,' he said, straightening up. He was keeping his voice light. 'Everyone's talking about it. I heard from Doctor Butts.'

'But he can't!'

John turned to me, very gently, with the kind of grave concern he might show if I were bereaved and he were comforting me. But all he said as he sat down next to me was, 'Shh, Meg. You'll upset the baby.'

I folded my arms over my chest. 'My father, the humanist, is going to burn a man at the stake.'

'Well, he must think it's necessary, Meg,' John said, still in the same voice.

'What do you mean necessary?' I ground out.

'He's the Lord Chancellor, Meg. Who am I to stand in his way?'

'He might listen to you. You could stop him.'

'I'm not a statesman. I don't want to do or say or think anything that might endanger us.'

'That makes you a coward.'

'Maybe,' he said, looking down at the baby, giving no sign that the insult had dented his composure. 'But the only thing that matters to me is our family. If I've learned anything in life, it's not to risk what you love.'

'I've just seen Will Dauncey try to talk to Father. He wasn't scared. Why are you?'

'Because I'm not a child like you and Will,' he answered unflappably. 'Because I remember how when you live under a weak king you live with fear. Because your father is the wisest adviser of a young king who's managed to make England strong and safe for the Tudors, and I trust him to keep things that way. If Thomas More says something is a danger to the land, I'm not going to question his judgement.'

He laughed without amusement. 'When old King Henry was still alive, we were invaded every year or two by armies fitted out by the Scots, or the Burgundians, or the French. Always with some lad as a figurehead, shouting that the Tudors were usurpers, claiming to be the rightful king come to claim back the throne. Most of them claiming to be me, oddly enough. But it didn't matter who they really were, because the magic of royalty is all in what people think you are. If their armies had been good enough, and they'd convinced enough people to follow them, any of those boys might have got lucky. Try and think what that felt like, Meg: not just for me, but for anyone. It might help you to understand.'

I was silenced, though still bursting with my private anger. His quiet sincerity reminded me of one of his long-ago improvisations to our Richard III story. It came flooding back now, his voice with the same bleak tone, murmuring: 'These matters are kings' games, as if it were stage players, and for the most part played upon scaffolds. In which poor men be but lookers on, and those that be wise will meddle no further. For they that sometime step up and play with them, when they cannot play their parts, only disorder the play and do themselves no good.'

'You mean, "those that be wise will meddle no further . . ."' I said, half-questioningly.

'Exactly,' he nodded, as if I'd agreed with him, and squeezed my hands.

'You mean, "let's pretend it's not happening",' I said dully.

He flinched. But he nodded. And then, with the baby blowing bubbles by the crackling fire, he tried to win me round to his way of thinking by telling me how he learned his reality.

'I used to be as wild as fire,' he said, staring into the fire. 'A reckless boy burning with the certainty that my every wish would come true if I only did enough to make it happen. A risk-taker. When we lost everything we'd been brought up to expect, and suddenly became just two boys being bundled away to the countryside to survive as best we could, I was more angry than I thought it was possible to be. Puffed up with poison and rage. A little snake stuck in a box, but waiting to strike when they opened the lid.

'Edward took it differently. He collapsed. He wept. He got ill. He prayed. I see why now. He was older. He was probably cleverer. He knew how lucky we were just to be alive. So he turned to God. But I couldn't see that then. I just couldn't understand how my big brother – the only family I had left – could cave in to Uncle Richard. I was mad with the idea that we'd been cheated, dying to plot his return from under the bedcovers, crazy for revenge. I was ten, remember. I was hardly going to be in control of any posse of cutthroats I might muster to bring Edward back as ruler of the land. My voice hadn't even broken. It was madness. And anyway, there wasn't even any point climbing out of the window at night to begin trying if he wasn't interested. He was the King, after all, not me. And he wouldn't listen. I could have killed him from frustration. I nearly did. They kept pulling me off him, shaking the life half out of him, in some miserable stone corridor in some castle somewhere. He wouldn't even fight back.

'The Guildfords would have taken us both. But I wouldn't go. I told Morton to find me somewhere else. I said I couldn't live with that coward. Perhaps he was a bit scared of the strutting little bully I was then. More likely he just felt sorry for me. So I stayed at Gipping with the Tyrrells. And my pride. It didn't win me a kingdom, though. It just lost me my brother.

'I was lonely after he went. And I got scared. Of course I did. I wasn't allowed to stay in touch with my mother or my sisters. And I wouldn't have anything to do with the one person in my family I was still permitted to know. I wouldn't give in, even when Archbishop Morton started wanting me to go to the Guildfords and make my peace with Edward. "No," I said. "I'll go abroad if I have to go somewhere. I'd rather go to my aunt's court in Burgundy than live with Edward again." That's where pride and ambition got me next. I'd lost my brother; then I gave up my country too.

'And it didn't stop there. Before I left for Burgundy, I started writing to my mother. She was at court again by then, all bustling and happy that the deal she and Morton had struck with Henry had made her daughter the Queen of England. I wrote her terrible letters. I accused her of forgetting her sons for the sake of her own ambition: of abandoning the truth, betraying her husband's memory, forgetting God. She was a difficult woman. But she didn't deserve the things I said to her. So she met me. And she pleaded with me. But I wouldn't forgive her. I slammed around and raged. I didn't mean to be so angry. I thought it was just a beginning. A negotiation. It wasn't just my ill manners; it was what we were brought up to: raging and blackmail were how she did things too, how everyone in my family did things. But we never finished our row – because King Henry found out we'd met. And he didn't play by our rules. When the old king got angry, it was a quiet, obstinate sort of anger. He said she'd broken their pact, so he was going to punish her. I didn't see her again. I was packed off to Burgundy without more ado. And she was sent over the river to the nunnery at Bermondsey. They monitored her letters. There was no way we could have written. And then she died.'

John stared into the fire. There were tears on his cheeks. He'd almost forgotten me. He was talking to himself. 'So my thrashing around lost me my mother too. And it lost her everything,' he murmured.

I squeezed his hand. Suddenly he looked properly at me – an electric flash of blue. He laughed, but a bad laugh, full of self-hatred, full of pain. 'And do you know what?' he went on. 'It was all for nothing. My whole one-boy rebellion. My whole willingness to turn on my family for the sake of an idea. It turned out to be a joke – a joke on me.'

'What do you mean?' I whispered.

'They didn't let my mother go to her funeral, but I saw Elizabeth before she died. When I heard her baby had been born dead, and that she was weakening too, I came running back from Burgundy. I got a *laissez-passer* in my groom's name, took his clothes and just rode off. I was lucky – I heard fast. She was my sister and the Queen of England and people talked about her in Burgundy. My aunt kept tabs on everything. And I was a man by then – twenty-nine – and just about wise enough to listen when my heart said 'be with your sister at her end'. But it was the same old recklessness too. I was homesick. I wanted to be where the air smelled of life, and people spoke English in the streets. I did it just because I could. I still craved that head-rush of danger.'

'What?' I quavered. But John wouldn't be prompted. He was in his past.

'I bribed a man to take a note . . . I got myself taken

302

in . . . she was in the State Apartments at the Tower . . . and she was very pale on her bed, with her red hair turning grey and wrinkles and bruises around her eyes, and her body bloated and coarsened so I might never have known her as the girl I'd last seen in the sanctuary at Westminster nearly twenty years before, except that when she saw me and smiled she suddenly looked young. Her face had been like my father's – beautiful and fleshy and sensual, with fat little laughing rosebud lips – and that's how it became again. And then she half-sat up in the bed and said, "Richard . . . I never imagined you'd come like this . . . God has brought you," with the most transforming look on her face, like a ray of light. There was something on her mind that made her hands flutter and her face twitch. She called a woman to bring her a box, her writing materials. She said, "There's something I've got to show you before I die." She stroked my face. "I never thought I'd see you again," she said. "Not like this. Not in peace." I had no idea my appearance at her side would bring her such joy. And when they brought the box she sent everyone away and had me pull out the parchment she wanted. She didn't have the strength to do it herself. "Look, Richard," she said. Weakly. Eagerly.

'It was an old document. It took my eyes a few seconds to adjust to the faded writing in the bad light. But once I began to follow what was on the page, I felt a rush of blood to the head. I was so dizzy I was grateful I wasn't standing. I couldn't have stayed on my feet.

'It was a letter she'd written me years before, in Henry's first years as king, during the uprisings. She'd never known from one day to the next whether one of those invading armies on one of those beaches might not turn out to have me at its head. However much Henry had sworn that Uncle Richard must have had me and Edward murdered, she'd never quite known if he was telling her the truth. They didn't trust each other. She'd never known, either, whether she'd have wanted me to be alive, because if I was, and I came back to claim the throne, then what would become of her children? So she'd written to me as a kind of private defence, in case that ever happened – a letter she'd never have shown her husband. It was her appeal to deflect the wrath of a vengeful returning brother. An appeal to my better judgement.

'What she'd written about was something that had happened many years before, before we were even born. Her letter said she'd seen proof that our father had already contracted one secret marriage before he'd secretly married our mother. That's what Uncle Richard had accused him of, when he deposed Edward and me; but I'd always assumed Uncle Richard had made it up. But what Elizabeth said was that Uncle Richard had been telling the truth. She'd actually seen the record: an agreement, binding in law, to marry Lady Eleanor Butler. Dated 1462, years before my parents married. Drawn up and signed by Robert Stillingfleet and the affianced couple. The written proof Bishop Stillingfleet had sworn to Parliament never existed. But then, by the time he talked about it, there was no one left to contradict him. The Lady Eleanor had died in the convent she'd been put into years before – Father must have got tired of her as soon as he'd had her, and moved on to some other pretty copper-haired war widow whose virtue was easier, and he must have got scared that the Lady Eleanor might try to make him honour his empty promise. And anyway, Stillingfleet had let the contract be burned.'

John turned back to me and the present. His eyes were still shocked now. 'I couldn't stop staring at the paper,' he whispered. 'I said, "but Elizabeth . . . this means . . . this means . . ." I was stammering like an idiot . . . and she said "yes," more calmly than me, but she'd had years longer to think about what it meant, "it means Father wasn't free to marry Mother when he did. It means he was a bigamist and we are a family of bastards, just as Uncle Richard said."

'"How did you see it?" I said.

'"Stillingfleet brought it to Mother." She laughed – our family laugh, a last little wolf-howl of defiance at fate. "After Father died. He told her she should pray for guidance from God; he must have half-believed it would make her give up her children's right to the throne. He can't have known Mother very well. Naturally she burned it. I watched her. I didn't try to stop her. I didn't try to stop Henry relegitimising me when he'd won the wars, either. Why would I? I was fed up with being a helpless girl in a war. I wanted to be Queen of England. We all knew Henry had almost no real claim to the throne; he needed me to be royal so my blood would legitimise him; he'd never have married a bastard."

'"Why are you telling me now?" I said.

'"Because I know you're the only one left who dreams of the old days. Edward's safe. Everyone else is dead. I kept it to give to you, because, if you didn't know the truth, you might go on thinking you had a claim to the throne. You might harm my boy. And I dread that happening. My children aren't like we were – not so hard; they were born in kinder times. My boy Arthur would have been a king to be proud of; a king of Camelot. But now he's dead" – she didn't flinch; she was made of stern stuff – "and there's just little Harry. Nine years old. As headstrong as Father ever was, but he's just a child. I don't want you to hurt him. I want you to keep him safe. Will you promise, Richard? And will you pray with me for God to bless Harry's reign?"

'I promised. And we prayed. And when she wanted to sleep – she didn't have much strength left – I kissed her and left with the letter in my pocket.

'I hardly noticed where I was on the way out. Everything that had sustained me since I was a child was falling away from me. It was as if I were dropping into an abyss, with nothing to catch a fingerhold on and save myself. In one moment I'd stopped being a king-in-waiting and been turned back to a man like any other – except that, because of everything I'd done, I was alone in the world.

'I wanted to stay; Elizabeth was my last family; but of course I couldn't. I wanted to go to Edward and beg his pardon; but I didn't know where to begin to find him, and I was scared to try. I wanted to be back in Burgundy, but I could never tell Aunt Margaret what I knew. I didn't know what to do.

'So I ended up in some tavern near Walbrook, drinking myself silly in my coat in a corner, and, when it got late enough and I was fuddled and despairing enough, I got the letter out and set fire to it at the table. Before I knew where I was, before it had even burned right up, two big broken-nosed thugs who'd been sitting at the next table had me down on the floor. They said I looked suspicious. They were yelling that I'd been burning a Lollard tract. They couldn't read, but they were pawing over the last scraps of the letter in my tankard, screeching, "A blasphemer, eh?" until I began to laugh at the sheer absurdity of it all and said to the biggest one, "Call the justice, then, you thieving thug." That sobered us all up. They kept my purse but they did march me round to the justice's house with my black eye and broken nose. He only lived round the corner.

'Your father was still very young then and building up his practice. Dealing with street drunks was the kind of case he did. I didn't recognise him when he came into the stable they'd put me in. When I'd first seen him at Morton's, he'd just been a boy. A page. But he recognised me straightaway. He got me out. He sent away the troublemakers.

He even lent me the money to get back to Burgundy. And he talked to me. He brought me in here, into this parlour, and we sat up half the night talking in front of this fire. He was curious about me. Morton had charged him with following my fate and helping me if he could. And Erasmus (I knew Erasmus from Burgundy; he was in my aunt's lover's household) had told me all about him – the rising young humanist lawyer. And he's an easy man to talk to. So I poured my troubled heart out to this stranger. Obviously I couldn't tell him my sister's dying secret – you're the first person I've ever told – but I told him a lot of the other things I'd been realising over my beers in the tavern. That I was homesick. That I was English, not Burgundian, and couldn't live all my life in a foreign land. That I'd got more pragmatic and knew neither I nor Edward would now come to the throne. That I wanted to live quietly and mend my ties with my brother. That I'd do anything to come back here.

'He listened and listened, and nodded and nodded. And he sent me back to Burgundy, but he promised to play his part in bringing me back to England. The deal was – I should put my fate in his hands, and promise never to meddle in affairs of state. Take no risks, and have no expectations, beyond the kind of personal happiness I would be unlikely to know otherwise.

'I'd spent more than ten years by then at the university in Louvain – I was fortunate that Burgundy was a place of learning, even back when Aunt Margaret married the Duke, so much so that my uncouth family of English fighting men thought of the court there as a kind of miracle, and called it Camelot. So I'd been lucky enough to have fallen into the world of books. I had an adult life. Studies. A passion to pursue. I didn't need my past. I had friends in the world of learning who didn't care where they came from, who gave themselves new names to mark their break with their past. Who even knows that Erasmus started life as Gerrit Gerritszoon? When More offered me his help, I suddenly realised that that was enough for me; that I truly wanted to be Johannes Clemens – John the Kind – and a new man in a new world.

'So I was happy to give up the Plantagenet dream. Now that I realised that the myth I'd grown up with of monarchs being anointed by God was just a cover for all the lies of the unscrupulous – one king a bigamist, one a successful usurper, one queen a bastard – it didn't mean anything to me anyway. All those kings and queens had cheated God and their people just as much as the Flanders street boys who wandered the courts of Europe, calling themselves Richard, Duke of York. And however much I'd hated my family's unscrupulousness, at that moment, when I realised that after their destruction I'd gone on behaving in a way that was just as hateful myself – and when I saw that what I wanted most was a personal connection in the world – I was ready to try what he suggested. So I became "More's boy".

'It worked. He did it – he and Erasmus in Burgundy. It took them till the old king died. But they succeeded in persuading the new King Henry that I believed in the Tudor monarchy, had no interest in politics, and would never be a threat. And they gave me a new life in England. I'd destroyed what was left of my family; but they even gave me a new family. Themselves. You.

'So you see, Meg,' John went on, drawing a gentle finger over my mouth, 'there's no criticism of your father's ideas that I could decently make. He's a subtle man. He knows how to work with unlikely allies and solve impossible problems. He's a natural politician and a champion of peace, and anyone who's lived through the turmoil I have can't help but value that. I don't pretend to understand how his mind works. But his existence is a guarantee that we can spend our lives living and loving each other, our child, our work. We should be grateful. Let's leave the affairs of state to him.'

Tommy stirred on the floor. I looked down at him, then up at my poor, bruised, beloved husband, with his eyes full of the suffering that I could see had bruised his spirit, and of hope that I would see his kind of reason. And my heart swelled with an adult's protectiveness of their shared helplessness. I stroked his arm. 'Oh, poor you, poor you . . . It's a miracle that you've come through so much,' I whispered wonderingly, 'and I do see now what you mean about Father, I do.' And I did appreciate better why he'd choose to rely utterly on Father, even if I didn't want to promise that I'd do the same myself.

'I'll get Tommy,' I said, and we sat for a while in front of the fire, me cradling Tommy, John cradling me, and when I stole a look up at my husband I saw a beatific expression of perfect peace on his lean face. The story he'd just told me was too extraordinary to take in all at once, but I could see I didn't need to do anything dramatic by way of acknowledgement. He'd become so modest in his demands on life that all he needed was this moment of quiet, loving togetherness.

'This is how I imagine us, always, Meg,' he said softly, with his eyes full of love. 'Peacefully giving Caesar his due, and God his, and being happy.'

How lucky my own life suddenly seemed. How easy. How small. With my head still spinning as I assimilated the details of his past, I turned and kissed him chastely on the lips, then lowered my lips to the baby's head, covered in black silk strands, smelling of milkiness.

'Doctor Butts is all taken up with saving the Bible men, you know,' John went on, musing, trusting, with a furrow to his brow. 'He hangs around Anne Boleyn's chambers, taking messages to the book smugglers. I spend half my days covering for him. And I worry for him. Of course, I don't think what he's doing makes him evil. I can see how intelligent and good he is with my own eyes. But I don't think he's wise; he doesn't seem to realise there's no point in needlessly seeking out trouble. He can do far more good with medicine than by messing around with the Bible men. It would be folly for him to get himself caught.'

I murmured something gentle – 'I see' or 'It would' – and rocked the baby. I made my body soft and pliant in his arms, but I was already starting to fret over some of the things he'd been telling me. John was pledging public allegiance to Father – but at the same time omitting to tell him how Dr Butts's mind was turning in private (which would have been natural if he'd been as outraged as I was by Father's bloodthirsty mania for religious purity, but sat oddly with the total trust in him that John was professing). And, when I thought back over his story, this wasn't the first time he'd told Father, his protector, less than the whole truth. Was it?

'John,' I said carefully, not sure if I'd understood that past omission right. 'Did you never think of telling Father – or Erasmus – that you'd found out you were illegitimate?'

I couldn't see his face, but I felt him lean down and kiss the top of my head. 'Whatever for?' he said, as peacefully as if he were talking about the weather. 'By then, none of it seemed to matter any more. The history Morton had already started rewriting made it irrelevant. I'd been John Clement for years.'

He touched my shoulders to make me half-turn my head and the baby's in my arms, and touched my nose with a gentle finger. He was perfectly relaxed; there was a glassy innocence in his eyes. 'And it didn't make any practical difference,' he went on. 'I still needed More's and Erasmus' protection, because I'd still have been at risk if anyone had found out my previous name. Royalty is about appearances. There's precious little reality in it. What would matter to a crowd looking for a Plantagenet king wouldn't be whatever I said my sister had told me on her deathbed, with no witnesses. All they'd care about is who they perceived me to be.'

I got up, hugging the baby, nodding as if I'd understood. It seemed blindingly obvious to me that Father should have been told; that he'd feel betrayed if he ever found out. But if John couldn't see that, perhaps it wasn't for me to start trying to explain. For now, there was too much else to think about.

He stood up too, and drew the pair of us into another hug. 'Besides, I couldn't have. It wasn't my secret to tell. It was Elizabeth's. And I couldn't dishonour her memory,' he added simply. I could hear he believed completely in what he was saying.

We walked upstairs together, the three of us, a muddle of arms and legs and tenderness and half-embraces, one within the other. My head felt just as muddled, with one great cloud of worries about Father and the burning partly displaced by this other confidence; tussling inside between my raging against Father, which I couldn't share with John, and, at the same time, an uneasy protectiveness of the man who'd done so much to help my husband, but had, as I saw it, been deceived by John's economy with the truth.

Perhaps that was how John survived change, I mused, putting Tommy gently down in his rocker – by learning to keep all the different truths in his life locked away in separate compartments.

But it was only after the candles were out and we were lying in the darkness, watching the fire die down, that the confusion gripping my mind coalesced into words.

Suddenly it was simple. I knew the question I wanted to ask.

I sat bolt upright with the shock of it, and I could feel John startle beside me.

'Why didn't you tell me before?' I asked.

I heard the beginning of a soothing bass rumble from the rumple of sheets below. But I disregarded it and plunged on.

'I've spent two years coming to terms with the idea that you'd once been a prince. That if your life had turned out differently you might have been king,' I said. 'Can you imagine how hard it was to learn to believe that? And now you suddenly say that what you told me before wasn't true . . .'

John sat up too, and put his arms round me in the darkness. 'Meg, listen,' he whispered, and his voice was full of love, but it didn't touch me any more. Suddenly everything I'd learned in that long day came rushing blackly back at me, like freezing Thames floodwater, two separate polluted streams of it coming together as they hit me and swept away the trust which I'd made the foundation of my married life. I'd had faith in John; I'd had faith in Father. But I'd been wrong on both counts. I was shivering.

'Meg, listen,' he muttered again, and the arms drew me in tighter to his shadow embrace, but I kept my arms wrapped tight about my knees, braced against the softness of him. 'You know everything now . . .'

'You should have told me the whole thing at once,' I said tightly. 'Back then.'

And there was sadness in his voice when he answered: 'I can see that now. I can see it would be a shock. I'm sorry. But when you shut old secrets away in your mind forever, and know there's no one you'll ever be able to trust with them, in a way you almost forget them yourself.

312

When all that was happening I never expected to get so close to anyone that one day I'd be able to tell them about it. I got used to living with loneliness a long time ago. And it takes time to unlearn the habits of loneliness, you know; to remember to bring to light the pieces of the past you've buried. To learn to trust. But I have told you now; told you things I've never told anyone. It's a sign of how close we are that I can. So don't be offended. Forgive me. Please.'

Hugging my knees even tighter, I said, without forgiveness: 'You're always saying we shouldn't have secrets. You say it every day, like a prayer. But you have so many of your own it makes me dizzy. And how can I be sure – now – how many more you've got? If you've forgotten this one for this long, what else might you suddenly confess to tomorrow, or the next day? Who might I be trying to believe you are by next week?'

'Oh Meg . . .' he whispered, stroking my unresponsive arms, 'I don't want you to think I have feet of clay . . . the last thing I wanted was to hurt you . . . you must see that . . . don't sound so cold . . . say you forgive me.'

I shook my head in the darkness. I needed time to think. 'Not yet,' I muttered. 'I'm probably just shocked. Let me let it all sink in a bit.'

'Say you still love me.'

'I do still love you . . .' I whispered; and he accepted the words as a truce, the best that could be expected in the circumstances, and drew me back down on the pillows next to him, and kissed me before his breathing quietened into sleep. '. . . whoever you are,' I muttered, completing the sentence once I knew he wouldn't hear.

My mind was racing with flickering, confused pictures of John, all with the features I knew animated by personalities I didn't, as if he'd been possessed by one shifting spirit after another throughout his past: my husband

313

embracing dying queens, fighting rough strangers, placing crowns on his head and grimacing under the weight. And taking crowns off his head and sauntering away, whistling. What was he dreaming of now, this man I thought I'd known, lying there so innocently beside me?

Perhaps I just couldn't cope with so much confusion. Unexpectedly I found the memory of Hans Holbein's square, sensible face coming into my mind. I clung to it with the relief that a drowning man would seize a piece of driftwood. Hans Holbein might be crude, but at least he wasn't scared of the truth. He'd had the integrity to paint Father as he saw him, with those cruel eyes looking sideways out of the frame above the fire in our parlour. That intentness of mind was exactly what John lacked. Feeling nostalgic, I let myself wonder whether Master Hans would ever come back now, from his faraway German home, to draw in the lutes and viols he'd sketched as possible improvements to our picture; to take Dame Alice off her weary knees and paint her reclining in the chair she wanted. It seemed unlikely, but I wished he would. I wished he were here to discuss all the things I was discovering now. He was the most straightforward person I'd ever met; and the only one of my generation whom I could imagine trying honestly to make sense of the way the world was turning upside down.

And that set me off on a new train of thought: wondering what Mad Davy would show me tomorrow.

13

It was just a room. A mean little room at the back of a mean little house, under All Hallows. But it was a room full of God.

'Bet you'd like to see how I make my remedies,' Davy had said – almost a taunt – when I took myself with cloak and basket round the apothecaries and stopped at his tatty display. He grinned for the passers-by. 'Bet you've never seen real unicorn's horn, eh, missis?'

The street boys cackled and poked each other with their elbows. I swallowed, ignored them, and nodded, wondering whether he was really just a lunatic after all, and he loped off eastwards, looking behind to make sure I was following.

He went on muttering. I caught some words on the wind as I hurried along behind, but nothing that made any sense. Once he turned round with a mad laugh and waved a dirty bottle taken from his pocket at me. 'Elixir of truth!' he shrieked cheerfully. 'Let's drink it!' Then he ducked into an alleyway, beckoning me forward with a bony finger, and pushed into his home.

It stank. There was bedding at the back, rolled up; and at the front of the room a frowsty old woman in a chair picked half-heartedly at some needlework. There was a table in the window with a dozen or so sloppy bottles, half-full of greyish, yellowish stuff, and basins with more of the same indeterminate liquids half-covered with cloths like children's games. Davy's games, I presumed. The old woman looked up and her eyes widened at the sight of me. But she hid her surprise reasonably well. She didn't put down her mending. 'Good morning, mistress,' she said with composure.

Davy took his craziness off like a cloak when he came indoors. 'We'll go to the room, Mother,' he said calmly. 'Will you let the others in later?'

We walked through the courtyard where two cats were hissing at each other and into the half-submerged cellar room at the back, whose walls were loaded with fire-wood, tools, bottles, a couple of shelves of foodstuffs and a couple of shelves, right at the back, of square shapes covered in cloth. There were three long trestle benches in the middle of the room.

'Sit down,' Davy said. 'Please. Can I get you something? Wine?' and he laughed, but a sane laugh now, perhaps even a little wry. 'Elixir of truth?'

'I've come to ask for the truth,' I said seriously, and was encouraged to see him sit down on another bench and nod back with equally serious simplicity. 'I think you know why. I want to know about the women you sent to me. The man who died. The Bible men and why my father hates them. I'm guessing you can tell me.'

He nodded. Considering. There was a gleam in those strange old eyes that I didn't remember seeing before.

'I've got a question for you first,' he said. 'What do you say when you pray?'

I paused. Watching his lips but not understanding the sounds they made. What kind of question was that?

'I mean it. Think,' he said. 'What words do you pray with?'

And the candle gloom of the church swept through me; the mighty, measured words of God. *Credo in unum Deum, Patrem omnipotentem, factorem coeli et terrae, visibilium omnium, et invisibilium. Et in unum Dominum, Jesum Christum, Filium Dei unigenitum. Et ex Patre natum ante omnia saecula. Deum de Deo, lumen de luminae, Deum verum de Deo vero. Genitum, non factum, consubstantialem Patri: per quem omnia facta sunt . . . Pater noster, quis es in coelis; sanctificetur nomen tuum: ad veniat regnum tuum: fiat voluntas tua, sicut in coelo, et in terra. Panem nostrum quotidianum da nobis hodie, et dimitte nobis debita nostra, sicut et nos dimittimus debitoribus nostris. Et ne nos inducas in tentationem.*

'You're thinking *paternosterquisesincoelis*, aren't you?' he said, watching my face. 'You're thinking *nenosinducasintentationem.*'

Then, without a word, he got up and went to the back of the room. I thought he was going to show me the books that seemed to be hidden under the cheesecloth wrappings on the shelf. But he ignored them. He pulled at the logs underneath, and from behind them came different cloth-wrapped packages. He brought one back to show me, unwrapping it as he went.

'Look.'

The book was octavo format, small enough to fit in a pocket or a bag. A loose piece of paper was inserted at the front. He pulled it out and put it under my nose. 'This is the *Paternoster* too,' he said roughly. 'I don't speak Latin. I don't know many people who do. This is the word of God for anyone who doesn't. This is the word of God, given to everyone who's been shut out of heaven by the priests. Do you recognise it?'

It was printed in neat Gothic type. Just a page. I looked at the first simple English words, '*Oure father which arte in heuene halowed be thy name*', and let it flutter back into my lap. I had a sinking feeling I'd gone too far in search of my own truth; there was a sickness in my stomach at the danger I was courting. But I could feel the exhilaration inside too – the thud of my heart, the lightness in my limbs. If I'd never understood the words of the Church until now, I'd have been transfigured by that sentence on the page.

'Show me more,' I said.

He gave me that bright sparrow look again, then opened the book for me: '*I am the floure of the felde, and lyles of the valeyes. As the aple-tre amonge the tres of the wood so is my beloved amonge the sons: in his shadow was my desire to sitt . . . Beholde my beloved sayde to me: up and haste my love, my dove, my bewtifull and come, for now is wynter gone and rayne departed and past . . . Up haste my love, my dove, in the holes of the rocke and secret places of the walles . . .*'

'"Up and haste my love, my dove, my beautiful . . ."' I echoed, aloud, surprised again to be moved by this unexpected loveliness of humdrum English words.

He nodded. Satisfied.

'You like it,' he said. 'I thought you would. I've been watching you for a long time. I know what you are, however much Latin and Greek you speak, however much you seem like one of them: you're an innocent at heart.

'Stay here for a bit, though, and you'll see the real innocents arrive: people who have never understood the Bible, because it's in Latin. Simple people who have gone to church all their lives, but not understood a word of what the priests are saying, just stood there muttering "Amen" and "God save me" and thinking the Host is a magic token. People who've been told they face hellfire unless they do whatever the priests want. People who've had to pay, and pay, and pay again to save themselves from what the priests tell them will be eternal hellfire. An angel for a Mass here. A mark for a wedding there. People who have always lived in mortal fear of the priests, because only the priests understand the word of God, and the priests always want more money than they have. People who come to me now for the books that show them they can know the truth for themselves, and are transformed by it.

'I'm not one of them – the innocents. My old dad was a Lollard. He believed in an English Bible for everyone who speaks English. So I never knew him. He died before I was born – at the stake. They did burnings, every now and then, even before your father. But at least because of my father I grew up knowing the Word of God. Some of it, at least. St James. He'd written it out, and they never managed to find the manuscript. My mother hid it. We learned it by heart.

'The Church is a blessing for the higher orders of society; for everyone else it's a dark mystery. A torment. Stay, and you'll see what hearing the Word of God for the first time can do. How knowing the truth of the Bible shows people they can be free from the tyranny of the Church.'

His face was blazing with intensity.

'But Davy,' I stammered, startled by the logic and force of his argument. 'My father's fighting the Bible men because he says they bring evil into the world. Are you saying you believe the Church is evil? And my father too?'

He cackled unpleasantly at the mention of Father, then collected himself. 'Look. What I believe is that no one in this struggle is truly evil. There are just two sides. On your father's side are the people who believe in tradition – who think all those centuries of Popes and princes of the Church and benefices and bribes are Christ's body on Earth. People who believe that the Princes of Rome need panthers and leopards and elephants and palaces and armies and to make their bastards into cardinals, and that

319

it's all right for them to pay for it by gouging fees for anathemas and fake relics from ordinary people. The people who turn a blind eye to the fact that enough wood to build a battleship is said to have come from the True Cross. And on the other side there are people – like me – who believe that being a Christian means they're allowed to have a simple conversation with God without having to pay a priest for the privilege. People who believe that if all you have to do is truly believe and your sins will be forgiven, that all these exorcisms the priests go in for – and all these Church hallowings of wine, bread, wax, water, salt, oil, incense, vestments, mitres, cross, pilgrim's staves, you name it – are no better than witch-craft. That a worldly Pope has no power to make a saint. That a Church full of lucky charms is no better than a synagogue of Satan. That's my side. I can't see why anyone would call that evil. If I can't understand the words, there's no more point in my saying "Paternoster" than "bibble babble", is there? And if I can't understand what they're saying in Church, and all I get is some priest jumping in my face telling me I'll be damned unless I give him my money, aren't I better off praying in a field? Or here?'

There was a tap at the door. 'Cover up,' Davy hissed, and I tweaked my hood over my bonnet. It was cold in the cellar. A tiny old man came in, with a cloak over him so shaggy and simple it looked more like a blanket. He gave me a fearful look. 'Don't worry,' Davy told him. 'She's new, but I know her.' The man nodded three or four times, and sat down with his arms wrapped round himself at the end of the farthest bench, but went on giving me wary glances.

They came in twos and threes after that, all poor folk, all huddled in thick worsteds and patched top gear. The last to arrive was the older of the two women who had been in my house. She looked startled to see me, but then she jutted her chin out defiantly and nodded. 'Welcome, missis,' she muttered, and the tiny old man calmed down and uncrossed his arms.

There was hardly any talk, just a mutter or two of greeting. When they were all assembled, Davy shut the door and read from the little book, in his cracked street-trader's voice. 'Come with a pure mind and, as the Scripture sayeth, with a single eye, unto the words of health and of eternal life,' he said, 'by which, if we repent and believe them, we are born anew, created afresh, and enjoy the fruits of the blood of Christ. That blood crieth not for vengeance, as the blood of Abel. Instead it hath purchased life, love, favour, grace, blessing, and whatsoever is promised in the Scriptures to them that believe and obey God.'

I looked sideways at the woman who'd brought the dying boy to me. There were tears coming silent and unbidden down her grey cheeks. I knew her to be in grief, but something about her rapturous expression suggested these were tears of joy. 'So shalt thou not despair,' Davy went on, 'but shall feel God as a kind and a merciful father; and his spirit shall dwell in thee, and shall be strong in thee, and the promise shall be given thee at the last.'

Now the little old man stepped forward, his fear of me forgotten, his face lit up with happiness. 'When I began to smell the word of God,' he began modestly, and the group turned towards him with a drawing-in of breath, 'it so exhilarated my heart – which before was wounded with the guilt of my sins until I was almost in despair – that immediately I felt a marvellous comfort and quietness, so much so that my bruised bones leapt for joy.

'The churchmen would say I've lost my faith. But I say this. Scripture has become more delicious to me than honey or the honeycomb, because in it I learn that all my torments, all my fasting, all my vigils, all the redemption of masses and pardons, being done without trust in Christ, who alone can save his people from their sins, these, I say, I learned to be nothing but a headlong rush away from the truth.' There were more quiet sobs of relief, and more wet cheeks, as he stepped up to kiss the book in Davy's hand.

Beyond a bit of banter in the street while I was buying something from a street trader, or a chat with one of the maids at home, I'd never have talked to people like these in the usual run of my life. Watching their faces light up with exaltation now, I realised I probably hadn't even thought of them as knowing how to talk other than in the cheeky chat of traders. Except when I was treating their wounds and ailments, that was; when I remembered that if you pricked the poor they bled just like the next man. But I certainly hadn't expected this depth of emotion, this passion for truth. I felt humbled by it.

They knew when to stop. When the only candle had burned down to its mark, they wrapped the books up and hid them behind the logs again and filed out, as quiet as they'd come, into the courtyard and off in their different directions. 'Will you take me home, Davy?' I asked, sitting on my bench, quiet with my impressions.

'I haven't told you answers to the questions you asked,' he said, as we slipped out into the alley. 'Showing you this was the best I could do.'

I nodded. 'It was a good answer,' I said, at peace with his new sane self now.

'You go up to the top, and left and left again into Walbrook. Best I don't go with you,' he said. He shouldered his bag. 'I've got business to do. Unicorn's horn business.' And he winked at me, then grinned crazily and danced off down the dirty little street, every inch the cheerful madman again.

He knocked at the door later the same day. The maid told me. 'The swivel-eyed loony came,' she said, with a contemptuous giggle. 'Mr Unicorn's Horn. He tried to sell me some medicine. And he took a penny off me for delivering you this from the Steelyard.'

There was a letter. It had the Steelyard stamp on the wax (they said all the banned books were smuggled into England by the Germans). It was from Hans Holbein in Basel. I gasped when I made out the author's name from the signature and the awkward handwriting in awkward French. After my rebellious moment of nostalgia for Master Hans last night, and the strange revelations of Davy's Bible meeting, the little letter felt like a sign from God. When I said his name under my breath I found myself remembering the intent locking of his eyes on mine before he walked away across the lawn for the last time; the hypnotic honesty of his gaze.

But the feeling didn't last. There was nothing much in Master Hans's letter – just a few clumsy phrases on the page, a reminder of the crudeness of the real man who'd sat in our house for so many months, stuffing bread and meat into his mouth so fast it hardly touched his cheeks before being swallowed into that capacious gut, and who belched behind his hands at the end of every gargantuan act of self-indulgence.

'*Dear mistress Meg*,' Master Hans wrote:

Please forgive me for not writing in English. I have forgotten too many words; French is easier. Master Erasmus asks me to offer my congratulations on the birth of your baby son and ask after your health and after the health of your husband. Master Erasmus likes the picture of your family. He is writing to your father to tell him as much. I am trying to settle back into Basel and get to know my family. It is a

323

*Protestant city now! I will go soon and paint Master
Erasmus again in his new home town. Please write
back soon – I would be very happy to take news of
you to him then.*

I nodded to myself, feeling my tongue click impatiently
against my teeth, remembering with a rush of ordinary
everyday disappointment the chaotic way he'd left his
pictures and thoughts and impulses scattered untidily on
table tops or imposed on the people he decided to like,
as well as with a hot burst of embarrassment at the
memory of pulling away from his kiss. I shook my head
resignedly and put the letter away in my apron. Maybe
I'd keep it. I'd been fond of him, after all. But there was
no point in building my memory of this man into the
image of someone who would have understood my life
now, or been able to help. It would be childish to make
a saint of him. I didn't think I would be replying. I'd have
to find my salvation for myself.

The salvation I found came from secrets. My own secrets,
not theirs. New secrets, hugged tight inside; my defence
against what else I might find out about my closest relatives. As winter turned into spring, summer to winter, I
took to dissembling as hard as any of them. The first
private act of my quiet rebellion was to go back to mad
Davy's conventicle, to worship the hunted God of the
Bible men.

It was surprisingly easy. John seemed relieved when I
went back to meeting him at the door of the house in the
afternoons with a brittle smile, asking everyday questions
about his work, and didn't mention his revelations again.
And Father seemed relieved that there were no more scenes
like the one over Hitton's burning, though my acquiescence came at a price. I avoided Chelsea, except in big

family groups, and I limited my brittle chats with Father to reports of black-haired, pink-cheeked Tommy's progress at eating and walking and, eventually, his first attempts at talking. Father kept his distance too; there were no more affectionate arms round my shoulders, no more kisses when we parted, just a cold watchfulness of eyes. It was as if we were all walking on ice, skating back prudently from the creakings and crackings we'd happened upon, looking for safer ground. So there was no one to ask difficult questions.

I left Tommy with a maid for an hour on some afternoons and slipped out. I sat at the back of Davy's cellar room and listened to the Bible readings, and the confessions, and the tears of joy. I didn't have to say anything. He hardly talked to me either, though I knew from the glitter in his eyes that my very presence was a secret triumph for him.

If he'd ever found out, Father would have taken my presence in Davy's cellar as an act of vindictiveness against him (and perhaps it was, though I preferred to think of it as a protest against his cruelty). And John would have thought me unforgivably reckless. I felt guilty myself to be running such risks when I had a child to live for. But I couldn't stop.

Part of me genuinely wanted to share the Bible men's simple act of worship. I wanted to hear that our lives were based on faith and hope and love. I wanted to be called to repent of my sins and to hear that the congregation – us, in that little cellar, and not the great men of the Church – was truly Christ's body on Earth. I left feeling uplifted, purified; a human being loved by a kindly God.

But I also knew, deep down, that even if I'd stopped going to Mass myself – the sonorous sounds of Latin and the solemnity of plainsong that I'd grown up loving now seemed tinged with cruelty – I'd never truly find my own God here. I couldn't believe in the ragings of Luther any more than in the fury of my father. Part of me knew that what I really wanted from those cellar meetings was just to be inspired by the willingness of so many fishwives and market women and tanners and weavers to endanger their lives for a taste of the truth. I wanted to believe that their passionate act of rebellion against what they believed to be the age-old lies of the Church was the same as the rebellion I was mounting against the lies I'd discovered in my life; but I knew in my heart they were different.

So it seemed as if God was pushing me into the secret that came next; beginning with a timid touch on my robe as I left Davy's house. I heard the muttered female voice even before I turned to see whose it was, very quietly repeating Davy's words from the cellar as if they were a secret code binding us together: 'God is like love or the wind, beyond our comprehension, infinite enough to bear being worshipped in an infinite number of ways, merciful enough not to care whether people pray to him in church or under a hedgerow, in Latin or English or Greek, crying or laughing.' I looked into her eyes. It was the mother of the dead boy. I still didn't know her name.

She still had the lines and pouches of bereavement, but her eyes had regained a little of the shrewdness that must once have given her face's charm. 'I've been wanting to ask you for ages, missis – why do you come?' she inquired, in an ordinary, if hushed, voice, as if we were old friends. 'I know who you are. So what are you getting yourself into with us?'

Something of the hurt I felt at what sounded like an attack on my honesty must have shown on my face. 'Oh, I don't mean what you think I mean,' she said hastily. 'I'm not saying you're spying.'

And she put a kindly, ragged arm through mine. 'I

know you're a good girl,' she confided. 'You must have your reasons for being here. Only I've got my own grown-up children' – and the shadow on her face for a moment reminded me that one of those children had been Mark; but then she smiled determinedly, she wasn't here to talk about that – 'and I know they get all sorts of ideas in their heads. You wouldn't believe the trouble some of them will go to to make their parents angry. And so I've been looking at you and wondering whether you're the same. Whether you're really here because of Our Father, or just because of *your* father, if you know what I mean.'

We both laughed (her at her own witticism; me partly shocked at her impudence, and partly, reluctantly, at the truth of what she was saying). In mid-laugh, she pointed a bony finger at my hand, which, when I looked down, I saw was dropping back down my body. I hadn't even been aware of moving it. 'See, you crossed yourself,' she said. 'You do, sometimes; that's the kind of thing I've been noticing inside. You're not really one of us, are you?'

I grinned sheepishly. She was sharp. 'You might be right,' I said. 'I hadn't thought . . .'

'Do yourself a favour, then. Stop coming. Keep yourself out of trouble; keep your kid safe,' she went on briskly. 'Got to look out for your family.'

Then she gave me a beady, questioning look. 'Mind you, there *is* something else you could do for us,' she said. I nodded. I liked her. I could see now that she'd been working round to this question all along; but I thought it was safe to trust her.

'Look after our sick,' she said swiftly, striking her deal. 'You've got healing hands. I could show you where. I could take you to them. That's something that would actually do us some good.'

And so I became the secret nurse of London's heretics. Instead of slipping out to Davy's cellar in the afternoons,

327

I started slipping out to St Paul's yard to meet my new friend (her name was Kate, I found out, though she was cautious enough not to tell me very much more), and off into the tenements and back alleys of London, to dose the ailing in their damp rooms with oil of cloves and herb poultices and sometimes, for the lonely, nothing more than a pipkin of hearty soup and a joke or two.

John didn't know who my patients were these days. But now that we started finding ourselves side by side in the parlour again at night, taking turns to grind up our roots or spices with pestle and mortar, I could see he was pleased I was beginning to find activities to fill my life again.

We'd gone on playing at being happy together through all those months; discussing the detail of his day over meals; watching little Tommy grow. But, for now, we'd stopped being man and wife. I'd taken to sleeping with the child in between us and complaining of headaches and backaches whenever he tried to touch me. Even if he looked just the man he'd been before, and went on behaving just as he always had, I felt uncertain of him; I didn't want to lay myself open to loving him in the way I had until recently, the kind of love that would make me vulnerable if there were more shocks and secrets in store. But he just looked resigned at my excuses, and hugged me to him like a child to its father. 'You're more fragile than you seem, little Meg,' he'd whisper; and I was partly reassured to know he still felt guilty at having deceived me, and was hoping to win me back gradually, through gentleness.

Now, as we weighed and measured and compared the symptoms of my poor and his rich patients, consulting his books for ideas or discussing whether oil of scorpions really could help against headaches, that shared enthusiasm began to deepen our relationship again from the grim banality of the winter.

I started staying downstairs again when Dr Butts dropped by, too, and I surprised myself by beginning to feel almost fond of the old man, for all his snobbish talk about expensive medicines for the rich, for all my hunch that he wasn't the great doctor he liked to think. It was the stories John had told me about him protecting protégés with Lutheran sympathies and visiting Wolsey that had first won my heart. He was brave, after his fashion. I was coming to appreciate his kindness, too. I liked it when Dr Butts came sniffing at my mixtures, offering advice that was always kindly meant and sometimes helpful; and John would look relieved when I thanked him prettily for it.

I was doing my best to emulate Margaret's genius for finding contentment in life as I found it. She'd made me feel it was foolish to worry over whether John's mind was second best. I was trying to conquer that feeling, just as I was trying to find ways to rebuild trust with John. Even if it felt imperfect now, I kept reminding myself, adding a pinch of something else into my medicine, that all my dreams had come true. I had the husband I'd wanted and the home I'd wanted, and Tommy, too, who illuminated my life in a way I'd never even dreamed possible. Surely I could learn to live with the ways in which reality differed from the dream. Surely we could find a compromise.

If I still felt secretly impatient that John and Dr Butts weren't working on any big scientific theories, beyond the correspondence with the Italian scholar that had arisen out of my idea, I tried to stifle it. How would Margaret have found contentment here? I wondered; and was pleased with myself when I hit on the notion that it might help them, and me, if I suggested more thoughts for them to feed into their correspondence with Vesalius. Dr Butts's pale eyes lit up with excitement and he began rubbing his hands under his beard on the night I said casually, 'Why don't you ask him to look into how much human anatomy

Galen really knew?' And John laughed in astonished delight, as if I'd hit on an important secret (although in fact it was a commonplace that the Galenic theories which had been handed down to us were all based on experiments with pigs, not people), when I went on, 'It might be less than we think.'

'You're an iconoclast, Meg,' John said, and, with a generous laugh: 'but you're quite right. Why didn't we think of that ourselves?'

As I began to feel more comfortable again in my marriage, I found myself able to appreciate the easy, humorous way John behaved around his new mentor. I surprised them one evening roaring over a story about a servant at the College of Physicians, Eddy, who'd told them a long story when he'd been taken on, about the wife who'd died at Worcester two years before, and his bitter prayers at her grave, but who'd been caught out in his lie when the supposedly dead wife had come looking for him just after they'd given him permission to marry again. There was something touching about the way they both turned to me as soon as they saw me, eager to share their story with me; the way each capped the other's phrases and both enjoyed each other's jokes.

'And then he said, "Well, if she's alive I'm a lucky man, because she's a good woman",' Butts chortled.

'And Butts told him: "Well, you're not such a good man if you're about to take another wife. Didn't you tell me she was dead?"' John picked up. 'But Eddy kept his wits about him. He didn't bat an eyelid at that, just said, deadpan, "Well, that's what they told me in Worcester." That made Butts cross. "So you admit you were lying when you told us both that you were at her grave yourself?" he said.'

'And do you know what he said then?' Butts spluttered, and they both started snorting at the memory:

'"Well of course I was there – but I was much too upset to look inside."'

On other nights, we were alone. As if he'd never stopped, John gently went back to filling those evenings with the stories he and Dr Butts heard every day about the court's cliques and plots and counter-plots. The Queen's men were Father's friends – the Duke of Norfolk, the Imperial Ambassador Chapuys, Bishop Fisher, Bishop Stokesley – ardent Catholics to a man, but their power was on the wane. The growing ranks of Father's enemies included almost everyone around Anne Boleyn, whose beauty and power grew by the day, although the matter of the King's divorce was still stalled. John laughed noncommittally when he said that Anne Boleyn had told one of Queen Catherine's Spanish ladies that she wished all Spaniards were in the sea, that she didn't care a fig for the Queen and would rather see her hang than acknowledge her as her mistress. The most important of the Lady's emerging circle of supporters was an outsider at court: Thomas Cromwell, a self-made man, a blacksmith's son from Putney who, before he entered Cardinal Wolsey's service, had been a mercenary in Italy and a wool-stapler in England and married an heiress. He had survived Wolsey's arrest and death and somehow dug himself in as an influential member of the King's council, although he didn't yet have any formal titles showing the extent of his power. His sympathies were with the Bible men, like Anne Boleyn's; he was the kind of man who wouldn't think twice about helping the King get out from under the Pope's control if it would help the King's marriage forward (and advance his own career). 'He has fierce little hawk's eyes,' John said, looking anxious. 'But he's a subtle man. A manipulator. A politician to rival your father. And he's out for your father's job.'

Finally, on a fresh April evening when there was bird-song on the air again, I began to feel I'd distanced myself too much from my husband through my secrets and my discontents – that I'd made myself the deceiver, while he, for all the secrets of his past, was offering nothing but innocent love. John and I walked under the budding apple trees together and he brought in a clump of primroses to scatter on our bed. When he pressed himself to me I murmured, 'I'm tired,' but my heart wasn't in it any more; we'd been estranged for too long, I thought, finally embracing him back. It was time to make peace. Afterwards he murmured, 'thank you,' and when he got up in the morning he spent longer than usual fussing around my side, tucking the quilts around me and kissing my head with a concerned look on his face. 'Stay inside, my love,' he whispered. 'You're so tired these days. And you've got so thin. Take a rest. Get your strength back.'

I almost did. But some instinct – some distrust of that concerned look on his face – told me not to stay at home. A thud in my heart told me I'd be missing something if I did. So once he'd gone and Tommy was tottering around in the kitchen with the nurse, I dressed and went out into the street. Which is where I found Davy, waiting to show me evil set loose in the streets of London.

14

The street was empty. It was as if there was a holiday.
There were no apothecaries out today – just Davy, sitting
in the church doorway with his bottles.

'You've come,' he said as I came out, as if we'd agreed
to meet. 'Let's go.'

We walked. There was a lift of life in the air and people
crowding down Cheapside all in the same direction. The
crowd thickened below St Paul's as we turned north
towards the steeple of St Bartholomew's Church and the
hospital. I didn't like to break the spell: the sunlight; the
smell of spring.

'Where are we going?' I asked in the end. He didn't
answer. It was a stupid question anyway. I could see we
were heading for Smithfield.

The crowd was getting solid now. We had to use elbows
to jostle through the burghers and errand-boys. A stake
was set up in the place of execution. There were a lot of
horsemen about, clanking their spurs, and the bench for
the gentry was packed. We stayed with the common
people. I'd known all along, I thought dully, looking at
the pitch barrel and the chains and the waiting logs.
'Who?' I asked.

He gave me a curious look. 'Bainham,' he said, as if I should have known. 'Sir James Bainham. Your family friend.'

I looked down. I remembered Sir James last year, standing so ill-at-ease waiting for Father in the parlour, trying to think of words of praise to say about my baby. I remembered Father's hard smile. For a split second I panicked, thinking there must be a mistake; but I knew really that there wasn't. It was all perfectly clear. There was nothing I could say or think now to soften the pain. Looking at my feet, being buffeted and kicked by legs busily pushing for a better view, I nodded. Of course.

Bainham came without a confessor, just a cartload of men-at-arms holding a chain around his middle. He was stripped to the waist, with white scars and red stripes down his back. His face was downturned so I couldn't see his expression. But I could see his skin was grey. The cart shrieked to a halt. The sergeants of the guard had to push and yell to get the crowd to give way.

'Shame,' yelled a woman's voice; and there was a low rumble of jeers and hisses as the men brought him to the stake.

'Doctor Simons was too scared to come with him,' I heard a fat man in front of me say, and spit, 'Couldn't convert him. Not going to risk a cobblestone in the head either. Bloody cowardly scavengers the lot of them.'

So it would be an ugly crowd. They said a mob could turn violent watching a popular man being killed.

Sir James put his arms round the wooden post. He stood on the pitch barrel. He watched the men build up the logs again. There was no fight in him. He was composed. He was ready to die. We were close and I could see his mouth begin to open. The spring wind caught some of his words and blew them away, but not the first. There was a deathly hush when he raised his voice to a bellow to announce: 'I come here accused and condemned for a heretic – Sir Thomas More being my accuser and my judge.'

My head was pounding with red shame. He was going to speak his mind before dying. 'Lawful . . . for every man and woman to have God's book in their mother tongue . . .' the voice was going defiantly on, coming in and out of my ears. There was a ragged cheer. 'Bishop of Rome . . . Antichrist . . .' – a more rousing cheer – 'no such thing as Purgatory; our souls go straight to Heaven and rest with Jesus Christ forever.' Applause. Catcalls.

I looked up and saw with a flash of fear that he seemed to be looking straight at me. He nodded. Our eyes locked. His were calm. I tried to breathe shallowly to compose myself. I didn't want to faint like some girl at a dance when he was dying with so much stoicism.

Another voice in the crowd, picking a fight; someone yelling the official truth in sharp London tones from beside Sir James. 'You're lying, heretic! You're denying the blessed sacrament of the altar!' I didn't know whose voice it was, but it was answered with a rumbling jeer.

Davy muttered, 'Master Pave, the town clerk. Scared out of his wits. Doesn't believe what he's saying himself.'

'I'm not denying the sacrament,' Sir James shouted, with a last barrister's flourish. 'I just dispute your idolatry. What makes you think that Christ, God and man could dwell in a piece of bread?' He raised his voice. 'The bread is not Christ. Christ's body is not chewed with teeth. The bread is just bread.'

Laughter. Banging. Appreciative foot-stamping. Cheers. 'Set fire to him and burn him,' Pave's voice came hastily back, and the flame moved its wobbly way along the trail of gunpowder.

Bainham looked down at it. He was greyer than ever now, a sickly dead colour even before the fire began to cook him. He raised his eyes and hands to heaven and said to Pave: 'God forgive you and show you more mercy than you show to me.' And then he looked at me again through the crowd, or I thought he did. 'The Lord forgive Sir Thomas More! And pray for me, all good people,' he said, and the fire burst into bright flower around him.

The crowd pressed forward around me, murmuring, and I lost sight of the flames. I felt Davy's arm strong against my back, holding my arm. 'Let's get out of here,' he said – a shout, but it came out a whisper against the tumult all around – and started pushing me, fainting and nauseous, against the human tide.

My face was wet.

'Keep walking,' he said, pulling my hood over my bonnet. 'And keep your head covered. People know you.'

When we were back on Cheapside, he said quietly, 'Did you really not know?' and looked into my eyes and saw the truth.

'God rest his soul,' he said, without crossing himself. 'Shall I tell you?' Taking my silence as an invitation, he began.

Father had James Bainham arrested at his chambers at Middle Temple soon after he married Fish's widow. He was accused of denying transubstantiation and of saying that a Turk, a Jew or a Saracen who trusted God and kept his laws was a good Christian. He was taken to Father's house – which must have been when I met him, waiting. Father tried to persuade him to recant. When he failed to make Bainham name other heretics at Middle Temple, he had the lawyer tied to the black mulberry tree in the garden and whipped, then sent to the Tower to be racked. Father went to the torture sessions in the Tower. They lamed him but they still couldn't make him talk.

They got him through his wife in the end. When she denied that Bainham kept Tyndale testaments at home, she was sent to the Fleet herself. He couldn't bear the idea of her being imprisoned on his account. So he denied his faith and accepted the shame of survival and let himself be taken to the Bishop of London to beg pardon for heresy, to persuade them to let her out.

'He used to come to us, you know,' Davy said, walking, watching my face with sly sideways glances. 'Sometimes. Like you did. I used to wonder if you'd meet one day. But, after all that, he stopped. And then he came back one more time after all, a couple of months ago. Without his wife. With his head bowed and burning with shame at his cowardice before God. He wept and he asked us to forgive him for what he'd done and he said he took on his shoulders the heavy burden of the Cross.'

Davy shook his head. 'I didn't see it myself, but they say he went back to church a week later. At St Augustine's. He stood up in his pew and waved his Tyndale Bible and confessed to the terrified congregation that he'd denied his God to save his life. It was a death sentence in itself to be holding up an English Bible. But he made doubly sure he couldn't be saved by weeping some more and begging for forgiveness for the cowardice that had made him pretend to return to the Church. He said he had to come back to the truth now, or the Word of God would damn him body and soul at the day of Judgement. And then he went home and wrote a letter to the Bishop of London telling him what he'd done. They couldn't do anything but burn him after that.'

I felt his eyes on me. I kept mine forward and tried to compose my face. I was trying with everything. Trying not to let myself think of Sir James's flesh cooking on the stake. Trying not to remember him walking kindly through Chelsea village with John, looking for ways he could help the refugees from the sweating sickness, or his vague, lost air in the parlour as he complimented me on Tommy's looks. Trying even harder not to recall Father's face or voice. With a different part of my shocked mind, which scarcely seemed to be functioning except to keep me walking forward and listening, but at the same time was also racing between questions, I was feeling my first prickle of suspicion about what Mad Davy had wanted of me and Sir James and any of the other inquirers after truth he might have drawn into his cellar and showed the word of God. Was he pleased Sir James had chosen this death? Was he pushing his flock to seek martyrdom – or at least those of us whose high rank would cause public scandal? Did he want blood, in his way, as much as Father?

'And then?' I said.

And then, Davy told me, Bishop Stokesley and Father interrogated Bainham, and Bainham carried on with his slow suicide. He said there were no dead saints and no point in praying to them. He said the Scriptures had been hidden from the people for eight hundred years because the Church had stolen the Bible from them. He went out of his way to be defiant. He told them there were two Churches today – the church of Christ militant, which could not be wrong, and Father's and Stokesley's Church, the church of the Antichrist, which could only be wrong.

When I reached home, I fled indoors and rushed to my room, and brought Tommy asleep from his crib to my bed, and curled the two of us up under the quilt and tried to calm the tremors through my whole being with the softness of his rose-flushed skin and the smoothness of his arms.

When that didn't work, and my stomach carried on churning and my blood pounding in my temples and my arms and legs shaking, I found myself rising again as the bell rang for Vespers and wrapping Tommy up before heading out to St Stephen's over the road. I was lonelier than ever before, with a chilly sense that there would never be anyone I could talk to about this. Dame Alice, Margaret – my witnessing of this horror would separate me from their innocence forever. I had a sinking feeling that John might have deliberately been trying to stop me going out just so I wouldn't find out about the day's burning; but whether or not that suspicion was justified, I knew in advance he wouldn't want to hear what I'd seen. I could go and seek comfort in Mad Davy's conventicle, but now that I'd begun to fear that Davy was looking for me to display public support for his beliefs, and to Hell with the consequences, that idea too filled me with a new kind of horror. There was just me and the sleeping child in my arms; no one else to trust. Except God. My own God; the true God, who couldn't be blamed for the brutality of men to each other. Suddenly all I wanted was the embrace of that innocent God, whose faith and love I'd denied myself for too long.

Tommy stirred in my arms but didn't wake as we slipped into the warm darkness, among the other worshippers, into air heavy with incense. The Bible pictures glowed in the candlelight. There was a muttering of people at the back and a murmuring of Latin from the robed men with their backs to us at the front, carrying out the beloved ritual of worship that St Augustine might have recognised, the thread that linked me and my child back to every believing brother and sister in history, right back to the Passion of Christ himself. It didn't concern me in the slightest if there were people praying, in their own way, in their own words, in rooms or fields or streets near me. Let them talk to God however they knew best. For me, though, God's home was here. And when I began to murmur the familiar words, '*Credo in unum Deum, Patrem omnipotentem, factorem coeli et terrae, visibilium omnium, et invisibilium,*' I found my heart taking hope – an abstract hope, with no application I could see in my life outside this building, but a hope nevertheless – that there could be joy in the world again.

'*Deum de Deo, lumen de lumine, Deum verum de Deo vero. Genitum, non factum, consubstantialem Patri: per quem omnia facta sunt*,' I whispered. And when the sacring bell rang, and every pair of eyes turned joyfully up to stare at the Host being held above the priest's head – the manifestation of God on Earth – I didn't care that perhaps half of the worshippers just thought they were warding off blindness or sudden death for today. I loved the cries of happiness and the kisses and the beggars rushing off into the street full of elation, slamming the door. This was what I'd always known – the sweetness and the solemnity of God in words I'd always loved. Like the rest of the faithful, I was filled with a blissful reverence for the ancient and familiar and awe-inspiring words that I didn't fully understand. I didn't have to understand. I only had to believe.

That reverence, that hope against hope, stayed with me as I let us back into the house. Tommy was beginning to rub little frost-reddened fists in his eyes as if he'd soon wake up.

The nurse took Tommy from me with a secretive smile. 'You come with me, young man,' she murmured at his sleeping head, grinning to herself. There was another little smile on the manservant's face as he followed them into the kitchen.

John was standing by the window of our bedchamber, freshened up after his day away, waiting. I stopped in the doorway and stared at him. I didn't know he'd be back so soon. The bed was strewn with spring flowers. There was a bath steaming by the fire. It was scented with lavender oil. There were petals floating in it. There were white embroidered linens on the bed. There was a hopeful smile on his face.

340

'It's my surprise,' he said, with the intimate voice that suggested he thought we would share a bath and make love again and fall asleep with our arms and legs wound around each other in a clean, springlike perfection of white lace.

The cloud of reverence in which I'd come to the house evaporated in a sizzle of rage.

It was unbearable, when the streets were full of smoke and ashes and the smell of human flesh – a burning John couldn't but know of. So was the knowing smirk on the nurse's face, and the knowledge that the servants had been creeping up here for hours with pails of water, trying not to clank, trying not to give away the secret that the master was about to come and take his obedient wife, chortling to themselves in the kitchen now at the idea of him spread-eagled over me on the bed, pumping away at me, while just down the road people were dragging James Bainham's roasted body away and sweeping up the charred faggots blowing in the wind by St Bartholomew's.

'I didn't ask for this,' I said numbly. 'It's a waste. I don't want to wash. I'm too tired.' I walked back towards the door. When I was already out of the room and at the top of the stairs, I said, 'I watched the burning, you know.'

His face bleached. His mouth formed the words, 'you went?' but no sound came out. I stood on the top stair, watching him watching me; watching his mind assimilate my news. The silence went on so long I couldn't imagine it ending.

Suddenly there was a rush of dark air between us and he was holding me as if I were a child, folding me against him, raining anxious kisses on top of the head I kept stubbornly turned down. 'You poor girl. You poor girl,' he was murmuring, over and over again, as if all I needed were comforting from him to make it all right; as if I had a grazed knee. There was something hypnotic about it. It was only when he whispered, in an agonised, helpless way, 'I'm so sorry. It must have been horrible. And I so didn't want you to know; I so didn't want you to be distressed,' that I found the strength to pull away.

'What's distressing is having had the truth kept from me,' I said coldly, disentangling myself, stepping back, meeting his eye. I didn't want his compassion. He heard what was on my mind at last: an accusation. I had the feeling he'd known all along I would feel like this. He looked down. 'I needed to know,' I pursued. 'You should have said.'

He stood before me, spreading his arms out wide in a gesture of bewilderment. 'How could I?' he said pleadingly, keeping his eyes on my face but not quite meeting my eyes. 'You've been so frail . . . and you were just beginning to become your old self again . . . we were just beginning . . .' He stopped, took breath, tried again; but he was looking disheartened now.

'What could I have said? What would have been the good of encouraging you to torment yourself?'

'Because there's no point in living a lie,' I snapped. 'Because it was someone we knew being chained up and set fire to. Because before they lit the flames he said he was dying because of Father.'

He looked appalled. He crossed himself. He dropped his hands so they hung limply by his sides. There was another silence.

'He walked through Chelsea with you,' I said cruelly, trying to shock a response out of him now, aware of my voice rising but not even caring any more if the servants heard. 'Don't you remember? He believed the same things Dr Butts does. That was his crime. That was what Father has had him killed for. You know that. So how can you just pretend nothing has happened? How can you come home and order a bath?'

He hushed me then; swished me back inside the

bedroom; shut the door. 'Listen to me,' he said, suddenly firm. 'Hear me out at least. We've talked about this before and you know how I feel. I don't believe in letting all the horrors of the world outside into our private life. I don't know today what to say or even think about the burning. Or about More, if it comes to that. But I don't have to. I'm a doctor. I'm a man with a wife and son whom I love and want to cherish forever. That's all I need to know. That's why I'm back now: because I want to show you my love, because I want to be with you and shut away the cruelty of the world outside. Nothing else matters if we have each other. If we can make each other happy.'

He was looking almost as though he believed I might agree – beginning to dart little pelading glances almost at my eyes. I didn't let him finish. 'We can't,' I said. 'Not without the truth.' And then I walked out of the room, and down the stairs, and back into the garden to watch the sun set.

There was no point in arguing any more. I could say, 'But don't you see?' until I lost my voice; the point was that he wouldn't see. It no longer seemed a problem that John's past had been a tangle of discarded identities and that I couldn't really know who any of them had been, or whether he had more secrets to reveal. The problem was that all those people with John's face were fool enough to think you could wash away the evil of a person being burned to death with a lavender bath.

Still, I half-thought he'd follow me. But he didn't. The bathwater was cold by the time I tiptoed back upstairs. A tray of syllabub and wine was untouched outside the bedroom door, and there was no sign of John. He must have gone to sleep in another room.

I dragged my medicine chest out from under the bed in the twilight. There were two things I needed to do.

First I took out the pennyroyal bottle and mixed up a dose just strong enough to bring on my monthly bleeding. I swallowed down the bitter, oily stuff and set my lips tight again. I didn't want there to be any consequences of John's lovemaking yesterday. I didn't want to feel his child growing inside me. I'd been wrong to believe we could find compromise and contentment.

Then, sticking my hand in the drawer where I kept Master Hans's mementoes, I pulled out the painter's letter of all those months before.

I'd started thinking of him again while I was standing in the dark of the church. A fond green summer memory. Not just Master Hans in the garden, under the mulberry tree, kissing me, folding me to his body with strong hands. But Master Hans's hands, which had set a prisoner in the garden free with a slash of a palette knife. It was light in the darkness, the memory of those hands cutting the man loose. It would never have occurred to me to have freed the prisoner until he'd done it; but afterwards I'd seen that I could have done it myself.

I wanted to think about the flash of that knife; not about my husband mincing about my room with his herbs and moral abdication. Perhaps John wasn't to blame for a past that might make a coward of anyone; but he could no longer command my respect.

In Master Hans, at least I knew one truly courageous man. It was high time I answered his letter.

15

'Do you remember,' Hans Holbein began, with his eyes on the line on the canvas in front of him, 'what you wrote in that first book of yours that Prosy and I illustrated?'

Erasmus waited, patiently, sitting at three-quarters face from the painter, looking left towards the pale light of the window, not moving as Holbein found words for his thought.

'. . . laughing at the way scholars glorify each other by giving each other the names of great men from ancient times . . . ?' Holbein went on.

Erasmus murmured encouragingly. He was even skinnier than last year, Holbein thought, and even more a martyr to the aches and pains that made him shift uneasily in his seat, trying obediently to stay still while also trying to move to ease his multiple discomforts. Holbein appreciated the old man's consideration for the demands of his art, and was touched by his uncomplaining stillness today. It was a miracle the old man was still here at all. (All he'd said about his white weightlessness was, with a laugh, 'Some fool of a doctor prescribed me two pills for purging my bile, and I followed his advice – like a fool. The only thing to do is send the doctors to the devil, commend yourself to Christ, and you'll be well in no time.' But he wasn't. He was fading away.)

'I always agreed with you about that,' Holbein said. 'Boastful idiots. Bloody stupid.'

Erasmus nodded, then stilled his head. It was clear there was more to come. But there was time to let the young hothead get it out in his own words.

Holbein blamed the bigots for the deterioration he could see in the old scholar's physical condition. Holbein hated all the bigots now, Protestants as much as the other kind and maybe more, and he could see that the bigots made Erasmus worry. They stopped him eating properly. Fretting over their stupidity interrupted his sleep. It was obvious that Erasmus had worried all last winter through the council at Marburg that had tried to settle the religious differences between Brother Martin's German reformers and the various quarrelsome Swiss factions, from states which had each settled on their own versions of the religious truth and promptly professed themselves horrified by the forms of worship all the others had chosen. And now he'd worried all through this summer while Protestants and Catholics met at the imperial Diet in Augsburg to try to stop Christendom splintering before their eyes. None of it had worked, of course; how could you stop these idiots taking things to extremes? It was a waste of good food and rest time to let the extremists put you off either simple pleasure. But it would be impossible for Erasmus, the last moderate intellectual left in civilisation, to take things that way. Now the scholar wanted his portrait done again to send to all the people he wrote to so energetically all around Europe, to remind them that his very existence symbolised moderation and hope for unity. Privately, Holbein thought it was too late to remind anyone of that. But he admired the effort the old man, whose first commission had got him started in life and

346

whom he'd hero-worshipped ever since, went on making. And he was happier than he could believe to be back in Freiburg, recording those sunken cheeks and sharp, sharp eyes and spindly shanks in their furry wrap for posterity, and hearing the old man's fears and secrets after dark.

'But,' Holbein blurted, 'there is one name I'd like to be called if I were going to get a name like that.'

He was grinning bashfully down at his feet now and his face was bright red. He was asking for a favour in the most tactful way he knew, but part of him felt he was making a pig's ear of it. He'd always known diplomacy wasn't his strong suit.

Erasmus blinked encouragingly.

'The name you were good enough, once, to call Albrecht Dürer, when you were recommending his work. Apelles. I'd like people to think of me as the Apelles of today.'

He was hot with relief when he saw Erasmus smile the smallest smile he could without changing the way his head was set, and murmur back, 'I never thought you were so ambitious, young Hans,' but kindly. Holbein could hear real affection in that voice. It made his heart rejoice. He needn't have worried so much. He wasn't going to bring any sharp mockery down on himself by asking. By now he should have known Erasmus liked and trusted him. The old man would never have told him all those things last night if he didn't.

Holbein still couldn't really believe what Erasmus had told him after supper, sitting up late, as ever, to the very end of the light of the very last candle. He'd been a bit drunk himself, maybe, as anyone would be after the bumping and bruising and boredom of a long day's boat ride, but Erasmus had been as sober as ever, with his goblet untouched beside him and his plate of food pushed to one side. The man seemed to live on air. So you couldn't put down what he'd said to a bit too much late-night worship at the Temple of Bacchus. It must be true, even if it was impossible.

Cosy catching-up talk had given way quickly to an anxious run-through of Erasmus' various attempts to bring the religious maniacs back to their senses. It was only when Holbein brought out of his bag the letter from Meg Clement in London that the old man's face completely changed. Holbein had known all along that Erasmus would be pleased his bidding had been done and contact had been re-established between Holbein and the Clement household. But there was real urgency on that old face, a hunger Holbein wouldn't have imagined the other man could feel.

'Excellent. Show me,' he said, and stuck out his hand for it.

'There's nothing much to see,' Holbein faltered, handing it over, feeling his fingers caress the pages Meg had touched protectively as they left his safe-keeping, fearing her luminously simple phrases would disappoint someone whose expectations were clearly so high.

'It doesn't matter,' Erasmus said shortly, and he smoothed the crumpled, much-opened document down on the table under the candle and devoured every clear French word. He sucked in air between his teeth as he read. 'Clement's been made an elect of the College of Physicians . . .' he muttered, and nodded approvingly. 'The baby's called Thomas. . . . And they're living at the Old Barge,' and here he looked straight into the heart of the flame for a moment, thinking a thought Holbein couldn't imagine. 'I spent a lot of time in that house myself, long ago,' he added inconsequentially.

He turned over. 'What's this,' he muttered, poking a thin index finger at the lines Holbein knew by heart after staring at them for many hours of every day in the weeks since the letter had arrived. 'Look, this bit, where she says: "*This is what I always wanted, or I thought it was. But London life is more complicated today than when I was a child, especially now that Father is in charge. It seems paradoxical, but sometimes I wish we were all back in the garden at Chelsea, wondering how your painting would turn out. These days it seems that things were simpler back then.*" So she feels it, then, the threat of today. She feels it.' And Erasmus sat, staring at the candle again and nodding his head several more times, thinking his private thoughts so that Holbein hardly dared move to fill up his own empty goblet or scratch the place on his leg where a flea had been giving him hell.

Finally the old man shook himself out of his reverie. He laughed his little goaty laugh and said, 'What must you think of me, a neglectful host!' and filled Holbein's goblet. He met the younger man's eye. 'Thank you,' he said simply as Holbein drained the liquid, relieved that the moment of tension was passing, wondering why Erasmus seemed even more acutely sensitive to Meg's every word than he was when he could surely scarcely remember her all these years later. Filling the painter's goblet again, Erasmus said, 'I'm glad you wrote. I didn't think you would. And I worry about them. I fear they may soon need help. I've wondered for a long time now how to find a discreet way to be in contact with them if it becomes necessary . . .'

And it was after that, late in the night, that the other story had come trickling out, the one Holbein couldn't believe he could have remembered right, the one in which John Clement, that Greek tutor and doctor with the remote, startling pale-blue eyes, and that infuriatingly quiet air of distinction that always made Hans Holbein feel as though he had twenty left thumbs and his breeches were falling down, was actually someone quite different, of royal stock, a prince of the old English blood who'd been brought up in Louvain under a false name in the care of the Duchess of Burgundy, and eventually settled back into anonymity in England when the present king came to the throne. Fuzzy though he might feel this morning, Holbein knew he hadn't imagined it: he could swear he remembered Erasmus leaning over with his eyes alight and hissing, practically into Holbein's ear: 'Richard, the Duke of York; that's who he once was.' Yes, it was all coming back now. The deal Erasmus described had been struck through the good offices of two young men of the New Thinking. One of the young men was Thomas More, the ex-page of the Archbishop of Canterbury, who was fast becoming a prominent lawyer and official in his own right in London. 'The other,' as Erasmus had gone on, twinkling merrily, 'was an orphaned ex-priest who'd never taken to the endless detail and prayer of holy orders; who found work instead under the Duchess of Burgundy's adviser, the Bishop of Cambrai. Yours truly,' and he'd sketched a modest bow. Both young men had been chosen by their masters for their diplomatic skills and discretion; they were given the task of discreetly protecting the man now known as John Clement for the rest of his life. Erasmus had studied in Louvain himself, once upon a time, so he already knew the young Englishman (back then, in Louvain, everyone knew Clement to be of noble blood, and half the university suspected him of being the love child of the Bishop of Cambrai and the Duchess herself). Erasmus was part of the same religious sect as the Bishop and the Duchess, Devotio Moderna. So he quickly acquired friends in high places. He was sent by his Bishop to London for the first time as long ago as 1499, while John Clement was still mastering Greek and astronomy in the Low Countries, to meet his English counterpart in their secret business. 'We walked from Greenwich to the royal palace at Eltham one day. More took me to meet today's King Henry – he was just a prince then, a younger brother, a ginger-haired boy of eight,' Erasmus recalled. 'More had met the royal princes many times already, I could see,' the old man went on, with his bitter-sweet smile, 'and he was a young man too, but he had all the ability to rise to the occasion that has made him a great man. He hadn't come empty-handed. He just happened to have brought with him some verses to read to the prince. When he brought them out of a pocket and started declaiming them, I felt absurdly unprepared. But it taught me something else, too: that he would rise in his career; that he was ambitious.'

'That's how we first knew each other, you see,' Erasmus finished wistfully, and he was staring into the candle again, seeing things that were no longer there. 'Everything else came later – that we became friends, and that the new learning we'd come to love swept the world, and that we were lucky enough to have some small part in shaping the way people learned to think. But my ties with Thomas More go a long way further back than that. Even what's happening now in the realm of religion hasn't stopped our friendship, though I will admit to finding some of the positions More adopts these days, well, difficult . . .'

Holbein leaned forward. This was something he'd wanted to ask for years. 'How has he changed?' he said curiously. 'What did he believe before?'

Erasmus paused to gather his thoughts, staring at the liver-spotted hands he'd stretched out in front of himself as if surprised by them. 'Well,' he said at last, 'when I first met Morus, he seemed like one of us. A humanist. No one could have been wittier at mocking the pointless mental gymnastics the old scholastic priests used to go in for – the kind of questions I call Quiddities and Formalities . . . all those tiresome debates about whether Christ could have come to earth as a woman, or a mule, and whether a mule could be crucified. In those days, no one could have been more eloquent about the need to do away with all that and renew the Church with some clarity and commonsense. So I'd never have expected the anger of some of his recent attacks on Luther,' and Erasmus sighed, more in sorrow than in anger. 'The sheer crassness of them . . .

'Then again, sometimes I think I misunderstood him back when I called him a man of the modern world. Morus was always old-fashioned in some respects. I remember him going through a very peculiar stage of wanting to be a monk when he shut himself up with a lot of weeping mystics, too; I could never understand the attraction of *that*. He got over it in the end, thanks be. But he still believes profoundly in authority. He's one of those lawyers of the old school who sees the laws of God and the laws of the land as the two sides of the same sword – both equally unalterable. He can't tolerate challenges to either. So maybe it's not as surprising as I still find it that he reacts with such terror to the likes of Martin Luther, saying that a man's personal connection with God is all that matters, and that we can do away with the mediation of the Church. He hears something more terrifying than most of us do in ideas like that. He hears the crackle of hellfire. He sees the darkness coming. We find his terror – and his overreactions – confusing because we think of him as an inquiring humanist. But I'd say the most charitable way to look at his behaviour now is to understand that he's never been a modern. His mindset is mediaeval through and through.'

Holbein nodded, savouring the word 'charitable', aware of the disappointment in the old man's voice. Erasmus shook himself.

'Anyway,' he said briskly, 'the point is that what these

religious quarrels have done – and my advancing age; we're none of us getting any younger, after all – is to make it harder for me to travel across Europe to see the More family and fulfil my obligations to John Clement without being indiscreet. I don't like to criticise my old friend Thomas More, but I can't entirely feel easy about the letters he sends me now. His perspective isn't what it was. But it wouldn't do for me to just start writing directly to Clement myself. Who knows who might read the letters? Still, I want to know he's well. Things won't get easier for him if the King and More fall out over faith. And it's still my duty to make sure that young man stays safe. So I'm grateful to you, young Hans,' he smiled, and the candlelight turned the lines stretching down his face into caverns and caves, 'more grateful than you can know.'

They didn't mention it again the next morning. Hans Holbein's head was pounding, as it often was in the early part of the day. Erasmus was calm and urbane and a little withdrawn as he sat in his robe, twisting and turning to get his pose right. Hans Holbein half-wondered if he'd imagined the whole fantastic story. He fussed over the fall of a hem. He took longer than usual to mix his colours. Bursts of last night – phrases, looks, pride at having won Erasmus' approval, and pricks of jealous pain, or incredulity, at the thought of Meg married to a man who might have been king – kept coming into his head. But he shut them out and tried to concentrate on today. He had to treasure his time with Erasmus. He had to let go of all the other thoughts crowding through his head.

This wasn't the place to think about how Meg's wistful line about the garden in Chelsea had almost made him pack his bags and head straight for the Rhine transport boat that would start a journey to London. It wasn't the place to think about the drudgery of the Basel printshops or what Elsbeth said when she found out how much of the Council Chamber payment he'd spent in the tavern or how much he'd paid for the cottage beside their house which he'd bought as an investment for the family.

It was easier to think about how to make himself the most famous and respected painter of his own day. However low he seemed to have fallen after his glorious three years in London, here, in these comfortable chambers in Freiburg, he was really winning the friendship of the greatest man in Europe. It was time to stop trying to quietly do the decent thing and getting stomped on in the process all the time by the presbyters and his wife and the world. It was time to ask for something for himself.

So he'd made his request. But now he didn't know what to do to follow through. He painted on, whistling through his teeth, increasingly embarrassed by his moment of greedy ambition. Erasmus had gone back into his dreams. His eyes were elsewhere.

'Do you want to take a rest now?' Holbein said nervously. He didn't want to tire his friend. Erasmus nodded gratefully and began to stir his limbs, stiff from so much stillness. He stood up and looked straight at Holbein. Holbein saw with relief that he was smiling.

'Have you never thought of going back to England?' Erasmus said, fixing Holbein with that luminous grey gaze. 'You were doing so well there. If you want fame, surely that's the place for you to go on building it?'

Holbein shook his head bashfully. 'I had to come home. The family. And my travel permit was running out.' He stopped. None of that was true. Well, it was true, but none of it was enough to have stopped him staying in London if he hadn't got into such a state about Meg. And now she was writing to him. She was nostalgic for her walks in the garden in Chelsea with him. There wasn't really any reason for him to stay home. Erasmus was right.

'Things have changed,' Erasmus said briskly. 'You've been back for three years now. It wouldn't be hard. You could easily get someone to write you a new travel permit.'

He was getting interested in the idea now, Holbein saw. His eyes were lighting up with possibilities Holbein wanted more than anything for him to point out. There was nothing Holbein wanted more right now than to be persuaded that a return trip to England was in everyone's best interests. But he needed someone else to persuade him.

'You have friends in high places there, after all,' Erasmus was going on. 'The Mores, of course. And now the new court circle. Obviously the new man, Thomas Cromwell, is no friend of the Mores.' But he's an astute man for all that. There's a reform parliament at work there that he's helping. There's just a possibility that he might steer England into some sort of bloodless, peaceful religious reformation – not like the violent shambles we've seen here. And you'd be well-placed to find commissions. Anne Boleyn's friends – I correspond with her father, the Earl of Wiltshire, who is an intelligent man. You've painted half the Boleyn circle already. It would be easy for you to find work.'

He grinned encouragingly at the younger man. Holbein was nodding, drinking in the words he wanted to hear, so delighted by them – and the fugitive mental picture he couldn't get out of his head, of himself holding out his arms under the shade of the mulberry tree as Meg ran across the garden into them – that he hardly stopped to wonder why Erasmus was pushing him to go. Surely the old scholar could see that Holbein's feelings for Meg were not ones that should be encouraged if you had the best interests of Meg's husband at heart? Or could he be so far removed from bodily things that he had no idea of the maelstrom Holbein had been plunged into in England – could it be that Erasmus simply didn't know what it meant to be in love?

'All you need is a really ringing endorsement,' Erasmus was adding, and the grey eyes had a mischievous glint in them now. He edged towards Holbein on unsteady legs. 'May I see your work?' he added inconsequentially, dodging round the easel.

Before Holbein could stop him, the old man was staring straight at the picture. He nodded and picked up a silverpoint pencil. 'Something like this,' he added, and grinned, and leaned down to write at the bottom of the canvas.

Holbein nearly snatched the pencil out of his hand. No one had ever dared do this to his work. But he stopped himself. It was Erasmus, after all, defacing his own likeness. So, in an agony of resentful indecision, Holbein restrained himself and peered round Erasmus' shoulder to see what he was doing.

There were four lines of Latin under the drawing. Holbein drew in his breath as he made out the agonisingly difficult writing: '*Pallas Apellaeam nuper mirata tabellam* . . .' His eyes widened. What Erasmus had written was: 'Pallas, recently admiring this Apellean picture, says that the library must keep it forever. Holbein shows his Daedalus-like art to the Muses, just as the great Erasmus shows a wealth of the highest intellect.'

He was still holding his breath. He called me Apelles, he thought. *He called me Apelles.* He made an effort to let air out of his chest.

'Will you really write that?' he asked, hardly daring to believe his luck. 'On the picture? About me?'

'Will you prove me right?' Erasmus asked, and twinkled merrily back at him. 'Will you go back to London?'

16

Events moved fast after Bainham's execution. As April drew to a close, Father's enemies closed in for their own kill.

We were silently at war at home too, in that tumultuous month. When I looked at John's face now I could no longer see the beauty that had once pulled me, like the tide towards the moon, into his arms. I recoiled in horror at even the memory of that – of having loved his sweetness, his softness, his sadness. It made my gut churn almost as much as the horror I felt for Father's descent into active evil. All I saw in John's features now was glassy-eyed, sinful stupidity; a cowardice and passivity that amounted to acquiescence in Father's sin. So I refused to look.

I stopped eating with him, avoiding dinner and supper and taking trays in my bed in the morning with the excuse that I was unwell (not entirely a lie; I was racked by the cramps in my stomach as the pennyroyal took effect and the untimely blood that might, in other circumstances, have made a baby came drenching out of me). I stalked out to church every morning with Tommy trotting sleepily beside me, avoiding any room where I heard footsteps in case they might be John's, to pay my respects to my God. Later, once I'd settled Tommy with his nurse and his toys in the kitchen or the garden, I'd stalk out again alone, with my basket on my arm, to meet the grey-faced yet oddly comforting Kate and start our day's perambulations among the rooms and tenements of her Bible brethren. It might have seemed odd to anyone else but Kate, the only person who knew of it, but it was the most honest compromise I could come up with, while my head was still whirling with the horror of all I now knew. I'd find a clearer way later, perhaps; confide in one of my family, except that Margaret was away at Esher and there was no one else who would do. Guidance will come, I muttered. God will provide. Meanwhile, my mixture of Latin worship and pastoral care for the Church's enemies was the best I could do.

Visiting the brethren meant I knew every rumour in London. Tiny George, the old man in the blanket cloak who'd said at my first meeting at Davy's that Scripture had become sweeter to him than honeycomb, and to whom I made a point of dropping off a little dish of honey whenever I could, was a mine of information. George lived in an attic above his married daughter's rooms at the cathedral end of Cheapside, and spent most of his days hanging around St Paul's churchyard, listening to street gossip, when he wasn't slipping up to Greenwich to hear the furious theological debates that sermons at the Chapel Royal were becoming. I didn't think George knew any more of my name than 'Mistress Meg', even now, but he'd long ago stopped being scared of me. When he wasn't praying, he liked nothing better than a long chat about the latest events. I was interested to see, now we were dropping in on him regularly to change the poultices on his leg ulcer, that he seemed to have stopped being scared of anything. I was always catching his rheumy eyes dancing with mischief and a hope I'd never imagined seeing on a Bible man's face.

It was through George I found out that Father was losing his battle against Thomas Cromwell – the rival royal servant who, unlike Thomas More, was willing to do whatever it took, even if that meant abandoning the Church of Rome, to marry the King to Anne Boleyn.

The story George whispered to us, pulling eagerly at our bread and honey on a glorious May morning, was this: A man Father had interrogated as a heretic – one of Cromwell's men – had escaped abroad and was publicly denouncing Father as a torturer. Father realised he couldn't work with Cromwell any more. The rivalry between them was too open. He tried to resign. The King wouldn't let Father go. Thomas More was too famous to be allowed to show public lack of confidence in royal policy. But Cromwell was out to get him. Cromwell was too clever to attack Father directly; instead, he was pushing the king to abolish the ecclesiastical courts where Father's friends, the bishops who supported Queen Catherine, dispensed Catholic justice. If Henry did that, and took all legal powers in the land for himself, he'd be able to push through his divorce. Almost more important for Father was that if there were no more ecclesiastical courts, there could be no more burnings. The bishops would no longer be able to make arrests for heresy, and Father's entire career as Chancellor and prosecutor of heresy would be undermined. 'Cromwell will have beaten bloody More fair and square,' as George put it, licking his fingers happily to get the last of the honey off, 'and we'll be safe forever.'

Hope was making the brethren as bold as hungry ravens, and fear was having the same effect on their opponents. At Greenwich the next Sunday, in front of the King, a preacher spoke openly in favour of the royal remarriage. That so infuriated the next preacher, Henry Elstow, that he lost his temper in the pulpit, making George and his daughter and all the others crammed inside gasp uneasily and crane their necks to see how the King would respond. 'You're trying to establish the royal succession through adultery,' Elstow yelled. 'And you're betraying the King to eternal perdition by doing so!'

'You could have heard a pin drop,' George recalled pleasurably. 'The King didn't move a muscle. But the Earl of Essex was sitting next to him, and he got up and yelled back: "You shameless friar! Hold your tongue or you'll be sewn up in a sack and thrown into the Thames!" Elstow didn't turn a hair. "Keep your threats for other courtiers," he said. "They don't scare us friars. We know we can get to Heaven by water as easily as by land." Bold as brass, he was.'

'Well I never,' Kate murmured, wrapping up yesterday's poultice and dropping it into the basket. 'They're properly rattled, aren't they?'

Davy woke us one May morning with a peacock scream. 'Even the King hates them! Even the King thinks they're more Roman than English!' he was bawling, and the traders eddying around him were bawling raucously back.

I rushed to my window. John's head pushed out of the next window at the same time, tousled and half-asleep, ready to yell something cross and pithy to the unruly street people about keeping their noise down. Then he realised what Davy must be saying.

'What are you talking about, Davy?' he yelled down.

'The King's order, Doctor John,' came Davy's insolent, cracked voice. 'He's told the bishops to give up their independent courts. It's goodbye to the princes of the church. And no more burnings. About bloody time too.'

John scratched his head and nodded it two or three times. 'I see,' he said, smiling in a good imitation of calm.

'Well, don't do that with your cap too often or you'll drop it in the sewer.'

But there was no smile on his face when he walked into my room, unbidden, just dread without words. I felt it too. It was enough to suspend the hostilities between us. We stumbled into our clothes and rushed downstairs. We walked out of the house together in a daze and wandered down Cheapside and to St Paul's Cross. There wasn't a priest anywhere to be seen, but there were people pouring into taverns all along Cheapside and down Ludgate Hill, laughing and joking and shouting for joy and drinking. 'Do you know what Anne Boleyn's had embroidered on her linen?' I heard one market woman squawk cheerfully. '"It's going to happen whether you like it or not." She's a clever little gold-digger all right.'

Davy saw me pass as we left the house and touched his cap ironically. He had a beer in his hand.

John didn't go to Dr Butts. I didn't go out with Kate. We stayed at home. We sat in the garden, consumed with our separate anxieties, in what passed for companionship. We watched Tommy play under the apple blossom and thought our two sets of parallel thoughts. At midday, after we'd watched him eat but not been able to manage much ourselves, a note was delivered from Father saying he would call later on his way home to Chelsea.

While John went to his parlour and pretended to read, I spent a few hours in the kitchen, feeling unreal, supervising the preparation of supper. Happy summer food. Yesterday's bird and leg of ham. Fresh greens. A dish of soft buttery egg. White soup with almonds. Junket. And I went out and bought Tommy a jumble from somewhere in the fizzing crowd. He liked the hard, curly dough and the dusting of seeds. He was enjoying himself on what must, to him, genuinely seem a holiday.

It would be the first time I would see Father since James Bainham's burning. I was expecting a ravaged face: black rings under eyes; lines; grey, punished skin. I'd spent the sunlight hours feeling stabs of pity for him finding himself in today's impossible position; I'd been imagining him coming broken to the house, asking humbly for advice; I'd imagined myself pleading, with warm tears in my eyes, for him to resign, and him softly agreeing and taking me in the embrace of a true father. I'd been surprised at the warmth that these mental pictures brought unbidden to my heart.

But, when Father turned up, his smile seemed as big and warm and all-embracing as ever, and his gestures as confident. His apparent confidence lit us up as his man took his outer robe and John poured drinks – water for Father, wine for us – and led us into the garden. I couldn't see what was in his heart. I was secretly relieved when, as soon as we were alone, the smile switched off. There was stubble on Father's chin, and his dark jaw jutted forward.

'This is a terrible business,' John said sympathetically, putting an arm on Father's back as I hung sullenly behind, watching.

Father nodded. He said nothing. He walked on, with John's hand resting on him, looking straight ahead.

'Our Saviour says that the children of darkness are more politic in their way than are the children of light,' he said, in a quiet voice from which all emotion had been stripped out. 'That's how it seems to me now.

'The court is full of traitors,' he added with more obvious bitterness. 'And Convocation is full of fools. I've never seen so many bishops so negligent of their duty. I took this job thinking I could advance the affairs of Christendom. But now,' he paused, then seemed to lose heart. 'But now.' And he stopped.

He composed himself and turned back towards the house, pacing himself so that John's hand, which he hadn't seemed to notice, nevertheless stayed lightly on his shoulder. But he didn't even glance at either of us. I thought he might be struggling to make his voice stay even. 'I feel myself growing old.'

He wasn't asking for a response from either of us, so we didn't give one. We ate in silence. I felt every pair of servant's eyes curiously on Father. 'Delicious,' he said mechanically, praising the bird and the ham. But he didn't touch the meat on his plate.

John waited until we'd shut the parlour door on the eyes and ears before saying, with his face full of almost unbearable compassion, 'You know we'll support you whatever you decide to do.'

My lips tightened. I didn't agree. There was only one thing I wanted Father to do, even if his defeat today meant he could no longer burn heretics, and that was to resign.

'There is still so much to do,' Father said. There was a gleam in his eye again; a gleam I hated. I could see he was going to ignore failure and stay on.

'You should resign,' I said into the silence, surprising myself almost as much as the other two. They turned to face me, with eyes wide open. 'You've done enough, Father. Your conscience should be telling you that.'

John stepped half in front of me, flashing me a warning look. But Father stepped round him to look me in the eye. 'Meg,' he said, with a hint of reproof, and the smile that didn't reach his eyes touched his lips. 'What do you know about politics?'

I said, stubbornly, ignoring my racing heart: 'I don't. I just know about burnings.'

John gasped. 'Meg hasn't been well,' he said hastily to Father.

'Yes. It made me ill to watch James Bainham die,' I

363

snapped back, suddenly shaking with feeling I hadn't managed to suppress. I felt my cheeks flush. I stepped forward to confront them.

They were wary now. Seeing me with new eyes, as the aggressor, the initiator. Their fear scared me. But I liked it too.

It was interesting seeing what they did next. John was still there, but it was as though he faded backwards into the shadows, while Father stepped forward. His jaw was out. He put his hands on his hips, mirroring my gesture. I wasn't of his blood; it must have been the years we'd spent living together, but I could have sworn that the angry man in front of me looked, at this moment, uncannily like me. He was certainly as ready as I was to give fight.

'He had to die,' Father shot out. 'He was spreading filth that would damn other people to hellfire.'

'It wouldn't!' I shot back. 'It was his own business what he believed! It's you who's risking hellfire by mistaking yourself for God!'

We stared into each other's eyes at last. Father's were slightly bloodshot. Neither of us moved. There was nowhere for us to move to.

'They jeered you when he said he was at the stake because of you,' I said. 'Londoners. Your people. They're coming to hate you.'

I was aware of John in the shadows, making soft, helpless gestures with his hands, but there were only two people in this fight.

'And I don't need to know much about politics to know that the King will come to hate you too. If he doesn't already,' I rushed on. My heart was racing. My tongue was on fire. 'You're trying to stop him doing what he wants. You've stopped being his loyal servant. It was you who always said that the wrath of the King means death.'

In the midst of my rage, I heard the pleading note come into my voice. 'I don't want you to die. You should resign while you've still got time.'

'The King doesn't want me to go,' he said, with dull hostility. 'I've tried.'

There was something in his voice for an instant that sounded like tiredness. But then I saw him straighten his back and assume his burden again. 'And that's as well,' he added stoutly. 'Because I believe it's God's will for me to stay. Not just to fight heresy. Because of the other matter. Because of John.'

It was the last straw. My moment of weakness passed. I exploded. 'You really think it's all up to you, don't you?' I sneered. 'You think you can save everyone. You think you and Morton have already saved England from a Plantagenet usurper and created an honest new dynasty that God would smile on. And now you don't just think you can save England again by stopping the King turning to what you call heresy; you even think you can save John from being forced into a kinghood he doesn't want. You think you have all the secrets of state in your hands, don't you? But do you know what? You're wrong.'

I could feel John's hands pawing the air hopelessly, and heard his voice murmur 'Meg' as if he wanted to stop me. But I didn't waste a glance on him.

I had Father's attention now. He was staring at me.

'You've never told him, have you, John?' I said. I was almost laughing with the pleasure of proving Father's ignorance. My voice was like a whip, flailing at them both. 'You've never told him that you know you're illegitimate. He's never realised he's been propping up an illusion all these years. And you're so,' and I hissed out the next word, *stupid*,' with every scrap of pent-up fury in my body, 'that you never even realised how much it mattered.'

'Meg . . .' John muttered, coming forward and trying

to wrap me into himself in the kind of embrace that would stop me from talking. But I stretched my head out from his warning arms and went on talking insistently at Father.

'Yes. He's illegitimate, Father. He was a bastard all along. He's known for years. He told me. He's never had any right to any throne, and nor did his brothers and sisters. Their father really was a bigamist; Richard Plantagenet wasn't a usurper. Your whole strategy has been built on a mistake. And that means your Archbishop Morton married Henry Tudor to a Plantagenet bastard, not a princess. And this king is as full of bastard blood as John is. You've been so proud of all the secrets you control; but you haven't ever known as much as you think. You haven't saved anyone from anything. You've just been juggling two lots of bastards and wondering why God keeps cursing the land that's ruled by one of them. You're not God or his agent. Just a man. As full of human frailty as the rest. And you've failed.'

I stopped. Paused for triumphant breath. Became aware that John had long ago stopped trying to silence my flow of words and had buried his head in my shoulder instead. Became aware of the hotness of my face. Became aware of the magnitude of the secret I'd given away. Felt a new flush, hotter still, pass over my face and throat and shoulders, and wondered if it might be the start of shame.

Father was staring at me as if dumbfounded.

There was a long silence.

Then he cleared his throat and said, very quietly, 'Is this true, John?'

John raised a stricken face from my shoulder. There were tears on his cheeks. He was being unmasked as a deceiver without having realised he was one. He was trying to form words; none came.

Father waited a moment or two more, watching him, letting the truth sink in.

'I see,' he said, surprisingly gently. He put a hand on John's shoulder, patted it; a gesture of comfort. 'My dear John.'

He turned to me. His face was inscrutable. 'Thank you,' he said quietly. 'You've set me free. If I have no duty to king or family, I can follow my own heart at last.' And then he was gone, into the dusk in the street, leaving me alone in the parlour with the husband whose secret I'd betrayed.

I heard about what followed in Chelsea from Dame Alice, two days later.

Father passed a restless night. The next morning, he said enigmatically over breakfast that if a man saw the things he should set his hand to sustaining decay through his fault and falling to ruin under him, then he should leave those things, draw himself aside, and serve God.

'The next I saw of him was when he came back from town in the afternoon,' she said, shaking her head in bewilderment, her cheerful voice unusually hushed. 'I was just leaving church when he walked in. He'd been to the King and resigned but he didn't know how to break the news. He's spent so much of his life in public, playing a role, that he's never really worked out how to be straightforward with his family, has he? So he didn't tell me straight, just made one of his jokes. He had his cap in his hand and he bowed at me and said: "May it please your ladyship to come forth now my lord is gone." I guessed right away, of course,' and she broke into a reluctant chuckle at the last part of her story. 'I've been around long enough to know he starts in with the jokes when he's in trouble. I would have guessed even if Henry Pattinson hadn't been there, and hadn't understood too, and wasn't dancing round in the aisle cackling, "Chancellor More is chancellor no more," like the fool he is.'

John and I were summoned to Chelsea with the rest of the family on the second day. The King, it turned out, had responded to Father's returning the seal of office with a formal little speech granting Father the right to spend the rest of his life preparing his soul in the service of God. That's what Father had said he wanted. But Henry made his displeasure felt. There were no rewards for Father's years of service. He left York Place empty-handed. We were called to the house in Chelsea for the practical purpose of reorganising the family finances.

John had spent two nights away from my bed, praying at St Stephen's by day, forgetting to come home to eat, slipping away from me with an animal's quiet pain in his eyes without talking.

I'd spent those long hours eaten up with remorse and horror at myself. I'd betrayed my husband's secret, ripped apart his life, and for what? A cheap revenge on someone else. Now I was forced to stop and look at myself, I didn't like what I saw. Was I less cruel than Father? Less stupidly unthinking than John? I didn't think so. I was vengeful and intolerant; a monster. 'I'd do anything to unsay what I said,' I wept, scrabbling at his door. 'Anything. I'm sorry. I'm sorry. I didn't mean to hurt you. I love you.'

All my apologies and entreaties and contrition failed to touch John. 'It's all right,' he kept saying, though he stayed on the other side of the door. 'I should have seen myself how important it was to tell him. I should have thought. It would have come out sooner or later. Don't torment yourself.'

He was kind; so much kinder than me, even in despair. But he didn't mean it was all right. His voice was shattered. I could hear he was heartbroken.

There'd been no answer either to my frantic note to Father, in which I'd found nothing better to say than,

'Father, I'm sorry, you're right, I didn't understand, I'm a foolish girl, please forgive me.'

None of the others knew about the row at my house. The first person I saw when we got out of the boat at Chelsea, after a silent hour on the water, was Will Roper, Margaret's husband, blond, red-eyed, floppy-haired, with tension lines on his pretty young face. He linked arms with both John and me as we walked up from the landing-stage, a compromise between the poise he was trying to learn as a Member of Parliament and his old puppyish ways. I didn't mind. His presence filled the empty, shamed space between me and John.

'He's going to talk to us all at dinner. You must be very understanding,' Will whispered – everyone was whispering, we discovered when we reached the house, and everyone talking only about 'him', without bothering with Father's name – 'he's being so brave. But he's taking it hard. He's even been talking about becoming a martyr; saying it would make him so happy if he could see that his wife and children would encourage him to die in a good cause that he would run merrily towards his death.' He shook his head, a sensible old head on young shoulders. 'I can understand why he'd take it that way, of course,' he added doubtfully.

They were all there at the table (except Elizabeth, of course, she was far away in Shropshire with her children; but William Dauncey, who'd been at Parliament, was at the end of the table with his face as foolish and chinless and his eyes as bright and watchful as I remembered). They all had reddish eyes and strained expressions on bloodless faces. Even Cecily didn't giggle; just held tightly on to Giles Heron's hand. And when young John – married to pretty Anne now but still living at home, since the times had been too troubled for Father to turn his head to carving out a career for his son – thought no one was looking, he kept putting a hand to his forehead to massage away his pain. I was briefly touched to see Anne, at his side, noticing his gesture and delving into her skirts to pull out a little cloth pouch for him; the vervain I'd taught her to treat him with. But there was no cheer among us. So John and I blended in; there was no need to explain our difficult silences.

My heart was wrung by the way Father looked, sitting between Margaret and Dame Alice at the head of the table – going through the motions of being as full of charm and attention as ever. I'd been so angry with him for so long that I'd forgotten his admirable strength, the reserves of dignity and grace in public that he'd naturally draw on in dark times. He was nodding courteously to Margaret and asking her for stories about her children; he was passing food to Dame Alice before the pageboys had time to reach for it. It was only when he raised his face to us that I could see the weariness of his expression and the emptiness in his eyes. At least, I thought, clutching at whatever comfort I could, he hadn't flinched away from me in the way I'd secretly feared.

Instead he stood up and came towards us both. 'Welcome,' he said graciously, smiling warmly, taking us to our places. 'My dear children. Thank you both for coming today.' Then he helped me settle on my seat, and murmured, 'Thank you for your note; you didn't need to write it. You helped me take a decision I should probably have taken before. Sometimes it just takes one nudge more to understand the best way forwards. I appreciate your honesty.'

I felt his arm linger on my back as he turned to John and helped him tuck his long legs under the table. I heard another murmur in John's ear, and when I looked round I saw that a few quiet words had been enough to make him, too, feel his guilt was absolved. Father went quietly back to his place. When, a moment later, a hand stretched under the table to take mine, I squeezed it back and, for the first time in too long, found John's eyes on mine with a light in them that might, I hoped, mean forgiveness.

The food was simple, even plainer than usual. There was no wine, just small beer and water, and no more than three or four dishes set at our table. Father cleared his throat to get our attention – it was easy enough, since everyone was giving him furtive glances the whole time and the table was all but silent – and, after saying Grace, said, as simply as he knew how, into our silence, 'I think you all know that I've made a decision which means my income will no longer be what it was. I've gathered all my children together today – I consider all of you my children – to ask your advice about how we can go on living and being together.'

I hadn't thought about money for a moment, but it was true; we all received allowances from Father and both the Wills spent half their week living at Chelsea. None of us knew how to respond. I looked at Margaret, and saw her looking sidelong at Will Dauncey, who was looking at Will Roper, who was looking at John. Dame Alice, who I noticed was wearing a plain dark dress with none of the opulence she usually favoured, was fidgeting with a piece of bread. Father looked around at our mournful faces with such a tender expression that it made me wonder, for a second, if he wasn't genuinely secretly relieved at his change in circumstances.

'Then let me share my thoughts with you,' he went on. 'You needn't worry: we aren't going to have to go out and gather bracken for the fire. We just need to be more careful. Those who can will perhaps be good enough to contribute to the costs of the household. And we can all save by gradually learning to eat more modestly.' Out of the corner of my eye, I saw Will Dauncey push away the dish of meat by his elbow.

'I plan to lead a quieter life in any case,' Father continued calmly, changing the subject. 'I get pains in my chest sometimes; my doctors have been telling me for years to do less.'

Will Dauncey saw his cue for courtly politeness. 'May we ask what your plans are, Sir?' he said, smiling and bowing his head.

'I shall . . .' Father paused, as if gathering his thoughts, 'pray more, and write more . . . Carry the cross in procession at the parish church at Chelsea . . . and, I hope, see more of all of you.'

And he smiled and bowed back at Will Dauncey with all the glowing warmth he was capable of.

Margaret slipped away from the table early. I followed her to her room a few minutes later, knowing she'd be as relieved as me to talk, knocked on the door and slipped inside without waiting for an answer. 'Who's that?' she called, more sharply than I'd expected. She was by the fire, kneeling on the floor, scrubbing at a rag in a pink-stained bowl. 'Oh, it's you, Meg,' she said, hurriedly putting herself between the bowl and me.

I looked away. 'I'm sorry,' I said awkwardly, imagining it was the rag from her monthly bleeding and wondering why she hadn't had a maid scrub it instead of doing it herself, 'I should have waited at the door.'

'It's all right; I don't mind you seeing,' she said, relaxing. 'I used to do it for Father when we lived here. And I feel so helpless now that I wanted to do it just to have something to do to help. But don't tell anyone else. It would embarrass him so.'

I looked again. The scraps of wet cloth sticking out of the bowl were rough enough to scrape the skin: Father's hair shirt. The sight of it made me want to cry. I found myself wishing I was gentle Margaret, and that it had been in my nature to willingly do Father this quiet domestic service for years to help him in his prayers, instead of myself, poking round his study when he wasn't there and recoiling in horror from his scourge and furious writings. 'Oh sweetheart,' I said, and we hugged, and found tears on our cheeks as we came apart that neither of us knew who had shed.

'Do you think he's really worried about money?' I asked, when we were both sitting on the floor watching the flames.

'I don't know,' she answered. 'I don't think he cares. Will says the bishops wrote to him today with an offer to find a lot of money – four thousand pounds – to pay him for his defence of the clergy in parliament. But he just laughed and said no. He told Will he'd rather they threw the money in the Thames. He said he looked for thanks to God, not bishops, and that he'd done his work for God's sake, not theirs.

'Do you know what I think, Meg?' she went on. 'I think he's relieved. I think he wants to live as plainly as possible because he doesn't have to do anything else any more. He's always wanted to devote himself to God. And now he's free of the world perhaps he can.'

There was something so wistful in the look she fixed on me that I nodded my agreement. We would both have loved that idea to be true.

But when I heard John's footsteps on the stairs and followed him back to the room we'd been put in to share (he hadn't objected, but I hadn't known if he would end up sharing it with me; I was mutely, abjectly grateful to find us both in there), I couldn't believe any more that Father's life would become simple. I stood with John at the window, watching the flickering light of Father's candle go down the path to the New Buildings to start his long night of prayer and thought.

'What do you think he'll be doing in there tonight?' I asked cautiously, and was warmed when I felt John's dry, warm hand on mine in the darkness. I was grateful that he wasn't gloating, as I might have done to him if our positions had been reversed on this subdued, unhappy May night: telling me that I had only myself to blame, and that I'd got what I wanted. 'What do you think he's thinking?'

'The same as before,' John said, carefully avoiding letting any intonation suggesting blame into his voice. 'Nothing's changed. I asked him. He's going to start another volume of arguments against Tyndale. It's his passion, Meg; what matters most to him in life. He's going to go on hunting heretics.'

Into the silence that fell then, in the starless, moonless, blackness of that summer night, I found my mind drifting back to the other confidence Margaret had shared with me. It was part of the rather shamefaced worry she'd started confessing to about whether Father's hundreds of courtly friends would still want to know our family now. 'I think we might get lonely,' Margaret had whispered. 'I think all kinds of people will just stop calling – even the ones who owe Father everything. For instance . . . do you remember Master Hans, the painter?' I'd nodded, mystified. 'Well, my maid says he's back in London. She saw him wandering round Smithfield yesterday. But he's staying at the Steelyard. I may be wrong, but I don't think you or I will be seeing Master Hans again any time soon.'

PART FOUR

After the Ambassadors

17

Hans Holbein watched a rat's tail whip against the drapes as a small, squat grey body scuttled away from the candle's light. The rooms were small and mean: bare boards on the floor, a rough table and bench and two chairs by the fire in the first room and a straw-filled pallet on the bedframe of the second room next to a wormy old chest. But that's what you got in Maiden Lane. That's why they let foreigners live around Cordwainers' Hall. There was no point in complaining too much. The house came recommended by Davy, the sharp-eyed manager of the underground market in religious books, and the Steelyard's most trusted London friend. It was safe here, and near the Steelyard, even if you'd be lucky to get half an hour's good light to draw by.

'There's no pot,' he said firmly. The old man nodded sadly. 'There's no carpet.' Another toothless, apologetic baring of gums. 'There's nothing to eat off.'

'They broke, didn't they,' the old man intoned. His voice was an irritating whine. There was a drip coming down from his nostrils which he didn't bother to wipe away. 'No point in buying new ones, see, not when the end of the world is nigh.'

Holbein laughed and put down his bundle. 'Well, I still

need to piss and eat until Judgement Day comes,' he said. 'Don't I?' he added, feeling secretly pleased that he was mastering the London idiom.

The old man nodded reluctantly, though he brightened when Holbein put the warm coins he'd already counted out into the gnarly old hand and pursued the advantage by saying: 'So you take that and go and get me what I need, and send your boy in every morning to clear up, and feed me when I'm home, and I don't know how much that will be, and I'll take your house for a year.'

His gait as he scuttled out before Holbein could change his mind reminded the painter of the rat.

Holbein thought: amazing how quickly a few coins stopped all that droning about Judgement Day. Fourteen suicides in London in fourteen days. The two giant fish pulled out of the Thames. Allhallows Church in Bread Street closed and its two priests imprisoned after they came to blows at the altar and wounded each other so that blood sprayed onto the altar cloth. That was a lot of bad-luck stories for less than an hour; and a lot of lugubrious shaking of the head; and a lot of mean little flashes of the eyes with the lip-smacking commentary: 'Bad times coming. Oh yes. And it's no surprise to me. Fifteen hundred years next spring since the Crucifixion and God's angry enough to smite us for our sins. Smite us good and proper. No wonder, with the way things are going down here.' It could be worse to have to listen to that all the time than to have to live without a chamber pot or a dish and cup. Holbein could only hope that, once he was installed in the room and the money was coming in regularly, the old man would stop going on about the Apocalypse and cheer up. He had enough problems of his own without the end of the world being nigh.

But the old man didn't calm down. Holbein could hear him from his room, muttering away to the rabbity, scared-looking young boy who did the work around the place.

There was a new story every day, chewed over with a mixture of terror and relish. The great red globe the brothers had seen suspended over the Charterhouse. The comets every night in the sky. The horse's head on fire. The flaming sword. The blue cross above the moon. If they'd been orthodox believers they'd have crossed themselves in mid-mumble. But they didn't cross themselves in this house. They thought it superstitious. Holbein thought that ironic. He found these secretive Lutheran types just as superstitious and bigoted as the other lot, the old-fashioned Catholics who loved poor Queen Catherine and went round muttering all the time about the Holy Maid of Kent and what she'd said to the King to put him off his idea of marrying the whore. 'You won't stay on the throne for more than a month if you do it,' she was supposed to have said. 'You won't be a king in the reputation of God even for that month; not even for one hour. And you'll die a villain's death.'

He'd heard that one in the alehouse every night for a month a few months after he got here last spring and settled in to paint the Steelyard men's portraits. It had happened in the autumn, when the King had taken Anne Boleyn with him to France to meet the French King and get him to talk the Pope into letting Henry annul his marriage. Henry and Anne had stopped at Canterbury, and walked in the garden. So it had been easy for the Holy Maid (or 'Mad Nun', as Holbein's landlord called her, remembering for once to sniff up his snot in his indignation) to slip into the garden from the chapel where she went into her trances and where her priestly minions bowed and scraped around her, writing down her every word, and start shouting at the King.

'It may be just my big German bone-head, but I admire her,' Holbein said to the old man one night, trying to make him look another way at the thing, trying to be reasonable. 'Elizabeth Barton. The nun. Of course, I don't believe she's a saint. But she was just a kitchen maid before she started having visions, and now look at her. We all talk about her all the time. She's famous up and down the land, and never has to lift a finger. Bishop Fisher weeps when he listens to her because he believes he's hearing the voice of God. It's not a bad return for a few prophecies.'

But the old man only looked disgusted. He didn't mind the King marrying again if it meant the government calming down about heresy, so he could go to his furtive prayer meetings at Davy's without fear of arrest and execution. 'She's as crazy as they get, that Barton,' he said with contempt. 'And as evil. She's the Shape of Things to Come. It's people like her they should be burning.' And the scared rabbit-boy in the corner shuffled his feet and stirred his pot and looked more frightened than ever.

It hadn't taken Holbein long to see that people here were as full of fear nowadays as they had been in Basel when he got back there. The only difference was that here they didn't know yet which way things were going to go. But they all had the terrors anyway, the pains in the gut, the hackles rising, the eyes flickering nervously towards the unknown, the horror of the beast slouching towards them.

He thought a lot about fear at the moment, sitting in his room at night, listening to the scuttling and the muttering about Merlin and dun cows and God knows what else and trying to concentrate on preparing his materials for the next day's work by the light of the single candle that the old man put in his room. He thought about fear not just when he heard the apocalyptic gossip on the street. It was everywhere. There was even fear on the faces of the Hanse merchants he'd painted behind the high walls of the Steelyard. You couldn't see the fear on Georg Gisze's stolid face in the portrait Holbein had just finished painting, but Holbein knew it was there. That look belied Gisze's imports of banned books for the underground trade here and his knowledge of the trouble he'd be in if the King's men ever caught him.

It was a relief to meet people who had no fear. But there were precious few of them. Apart from Kratzer, he'd only really come across two in his year here. Thomas Boleyn, now the Earl of Wiltshire – Anne Boleyn's father – one of Erasmus' humanist correspondents, to whom he'd taken a book from the old thinker and whose merry face had reminded him of a child's waiting for a present it knows it will get. And Thomas Cromwell, the coming man in the King's entourage, Thomas More's enemy, a pork-barrel of power with narrow eyes looking consideringly out at the world. He wasn't afraid of anything. He was going to become the King's secretary if he had to kill half of England and finish off More with his own hands to get the job. That was who Cromwell had talked about first, with his street toughness, when Wiltshire had sent him to Cromwell's home to pay his respects as a first step towards getting a commission: 'Yes. Holbein. I remember you. You painted More, didn't you?' Flashing those Thames-coloured eyes – mud with glints – and making Holbein think his own name might be on one of those lists of people being investigated. Holbein had kept his head straight and his eyes steady and answered, 'Yes', in his firmest voice, and 'No', when Cromwell had asked, 'And have you been to see him since you got back?' and smiled quietly back when Cromwell had clapped him on the shoulder and said, 'Wise. Not the man to know these days,' as if he agreed and didn't feel remorse at his own cowardice in failing to visit his biggest benefactor now he was down on his luck. Holbein didn't think of himself as a man who scared easily. But he'd felt his own little prickle of fear.

So his landlord's daily horrors were beginning to grate on him. He laughed the old fool's nonsense off as genially as he could, just as he laughed off the man's invitations to go and pray with the other bigots-in-training in Davy's backyard. What he didn't like was that he couldn't help himself, every now and then, watching the sky for comets too.

'You should have stayed with me,' Kratzer told him over a cup of beer in his warm parlour, where Holbein's portrait of him, looking seriously out of the right of the picture over his astronomical instruments, had pride of place above the fireplace. They were celebrating Holbein finishing his biggest commission yet: two monumental paintings for the Steelyard's long, timbered banqueting hall. He'd illustrated the merchants' motto – '*gold is the father of deception and the son of sorrow; he who lacks it is sad; he who has it is uneasy*' – with two enormous paintings, one showing the Triumph of Riches and the other the Triumph of Poverty. Kratzer had popped in and out as he painted, full of ideas, fizzing with energy, suggesting things, chatting, bringing food and ale; his dearest friend. 'I don't know what you're doing in that dingy hellhole,' the astronomer went on. 'Your landlord's family aren't wrong about everything: the heavens *are* full of warnings. Sometimes when I look at the stars I believe the end of the world is upon us too. But that's not the point. You've got rats, for God's sake. Fleas. Bedbugs. Flat ale. And stale bread.'

Holbein only shook his head. 'There are always two ways to look at everything,' he said sententiously (he had had quite a lot of beer by that time in the evening). 'On the one hand, fair enough, it's not a great place to live. On the other . . .'

'What?' the older man asked, his big raw features alive with sarcasm. 'What other hand?'

'Well,' Holbein said, leaning forward to pour more beer for Kratzer, 'let's just say there are things about it that suit me.'

He couldn't tell Kratzer what he liked about it. He

382

couldn't tell anyone. His obsession was like a sickness – too private and shaming to share.

It was what he thought about in the poky little rooms tossing and turning all night long, unable to rest; what he thought about when he got up from the dusty straw sack with the rough blankets, scratching at himself and rubbing his eyes; what he thought about when he relieved himself in the yard and splashed water on his face and scrubbed at his painty hands; what he dreamed of, every minute of every day, until he felt his head would burst. The morning walks: through alleyways and down quiet lanes, as if by choosing the most inconspicuous route he could somehow prevent even himself from noticing what he was doing, skulking round corners trying to keep his bulk out of people's way and avoiding their eyes. His daily trip was to the pissing conduit fifty paces from the entrance of St Stephen's Walbrook, which he had to reach in time to see her slip over the road from her house and through the church door with her eyes down. Her. Meg. Mistress Meg Clement. (Letting his mind conjure up her married name always made him wince; but he did it, to try and keep reality in the picture.) His long wait, pretending to relieve himself, or hanging round looking at what they were selling on the street, and whistling to himself to keep himself warm until she came out, shriven, in a cloud of incense, with the small dark boy at her side. The second glimpse of her as agonisingly short as the first. And then his second scuttle home to resume his life.

He felt dirtied by it. He was horrified by what he was becoming, creeping around town like his landlord in his dirty little house, as if he'd become the kind of ruffian who screwed little girls in back alleys, or picked pockets, or knifed old men for their purses. But he also felt so exhilarated by those two moments every morning that there was no way he could give them up. Those glimpses of her were shafts of light in his darkness. He carried them with him all day: the plane of her cheekbones, thinner now and more drawn than before; the few prematurely silver hairs he could see in the black hair peeping out from under her bonnet; the lanky, careless way her thin hips moved as she covered the ground. The sight of the little boy toddling along beside her pained him; so did the soft looks she sometimes gave the child as she tightened her grip on his hand. He tried not to think about them. But those images were burned into his brain too. His sightings of this ghostly Meg, seen as if behind glass, were the purpose and crystal-hard light of his life.

He knew he deserved the sour things Erasmus had started writing about him to Kratzer. He knew he was an ingrate who had failed to show respect to the man who had taken him in and set his career in motion. He should have been to see More. He knew himself to be a coward (though he often excused himself for his failing; he was a poor man with a future to think of, a reputation to build, clients to find, mouths to feed; he couldn't afford the luxury of being seen visiting a man committing political suicide as More was by refusing to serve the king; the choices More had made weren't his fault). Sometimes he told himself that Erasmus wouldn't be quite so disappointed in him if he realised that his painter disciple was, at least in part, fulfilling his promise to look out for Meg and her family; but mostly he was still enough in control of himself to know that the reason he couldn't tell Erasmus this personally was because there was nothing in what he was doing now that would please his old friend. What he was doing was for himself and no one else. The love he was trapped in was like a sickness, or a madness.

It wasn't what he'd meant to do in London – hang round in this limbo waiting for God to show him a way forward. He'd been so excited at the idea of seeing her again. He'd meant to do what Erasmus wanted and go openly to More's house, then Meg's house, but when he'd reached the Steelyard and Davy the books man had told him the news about More walking out of his job (watching him carefully, like everyone did here nowadays, as if there'd be a secret to be unravelled in the way he reacted) he'd needed more time to assess the situation. He was on unfamiliar ground. It seemed more prudent to find lodgings through the Steelyard. He didn't want to jeopardise his friendships with those in high places who were positioning themselves to deserve yet more greatness by advertising his reliance on More. There would be time when he was established again in London to negotiate a meeting with his old benefactor. Still, it had seemed like a God-given opportunity when the old man first said, 'You stayed with Thomas More before, eh? You lived with him? His daughter cured the boy here of the sweating sickness.' Holbein hadn't ever heard the boy say a word before but suddenly a mumbled story came out: the father who'd died of the sweat at Deptford; the rest of the family dying of it in the country; and him, left alone and expecting God to take him too, put into the gatehouse by the dark-haired lady, with a blanket and a bottle of physic and a hug and an agonised, frustrated look on her face. The physic cured the boy. He drank it when he got hot and his head started to ache and he threw off the blanket and thought he was done for. But he woke up the next morning, drenched yet alive, and stumbled off back to London and his granddad. And that was how he started going to the prayer meetings with the old man: to give thanks to God for sparing him. She was a good woman. Shy but kind. Looked hard, as if she didn't want to know people; but she had a heart hidden away underneath. She was in London now with a family of her own. The boy sometimes went and looked at her outside the church by her new house and said his own private prayers for her.

'I could show you where she lives,' he said, with a burst of confidence; then swallowed his Adam's apple and stared at his feet and went a miserable crimson.

'Tomorrow morning,' Holbein said, and gave the boy a golden angel, which made him go even redder.

It had been that easy. And then, after he'd seen her for the first time, he'd lost his nerve forever. He couldn't go and speak to her. (What if she wanted him to visit her father? What if she wanted to know how long he'd been here? What if she knew he had feet of clay?) But he couldn't go away either. And the trap was sprung. He kept hoping weakly that he'd wake up one morning not feeling like this. Find the strength not to go and hang around watching for her. He went to bed every night telling himself he wouldn't go tomorrow morning. He went to bed every night knowing he was telling himself lies. The truth: he couldn't wake up early enough to begin savouring the minutes leading up to the moment when he could set off. He couldn't even move lodgings now. There was a complicity about his relationship with the old man and the boy. They knew where he went on his own every morning. When the boy dumped his bread and ale on the table in the morning, he knew whose face Holbein had seen. He didn't say anything, but Holbein liked the notion that they were companions in their unspoken, unseen love for Meg. That was enough to make it tolerable to share living space with an old goat with rank breath who told him every night, in the same querulous voice, that Henry would be driven from his kingdom, or that the priests would rule for three days and three nights; or that the white lion would kill the king; or that the pope was about to arrive in England. Almost enough, anyway. There was no one else he could tell. He was stuck, frozen in time like a fly in amber.

Kratzer often gave him the kind of calm look these days that said, 'I'm not fooled; I know something's up' louder

386

than any words. But he didn't go further than that. He was a man of subtlety for all his frank talking, Kratzer; he knew when not to stick his nose in.

Holbein began the double portrait Kratzer had wangled for him on the day after Queen Anne's coronation ended.

They'd been dining together just before the beginning of Easter Week when Kratzer had suggested it. But he'd had too much work between that Easter Sunday – 12 April 1533, when, within days of the bishops knuckling under and accepting that King Henry's first marriage had been invalid, and Cromwell pushing through the law that ended the common era of Christianity by denying Queen Catherine the right to appeal to Rome against the decision, Anne had been declared Queen from the pulpit of the King's chapel at Greenwich – and the Whitsun weekend in May when the new queen had been brought to London to be crowned to have had time to think of new commissions. He'd been working on his contribution to the firework-studded four-day coronation, for the pleasure of the sullen, sparse crowd of Londoners who turned out to watch.

The Hanse Merchants, who had reluctantly undertaken to pay for the decoration of the corner of Gracechurch Street for the Whitsun weekend, put the coronation work his way.

Holbein was proud of the scene he had designed. He made Mount Parnassus, with a white marble fountain of Helicon, and four streams meeting in a cup above the fountain, and Rhenish wine flowing up and down (and into the mouths of passers-by, or their cups if they'd had the wit to bring cups) until nightfall. He had a pretty golden-haired Apollo on top of the mountain, and a pretty Calliope at his feet, and a muse on each of the mountain's four sides, each playing music and praising the new Queen. Kratzer, who'd been in London so long now that he knew almost everyone

387

in the city, found an out-of-work poet to compose the necessary poetry, epigrams and jokes; he also found a scrivener fallen on hard times who wrote out the best bits in gold letters so that those who were able to could appreciate them in writing.

Before the city was even cleaned up after the tight-lipped, reluctant city people who hadn't really wanted to celebrate, first thing in the morning, Kratzer took him to meet his important sitters and introduced them. Kratzer had a big bag full of stuff on his back – props for the picture – and a big smile on his face. The two Frenchmen who were to be in the picture were younger than Holbein, in their late twenties, with the finest of velvets and cambrics and silks against their peachy skins and the noblest of faces and the purest French on their lips and the longest and largest of titles. Holbein might have felt intimidated by their effortless loveliness and aristocratic virtue – in this grand and unfamiliar room in Bridewell Palace, full of the most beautiful of furniture and objets d'art, with fine chased goblets of wine laid out on a table – but for Kratzer and his absolute confidence in the levelling power of learning. Kratzer bowed low and was a little more elegant than usual in his dress, but he was fizzing with words and ideas as if the Frenchmen were old friends. He spoke French with the same fluency but execrable accent which he brought to English. He didn't care; what he had to say was more important to him than the accent he said it in. And Holbein saw, as the Frenchmen responded, that although they didn't truly know Kratzer they paid him the compliment of treating him like an old friend too. He might have been born the son of a Munich sawsmith, but he'd become a learned and respected man; he'd been an astronomer in the King's service for fifteen years now; he'd studied at Cologne and taught at Oxford; and he was the friend of Erasmus and Pieter Gillis and Thomas More and most of the scholars of Europe.

'We four are united by our shared love of learning,' as the French King's fresh-faced ambassador to London, Jean de Dinteville – Sieur de Polisy, Bailly de Troyes and Maitre d'hotel of the French court – elegantly put it. 'We are honoured to make your acquaintance.' And Holbein felt his back relax a little, and he almost forgot to bow as he turned to drop his bag, begin his preparations, and examine the scene.

'I've got some ideas,' Kratzer said to him, a hissed aside. 'Don't forget to ask me. I've brought some stuff to help.' Holbein nodded calmly, and laid his book and silverpoint pencil out on the table behind him next to a few of the props he had brought. His hands weren't sweating any more. His nerves had gone.

Alongside de Dinteville was Georges de Selve, the twenty-five-year-old Bishop of Lavaur who had just been sent over from Paris to help the ambassador cope with King Henry's rages whenever he had to be told that the French King couldn't, or wouldn't, help make the Pope see sense over the King's marriage. ('Oh, his tempers,' de Dinteville was saying ruefully, shaking his elegant head. 'They're quite debilitating. I haven't had a week without being ill since I got here in February.') The two wanted a big impressive record of their mission, as tall as a tall man and square. They were prepared to pay lavishly. Holbein had had ten Baltic oak panels prepared and put together in advance to suit the grandeur of the commission. The giant square was already up against his easel, eighty inches tall and wide, which Kratzer had sent to the ambassador's home in advance.

Holbein let the three men talk and sip at their wine while he watched them and wondered how to compose his picture to show the Frenchmen at their best. The bishop had pink cheeks above his beard, a black bonnet and a gown the glowing purplish-brown colour of mulberries; the ambassador liquid eyes, furs, scarlet sleeves and fine hands below his lace ruffles. Their backs had the straight poise of years of command and fearless inquiry. Their eyes sparkled with intelligence. They were both men of learning and subtlety, versed in every modern liberal art. He couldn't see anything but that poise; but he sensed the fear in them as he paced and sketched and stared.

The three others were talking about the coronation. Both the Frenchmen had been part of the court entourage. Representing France at the event had been part of the reason for the young bishop to be in London. If the child the new queen was carrying turned out to be a son – making the royal dynasty safe – it would be an event people would remember for generations to come. France, the go-between in King Henry's so far unsuccessful negotiations with the Pope, needed to be well-represented. Holbein was only half-listening. It was easy to shut out the French words after so long hearing nothing but English and German. He was trying to focus on getting a first glimmering of his layout: the ambassador on the left; the bishop on the right; their faces turned to him; the accoutrements of nobility and learning scattered around them in ways he couldn't yet picture – he wasn't quite sure yet what props Kratzer had brought with him; and a *memento mori* of some sort grinning down from the centre of the piece. But it seemed commonplace to him; like any old bookplate. He needed something more.

'He wasn't there, did you see?' he heard, and lifted his head. Then he lowered it cautiously again and carried on laying lines on paper. 'They said beforehand he wouldn't go, but I didn't believe he'd have the nerve to snub the new queen.'

They were talking about More. Holbein almost held his breath.

'He told Bishop Tunstall he couldn't afford a new gown,' the French bishop said, and Holbein saw out of the corner of his eye that the young man looked bewildered; it could never have occurred to de Selve to excuse himself from anything on grounds of poverty. 'Tunstall and two friends sent him some money for clothes. They knew how important it was for him to be seen there. He took their twenty pounds.'

Kratzer knew the power of money over a man; Kratzer traded in Toulouse woad and Gascon wine (the wine they were sipping now might even be stuff he'd provided); he had an interest in prospecting for metal ores in Cornwall. But Kratzer shook his head understandingly. 'More's a rich man,' he said in his heavily accented French. 'He stayed away on principle. There's another story going around. Perhaps you've heard it?'

They shook their heads. They drew closer.

'I had it from Will Roper the other day,' Kratzer said, pink with secret pleasure at knowing. 'I saw him in the street. More wrote back to Tunstall. He reminded him of the story of the Emperor Tiberius being faced with the dilemma of having to sentence a virgin to death for a crime for which virgins couldn't be punished. He recalled how Tiberius's advisers had suggested that the Emperor first deflower the woman, then kill her. And he finished by telling Tunstall to watch out for his own virginity. He wrote: "*I can't know whether I'll be devoured. But even if I am I'll know I haven't been deflowered*".'

All three men laughed, then sighed and shook their heads. 'A proud and honourable man,' the Bishop, de Selve, said.

Why didn't Kratzer tell me that? Holbein thought. He knows I love More and his family. He knows I admire his honesty. Then he felt a prickle of doubt. Kratzer didn't know that. He knew that Holbein hadn't been to see them. He'd read Holbein bits of Erasmus' letters criticising him for failing to go. Perhaps he'd been hinting that Holbein should go? Perhaps Kratzer himself saw more of the Mores than he realised? Perhaps Kratzer thought him a coward, but was too polite to say so? He moved closer, holding up his book like a shield of invisibility.

'We live in dangerous times,' he heard. One of the Frenchmen. 'If they're hunting down scholars of More's eminence for not agreeing with whatever the authorities tell them to believe – even here, in what I've always taken to be the most moderate of lands – then it's the end of the era we were born into.'

He saw Kratzer nod. 'The bigots are winning,' he said gloomily. 'Both kinds of bigots . . .'

The ambassador finished his sentence for him: 'And the only losers are the learned.'

They all shook their heads.

Holbein stared down again at his sketch then up at the trio in front of him. He was hot with shame now; hot with the sudden certainty that, by not going to see More when he first got to England, he'd compromised himself. He'd revealed himself as a small man, he saw now: someone incapable of big gestures and generosity of spirit. One of the fearful. The knowledge churned poisonously in his gut. He'd failed the man who'd done most for him, the man with the rough chin and the luminous eyes and the mellifluous voice and the fascination with ideas and words, the one Englishman with whom discussing your thoughts was truly a pleasure and an adventure. Perhaps it was the dawning realisation that all the learned men in this room thought the uncertain future of More was symptomatic of the woes of the age that was crystallising the anxiety he'd suppressed for so long. Or perhaps it was just the sight of the bishop plucking with one hand at his mulberry velvet skirts, with the expression of regret still on his face at the idea of witnessing the death of learning, which gave Holbein the first flickering of his idea.

'Of all the dates people give when they talk about the

end of the world coming, of all the dates my colleagues give when they look at the darkness of the skies . . .' Kratzer was saying, 'do you know which one I'd say was the most significant?'

Mulberry, Holbein thought, excited without yet knowing quite why, only half-listening to Kratzer's French. Morus. The skull that Meg had once hidden under a table in Chelsea, on top of all his dangerous sketches, was on the table right behind him. He wasn't sure yet, but he was beginning to get that rush of euphoria that meant a big thought. Hovering somewhere just out of reach of his mind was a shape; the shape of learning and fear; the shape of everything that was hidden in the stars. It was just possible that this was going to be a great picture.

'It's not any of these false dates they talk about on the street. It's simpler by far. It was Good Friday this year,' Kratzer went on, looking round with that big, bony, serious yet mischievous look that he had when visited by an idea: reckless, impelled to get the idea out and see what those around thought of it. 'One and a half thousand years after Christ's death; with the churches all in mourning. The last day of the universal church, too; the day before Anne was proclaimed Queen and England broke away from Rome. What kind of God I personally believe in doesn't matter here; the point is, that was the day they let the darkness in. And only the good Lord knows what will come of it all.'

'Kratzer,' Holbein called urgently, before the Frenchmen could respond, breaking into the conversation then blushing at his own uncouthness and muttering, 'I'm sorry to interrupt,' before going on in the same preoccupied tone, slightly too loud: 'Kratzer. Can I get your stuff out of your bag?'

Kratzer waved an arm without really paying attention. He was lost in his lament; starting now about what the heavens said about the troubled state of things on earth today.

Holbein emptied the astrologer's bag on the table, in the grip of the thought beginning to take shape, not caring now if the objects rattled. Kratzer's astrolabe and the white decagonal sundial he'd painted before, when he painted Kratzer. Yes. A couple of globes – earthly and heavenly – and more astronomical instruments that he didn't recognise. Yes. Books. Yes. And a lute on a chair which he could borrow. Everything he needed to show the quadrivium of higher learning: astronomy, geometry, arithmetic and music, the four mathematical arts of harmony and precision. Everything he needed to celebrate culture and scholarship.

He pulled them all together. Looked at them. Yanked open his own bag where the strip of Turkey carpet was wrapped round all his paints and bottles and jars and boxes. Spun it away from the encumbrances so that the paints and bottles and jars and boxes fell where they lay. Spread it on the table, enjoying the rich red glow of its patterns under his fingers. Began building a display on it, under the gentle, tormented face of the Christ figure on the crucifix nailed to the wall. Instruments to measure the heavens on the Turkey carpet on the table's top layer; instruments of earthly life – the lute, the globe of the world (he'd paint it turned towards France, of course), and Kratzer's arithmetic book and Lutheran hymnal on the lower layer. He was beginning to see it come together: a picture that would convey the things of heaven and earth, not just by painting these objects but in more subtle ways; ways that Kratzer would help him plot; ways that would impress the greatest minds in Europe.

His hands were shaking. If this picture came off – if he managed to convey all the things in it that were bursting through his head now – it might be not just the perfect way to fame and fortune. It might be the way to make his peace with the Mores. Just possibly, it could even be the way to win the right to see Meg again. He looked up, breath coming fast, eyes sizing up the lute that he was about to stride over and grab to add to his tableau. He'd forgotten the others. He was almost surprised to see three pairs of astonished eyes staring at him.

Kratzer came home with him and tiptoed up the bare stairs to Holbein's rooms behind him. Holbein was silent and preoccupied, striding ahead, carrying the bag. 'Look.' Holbein shoved the sketch under Kratzer's nose as soon as the other man had sat down in the dying light of the window. 'This is my idea. You've got to help me make it better.'

'Aren't you offering me a drink, at least?' Kratzer said, half-laughing, not taking the younger man's enthusiasm seriously enough, not looking at the drawing. 'To get me thinking?'

Holbein stifled an impatient rejoinder. He took a deep breath. Kratzer was still glowing with the pleasure of having done him a good turn and the joy of having spent an afternoon in conversation with intelligent men. He didn't realise that his real work was yet to come. 'All right,' Holbein said, consciously taking a few deep breaths and summoning what patience he could. He went to the door and yelled hastily downstairs to the boy, 'Fetch us some pies and some beer,' then came back, stood behind Kratzer's shoulder and looked down at the rough picture: the two Frenchmen, de Dinteville on the left, de Selve on the right, with the tableful of implements between them. The light was going already, even on this June evening, making the sketch look grey and blurry. He lit a candle. 'Look properly, Nicholas, before it gets too dark,' he said pleadingly. 'They'll bring the food up in a minute.'

And, to his intense happiness, the astronomer at last heeded the urgency in his voice, nodded more seriously, and turned his head down to examine the picture properly.

By the time the boy came stumbling up the stairs to set

out the food, the two men were lost in their idea. They were leaning towards each other over the rough table, over a pencil sketch, and jabbering together in loud German. They ignored him. Ignored the food too. He slunk out, shaking his head. It was true what they said about foreigners. An excitable, unpredictable lot. They hadn't even tipped him for his service.

'If you're going to make it a Good Friday picture, you'll need to borrow some Lenten things from the chapel at Bridewell,' Kratzer was saying, very fast. 'It's June. They won't mind. We could take their Lenten veil, for instance. Hang it behind the table. That would probably be enough.'

Holbein nodded, beguiled away from his bigger aim by this practical idea. 'We could set it as if it were the end of Tenebrae,' he said, catching Kratzer's thought. Tenebrae: the Darkenings, the ceremony that began Good Friday, and Wednesday and Thursday of Holy Week too, in which the priest gradually extinguished all the candles in the church. On Good Friday, the darkest of days, the priest gradually uncovered the crucifix, hidden by the green Lenten veil, as the candles went out, before beginning the veneration of the cross. He crept barefoot on hands and knees to kiss the foot of the cross, followed by the laity. Once the veneration – the Creeping of the Cross, they called it in London – was complete, Christ's burial was represented: the cross washed in water and wine and placed in a mock sepulchre – some box or nook somewhere in the church – until Easter Day dawned and the sepulchre was ritually opened to mark the miracle of the day. Showing the curtain as it was at the end of Tenebrae, tweaked back just enough to reveal the cross in deep shadow, would immediately signal to anyone looking at the picture what the thought behind the picture was.

He almost laughed with pleasure. Then he shook himself. 'But I want more from you,' he said, mock-sternly. He looked around, saw the beer, gave it a surprised glance, drank deep, and paused for breath. 'Something only you can help with,' he added. 'I want you to set your astrological instruments to show the time and day we're talking about. The darkest hour: the fourth hour in the afternoon, when Christ died on the Cross.' Kratzer nodded, as if to say, that should be easy enough. 'And I also want you to show me how to put every influence in the skies this year, on that day, at that time – like we were saying, more than a thousand years afterwards – into the picture,' Holbein went on.

Kratzer looked up from his own tankard with a comical froth moustache on his upper lip. Holbein didn't think to laugh. There was no expression on the astronomer's face. He was in the moment; thinking only how this could be done.

'What, make it a horoscope of that date this year, you mean?' Kratzer asked, consideringly. Humanists weren't supposed to trust horoscopes; but Thomas More and Pico della Mirandola before him had been so vigorously commonsensical about denouncing them as superstitious folly that many others had been perversely reminded of the store they'd always set by the predictions. Kratzer, like most people, enjoyed thinking about astrology, Holbein remembered from the hours he and Kratzer had spent together long ago designing that floating astronomical ceiling for the King; it had been full of astrological hints. So he wasn't surprised to see Kratzer's face break into a grin. The astronomer grabbed the picture. 'Pencil,' he ordered. Lightly he sketched over it the shape used by every astrologer casting a chart: the horoscope square, a square with a second square set slantwise inside it, and a third square upright again, with sides half as long as the first, inside that. That gave twelve spaces for the twelve astrological houses through which the planets moved: twelve domiciles from which planetary influences malign and benign could exert their power.

'You'll have to add an extra bit of wood at the side here,' Kratzer muttered, squeezing his left-hand line for the outside square a little inwards; 'we'll keep that crucifix right out of the horoscope square, if you don't mind.' Holbein nodded. He could see the force of the argument. It wouldn't be prudent to put Christ into an astrological chart. The rough lines Kratzer was sketching in showed the first house, beginning with the ascendant – the horizon line at the time of the chart – starting from de Dinteville's dagger.

'Look,' Kratzer said. He was scribbling signs on his lines. 'This is where the most important planets were. It's just from memory; I'll do it properly later. But this is something I've been thinking about; it's what I mean whenever I say the heavens have been full of warnings.' Holbein looked closer. He couldn't decipher the signs.

'I'll just tell you the important bits. The very beginning of Libra: in the ascendant,' Kratzer said, pointing at his stylised scribble of scales, 'in the second degree. The first degree is combatant; they draw it as a man holding a javelin in each hand. But the second degree is what they call the cleric, and they draw him with a censer, because they say Christ was born when the second degree of Libra was rising. So, a time when religion and fighting was on men's minds.'

'Then Jupiter. Jupiter is what we associate with Christ: the mightiest and most benevolent of the planets. And do you see where it is?' His finger pointed at the bottom of the horoscope square: 'Down here, in the third house, and within three degrees of falling into the lowest and darkest place of all; pretty much as inauspicious a position as it could possibly be in.'

'Finally, Saturn,' Kratzer said. 'Planet of misery and malevolence. Here,' and the finger jabbed upwards, 'in the ninth degree of Cancer. Overhead. Near to mid-heaven. At its zenith, just at the time when the planet of Christ has sunk as low as it can be.' He looked up, bony head slightly

398

cocked to the left, expecting praise. 'The darkest set of influences imaginable,' he added cheerfully. Holbein stared, nodded; felt his brain whir with ideas.

'There are plenty of other things too, though,' Kratzer said, leaning over to pull something else to draw on from Holbein's bag. He began to sketch a six-sided figure. A hexagon.

By the time the silent boy came to take away the plates and bring more beer, there were half a dozen drawings on the table, propped up against the tankards: hexagons, sketches of skulls, and several two-line scribbles shaped like wedges of pie with the number twenty-seven marked inside their two lines. This time Holbein, half-aware of the feet padding around the table, dragged himself away from the conversation for long enough to put a hand in his purse and slip the boy a coin. That was enough to bring the boy gratefully back a third time, an hour later, to clear away the tankards. He found both men asleep in their chairs, fully dressed and snoring, and the table and the floor so littered with drawings that the room looked as though a freak summer snowfall had hit it. The boy shook his head, extinguished the candle still burning at the table, and tiptoed away with the tankards in his hands.

Kratzer and Holbein woke up groaning in the midsummer dawn to a shout of birdsong. Kratzer moaned and put his hands over his eyes from where he was slumped backwards on his chair. Holbein snuffled, stirred, took two shambling steps over to his bed and collapsed fully clothed on the mattress to try and sleep out the night.

But it was too late. Ten minutes later they were staring blearily at each other, feeling their aches and pains with tired hands. 'It's morning all right,' Kratzer said, his voice blurred. 'No hiding from it. Let's go and find some food.' They pulled themselves up. Saw the pictures. And Holbein's face lit up as recollection flooded back about what they'd been doing before they passed out. 'It was worth sitting up late,' he said. 'This is good stuff.'

They were whistling so loudly as they tramped down the stairs, with the papers in their hands, that they woke the boy from his light sleep by the embers in the kitchen. It was going to be another beautiful day.

The painting raced ahead. There was no time to think of anything else. Kratzer came back so often to Holbein's place that the old man put a second mattress in the room. At dawn, the pair got up, splashed in the water butt in the yard, and went off to buy bread and ale before marching off past the traders setting up their benches, eating as they went, to Bridewell in the clear morning light. There was simply no time any more for loitering outside St Stephen Walbrook, waiting for Meg. She prayed too late; he just couldn't make that trip in the wrong direction when he had so much else on. Holbein scarcely even thought of what he'd done in the mornings before this painting began; he was filled with light; too busy and happy to remember even to eat until ravenous pangs overcame him as he and Kratzer walked back into the street during the burning afternoons, suddenly filled with divine appetite for bread, cheese and beer. The ambassadors were delighted with their artist's and astrologer's theme and ingenious ideas. They arranged for a green Lenten veil to be brought up from the chapel and hung behind them. For all their Catholic sensibilities, they even agreed to leave Kratzer's hymnal in the picture, turned to Luther's German-language rendering of 'Veni Sancte Spiritus' to strengthen the notion of religious difference being the theme of the time.

The ambassadors were fascinated, too, by the examples Kratzer gave them, over the many goblets of wine with which the painter and his sitters relaxed and stretched their limbs between work sessions, of the spiritual power of the hexagons and six-pointed shapes that Holbein was scattering through the work. Hexagons were beloved by astrologers (signifying planets in harmonious conjunction with each other) and by alchemists (for whom they signified the harmonious union of the sun, gold, the Lion – Leo – and kinghood on the one hand, and the moon, silver, the Crab – Cancer – and the feminine on the other; a marriage illustrated in books by pictures of a king and a queen holding flower stems which, with the help of a falling bird in whose beak is a third stem, combine to make a six-pointed star, with a bigger six-pointed star hovering over the whole picture). Holbein's hexagrams and stars were in the spirit of the marble floor at Westminster Abbey, which he was painting now as if it were under the ambassadors' feet. The hexagon at the heart of that floor – the place where a king being crowned at the Abbey would stand as the Holy Spirit descended on him – symbolised the six days in which God created the universe and everything within it. Holbein's hexagons represented the focus of the creative act. They were his rendering of the Holy Spirit; his way of showing the faint hope that all mankind could again be blessed by a shared understanding of God.

The ambassadors chuckled over the many imaginative ways and places in which Holbein and Kratzer managed to put the number twenty-seven and the angle of twenty-seven degrees – a reminder of the altitude of the sun at the time Christ died on the afternoon of the first Good Friday – into the picture. Their only stipulation was that Holbein buy the extra strip of wood for the side of the picture – a place of honour for the sacred image of the crucifix at its left-most edge, away from the game with the horoscope. He attached it himself, proud to think of the shape the picture was taking, with his mind singing louder than the birds outside the window and the boys selling the first strawberries on the street.

401

It was only a few weeks into the job, when the boards were already covered with colour and the red underlay on the bishop's robe was almost dry, that they had the other idea. Afterwards, Holbein couldn't quite say whose idea it had been. Perhaps de Dinteville had been called away to see the King, or to be checked over by the doctor, as he sometimes was, but the other three of them had all been talking. They'd all been contributing. That was one of the joys of working in this group – their minds all sparked off each other's, sharpening each other's wit, just as he remembered it happening with Thomas More or Erasmus. So perhaps it was his idea as much as anyone's. It was certainly he who had thought of the shape that the conceit could take.

'What about the *memento mori*?' one of the Frenchmen had said, stretching arms and legs after Holbein had made them both stand immobile for what they clearly felt was too long. 'What will you use for that?'

Holbein's eye went to the skull on his work table, littered with bottles and papers and jars and odds and ends of cloth. The skull was the classic way to mark human decay; to show how vain are scholarship and power when confronted by the inevitability of death. Anyone exalted by looking at a portrait must be reminded that they should not forget the end to come or their fear of God. 'I was once what you are, and you will one day be what I am,' was the *memento mori*'s message. 'Pray for me.' Why not a skull?

Yet suddenly he wasn't sure. Suddenly his head was full of Meg's long-ago voice, urging him to amuse her father by including a less obvious *memento mori*; suddenly he remembered the picture of More, with the rope that had ended up serving as *memento mori* dangling behind that other green curtain. When this picture was finished, he wanted to show it to More and Meg as a way of explaining himself; as a way of apologising for not coming to them before. Might there be something that would impress them that he could come up with here, too? Perhaps a skull was too obvious? Might the ambassadors laugh behind his back at his hackneyed imagination if he suggested it?

He hesitated.

It was the Bishop who spoke next. He remembered that. 'I would imagine that an artist with as fertile an imagination as yours wants something striking and unusual enough to be proud of as your *memento mori*,' he said with great courtesy. It was an invitation to think further. Holbein seized on the permission.

'For all its secrets . . . however much we talk about religion and things of the spirit . . . this is a very worldly picture,' Holbein said, feeling uneasily that he was edging towards taboo, trying to choose his words carefully. 'Its subjects,' he bowed slightly, 'are noblemen of the highest degree . . . anyone who looked at it would be impressed both by the breadth of their learning and by their elevated position . . .'

He didn't know himself quite what he was driving at.

'You don't know how to remind us that even we noblemen, in our velvet robes, must die, do you?' de Selve said, and his young face broke into the most understanding of smiles. 'But Master Hans, you mustn't let yourself be over-impressed by our station in life. I can't talk for my colleague, but I would imagine he feels like me; and personally I never forget that I must one day meet my Maker. Earthly life, after all, is only men in a cave, believing that reality is the shadows they see cast on the walls. I want you to play the part of the philosopher who gets out of the cave, and sees the bigger reality.'

He laughed at Holbein's bewilderment. 'Here, Master Hans. So far your picture shows two men looking at some very golden shadows on a cave wall and taking them for reality. Look at us!' and he strode round, robe swishing at his ankles, to where Holbein stood behind his easel, and pointed out the velvet, the fine gold chasing on de Dinteville's dagger and the jewels, marks of favour, dangling at wrist and cap and neck.

Hardly knowing how he dared, Holbein laughed too. He said, full of relief: 'It's true. You couldn't look grander.'

'So,' the Bishop pursued. 'A good *memento mori* would be one which excluded and overshadowed us as completely as possible; which pushed us to the background of the picture. Which reminded us that God is waiting, behind all our earthly baubles. And the work you've done on us men watching the cave wall is so striking, so true to life, and so full of spirit and wit that you will need to find something truly extraordinary to eclipse us.'

He wandered back to his place. 'I wonder what you'll come up with,' he added easily. 'I can assure you we won't be offended, whatever it is. I'm looking forward to making fresh discoveries about the power of your mind.'

And now it was Kratzer who was leaning forward, with an intensity that Holbein knew from his own moments of almost panicky grasping at an idea.

'I know,' Kratzer said, grasping the skull. 'I think I know. We have to go back to the twenty-seven degrees.

'Look,' Kratzer went on. He couldn't draw, but he was a wonder at angles. He took Holbein's notebook and sketched in stick figures representing the picture – two ambassadors and the table loaded with scribbly instruments between them. Then, with a much heavier hand, he drew a horizontal line bisecting the sketch. 'This is my lower line,' he said. 'And this is my upper line.' He took an instrument and measured a second line diverging from this horizontal axis – like a slice of pie – moving upwards and leftward across the image. His line reached the top left-hand corner just at the spot where Holbein's shadowy crucifix peeped out from behind the green Lenten veil.

'I knew that would work,' Kratzer said with satisfaction. 'Now, here's my point. Stand at the right-hand side of this picture and look upward along this line and you will see the crucifix – a hope of God, eternity, salvation, even if it's in shadow and in doubt. Your *memento mori* should be a reflection of that. Something that you'll see by looking downwards from the same point, at a reflection of the same angle. The opposite of the hope of salvation. Something – here,' and he drew the downward line, like a second slice of pie, to a place somewhere below the two central figures' feet.

'To be honest,' Holbein said, understanding better and better what was needed now, and with the glimmering of an idea of how to achieve it. 'I can't think of anything simpler or better for the purpose than a skull.'

But not an ordinary skull, painted in an ordinary way. Holbein was almost certain that he knew how to do what he needed to do. He'd spent enough time doing special effects as a jobbing draughtsman back home that he'd tried every trick in the book. Quietly, he thanked God, and his father, for that long apprenticeship in the art of the possible.

They stopped painting while a servant was sent out to buy a good thin piece of clear glass. The Bishop could have returned to his books or his correspondence, but he was too intrigued by the fever gripping Holbein and the others to want to leave.

The servant came back with the glass. Holbein mixed up a palette of paints to depict his familiar old skull prop: browns and greys and shadows. His hands were itching to begin. On the glass, he laid down lines – the shadows of eye sockets, broken nose and jaw. He almost cursed with impatience, under his breath, as he waited for the paint to dry. Kratzer and the Bishop, not wanting to disturb his train of thought, stood back at the window, watching the world go by, or turning back to watch him and his inspiration.

'Do you have a candle?' Holbein asked. He went to the window, but not to join the others. Instead, he reached past them, grabbed the curtains and yanked them shut.

In the semi-darkness, followed by the other two men, he went to the big painting at his easel. Once at his place, he measured off the twenty-seven degree angle upwards, leading from the right-hand side of the image up to the crucified Christ. On his real picture, the starting point was much lower than half-way down the painting; Holbein made it somewhere around the Bishop's velvet-clad knee. Then he measured the twenty-seven degrees leading down from that right-hand starting point, and painted – freehand, with the thinnest line imaginable (he wasn't known as Apelles for nothing, after all) – a perfectly straight line down towards the bottom left-hand corner of the picture.

Then he lit the candle. 'Hold this,' he told Kratzer, brusquely. Kratzer took it. Holbein held his painting on glass of the skull up, at an angle, against the big painting. 'Move the candle close to the glass,' he said. Kratzer obeyed, and as the candle moved it cast a long shadow up the twenty-seven degree line, up the painting. The Bishop moved closer.

'Look,' Holbein said. They gasped. There it was: the most enigmatic *memento mori* imaginable. The distorted shadow of a skull, cast at twenty-seven degrees from the horizontal. A mysterious, flickering, slightly menacing shape, with something of the night about it even before you realised what it was. And then, once your eye and brain did seize it, once you shifted to the strange sideways angle at the edge of the painting that you needed to be at if the skull was to take realistic shape, once the real-life subjects of the picture – the ambassadors – had faded to insignificant two-dimensional blobs of paint and pomp that your eye couldn't follow, then the *memento mori* became a bizarre, provoking puzzle; an eye-catching proof that you

406

were in the presence of sacred mysteries while you looked at this picture, whether your eye was led upwards to the shaded, suffering presence of possible eternal life or downwards to the shadowy, distorted certainty of death.

'I'll paint this in, shall I?' he said; a question, but he already knew the answer.

'Yes,' said Kratzer simply.

'Excellent,' said the Bishop.

'Come on, hold the candle yourself so I can take a look from the right,' Kratzer said impatiently. They swapped. Kratzer shuffled round with a hand over one eye, squinting to the left, raising and lowering his head until he got himself into the one place at which the skull undistorted itself and became the only truly drawn figure on the entire canvas.

Then he nodded, and grinned. 'Yes,' he said. 'Oui, oui, oui! It really works. This will be the most unusual picture ever painted. You're a genius, my friend!'

For a glorious moment, Holbein knew it. Every clever detail he and Kratzer had thought of was part of the same sombre message: he was showing a world which had once been united by religious harmony but was now being destroyed by nationalist ugliness and factional feuding. He was using the things of this earthly life to tell a solemn story about the divisions rending God's universe asunder. He'd seen a deeper kind of truth, and revealed it.

It was only much later that evening – after a self-congratulatory stop at the alehouse with Kratzer – that Holbein made his way back up Ludgate Hill towards his lodgings. For once he was alone. Kratzer had burped sleepily as they left and said it was time he slept in his own bed for once; he was getting smelly enough to make a change of linen urgently necessary. 'You don't need me to talk to tonight,' he slurred, 'we've solved all the problems in this painting now.' And he wandered off down the alley to the river.

Holbein was listening to the drunks and the nightingales sing as his feet planted themselves, one in front of the other, on the filth of the street. His heart was singing too. No one had commented on the symbolism for the painting that he'd first thought of – the simplest game of all – in which every one of the strong diagonals around which he'd constructed his painting led to the mulberry skirt of de Selve's robe. His own idea had been for the true meaning of the painting to be mulberry colour – *morus* to those who spoke Latin, like the tree More grew in his own back garden and, symbolically, on his coat of arms: More's name for himself. The lesson he wanted to learn from making this painting was one anyone who saw it could also remember: that every eye would be drawn to the colour that was an eternal reminder of More; that *'memento mori'* can also mean just 'Remember More'. That would have been enough for him before he'd begun the intellectual voyage of discovery that he'd made in the past few weeks with Kratzer and the Frenchmen. But now, with all the extra layers of meaning and wisdom that four intelligent men had managed to pack into it, his painting was going to be a more elaborate triumph. He grinned, slowed down as he skirted the cathedral, and filled his lungs with hot, smelly, happy night air. It was time to start taking more exercise, he was thinking cheerfully; it was bad to be so breathless after nothing worse than that small hill.

He hardly noticed the tall, thin figure in a cloak disengage itself from a wall near his house as he turned into Maiden Lane. There were always stray people about on a summer evening, taking the air, thinking their thoughts, weren't there? He hardly heard the light footsteps patter along behind his.

For a few minutes, at least. And then he began to worry. The street was deserted. He didn't want to have to fight for his life without hope of help if this was a footpad attack. He whipped around, ready to attack.

But the face staring wide-eyed back at him from under the hood of the cloak stopped him in his tracks. It was a well-bred face; a face from his dreams, if a strangely unfamiliar one now. A woman's face – at least as far as he could tell in what was left of the twilight.

He froze. His heart was beating even louder now. He didn't know his mouth had opened until he found himself speaking. Gargling, more like: with the air suddenly rasping into his lungs making him realise he hadn't breathed for several agonisingly long seconds.

And the word his lips were forming, independent of anything he could recognise as his own will, was: 'Meg . . . ?'

But, before he could move forward to grab her shoulders, the stranger with Meg's face had taken to her heels and fled off away from St Paul's, vanishing eastward into the evening's uncertain light. Hans Holbein's head was spinning. It couldn't really have been her, could it? Could it? Or was it just a drunken mirage – his brain playing tricks on him? He'd never know now. He was a little tipsy, alone under the stars in Maiden Lane, and all he had in his hands were shadows.

18

When I saw him back outside my house the next morning, as if he'd never been away, a great rush of joy went through my body. It was as if I'd been drenched in sunlight.

And then I almost laughed at the sight of him, waiting for me to go to church and congratulating himself on his subtle hiding place. It was typical of Master Hans that he'd choose to wait by the pissing conduit as if about to relieve himself. I think he genuinely believed that would make him invisible to a lady; he couldn't imagine I'd actually be able to see him doing something so physical. It had made me laugh quietly into my psalter the first time I'd seen him hanging round up there, nearly a year ago, stealing glances at me from under his golden eyelashes. But perhaps my laughter had been relief as much as anything else: relief that he'd turned up, that he was there, undecided, wavering, so nervous of our family disgrace that he didn't dare come up to me and say good day in a straightforward way, but at least wanting to resume a friendship from before our lives went dark enough to hover nervously at the corner of the street for hours on end. I'd found the comical sight of him strangely comforting. I scarcely admitted it to myself at the time but gradually, as the season rolled by and he went on faithfully being there, I'd found myself dressing up for my early morning church outings more carefully than before: dressing up to look more elegant, but also to look wistful, sadder, thinner, paler, and more tragic than before; and sighing gently as I unseeingly passed him by. Things were certainly bad enough to sigh and look wistful anyway; it wasn't that I was pretending to have these feelings. But for reasons I didn't completely understand myself it was reassuring to know someone was watching me feel that way.

So I couldn't believe it when, suddenly, he wasn't there one morning in spring. And then not the next morning, or the next. He just stopped coming. I looked and looked for him, scared by the emptiness inside me at the idea he'd gone for good. But however hard I looked, he wasn't there.

Perhaps I shouldn't have been surprised that Davy knew him. Davy always knew everything. Davy sidled up to me in the street one day after church, as I was furtively looking round while pretending to trail home without thinking of a thing. 'Your admirer's stopped hanging round, innee,' Davy said. He put his head on one side. He looked inquiringly at me. I shrugged as if I didn't know what he was talking about, but I kept my face soft and welcoming. I didn't talk much to Davy these days – I'd stopped buying medicine or going on the street more than I had to so there were few chances of accidental meetings; our family disgrace made me want to keep away from crowds of people in case of chance unpleasantnesses; and in any case Davy didn't try that hard to keep my friendship either. Perhaps cynically, I thought it was because Father no longer held his job. I thought it was because there was no point in converting me to heresy any more; I'd stopped being a prize worth winning. He never gave any sign, for instance, of knowing that when he saw me and Kate in the street, with baskets on our arms, we might be on our way to tend his flock. I still treated the Lutheran sick, from time to time, even if I went out less than before. There weren't so many of them so afraid of the authorities any more that they chose to exist underground, among their own. And I didn't want to bring more danger down on my family; things were bad enough as they were. But at the same time I didn't want to lose altogether the quiet companionship I'd developed with my fellow nurse, the flicker of something maternal I sometimes surprised in Kate's grey eyes. So I looked about for people from outside Davy's cellar to treat; and brought Kate with me sometimes when I dressed the sores of the poor of St Stephen's and fed broth to the elderly. Still, in my new circumstances a grateful-ish smile was politic; people with as few friends as we had these days couldn't afford to toss their heads and be high and mighty to street salesmen any more, even if they were being impertinent.

'Master Hans, I mean,' Davy went on, giving me another little nod as he watched me keep my face impassive at the mention of that name. 'Holbein.' Davy was like a city bird, a sparrow or a raven, I thought: all chirps and dirty feathers and knowing looks and sudden bursts of intent intelligence. 'Living over at Maiden Lane,' and he gestured towards St Paul's. 'Not surprising he can't find the time at the moment though. They say he's working down Fleet way now. Painting the French ambassador. Early starts.'

The French ambassador had put up at Bridewell Palace, I knew; over the Fleet, and even further west than Maiden Lane. 'Oh,' I said, and felt myself blushing with relief. Davy smiled secretively at his feet. 'Nice to talk to you, anyway, Mistress Meg,' he said, and ambled off without looking back. I thought about it a lot afterwards but I couldn't work out why, if Davy was acting

412

as agent provocateur for some enemy of my father's, as he might easily be, he'd have been interested in telling me that particular piece of comforting information. The only explanation that seemed remotely plausible was that he was being kind. It was as if he were sorry for me. Or was that just me being naïve?

A lot of things were confusing just then. Perhaps it was the spring playing tricks on me. Perhaps it was the fear for Father and the rest of us that ran through everything now. Perhaps it was not having anyone much to talk to, with old friends keeping a watchful distance, and the servants so tricky and easy to take offence and leaving faster than I could hire new ones. Or perhaps it was John being out of the house so much and our love, which had lost its old innocence, still so watchful and cautious and threadbare of trust. The spring weeks of war were over, at least, and we'd gone back to trying to be good to each other – though now it was me, full of remorse, who was trying to make up to him for my betrayal. I didn't know what to do to take the sad, lost look off his face. Whenever I apologised, he'd just smile gently and say, 'It doesn't matter', and 'Don't worry, Meg', and 'It was bound to come out sooner or later', with the generous kindness I was only now realising I loved, but with none of the warmth I now realised I missed. So I tried subtler ways of feeling towards re-establishing his trust. I pounded his medicines for him. I embroidered his linens and strewed lavender in his chests. And he thanked me for each gesture with wistful, remote smiles and small chaste kisses on my head or cheeks. But, though he'd come back to sleep in my bed since we returned from Chelsea, he slept exhaustedly at the extreme edge of it, as far as possible from me, with his back turned. I couldn't see his heart. What everyday conversations we had at table, over the meals that I supervised with more anxious care than ever before,

413

were fitful and broken. And he left the house every day to meet Dr Butts far earlier than he ever had before, and never brought him inside our house in the evenings. How could I have been so suspicious of him? I wondered, now that my fear he might have more secrets to hurt me with had faded away, now that there seemed nothing more desirable than taking refuge from the cares of the world in private love, as I tried to win back the ease we'd once had with each other. Often it felt hopeless, struggling to find a way out of this cloud of contrition and regret, penitence and discouragement; with too little chance of success, and too much my own stupid fault to be bearable.

I drew what hope I could from a murmured conversation I overheard between him and Butts, holding their horses' bridles, saying goodbye to each other under my window one evening. 'Give my regards to your lovely wife, dear boy,' I heard the doctor say archly, while I drew as close to the window as I dared, hoping to hear what John would say without being seen; 'I hope she's well?' He must wonder why he wasn't invited in any more. He must be angling for information. Perhaps that harmless old man might even worry that it was his fault; that he'd somehow given offence. The thought wrung my heart. 'As well as can be expected,' John was saying, quietly, loyally. 'Of course these are hard times for all of us.' Then he laughed, gently, more to himself than to Butts but with genuine warmth. 'I'm learning that marriage is a bit like medicine, Dr Butts,' he went on. 'If you open your heart to someone, whether it's a doctor or a wife, it's inevitable that you expose yourself to pain. Shocks. Disappointments. Luckily I can see that the healing process is very similar in both cases too. If you have faith in your remedy, and go on doing your honest best to achieve a cure for long enough, you find the right way in the end.' They both chuckled, and Butts reached up to pat John sympathetically on the shoulder before setting off for his own home. Did that mean, I wondered, heart racing, that John knew he'd forgive me as soon as his hurt had healed; that he felt his wound knitting back together; that it was just a question of time? 'We must ask you in for a meal again,' John called after his colleague, mounted now, retreating into the twilight. 'Soon.'

Meanwhile, Tommy was my consolation: rising four now, with a peachy skin and that elegant little nose that would one day be his father's great beak, and John's elegant hands too, lisping and running determinedly round the garden. But whether there'd be any more children, even if John were to find his old joy in me, I couldn't have said. However modest the dose of pennyroyal I'd taken in my angry attempt to purge my womb of his baby, it had set off its own fury of bleeding and pain. It was beyond my medical knowledge to try to treat myself. All I could do was hope that my sickness, like so much else in my life, would cure itself. So perhaps it was no wonder that everything seemed so confusing. Distinguishing reasons had become too complicated for my overtaxed mind.

And perhaps that's why I missed the sight of Master Hans looking nervously at me out of the corner of his eyes so much that I took a chance and went to Maiden Lane one evening. Perhaps I was missing the hearty simplicity, the joyous lust for life that I remembered in him. I didn't go just once, if I'm to be honest about it. I went several times. Time after time, as spring deepened into summer, whispering to the maid that I was just off to stretch my legs if the master asked where I was, slipping away in the warm dusk on my private business and coming back as quietly as I could more than an hour later.

It took two or three visits before I saw his back in the shadows and identified the house where he'd taken rooms. After that I went past, as if by chance, whenever I could get away. Sometimes I saw that solid, purposeful back again; more often I didn't. I had a lot of time on my hands. It was something to do; something to keep me feeling alive.

But I'd have given anything to avoid running into him on the street. Anything. I ran home afterwards with my heart beating as if it would burst and a lump of shame swelling so big in my throat that it seemed to be pushing out into my mouth. I stayed awake, pacing around in the dark garden until the city was completely quiet except for the occasional wavering footsteps of a drunk, shutting my eyes against the recurring nausea of embarrassment at the memory. His hands on me. His eyes boring into mine. Hands on my shoulders. His voice, a bit slurred, a bit drunk, muttering: 'Meg . . . ?'

Still, one good thing had come out of it. He was here this morning. I saw him hanging round outside the church door from my bedroom window ten minutes before the bell rang for Matins. He wasn't taking any chances today. He had no intention of missing me. And, through the window, as he stared up, he was exactly as he'd always been: big, gingery, capable, determined, and so visibly ill at ease and anxious about what he might or might not have seen the night before that my heart warmed painfully towards him. My heart was lurching like a lunatic's anyway.

'Tommy, you'll have more fun playing in the orchard than coming to church on a beautiful morning like this,' I said, pulling my lovely little dark boy off the bed with my hands under his armpits and swinging him against my dress, loving the small, solid barrel-chested strength of him.

'But I lub Matins with you, Muvver,' he lisped indignantly in his treble voice. '*Pater noster quis es in coelis*. I know it all.'

416

I kissed the top of his head, put him down on the floor and placed his hand in the maid's. 'Yes, I know, you're doing really well. But today you and Jennet go and water the apple trees,' I said briskly, with not a moment's regret. 'You'll be pleased you did when we have apple pie in the autumn.' And, as they went downstairs, I whisked quickly over to the glass on the wall to look guiltily at my face: the pallor and pinched panic of so many recent days vanished; instead a flush of what I feared might be excitement on my cheeks. Sparkling eyes. Pink lips. I looked better than I had for months.

I sprinkled sweet rosewater on my cuff before picking up my psalter. Absent-mindedly; I swear I didn't mean to. Then I slipped away down the stairs to Mass feeling my feet almost fly over the boards. I couldn't explain even to myself why I was suddenly almost floating.

I pretended not to see him on the way into church. Under the brilliant sunshine, under the pretty whiteness of my lace and bonnet, I stared at my feet, looking soulful. It wasn't just pretence; I needed to compose myself. I needed a moment alone with God.

And then, somewhere in that moment with God, in the welcoming of candle and shadow and incense and holiness and peace, I decided to brazen it out. On the way out, after I'd blinked into the sunlight and seen that the crowds were already pressing up and down the road and no one was paying particular attention to me, I raised my eyes straight to the waiting figure down the way from me and watched him blush a deep pinky-red that clashed with his dirty blond hair.

'Master Hans!' I exclaimed, a little unkindly, a little theatrically, but with the welcome in my eyes undercutting any tartness. 'You're back in London! What a surprise!'

He was thunderstruck.

He stood for a long moment as if turned to stone. Only his big, solid snubby face – like a child's, like a great adult version of Tommy's, I suddenly saw, with a surprised stab of almost maternal affection – was too open to hide the emotions chasing through his heart. I saw fear and embarrassment on that face, struggling with something else, making his eyes open wide and his neck tighten and his teeth chew at his lower lip.

I didn't mind. All the fear that I'd found went with living in the darkness of the King's disfavour meant I'd learned more about the kind of life calculations other people had always had to make: who they should or shouldn't be seen with if their careers were to prosper; how to keep themselves on the up; how to avoid the shadow of someone else's misfortune falling on them. I'd never needed to think about that before trouble came to us: we'd been so settled. Now, watching Master Hans, I felt sympathy for his dilemma.

It was the something else in his heart that won, though. As he finally conquered himself and rushed forward to greet me, his arms came out as if he would embrace me and a look of pure, innocent joy suffused his features.

'Mistress Meg!' he said, with happiness powering those broad shoulders forward. He came to a halt towering over me, very close, so I could smell the familiar painty smell that always came off him, but when it came to it he didn't quite dare put his arms around me. 'I've come . . .' and he fell silent, and blushed again, and shuffled his feet, 'I'm here . . .'

Once upon a time, I remembered dreamily, I'd found his uncourtly straightforwardness both uncouth and often, unintentionally, funny. But after all this time living uneasily with the secrets inside my own family, avoiding them – my husband and father and sisters – with gentle words and polite skating around on the surface of our lives, and

418

becoming aware of so many people outside our family stepping quietly to the other side of the road and looking the other way when we passed, I was rejoicing in the visible play of honest emotions on this man's intelligent face.

'I'm joking, Master Hans,' I said gently. His discomfiture was allowing me to feel mistress of the situation, so much so that I even dared to put a reassuring hand on his arm. I liked the feel of muscle under my hand, and the start he suppressed at my touch. 'I've seen you in the street. I knew you were here.'

Another wave of crimson. His mouth opened again, gasping for air. Was he realising for the first time that I might have been watching him watching me from the street for all those months? My confidence was growing; I felt almost playful as I watched him.

'Last night, you mean?' he spluttered, and now it was suddenly my turn to feel heat sweep over my face and body. I'd forgotten last night. Or, if I hadn't quite forgotten it, I'd never have expected him to bring it up to my face. 'In Maiden Lane? Was that you?'

'I . . . Last night?' I said faintly, playing for time. 'Maiden Lane?'

It was in my mind to deny it. Pretending things weren't happening was coming to seem quite natural. But the eyes fixed on me were full of knowledge. And it didn't seem in the spirit of this meeting to hide from the truth completely.

'Heavens. Was it you who stopped me?' I asked, trying a light smile. 'And there I was thinking it must be a footpad. I was so scared I ran away without even looking . . .' It sounded unconvincing. We both remembered staring into each other's eyes. 'I was coming back from Mass at St Paul's,' I went on hesitantly, feeling my way towards the truth. That sounded weak too. So I blurted, in an

419

embarrassed rush, 'and I'd heard somewhere that you were living there, so I took a look . . .'

I was mortified by the delighted understanding that was dawning on his face now.

'You came to see where I lived?' he said, completely failing to whisper, so loud that a man passing by with a bottle of oil turned to look at us. 'You did that?'

'Well, I was intrigued that you'd been living just down the road for a year and hadn't come to call!' I answered, nettled enough to feel safer going on the attack.

He nodded his head, then shook it, and scuffed the toe of one big boot against another. 'Yes,' he said, with shame written all over him. 'I know. I can explain . . . but you must think . . . you know, Erasmus wanted me to come straightaway . . . but I wanted to set myself up first . . . get myself straight . . . so you'd admire what I'm making of myself.'

His English was better than before. He even had a slight London twang. And I saw he'd learned at least a touch of English hypocrisy too: he wasn't going to mention Father's downfall. I felt my heart melt at the transparency of his wish to steer clear of that painful subject and whether it had affected his plans to see us after he got back to England.

'But I've come now,' he said, eager as a puppy, and his face lightened. He'd suddenly remembered something; whatever it was that had given him the courage to come back to the street outside my home. 'I've come, and I've got something to show you. Something I've done. A picture I'm proud of. I think you'll like it. I hope you'll like it. And your father.' He paused. 'And your husband, of course,' he added unwillingly. He took a deep breath and stood up straight. 'I want to invite you . . . all . . . to my lodgings to see it.'

I was awash with tenderness now. 'We'd love to,' I said

warmly, knowing that my smile was going to put just that look of bliss on his face. 'Truly.' He glowed, and the eyes fixed on mine were smiling. Then he recollected himself, as if our entire conversation had been a happy daydream he'd got caught up in and he was coming back to reality. He looked round, looked up at the sun, stepped back from me and did a little bobbing bow as if he were about to move hastily away.

'But Master Hans,' I said, catching the meaning behind his movement, not wanting to end this conversation that was bringing back the ease of the old days with such painfully nostalgic force, 'won't you come in and take a glass of something with me? We have so much to catch up on after all this time. There's so much I want to ask you about what you've been doing,' and I let my voice trail wistfully away. (Had I always known the flirtatious ways that seemed to be coming so naturally now? I wondered, catching myself.)

'I should be off,' he said hastily, with embarrassment making him suddenly boorish. He cast a queasy look at my front door. I was almost hurt, until it occurred to me that perhaps he didn't want to see the reality of my married life behind that door, a thought that brought a lump to my throat. 'Work,' he went on, staccato. 'And I've kept you too long.'

He was shuffling backwards now, squinting up against the sun. 'It's good to see you, Mistress Meg,' he said awkwardly. 'Sunday at noon?' And before I could answer he'd flipped around and was striding off, planting one muscular leg after another on the flagstones at a speed that wouldn't have taken much increasing to turn into a run.

I planned the Sunday visit carefully. I told John I wanted to go to Mass with Father at St Paul's. I left my husband with Tommy at home. I told Father that John couldn't join us at church because he was busy with his work. I only told Father about the plan to call in on Master Hans in Maiden Lane once we were shriven and on our way out of the churchyard. I didn't want to deceive John; but I thought Master Hans would be more at ease with just the two of us.

'Our old friend Hans Holbein!' Father had said, with his new quietness, though with every appearance of pleasure, 'now that's a surprise.' He must have known Master Hans had gone from making the portrait of Thomas Elyot, our friend, to painting almost every one of our foes in the Boleyn circle as the fashion for portraiture developed. But he didn't make any further comment, just walked on humming under his breath in the intense July sunshine. He looked so pale in the fierce light that I remembered Dame Alice's worries about the pains in his chest and his bad sleep. I didn't dare ask him to his face, though; I knew how he hated to lose his dignity.

Master Hans wasn't exactly at ease. He was watching out for us on the street corner. His face lit up when he saw us, though he skittered round me without meeting my eyes before bowing enthusiastically at Father (but, I wondered, was he secretly noticing how Father seemed to have shrunk into himself, getting shorter and stringier and thinner in the face by the week, with grey in his strong black hair?). Master Hans only paused for a minute to bask in the glow of Father's smile – which was still as powerful and golden and enchanting as ever – before hurrying us into his doorway. I thought perhaps he didn't want to be seen in the street with us. He lived in upstairs rooms at the end of a dingy staircase. There was silence downstairs, and no welcoming smells of cooking. 'They've gone out,' he said shiftily as he shepherded us up the stairs, 'the old man and the boy who do for me. But they've left food for us in my rooms.'

There was a table with wooden platters groaning with bread and cheese and beef and a big jug of ale and a glitter of newly polished pewter, and a cloud of tiny wildflowers on wiry stems in another big jug. Someone in this all-male household had made an effort to please. There was too much food for just three of us. However much Master Hans might wolf down, I was so nervous my appetite had gone completely, and Father, who'd always been abstemious anyway, scarcely ate a thing any more.

Then I realised I was the only one who was looking at the food and worrying about the social arrangements. Master Hans was worrying about his picture. 'This is what I wanted to show you,' he said urgently, not bothering with politeness and pleasantries, getting his arm under Father's elbow as we entered the room and drawing him straight to the room's side wall, where, at this time of day, sunlight slanted through the open window. The painting took up almost all of it: a huge square thing on big wooden boards, bigger than the door frame, taller than a man, propped up on a bench.

Father looked at the picture glowing against that dingy wall. It showed two young men in court clothes, standing on either side of a table.

There was a long pause. I gazed at it too. Technically the painting was even more accomplished than the earlier pictures that I'd seen. But there was something new in it that I didn't altogether like: less of Master Hans's old, rich, straightforward simplicity; instead, some more subtle intelligence whispering stories beneath the surface that I could sense were there but couldn't make out. The composition seemed crowded to me; the centre piled with detail; and with a long, mysterious scar at the bottom, sloping sharply upwards and to the right.

But I could see Father liked it. He was entering into the spirit of this game. He was puzzling out the secret stories in the picture. He moved to the far right of it. He squinted back down from there at the sloping scar, moving around until he found exactly the right place from which to view it. And suddenly he grunted with satisfaction. He'd solved the visual puzzle. 'I see,' he said to himself, then, to me, 'it's a skull, if you look at it from here,' – pause – 'and if you look at it from here you can't see anything much of the rest of the painting; the Frenchmen become shadows on the wall; like Plato's cave.' We all paused, and I could see a wistful memory of Erasmus enjoying his favourite story, about the men in the cave believing the shadows on the wall to be reality, while only the philosopher who got out of the cave seeing the bigger truth, come to each of us.

Then, stepping back to look again at the painted astronomical instruments on the table, Father turned to Master Hans to say, 'It's about angles, isn't it? It's an astronomer's painting.' Then he stepped back up to the painting to see the skull, stopped squinting downwards and started looking upwards at the same angle, with his eye following the natural upward diagonal in the portrait, from the hand of one sitter and upward along the sloping red slashed-satin arm of the other to . . . Now what was that behind the green Lenten curtain at the end of the upward diagonal? Father moved leftward. I shuffled along behind him, drawn despite myself into the game.

It was a crucifix. In deep shadow. Almost invisible. Almost covered by the veil. As if it were Good Friday and the priest had just begun to twitch back the curtain.

Father paused again and looked at Master Hans with growing appreciation. 'You've become an astronomer, Master Hans,' he said, and his voice was as relaxed as if five years hadn't gone by since he'd last been in a room with the German and as if we weren't all now in a room with hardly a word spoken between us to explain ourselves. 'And,' he gave Master Hans a searching look, 'a theologian; and perhaps an astrologer too?'

Master Hans nodded. Father darted to the middle of the picture. He was eyeing the angle at which an arithmetic book showing a division sum under the German word *dividirt* was held open by a set square; and the very similar angle at which one side of an open hymnal in German was raised from the table by a bundle of four flutes.

'The same angle,' he said; a question. Master Hans nodded, intent, delighted, watching Father's quick mind work out answers. 'And the same angle as the big lines taking you from the skull to the crucifix – your *memento mori*?'

Master Hans nodded again, almost bursting with excitement. They were almost hissing at each other now, lost in their play of minds.

'What angle is it?'

'Twenty-seven degrees.'

'And we're to think of grief: Lent, and Good Friday, and Christ behind the curtain . . .'

Father wrapped one crooked arm around his waist, with the hand catching the elbow of his other arm. His second hand was cupping his chin. He was deep in thought.

Master Hans couldn't wait. 'Twenty-seven degrees was the altitude of the sun this Good Friday, in mid-afternoon, at the time Christ died,' he blurted. 'The skull is a record of the shadows cast by that sun: not just the usual *memento mori*,' and he flashed a little shared-secret grin at me as he said the phrase '*memento mori*'.

Father smiled. A new smile. A degree of infectious joy to match Master Hans's own. 'This Good Friday. The Easter weekend when the Lady Anne was proclaimed . . .' He couldn't finish the sentence with the word 'Queen', but he'd seen the secret sense of the picture: Master Hans was grieving as he was for the destruction of the common Church and the darkness into which life was slipping. He'd portrayed the time of Anne Boleyn's rise as the end of the civilisation we knew.

'Yes!' Master Hans was saying, and, unable to restrain himself any longer, like an errant schoolboy forgiven, or a friend, he stepped forward and clapped his big bear-paw on Father's shoulder. 'I knew you'd see.'

How had I thought the room dingy? The air was full of doves as we sat down to eat; the ale golden as honey. And suddenly we could talk, as we hadn't been able to for months. The picture glowed before us and Father and I went on hunting for elements of the games Master Hans had been playing – an inexhaustible stream of inventiveness. There were big thoughts, part of his idea that the times were full of foreboding and that civilised life was being torn apart by religious strife. The marble floor looked like the Westminster Abbey pavement where kings were anointed, a marriage of heaven and earth; and there were magical hexagons at the top and bottom of the picture, a mathematical device signifying the otherworldly, and, as Master Hans showed us when we didn't understand quickly enough, the composition also contained a hidden astrology square of the dark planetary configurations on that day when Father's fate had been sealed. There were details, too, that struck me from time to time, making me so fond of Master Hans that once I had to choke on my bread and cheese and lean into my ale to hide my feelings. There was something endearing about the little hints of flattery to the Frenchman who'd commissioned him – Polisy marked as an important place in France on the same globe, say. And I loved the spelling mistakes his German pronunciation led him astray on: 'Pritannia' for Britanny and 'Baris' for Paris on the terrestrial globe.

'You were once going to come back and do some final alterations to our portrait, Master Hans,' Father said, stretching contentedly back in his seat, pushing away his wooden board. 'Do you remember? But it was a long time ago, and I hardly like to ask you now. You've become a busy man. Perhaps you don't have time . . .'

We all knew nothing more need be done to the painting. It didn't need the lutes and chairs Father had once asked for. What he was really talking about was a tentative proposal for more meetings; a new friendship. And Master Hans glowed with the pleasure of it. He loved Father, I could see. He and Father made each other playful; gave each other ideas; were more alive together. And I loved him for bringing to Father – already somehow less shrunken, less grey, with less of an air of being away from this world – this renewed willingness to engage with happiness.

But then Master Hans's face clouded with the returning memory of how things actually were nowadays.

'I would like to,' he said, but a little too carefully, 'very much.'

He didn't offer a date. Father didn't ask. But I felt him shrink back into himself, wounded.

So, slightly surprising myself, I took charge. 'You and I can work out a date between ourselves,' I said to Master Hans. 'We don't want to bother Father with details. We can write to each other. You probably have a lot of commissions, but maybe towards the end of the summer . . .' He was still looking torn: wistful, but faintly alarmed too. And then it occurred to me that he might not want to be seen going to Chelsea, or for that matter to my house, in the middle of town, where everyone saw every-thing and the walls had ears. I should be sensitive to that. 'Maybe we could all go and stay with the Ropers? Margaret lives in Eltham now, near the palace,' I added, on a burst of inspiration. 'It's beautiful. Well Hall, it's called. She's making a wonderful Kentish garden. You'd love it.'

I'd been right. He'd been scared. But he wanted to see us. His face cleared. He beamed, and I was aware of Father's shoulders relaxing. 'Yes. Eltham. We'll write,' Master Hans promised, and he leaned forward almost as if he were going to start clapping me energetically on the shoulder. 'I'll make a fortnight to do it. I'll enjoy it.'

It was only after we'd left and Father had turned downhill towards the river and I was slipping back home with my hood up that I saw, with my mind's eye, the other *memento mori* that Master Hans had also built into his picture: one so simple and elegant that I couldn't believe I hadn't noticed it straightaway, and one that represented the biggest homage to Father of all. Those strong diagonal lines radiating from the eye-level point at the right of the picture, downward to the skull and upward to the crucifix, met at the picture's rightmost edge: in the purple-brown velvet coat of the French bishop. All those portents of doom connected with religious discord and political disharmony came back to the same point. A mulberry-coloured gown with a mulberry pattern. Morus; Father's favourite pun on his own name. Holbein hadn't forgotten us, even if he was trying to build a future in the other camp, with the people who had tomorrow in their grasp. What his picture was saying, over and over again, was: Remember More.

He didn't see Father primarily as the burner of Protestants he'd briefly become, the man I'd hated. Master Hans's vision was bigger and more generous. His picture was mourning the vanishing world of intellectual tolerance which Father had once been part of. Master Hans, for all his long absence and silence, was our true friend.

*   *   *

I was so uplifted by the way things had turned out that it was easy to tell John about the meeting and the picture. Decorously, tactful as ever, he asked no awkward questions about how I'd made contact with Master Hans in the first place. 'I'm pleased it made your father happy,' he said, when I'd got my bubbly story out, and there was a hint of real pleasure in his sky-blue eyes at the sudden light-heartedness in me. John loved Father. And he loved it when I could overcome all my ambivalence about the man who had raised me and be happy with him, enough that he could forgive, or ignore, the way I must have kept him out of my secret plan to put the two other men together again. I might not have been so generous, I thought with a pang. I'd overlooked that easygoing generosity at the heart of him for so long, once I'd started to feel uncomfortable with his anything-for-a-quiet-life lack of energy and ambition, his reluctance to question the things in life I felt were wrong. But now everything suddenly seemed simpler. We only needed a flash of joy to fill our lives with sunlight. The moment of ease we shared that day might have been fleeting, but it seemed to mark a change for the better. John pulled me to him in the bed that night, running his hands through my dark hair and over my breasts and murmuring how he'd missed me, I responded with a kiss and felt my body begin to tingle. When, what seemed like hours later, we drew apart, I could see starlight reflected in his eyes; when he kissed me and muttered, 'my love,' I whispered back, 'I love you,' and meant it enough to make all the anxious silences and chills and hesitations of the last year vanish as if they'd never been. It felt like at least the beginning of a new beginning. It felt as though he really might trust me again, however badly I'd betrayed him to Father. I slept soundly that night for the first time I could remember.

By the time we set off for dinner at Chelsea the next

evening, I'd already written to Margaret and Master Hans about when we might go to Well Hall. I was suddenly full of good cheer, with enough energy to join Tommy in a sliding race round the stone flags of our corridor until we both fell over screaming with relieved laughter. The right time would be September, I thought: when the weather began to turn; when this summer of waiting was coming to an end. A trip to Eltham would be something to take Father's mind off the time he was dreading most: the day when the royal baby that the new Queen was carrying would be born and, with the first cry of a new prince to continue the Tudor dynasty, the King would have won the mad gamble on which he'd staked the future of Christendom. And Father's last hope that the false marriage and everything that had gone with it could somehow be undone would finally crumble to dust.

We have to learn to live with that future, I found myself thinking. If we expect less, we won't be disappointed. We can do that. Perhaps even Father can.

Dame Alice bustled us into supper, old-fashioned style, with servants at the lower table and us sitting above them in the great hall in Chelsea. I'd got so used to dining in our more intimate way, in the parlour, without eyes on us, that I didn't like eating communally any more. I'd learned to love privacy. But it was good to feel her embrace and see her twinkling eyes and merry, undaunted face.

There was no sign of Father yet. Just young John and Anne, Cecily and Giles, showing signs of the wispy tension that usually hung about us all these days: bitten finger-nails; rictus smiles. Poor John: with no hope of advancement in a political career of his own, he was still living here as a child even though he'd turned twenty and had a wife. But he was doing his stoical best to keep busy. Father was creating work for him. He'd got him translating bits of continental writing reaffirming the unity of the Catholic Church and restating the importance of the Eucharist in sacramental life. The Rastells were going to publish it. No one liked to point out that they'd have to do a very thorough editing job on John's imperfect translation; he looked stressed enough without being teased. Now that my own mood had lifted, I was more aware than usual of the rest of the family's raised shoulders and forced cheerfulness as they waited for Father. 'He's writing, still,' Dame Alice said mock-crossly to the younger generation, trying to dissipate the anxiety. 'It's all this fuss about the book. He's been writing defences for weeks. But the man's got to eat. I'll send for him.'

But he appeared before she could. And, even if he had been writing one of his many detailed letters to Cromwell's men, explaining why his latest anti-heresy outpouring, published at Easter, hadn't actually been a veiled attack on the new direction of government policy, more tolerant towards heresy, there was no sign of it on his face. His smile cheered everyone in the room and lifted their mood, just as it always had. 'Welcome,' he said simply. 'Shall we eat?'

But something wasn't right about him. Meeting Master Hans hadn't worked quite the same magic on him as it had on me. Once we were at table, he opened his Bible to choose a text to read to us in his usual way. The book fell open, apparently by itself, at the Psalms. He glanced down. Stopped. 'So be it,' he said, and lowered his head to it. And something in his eyes made the hair stand up on the back of my neck.

'*Posuisti tenebras et facta est nox in ipsa pertransibunt omnes bestiae silvae. Catuli leonum rugientes ut rapiant et quaerant a Deo escam sibi*,' he read, almost in a whisper, so that the silence about him deepened and everyone drew forward to hear better. ('Thou hast, good Lord, set the darkness and made the night. And in the night walk all the beasts of the woods: the whelps of the lions roaring and calling unto God for their meat.')

Dame Alice, who was usually slow to follow Latin, had no trouble with these verses. I got the feeling she'd heard them many times before. Perhaps this was what he read for comfort when he woke screaming from his nightmares. Or perhaps this was the stuff of his nightmares. There was a sick look about her as she leaned forward to do one of her comical scolding routines: 'Come, husband! That's enough of your gloom! You'll curdle the cream!'

From very far away, I saw the others frozen into their polite smiles; not wanting to say a word out of place; desperate not to do the wrong thing. We could all see something was amiss. Under the table, I felt John squeeze my hand.

That's when we heard the knock at the front door. First one, then a whole volley: so loud and insistent that they sounded like blows from an iron fist. They were almost louder than the race of my heartbeat. I saw Anne Cresacre's big round eyes widen until she looked like a terrified owl, and wondered through the drumming in my chest if I was wearing the same foolish expression.

One of the servants rushed to answer. We could hear his scurrying footsteps behind the arras; the creak and shriek of the bolts and bars; then more solid men's footsteps coming back behind him.

The two newcomers who stepped stolidly through the door were strangers; men in cloaks.

'Sir Thomas,' one of them said in ringing tones, moving forward, feeling in his pouch for a document.

Father rose to his feet. A true man of public service, he'd somehow managed to put a politely welcoming smile back on his face. The rest of us stayed crouched, frozen in our chairs.

The man completed his stride across the room and up

to the dais. He held out a sealed document. 'From His Majesty,' he said, still too loudly. Father took it but didn't open it, and the inquiring look he gave his interlocutor was full of mute challenge.

'It says that you're required to present yourself to the royal commissioners,' the man said, and, when Father didn't respond, added, as sternly as if he were reading a death sentence: 'at once.'

It was the book, I thought, with a terrible resignation gripping my heart; Father's last challenge against the new political order; one blow too many in his lonely war. Cromwell wasn't going to forgive him. It was the beginning of the end.

Very slowly, Father bowed his head. He still had a little smile playing on his face. Through the fear paralysing me, I found myself thinking how I hated that perpetual little smile, which masked whatever he was really feeling and hid him from us. Very slowly, he got up.

Dame Alice rose to her feet too, returning to life as she stepped out of our immobile scene of terror. There was nothing like a smile on her face: just utter determination.

'Wait,' she said, with breathtaking calm, addressing the man and the other one skulking behind him below the dais among the servants. 'Sit down, both of you. I'll need to prepare some things for my husband to take. Let us give you something to eat and drink while you wait.'

The man who'd addressed Father – clearly the leader – paused for a moment. Father nodded at him. He nodded at Dame Alice.

'We'll eat in the kitchen,' he said, and gestured at the servant who'd brought him in to show him the way.

There was dead silence in the hall as we listened to them clattering away. Just eyes moving from their fixed position staring at plates to snatch looks at the next person up or at Father, still standing with that absent smile on

433

his lips, or at Dame Alice, looking fiercely round as if willing everyone to stay calm in the face of catastrophe; just breathe, carefully controlled, in and out, to stop the moments passing too fast into a future none of us could bear to enter.

Except for the sound of sobbing, which I heard from behind heartbeats and breath: a little whinny of hysteria; then a helpless, hopeless keening on a single treble note. I looked around for the source of the noise but all I saw were blank faces staring back at me.

It seemed an age before I realised that the noises were coming out of my own chest, as if independently of my will. That it was my cheeks that were wet with tears I couldn't stop flowing out of my wide-open eyes. That everyone was staring at me because I was the only person in the entire room to display signs of grief.

'Meg,' Father said, and all the eyes turned to him. The smile had gone. There was a kind of softness in his eyes that I didn't understand. There was a kind of hardness too. 'My dear girl. Stop crying.'

I looked at him, made an effort to master my body's rebellion, hiccupped and fell silent. I felt John drop my hand, reach for a cloth and turn to me to wipe the tears, very gently, from my cheeks.

'Meg. All of you,' Father said, and the silence deepened. He stood taller. 'You mustn't give way to fear. These are hard times for our household. You never know when you'll need every ounce of courage you possess.' He paused. He was struggling within himself, finding it hard to say what was to come next.

'But it isn't now,' he went on, still uncannily calm, but with strain visible on his powerful features. 'That wasn't real. It was just a rehearsal. Those men didn't come from the king. I got them from John Rastell. They're actors.'

Into the sudden buzz and movement at the servants'

table, Dame Alice turned furiously to her husband. Then everyone spoke at once. Everyone except me, that is. Now it was my turn to be frozen with shock.

'You mean – you haven't been arrested?' I heard young John boom breathlessly.

'You hired actors?' Cecily yelped.

'You scared her,' I heard from next to me. My John's voice, but a monotone whose murderous fury was utterly unfamiliar. 'For nothing.' Then there was a dark rush of air at my side, and, too astonished to take breath, I became aware of John flying towards Father, with a dangerous, wild-eyed look about him that I'd never seen before, drawing back a fist and hissing, 'I'll take that smile off your face!', smashing him full in the jaw. There was a dull thud. Father reeled on the dais, clutching at his face, spitting out blood. A tooth landed near his feet. John stepped back too, holding his fist in his other hand, looking down in what seemed to be surprise at the blood on his own split knuckles.

Silence followed. Father recovered his composure first. Still holding a hand to his face, but with no apparent anger, he said through thickened lips to John: 'So there's still a touch of the wild boy in you after all.'

John just went on standing there, not responding, watching his own hands.

'Well, you deserved it!' Dame Alice squawked, suddenly finding her voice, and her outraged tones gave the rest of us a chance to take breath and move our frozen limbs again. 'You scared us all half out of our wits! Don't you dare tell me this is just one of your jokes!'

'Shh, wife,' he said, half-soothing, half-warning, making a visible effort to put down the hand that had been cradling his mashed jaw and turning slowly towards her instead, putting an arm round her stiff waist and a kiss on her red, angry cheek in front of everyone. In horrible fascination,

I stared at the bloody kiss mark on her face and his puffy, distended mouth going blue on one side. He took no more notice of his injury, but I thought he was almost relieved by the outbreak of rage on all sides; it was an easier emotion for him to manage than the grief that had threatened to overwhelm us before. He was performing now, before a courtroom of his own making, carrying us all along on the tide of our feelings towards the point he wanted us to understand. 'It wasn't a joke. As I said, it was a rehearsal.

'Some of you find it easy to put out of your minds how precarious our position here is,' he went on, and he included Dame Alice in the stern look he flashed around the room. 'There's nothing to joke about in what might become of us. We really are walking through the woods in God's darkness. The sounds we hear on all sides really are lions roaring for their meat. Our ordeal might begin at any moment. You need to be prepared for the worst. We need to be ready to meet our fate with dignity.'

He was pale and set. There was no joking in his tone. And when his eyes turned to me and John, who was still standing up and looking stunned, they were almost accusing.

'I don't want to see tears if it happens. I don't want brawling. I want dignity. I want us all to take comfort from the knowledge that God will provide.' Then he softened, and, sliding his body around John, came to stand by me. 'Don't unman me, Meg,' he said, more gently. 'Will you promise?'

I nodded mutely, so full of emotions I couldn't name that I was incapable of words.

'Amen to that,' he said. 'Thank you.'

Then he bowed, and walked down the hall past the servants. 'Thank you all for sharing supper with me,' he said from the doorway, with a strange return to everyday courtesy, 'now I have work to do. If you'll excuse me.'

No one knew what to say after he'd gone. Through the window, I could see his candle bobbing determinedly away towards the New Building. Our food was untouched on the table. But none of us had any appetite for meat.

'Well!' said Dame Alice. Even she was at a loss for words. She looked round at the goggle-eyed servants. 'Finish your meal,' she said kindly to them, then turned to us. 'Will you join me in the parlour, children?'

It was a relief to be away from all the eyes and the hubbub of excited conversation that broke out as soon as we walked away from the table. John put an arm round me in the corridor and squeezed me comfortingly. 'Well, at least we both disgraced ourselves!' he whispered, and although he spoke with a hint of humour I could still see a glint in his eye and rope-like tension in his muscles as he strode along – my first indication of the long-suppressed fighting instinct which I'd never quite believed so gentle a man could have. 'You were quite right to cry. But let's calm down now.'

I sniffed, partly comforted, and tried smiling back as I trotted along a bit faster, trying to keep pace with his seven-league strides. 'Thank you for standing up for me . . . no one's ever done anything like that for me before . . . does your hand hurt?' I asked, feeling an ache of proud tenderness for my defender. But he didn't care about his hand. He was still lit up with the force of his attack. 'Not yet. It might later,' he said, baring his teeth in an unfamiliar, dashing, glittering buccaneer's grin.

'Well, that was just the end!' I heard Dame Alice say, as we reached the peace of the parlour, where a fire was burning, and everyone began settling in chairs and on cushions and muttering to each other in an odd mood, somewhere between excitement and panic. 'I'd never have thought he could be so cruel! I declare the man's taking leave of his senses at last!'

'I'm not so sure about that,' John said, striding over to stand next to her, beside the fire, electric with his newfound energy. And there was so much quiet authority in his voice now that every other voice in the room fell silent as we turned to him for an explanation. 'I've got an idea about why he did it. But first,' he looked kindly down at Dame Alice, fuming in her chair, 'tell me, do you know what the dreams he's been having are about?'

She looked relieved to be asked. She'd been saying Father had been sleeping badly for weeks; but none of us had shown interest in knowing more until now. 'It's terrible,' she said frankly, and I noticed the blue rings under her eyes. 'I don't know what to do with him. He screams in his sleep. And he wakes up with his eyes staring open and the bed drenched in sweat. Sometimes he tells me things before he's properly awake. Horrible things. About torturers. Sometimes he's been on the rack. Sometimes they're coming at him with knives to disembowel him. Sometimes he's staring as they tear his heart out of his body and wave it in front of him. But as soon as daylight comes he won't talk about it. He just pretends it never happened.

'I blame that Elizabeth Barton,' she went on. 'The nun. The Maid of Kent. You know: the miracle woman. He's been like this ever since he went to visit her. He spent a whole day alone with her. Praying. And he wouldn't say afterwards what they talked about. Just that she said that when the Devil came to her he fluttered around her like a bird. But that's when it all started. She's been here twice since, trying to get to him. I showed her the door, of course. I wasn't having her in my house, stirring him up with her talk. But he's still having the dreams.'

Cecily and I exchanged shocked glances. We had sceptical London views about the Holy Maid of Kent: that she was a troublemaker and a rabble-rouser and probably a fraud. I had no idea what could have impelled Father to meet her. It was many steps further down the road towards Catholic mysticism than I'd imagined him going – a long way towards what we'd been brought up to despise as superstition. I looked away from Cecily, not wanting to reveal my mind through my eyes, but I was aware of her furtively crossing herself.

Dame Alice wanted John to go on. 'So why do you think he did it? The . . . thing . . . tonight with actors?' she prompted, and I could see her fury with Father had softened while she was describing his nightmares, though she still had the light of battle flickering in her eye. 'You said you had an idea.'

'Because he wanted to show us he's afraid, but he couldn't find the words to tell us,' John said simply. 'He's an old-fashioned man at heart. He grew up in a time when people lived in the public eye all the time, and they each had their public role to play, and they did it perfectly. The only time you ever saw people wail and beat their breasts and display their feelings was on stage. The mummers' plays and all the holy days of pageants and disguisings and misrule were the only good excuse there used to be for a bit of riot and upheaval – the only chance for people to go wild. So what I think is that – now he's lost his own public role, and been left alone with his thoughts, and he's trapped with all these terrors he doesn't know how to discuss – he took refuge in the only way he knew to show us his feelings. He got in the mummers.'

Everyone was staring at John with dumbfounded expressions. Except the Dame. She was nodding, as if it made perfect sense to her. She and John were from the age of mummers too.

'You're saying,' she said, and her face had softened, 'that what he was doing out there was putting on a kind of mystery play for us of what's in his heart . . .'

We'd never heard her so poetical. 'Yes,' John said, with a conviction that no one would gainsay. He was too obviously right. 'I shouldn't have hit him. I thought he was being cruel. But he must just be desperate.'

I saw tears gather in Cecily's eyes, and the dawning of sympathy on every other face. 'That's a clever idea,' Giles Heron murmured, and his well-modulated politician's voice vibrated with respect for John. 'I'd never have thought it out for myself.'

'Oh, poor Father,' Anne whispered.

'Could I leave him a draught?' John asked practically, turning back to Alice, 'to help him sleep?'

She shook her head. 'He'd never take it,' she said. 'I can't tell you how often I've suggested that. But he just starts talking about the will of God. He's impossible.'

She crossed herself.

'Well, Amen to that,' John said with resignation. He'd known it was what she'd say. 'But he'd be more reasonable if only he could get some rest.'

John let me bind his knuckles when we got home. He lay on the bed with his arm awkwardly outstretched as I cleaned and bandaged. 'How could you go from hitting him to understanding him so fast?' I asked tenderly, admiringly, gratefully. But when I lifted my hand to stroke his face, I saw he was asleep.

Master Hans's note came the next day. He would come to Well Hall in the last week of September.

I let it drop back to the table. I'd pinned all kinds of hopes on the remaking of the portrait and the renewal of our friendship with Master Hans. But, after last night's uproar, I couldn't believe any more (even if I carried on hoping) that the trip would really mark a new beginning for Father. He had no intention of retiring quietly, picking up the threads of whatever old friendships were still on offer now he was just a private citizen, or doing what he'd said he wanted to do when he first resigned: taking to his prayers and serving God. He didn't know how to live a private life. John had proved that. Father had taken the loss of the Chancellorship as liberation from the constraints of doing the King's bidding, but not as a cue to leave the public stage. And I woke up gloomily sure that, however frightened he was, he'd go on stubbornly fighting for the Catholic Church. He'd be a crusader to the last.

My mood was linked to the unsettling moment I'd had on the boat ride home, hugged tight next to a John who was still sitting prouder and taller than usual, and sneaking admiring looks up at him. I didn't know if it was the heat of the night air, or the fluttering of birds and bats on the shore reminding me of the Devil visiting Elizabeth Barton, or just my mind being fuddled with the wine and emotion of the evening. But once John's eyelids began to droop, I'd looked back at the night sky above the Chelsea house – and, for a long, bewildering moment, I could have sworn I'd seen a long comet tail trailing back from a blood-red orb hovering over the house. No one else saw it. The boatman was grunting and watching his oars dipping rhythmically into the water. When I nudged John, wrapped up beside me in his cloak, he took a moment or two to respond. By the time I'd hissed 'look' into his ear, and pointed back at the sky, and got him to turn round to follow my finger, what I thought I'd seen had vanished. All that was left was the innocent white full moon, and a wisp of cloud, and the shadows.

19

The leaves were turning red and the roads to mud as Hans Holbein rode uneasily out of London, mounted on an unfamiliar horse borrowed from the Steelyard, with his packs bumping behind him across the animal's stout withers. He was leaving for Well Hall earlier than he'd originally planned, yet autumn was already on its way and there was a chill in the air.

He'd spent all summer thinking about this. He'd stopped haunting Bucklersbury hoping for a glimpse of Meg – a man had to show some restraint – but nothing could stop him dreaming every night of arriving triumphantly at Well Hall on 21 September and of her rushing out to meet him with a face radiant with happiness.

Pride was all that had stopped him trying to see Meg now, early, outside those dreams. But it was a pride fierce enough for him to catch himself on every stray thought that his rebellious mind began to form, every wisp of every idea of somehow bringing the meeting in the quiet safety of the countryside forward. Stop, he'd been telling himself sternly, each time he found himself daydreaming. Late September is soon enough. After that, we'll see. The important thing is to make the painting perfect.

But in the end he'd not been able to be so patient. It was his interview with Thomas Cromwell on the morning of 7 September in London that had finally made up his mind that he should rush things after all.

Holbein had been asked days earlier to visit the politician to discuss painting his portrait. He'd woken up to a glorious golden late-summer dawn and walked through the quiet streets, so full of anticipation at the prospect of the important commission to come that he scarcely noticed the sights and sounds around him. It was only when he was being ushered into Cromwell's chambers and beginning the affable bow he'd been rehearsing in his mind since he left his rooms that he realised he'd been walking for the best part of an hour through a frenzy of bells ringing from every church tower in London and Westminster.

The narrow eyes in the big slab of a face were watching him with what Holbein thought was amusement. The man at the table stopped writing and put down his quill. But he didn't get up, or answer Holbein's bow, just jerked a thumb at the window, behind which the bells were going crazy. 'So. God be praised,' Cromwell said drily, and smiled his cunning, lopsided smile. Holbein straightened up, wrong-footed by having his courtesy ignored, and looked carefully at the other man for guidance as to how to respond. 'God has smiled on the King and Queen, Master Hans,' Cromwell said, with exaggerated patience, and Holbein understood uncomfortably that it was his own ignorance that was tickling the politician. 'Can't you hear the bells?'

'Do you mean – the prince is born?' Holbein said, and quickly stretched his mouth into his broadest possible smile. Cromwell was making him just as nervous today as he had the last time they'd met. He was the kind of man, Holbein felt, who could never let an encounter with another man pass without establishing that he was tougher than them, superior to them, in some important way. Holbein had met plenty of brawny bullies like this in taverns in his time, and he knew he preferred to steer clear of them. He didn't enjoy pointless arm-wrestling. Still, this news would please Cromwell. And he'd associate Holbein with that moment of good fortune forever; so Holbein should rejoice.

'Not exactly,' Cromwell said, even more drily, and now Holbein could see something wolfish in the man's grin. It was very far from an expression of joy. 'Today we are celebrating the birth of the . . . *Princess*. Princess Elizabeth.'

'God be praised! Long live Princess Elizabeth!' Holbein burbled hastily, and bowed again. Inside he was cursing his bad luck. To be here at the very hour when a daughter was born – meaning that the King had, despite setting all Europe by its ears through the break with the Church of Rome, failed to get an heir and secure his Tudor dynasty, and Cromwell, the statesman who had done most to guide the King down that risky path, must be feeling anxious about whether his policy was now going terribly wrong – was no way to begin his professional relationship with the man.

Cromwell bared his teeth again. 'Well, to business,' he said, unceremonious as ever, and turned the conversation to practicalities: the size he wanted his picture to be and the date he could make himself available to be painted. 'The first day of October,' he specified laconically. He didn't offer alternatives. It was clear he could see no reason why a painter wouldn't drop everything else to paint him.

Holbein swallowed, and nodded, and looked down at the papers on Cromwell's desk. It would mean coming back early from his quiet week with the Mores. 'I'll be here,' he said, with more enthusiasm than he felt. There was no more to be discussed. Cromwell felt for paper, wrote him a new three-line *laissez passer*, sanded it and handed it over. Holbein bowed, murmuring thanks, and left.

Only when he was already outside, listening to the bells again while folding the paper into his pouch, did he notice there were other words on the back. Cromwell must have turned over the page he'd been writing as Holbein walked in to hide it from him, then forgotten what he'd done and reused the other side. There was just one sentence: '*Soon: look into Master More's friendship with the Maid of Kent.*'

Was persecuting More going to be Cromwell's way of venting his anger, now that the birth of a princess had put a question mark over his own career rise? Holbein wondered. He didn't know the answer, though the prickling down his spine made him feel that the danger More was in was coming closer. But he did, suddenly, know what he had to do. He went home and wrote a hasty note asking Margaret Roper if he could come to stay immediately to begin preparing the portrait, as he'd have to be back in town earlier than he'd thought. It wasn't what he'd dreamed of: Meg wouldn't get to Well Hall for days yet. But at least he'd have time with the Ropers and time to make the picture a perfect gesture of respect for More. He was already having a new idea about how to do that. He'd borrowed the horse, planned his route, gone and bought some extra materials – including several large planks of wood – and packed his bag by the time Margaret Roper's welcoming reply came. There was nothing left to do but set off.

She was a little woman, Margaret Roper: dark and sweet-faced, full-bodied now from the birth of the third baby in her arms (a second girl, called Alice in honour of the More children's stepmother), but basically a scrawny scrap with a long nose and sallow skin and a prim, studious air. Her thoughtful eyes (with anxious wrinkles he didn't remember

445

from before) and long nose were not unlike Meg's, but she had none of her stepsister's fascinating bony, rangy sharpness. No glitter in her eyes. No hidden wounds in her heart, except those put there by her family's current misfortunes. A nice, kind girl, and certainly a good wife, but not what Holbein would ever have called attractive.

But she was delighted to see him. She rushed out of the house – a solid new redbrick edifice which Holbein could tell at first glance would be comfortable and free of draughts and full of pretty tapestries and cushions and the tantalising smells of good food – into the lush garden to greet him. She was holding the baby. She'd been watching for him from the nursery window.

'It's so good to see you, Master Hans!' she cried in her soft, forgiving voice, squinting up against the afternoon sun at him as he tried to make a leg, exhausted from the unaccustomed exercise of riding, swing effortlessly over his horse's back and dismount elegantly. 'We've been so excited that you're coming. It will be just like the old days again for a while.'

He slithered to the ground, bringing one of the bags clattering down with him and looking a bit startled at the noise.

She laughed kindly. 'It's been years, hasn't it? Far too long – but you look just the same. A bit more sleek and prosperous, of course. And tired from your journey. Let's get someone to look after your horse and take your things into the house and get you some refreshment quickly. You must need feeding.'

She wafted him to the open door and into the welcome gloom, where the smell of roasting meat made his mouth begin to water. She had a gift for hospitality: he felt enfolded in affection already, so that he knew it didn't matter that with all the new impressions crowding in on him he wasn't taking in everything her soft voice was saying; just odd,

446

welcome words, like 'Ale or wine?' and 'Little Alice sleeps beautifully . . . only Tommy and Jane adore her and keep waking her up to hold her,' and 'Do you like pigeon?'

He had a pretty parlour with a great mullioned window that let in a torrent of late summer light and was fringed on one side by a luscious vine casting dapply, dancing shadows into the doorway. His bedchamber and privy were directly behind it: clean, comfortable, simple. He let out a great happy sigh. This visit was going to be a joy.

'It'll be very quiet for you for a bit, Master Hans,' Margaret said, a bit apologetically, as she showed him the rooms and a groom brought in his pile of bags. 'Just me, and Will when he's not in town. Father and the Dame' – she dimpled affectionately at the pet name for her step-mother – 'will be here in a week or so – they were delighted you were coming sooner than they thought. And Cecily and Meg say they'll try and come early too, though they can't answer for their husbands. But my brother John is held up in town with Anne. And we're not sure about the Daunceys, though Elizabeth says they'll come when they can. We don't see much of them these days . . .' She paused, looking wistful.

Holbein could just imagine why. He remembered William Dauncey with no great affection from Chelsea: a whey-faced youth with pretentious ways, obsessed by his own personal advancement, unwilling to share a word with a humble painter whose friendship could have no possible bearing on William Dauncey's career and so who wasn't worth speaking to. He wouldn't imagine that someone like that would take the risk of having too much to do with a father-in-law who had fallen into the deep shadow More had – even one who had done so much to start Dauncey's parliamentary career. He'd heard Dauncey had been the only MP from what Cromwell sneeringly called the 'Chelsea group' not to have spoken out against Cromwell's Act of

Restraint of Appeals that spring, the law that broke the unity of the Catholic Church and stopped Queen Catherine appealing to Rome against her divorce decree. It made him angry to think of the disloyalty of it. It was easy to see why his pretty wife, as Holbein recalled, had been more than a bit in love with John Clement.

'It's because they live outside London,' Margaret was going on, rushing to excuse them. 'I know how hard it is to keep up, if you're far away and your children are with you and there's really no reason to go to town . . . I try to make the effort. I go and see them sometimes. But they hardly ever come here, and Meg says she hasn't seen them since she married, except William occasionally at dinner at Chelsea while parliament's sitting. Still,' she sighed, 'it's not surprising really. Elizabeth has three lovely children now: another Tommy, like mine, and another Jane, and now little Henry too. You won't have seen any of them, will you? We were all still just about to have them when you left. Well, you'll be overwhelmed. We all are. They're a handful. No wonder she doesn't like to travel with them.'

She stopped, and put the dimply smile back on her face. 'Listen to me running on, tiring you out with family gossip,' she added apologetically. 'All I mean is that when they do come it will be a pleasure for all of us: our first proper reunion in years.'

'I'll enjoy that,' Holbein said heartily, relaxing into the soft atmosphere she created, liking her more and more.

But there was a sudden shadow on her face. She was looking doubtfully round at the mountain of stuff the groom was piling up. Holbein's box of paints, ready for mixing. His tool kit with hammers and saws and nails. His bag of clothes. His poacher's bag with the sketchbook and silverpoint pencils and crayons. His Turkey carpet. He'd brought almost everything he possessed, except the skull. In fact, he'd alarmed the old man so much by packing

448

everything up to go that he'd had to pay a month's rent in advance as proof he was planning to come back to Maiden Lane. And then there were the boards: great big things, from the same timber merchant who'd sold him the Baltic pine for the ambassadors, now being propped gently against the clean limewashed wall. How had he ever got so many packages on the back of a single horse?

'You do know the picture's still in Chelsea, don't you, Master Hans?' Margaret said, looking as though she felt guilty at having misled him over something important. 'Father is bringing it with him. And I've been so excited at the thought that we'd see you that I'd almost forgotten that you're here on business. I'm worried that you'll think you're wasting your time with me – though I've got lots of gardens to show you, and the countryside around here is lovely. It's just that you won't be able to do much painting till he gets here with the picture.'

Holbein laughed, a big reassuring belly-laugh that was an expression of much more than just his wish to banish the anxious look from her face. He was full of the idea of the picture he was about to make, in the sunshine pouring through this window into this lovely room that she'd so generously made his. It was going to be a triumph: a fearless, peerless depiction of the truth. He was fed up with skulking around being scared among the fearful. He was itching to start.

'Don't you worry about that, Mistress Margaret,' he said, as kindly as he could, as if she were a nice child he was making friends with. 'Look.' And he pointed at the boards against the wall. 'I've been thinking, and I've had an idea. I'm a better painter now than I used to be. I've learned a few new tricks along the way. I've found new ways of making my painting more true to life. It would be pointless just to make a few changes to an old picture, and not use all that knowledge. So I've brought everything

449

I need to make a new one from scratch. It will mean working much harder than I'd planned while I'm here – it would have been so easy to just fix the background of your father's painting while I enjoyed sitting around talking with all of you for a couple of weeks – but we'll all be happier if I do it this way, because this painting will be far better than the one I did before. But I'll need to do lots of planning and preparation. So I'll be busy enough until the others get here.'

Her mouth was an O of astonishment: not quite the overjoyed reaction he'd expected. Perhaps she'd got out of the habit of expecting people to go out of their way to do kindnesses to her now ill-starred family? Or perhaps she was worried about money?

'Look, I lived with your family for months,' he went on hastily. 'You were all kinder to me than I'd ever expected anyone to be. This is the only way I have to repay my debt. And,' he gulped as he said it – he hadn't thought about this: was it too crazy an offer for a man with his way to make in the world? – 'it won't cost you anything. You'll get two paintings for the price of one; maybe one for here and one for Chelsea. It's my thank you. It's a present.'

He still didn't know which question he'd answered with his awkward little speech. But when he saw the sweetness suffusing her face and turning her cheeks a surprised, happy pink, he felt that his gesture of generosity had been worth it. If he was going to have the courage of his convictions, and do the right thing at last by the people his heart was drawn to before the fate he suspected lay ahead finally caught them up, he might as well go the whole hog.

He had time to think out his plan in more detail as he sawed his boards and joined them together; as he planed and sanded and primed them; as he played with the Roper children or listened to their high, thin, happy voices playing out of sight in the garden; as he dug out his last little copy of the original picture to work from; as he walked with Margaret and her scampering children under the canopy of golden leaves that ran down the long path to her barn and back and she pointed out the flowers and herbs that she'd planted; as he sketched the outline of the picture he was going to make.

His idea was so big that it seemed like a great storm all around him, muffling the rest of the world, crackling with sparks of energy and booming in his ears as he planned, walked, ate and talked. His painting would be a rejection of fear. He was going to draw on every ounce of knowledge he possessed and show everything, in ways both open and veiled, as he'd learned to by painting the ambassadors: the truth, the whole truth, nothing but the truth. This would be a picture of a family he loved and had finally found the courage to come back to, but it would contain far, far more than the simple scene he'd painted before. It would be an expression of the anguish filling his soul at the world going mad. It would show his sorrow at the way all the humanistic harmony that Erasmus had striven for – the life of debate and serene tolerance that he, Holbein, had once found so uplifting and full of hope – was being thrown away, both by the Protestant bigots whose excesses had lost his respect at home, and now by English politicians who were proving themselves ready to do anything, and believe anything, that would win them advancement by slaking a king's lust.

Even if More had been part of that political battle while he was Lord Chancellor – and had been brought down by the passion with which he'd defended the old faith – he was still a man of principle. He'd had the grace in the end to withdraw from politics with his honour intact. You only had to look at him to see that he was really still part of

Erasmus' world: a wit, a thinker, a humane and efficient lawyer whose reputation for kindly justice had taken decades to build up and hadn't been tarnished beyond repair by his recent Catholic excesses. That's why so many people on the streets in London still spoke fondly of him. Holbein couldn't imagine More behaving in the overbearing, bullying way of Cromwell, that natural-born thug who would no more resign from power on a point of principle than he'd let himself be willingly fed to the wolves. Holbein knew More to be innately a finer kind of person: someone who played the lute with his wife and watched the movements of the stars through the heavens. Whatever you thought about the burnings More had ordered, there was no avoiding the conclusion that the men who'd pushed the King's second marriage – and now found their designs unmade by God sending the Queen a daughter and consigning the dynasty to history – hadn't exactly been blessed by the good Lord either.

Holbein was determined to get every scrap of his disillusionment and anger in. He was going to show that the bullying ways of this king were condemning the Tudors to futility as surely as the violent cheating of the Plantaganets had an earlier dynasty. He was going to show humanism being destroyed by the madness, and More's fate and that of England being bleak and intertwined as the bigots took over. He was going to show the magic in More's mind being ignored and belittled. He was going to show the destructiveness of fear. He was going to show every trait and tic of the family that had welcomed him into their home and made him one of them. And he was going to make this ultimate gesture of respect one that everyone he loved could understand: More, his children . . . and, of course, Meg.

Meg, who he'd see in just a few days. Meg, whose failure to produce three children – as he now realised her sisters all had in five years of marriage – might just possibly mean that her marriage was now barren of love (a thought so wildly intoxicating that he could hardly bear to let it into his mind). Meg, whose respect he wanted almost more than anything else. Meg, who was at the back of every thought he'd had for years. If he was to be really honest, this painting was going to be a love letter to her as much as anything else. But he didn't dare let himself dwell too much on that. For now, he was happy to lose himself in the idea he'd lay it at her feet later. He couldn't get ahead of himself.

He felt all-powerful, unstoppable, walking on air. Even the fact that he didn't have the vast learning of Kratzer to help him stuff this painting with the subtle allusions to the life of the mind that had distinguished the portrait of the ambassadors didn't bother him. He was full of sublime confidence that he'd somehow be shown the way – so confident that, when fate brought his way just the bits of knowledge he needed, he was hardly even surprised.

Dinner with Will Roper, back home from parliament for a Sunday of rest, looking older now, hiding his youthful blondness with a long, shaggy beard. When Holbein asked him how London was taking the birth of a princess, a gleam of I-told-you-so Catholic feeling in the parliamentarian's eyes made him seem a mischievous boy again for a moment. But then he sighed, and went back to looking like the greybeard he was imitating. 'It came too late for Father,' he said heavily. 'He's already flown too close to the sun.'

The unqualified sadness in Roper's eyes made Holbein aware of how easy it was to be with these More children, the ones who loved their father with the same painful simplicity they loved their own children and – unlike impetuous, critical, hard-to-please Meg – never, ever questioned the rightness of their father's actions. 'Icarus,' he said to Will Roper, a little hesitantly, and marked that thought down in his head for private consideration.

In the garden with Margaret Roper. 'I wish Father could be at peace out of the public eye,' she said wistfully, looking at the first leaves of winter fluttering down. And then, bookish creature that she was, she found a classical quotation for her mood, and murmured it to Holbein. '"*If I were allowed to change fate according to my will, I would move my sails with a gentle zephyr, so that the spars would not be strained to breaking point by strong winds. A calm breeze would ripple softly along the sides of my rocking ship.*"' Her voice trailed away.

'That's beautiful,' Holbein said, awe-struck for the thousandth time at the erudition of these young women. 'What's it from?'

'Seneca's *Oedipus*,' she said, not quite adding, 'of course', but looking faintly surprised, as if everyone must know that.

His spine tingled. His instinct told him he was on to something here. 'I like it,' he said. 'Will you read me more Seneca after supper?'

And so she told him, by the fireside, about Seneca, a classical scholar-statesmen who, after being disgraced and forced to leave his job running Nero's government, had devoted his retirement to writing. But Seneca's acerbic thoughts didn't please the frivolous emperor. After writing the *Epistolae morales*, which advocated stoic resignation in the face of public vices, he was forced to commit suicide.

At the same hearth, in a later episode of the same fitful evening conversation, on that evening or another – they were beginning to blend into each other in Holbein's preoccupied mind – he heard about another philosopher who died at a king's hands: Boethius, servant of King Theodoric of Italy. Boethius wrote *The Consolation of Philosophy* after he'd been thrown into prison for subversion and witchcraft. He discussed good and evil, fame and fortune, suffering and injustice, and concluded that happiness lay only in the serene contemplation of God. But he was executed anyway. Holbein noted the names.

He couldn't stop watching little Margaret's hands as she talked. She kept her face as serene as she could, stopping the conversation from time to time to tend to one of the sleepy children she liked to keep in her arms or cuddle next to her while watching the flames. She was a gallant creature. She wanted to be happy. She wasn't going to let herself, or her children, be easily downcast. But her hands told a different story. They were busy, fretful, fidgety hands. They had bitten nails. They were the hands of a daughter wondering whether her father would meet the same fate as the philosophers of antiquity who had crossed their kings. They tweaked at things: a child's hair, a tassel, a burr from the garden. And when she finished her Boethius story, she was gripping the book she'd brought to show him so tightly that her knuckles were white.

When he started laying paint on the great wooden blank that would be his picture – he knew its predecessor so well that he could get a lot of the basic work done now, as the family was arriving, using his memory and his drawings – Holbein kept the sketchy outline figures in the family group approximately as they had been before. He kept the same line of bodies and faces surrounding More, who would still be looking gently down at a seated Margaret Roper. What he changed first was the hands. The new picture would be a study of hands. A long diagonal line of hands pointing and prodding, poking and plucking in a great downward sweep from the top left to the bottom right of the composition. Busy, fretful, fidgety hands. Hands that betrayed fear.

Margaret Roper's nervy hands, at the centre of the

455

picture, pointed to the words in the book she was holding: words that would show More's wish to devote himself to learning and prayer now he'd been disgraced by leaving office. He chose the wistful words she'd quoted from Seneca's *Oedipus*. And, on the facing page, he put the lines she'd found him from Icarus on the futility of ambition as another wistful comment on More's fate: *"'madly he makes for the stars, and, relying on his new limbs, tries to outdo the real birds. Thus, the boy trusts too much to his false wings.'"*

Next Holbein turned the clock back to the time of the first family portrait. Literally. There'd been a clock in the old picture, but now he gave it more prominence by moving it to the top centre of his space and painting its door open, as if it had just been wound or adjusted, to suggest that he was changing the time. The one hand that he put on the clock face pointed to just before twelve noon, by which he meant just before the present day. To show when he meant to turn time back to, he painted the clock's lower weight directly above the number fifty, the birthday More had commemorated with the original portrait. He wanted the family to understand that this was a wry look back at the household as it had been a few years before 'noon', or 'now', as a starting-point for charting the misfortunes that had befallen them since.

It was easy enough to paint in signs of More's fall from royal grace since the time of the first painting. Holbein skewed the pendant Tudor rose at the end of the ex-chancellor's chain of office, and reversed half the s-links in the chain in a vaguely disturbing way that could never happen in nature. All around, he scattered a host of other impossible, unsettling details conveying a world in which nature was being turned topsy-turvy: a vase with one handle upside-down; a monkey clinging to Dame Alice's skirts.

Other affectionate jokes came bubbling into his mind. He drew young John (to put it kindly, never the cleverest of the More brood) standing, staring intently but a bit vacantly at a book as if he couldn't quite make out the words. Then, chuckling to himself, he put one of the young man's characteristic spelling mistakes into the name he wrote above the painted figure's head, making it read 'Joannes Morus Thomae Filuis'. When he saw Cecily again, the first of the other More children to arrive at Well Hall with her own three infants, including a black-haired Tommy, the same age as Margaret's Tommy, and he remembered how close she and Margaret Roper had always been, and saw how well their children also got on – now bedding down together with a lot of shrieking and toddler horse-play in a chamber full of straw pallets where all the under-five cousins were going to sleep and play – he hit on a French pun that he thought even the subtle ambassadors would have appreciated. '*Etre dans la manche de quelqu'un*', he laughed to himself. It meant 'to be close friends', but what the words literally meant was 'to be in someone's sleeve'. So he mixed up the rich material of the two sisters' clothes in the picture, where they were sitting side by side, so that each of the fruitful, childbearing women was shown wearing sleeves in the contrasting material of the other's comfortably loosened bodice. He thought they'd appreciate being remembered as friends.

'It's getting impossible to drag you out of here, Master Hans,' Cecily laughed as she brought him a jug and plate of bread and cheese. She had the same pointy dark face as her older sister, and the same dimples when she smiled. 'You've been locked up for three days without a breath of air. Father will be here tomorrow and you'll have to come out of your lair then. But won't you join us to eat now?'

'Later,' Holbein said, staring distractedly at his work, then, realising how rude he must sound, looking guiltily away from it and into her eyes. 'Later, definitely,' he added more gently.

But he didn't join them later. He was getting intoxicated by the boldness of his truth-telling. And it had just dawned on him how to paint his biggest and most dangerous idea: to make the painting a metaphor for the misfortunes that York and Tudor houses had brought on themselves, which in turn had brought misfortune down on More's head. His picture would show that, after all the bloodshed of the Plantagenet years, the nation was no better off now. In spite of all Henry's attempts to sire a male successor, his self-indulgence had doomed his own line to extinction too. Now only frustration reigned. Before More arrived, Holbein was determined to get enough of this down to show him. And he could use members of the household to do it.

The old picture had already had the Fool, Henry Pattinson, at its centre, between More and Margaret, staring straight out at the viewer as if daring them to remark on his squat gingery resemblance to the King. But this time Holbein dressed him up in earnest as Henry Tudor. He strengthened the resemblance with the real King's swagger and assertive royal stance, and put Tudor red and white roses in the Fool's cap and a sword at his belt (another chance to show hands playing nervously with the hilt).

If he was going to have Henricius Pattinson personify the Tudor dynasty, he needed to depict someone else personifying the Plantagenets. And only one face fitted the bill.

What had been a doorway in the top right-hand corner of the first picture, leading to an outer room where a secretary could be glimpsed crouched over a distant table, he now transformed into something altogether more enigmatic to draw the eye and intrigue the mind's eye: an optical illusion that could be viewed either as an open doorway or the edge of a door. Then, deliberately, he began sketching in an altogether new face and figure inside the mysterious space – the only person not in the first picture at all.

Holbein's racing hand gave life to the three-quarter-length figure standing wistfully in his impossible doorway, leaning forward to observe a family group he didn't belong to. He gave the man he was painting dark clothes in anti-quated fashion; then a sword and shield for the bloody business of kingship, and finally a sealed scroll for secrecy. He gave him the anxious, pinched expression on the famous portrait always published with More's history of the murderous hunchback Plantagenet, Richard III. He gave him a deathly pallor that contrasted with the living complexions of the rest of his subjects. But what made Holbein's hand shake as he drew in the face was that he was giving this ghostly Plantagenet the familiar black hair and aquiline nose and sky-blue eyes of John Clement. Remembering Erasmus' late-night revelations back in Freiburg about Clement's true identity, he was making a mirror image to his full-blooded burlesque of the Tudor king out of the man that some members of this family knew to be a Plantagenet descendant who could never be king.

He knew this was a gamble. A swagger. A boast. He knew More and Meg might be horrified to see this secret revealed in paint. But the reckless belief that had taken hold of him and was moving his brush across the boards almost independently of his will was that this revelation would prove to the Mores that he was one of them. A man of intellectual substance to match theirs. One of the elect. A person of integrity, so close to Erasmus that he could be trusted with any secret. And someone Meg could turn to with her most private troubles.

Sweating, almost dancing from paint table to wooden rectangle, determined to race the idea into being before the light faded altogether, he painted the words 'Johanes Heresius' – John the Heir – above the figure's head. Would that be enough to make his point clear? His hand jerked on. On the table beside the doorway into the other world that was Johanes Heresius' home, he painted a vase of flowers. Not real flowers. Punning flowers: unbelievable blueish-purple peonies, an extra clue marrying the French word '*peon*', or physician, and the colour of the blood royal. Would that be enough? His hand – full of the trembling madness of inspiration now – led him back again to Margaret Roper's fidgety fingers. He scrubbed at them and repainted them so her right index finger pointed directly at the word 'Oedipus'. He knew more about the story of Oedipus after the recent firelight evenings – the man who won the crown of Thebes by unknowingly murdering his own father, and thus unleashed an appalling wave of tragedies, had been a murderous usurper just as Holbein felt Plantagenet and Tudor kings alike to be. He used Cecily's twitching fingers to show he had two doomed dynasties in mind, making her count, one, two, with the fingers of her left hand against the palm of the right. Moving up the diagonal of hands, he turned to Sir Thomas. First he painted in more of the rough undergarment to which his rich red velvet sleeves were attached, to make the contrast between them more obviously a visual version of another French pun that would have amused the ambassadors. The expression he was thinking of now was a joke about More's reduced circumstances in retirement. '*Il fait le richard*' could mean 'he's posing as a rich man' – an appropriate comment in view of that red velvet and dirty wool contrast. But it could also just mean – appropriately for the author of a history of the Plantagenet usurper – 'he makes Richard'. To emphasise that second meaning, Holbein changed the configuration of More's arms from what it had been in the first painting, and added three fingers peeping out from the politician's black furry muff to signify 'Richard III'.

He could hardly see now. The light had faded and he was peering at the darkening picture through shadows. Turning to light a candle, he realised his energy was completely exhausted. He was hungry and thirsty. His legs ached from hours of standing and his arms from more nonstop hours of lifting a brush without pausing for breath than he ever remembered. He fumbled for the wooden tray of bread and cheese Cecily had left, then realised he'd eaten the lot hours before. There was just a bit of small beer left. He drank it down, then turned back to stare obsessively, admiringly, lovingly at the picture, moving his flickering light up and down to examine each of the details that he'd worked out in that day's frenzy of creativity. He liked it. He loved it. It was still rough. There were still great empty patches on it. But he'd fill them. And what he'd done so far would be enough to show More.

Slipping out into the stairwell, he could hear the sleepy sounds of sisterly chat coming from the fireside in Margaret's parlour. But he knew he wouldn't find the energy to join the women this evening. All he could imagine doing now was sneaking into the kitchen to fill himself up with great chunks of Margaret's fresh bread and salty cheese, downing a big tankard of something pleasantly alcoholic, then throwing himself onto his bed fully dressed to catch up with his sleep.

Thomas More stood in front of the canvas for a long time. It wasn't like when he'd seen the other picture. He didn't move excitedly from corner to corner of the painting, looking for secrets and clues. He just stared.

Holbein hovered beside him, hardly breathing, sneaking sidelong glances at the older man whenever he dared, learning enough from that immobile face to see that at

461

least More's eyes were flickering over the paint, looking down the diagonal of hands; reading the texts; gazing at the red-cheeked Henry VIII and the ghostly Richard III with John Clement's face.

Every second of silence was making Holbein feel sicker. His hands were clammy. His stomach was full of black churning acid. He wanted to groan and hide his head in his arms and bash it against a wall to stop the blood drumming in his temples. How could he have gone to bed so pleased with himself? How could he have taken such liberties? Why hadn't he seen that what he was doing was terribly wrong? Why was he such a fool?

When More finally turned to face him, still expressionless, Holbein was ready to start mumbling apologies; to run out of the room, out of the house, out of his life.

So he almost didn't understand when More whispered: 'So you understand.'

And he was taken completely by surprise by the arms wrapping themselves round him in an awkward, bristly man's hug.

After a few minutes, More stepped back. Looked down. Put a hand to the bridge of his powerful nose and squeezed the corners of his eyes. The hand came away wet. But Holbein couldn't believe he was weeping until More said, a little shakily: 'The wine of angels . . . Do you know that's what the monks at the Charterhouse call tears?'

Holbein shook his head, trying not to let his own bewilderment show, trying not to think at all about anything except keeping his eyes fixed kindly on his hero to help him find his own way back to poise.

'I spent a year with them when I was young,' More went on, his voice gradually regaining its strength. 'I thought I wanted to become one of them. I sometimes still think I made the wrong choice by deciding not to. But Erasmus said I was mad. He couldn't be doing with all the visions and visitations. Or the tears.' He laughed wist-fully. 'Or the fish dinners, come to that. He kept saying, "But why do you think it's Godly to go round smelling like an otter?"'

Holbein could just imagine Erasmus' thin nose wrink-ling fastidiously as he made that remark. He burst out laughing: a laugh that was full of his own dawning real-isation that instead of being thrown out of the house he was being embraced as an intimate; a great gust of relief.

'I miss him, you know,' More said, smiling with the painter but still sounding lost. 'He's the last of the old friends from those times. I don't hear much from him any more. And it can be a lonely business keeping secrets.'

He stopped. Got a grip on himself. Beamed the full beam of his public charm on Holbein. 'Well, Master Hans, I won't talk more now,' he added more forcefully. (Though not forcefully enough to stop Holbein, now awash with a great tide of warmth and love and happiness, suddenly notice how thin the other man had got and how many grey hairs there were on his head. How did I not see that before? he wondered. He's getting old.) 'I should clean up' – More gestured ruefully down at his mud-spattered riding boots – 'and I don't want to hold you up. You have a painting to finish!'

But he stopped at the door for a final word. 'I'm glad Erasmus told you,' he said, looking Holbein straight in the eye.

Holbein was surprised, when he turned back to his work, to find his hands shaking so hard he couldn't pick up the paintbrush.

He needed to calm down. He managed to get working quietly on the figure of old Sir John More, who'd died a couple of winters back. That was just the sort of good, simple hard work he needed now: nothing more intellec-tually demanding than copying and accurate colouring.

But he was almost relieved when the children came to interrupt him: a giggling tumble of raven-haired Tommies and Janes and their gurgling toddler siblings.

He didn't hear a sound at first. He just had an instinct he was being watched. And when he turned round there they were, bright-eyed and mischievous, peeping at him from the doorway. They scuttled back in mock-alarm for a minute, but he could see they weren't really scared of him at all. They knew he was harmless.

Within minutes they were swarming all over the room, getting under the table, standing on the stool, touching the picture, tugging at curtains, sticking their heads into bags, putting their fingers in his paints, smearing the expen-sive colours on each other and, roaring with laughter, presenting their tummies to him to be tickled. 'Hey!' he yelled comically, flicking at them with a rag. 'Don't do that! Ach, you naughty little monkeys!' But it only made them shriek more excitedly.

He didn't really mind. He let them swarm. Looking at them romp around underfoot, it occurred to him that there seemed to be more of them now than there had been the last time he'd counted, at breakfast. He hadn't heard a thing, but another group of grown-ups must have arrived with them while he'd been with More.

He looked more closely at the child sitting eagerly on his foot and clutching at his calf, clearly hoping that Holbein would start walking and give him a ride round the room. This little boy had the black pudding-bowl hair and the dark eyes and the long, bony face that all the cousins shared. But, unlike the rest of them – who had the long, thin straight noses with slightly downward-pointing tips that the whole family seemed to have inherited from More – this child's nose was already distinctly aquiline.

464

Holbein could swear he knew this child's face from somewhere. He racked his brains, going through every set of features he'd ever scrutinised with his keen painter's eyes. Then light began to dawn. Surely this was the solemn little boy he'd seen Meg walk across the road to church with in London so many times in the last year? John Clement's son? Tommy?

He felt his hands start shaking again. Could he have missed Meg arriving?

Urgently, he put his hands under the boy's arms, pulled him off his foot and lifted him, squirming and squeaking, up to his own eye level.

'Is your name Tommy?' he asked. The child giggled and nodded his head. 'I thought so!' Holbein said triumphantly. 'And have you just arrived this morning?' Another beaming smile of agreement. 'With your mother?' The little legs kicked the air for joy. 'Yeth!' the boy lisped delightedly. 'With my muvver!'

Holbein put him down. 'Well, I want to say hello to her,' he said firmly. 'Right now. So come on, Tommy, take me to her. And the rest of you: out of here.'

He shooed them all out, shut the door firmly behind them, and headed off for the parlour at the back of the squeaking, joyous pack of children with his heart thudding eagerly in his chest.

There was a buzz of cosy women's voices in the parlour, and four heads in a semicircle with their backs to the door.

Margaret Roper's was the first to turn at the sound of the children. 'Shhh, children,' she called gently. 'You're getting far too excited.'

Then she saw Holbein, skulking nervously in the doorway. 'Master Hans!' she said, and the three other bonnets also turned his way. He heard her voice say, 'Come in, come in,' as if from far away; he was already staring hungrily at the faces under the bonnets. He saw Cecily and Dame Alice; he did two polite half-bows to them before turning, with almost painful anticipation, towards the last face.

He blinked. Perhaps it was the drumbeat of his heart that was stopping him thinking and seeing straight, but he was having trouble making Meg's features come into focus in the face swimming in front of him.

It took him a few more seconds to realise why. It wasn't Meg at all, even though the child who looked like a miniature John Clement was clinging to her skirts. It was Elizabeth.

It was all falling into place. He'd always known Elizabeth had been in love with Clement. But he hadn't realised until now that Clement might actually have fathered her child.

He paced furiously through the garden, bursting with pity for Meg, raging against the deceiver she'd been gullible enough to marry, and feeling a nameless, shameful excitement at the unfathomable possibilities his discovery might open up. How humiliated she must have felt when she realised the truth, he thought, stamping his feet heavily down the path. How she must hate her husband. How she must resent Elizabeth. A woman as honest as Meg would never again dream of touching a man who'd humiliated her so openly. No wonder she always looked sad to the bottom of her soul when she left her house to pray. No wonder her marriage had been barren since the birth of that first child.

His head was still swimming with indignation when he slipped back into the house, quietly so as not to alert the others, tiptoeing back into his parlour as if, by making no noise, he might avoid stirring up any more of the family's secrets.

He couldn't paint Meg and Elizabeth now in the same

way he had before. His discovery had made them part of his picture of barren futility. It was all the same story; all the workings of the same implacable fate. Almost without knowing what his hands were doing, he found himself transposing the two figures on the left-hand side of the canvas so that Meg was standing forlornly at the very edge of the picture, holding a book with blank pages; and a sly, determined Elizabeth was pushing her out of the way, pulling a glove suggestively off her hand and giving the ghostly John a bold stare from across the room.

It worked. It was the extra element his painting had needed. These two standing forms, a picture of discord and disharmony, now made a perfect contrast with the two happy, fulfilled sisters sitting in the opposite corner wearing swapped sleeves. To reinforce the disharmony between Meg and Elizabeth, he drew in a viol on top of the cupboard behind them with the point of its bow turned back to front. Then he put a plate next to it, between the outlines of their two heads. Another French pun, *'pas dans la meme assiette'*, meant 'at odds', but it also literally meant 'not in the same plate'.

How else to tell his story? He added books. He put Boethius' *Consolation of Philosophy* on the cupboard near Meg. And finally, with heavy irony, he painted the title of Seneca's *Epistulae Morales* on the spine of the book under Elizabeth Dauncey's deceitful arm.

He stopped and scratched his head, wondering what to do next. He felt flat when he realised that he'd probably finished. Wearily, he poured out water and oil and began the slow job of cleaning his tools. He didn't want to eat, or drink, or think any more. He didn't even want to sleep. He just wanted Meg to arrive.

The last little cavalcade of horses and ponies of the day arrived as the sun set. Young John, his wife Anne, and their three children in front; Meg and her little Tommy bringing up the rear.

Holbein was waiting for them in the garden, standing under the mulberry tree Margaret Roper had planted in her father's honour, patiently watching the shadows lengthen.

The rest of the family came pouring out of the house to greet the newcomers when they heard hooves and snorting and the creak of saddle leather in the courtyard. But Holbein made sure he got to Meg first, so that it was his chest her tired arms in their simple brown wool sleeves could cling to as she slithered gratefully to the ground. If there'd been no other reward for being there but the shy smile she flashed him now, from under her lashes, as he stood in front of her, forgetting to take his hands off her waist in the sheer joy of seeing her face again, he thought it would be enough. Then she laughed and stepped back, deftly freeing herself from him. 'I'm glad to see you,' she murmured, before turning to her sleepy child with John Clement's aquiline nose, who was slumped on the pony beside her – 'Come on, Tommy' – and putting out her arms to help him down too. There was a new timidity between him and Meg, he thought, trotting proprietori- ally indoors behind mother and child. But there was also a new radiance in the way she looked at him – as if he could offer a hope of salvation she hadn't dreamed might come her way – that filled him with a great hope he didn't dare put words to.

Holbein wouldn't have had the nerve to try to separate Meg from her family until all the greetings and huggings and welcomings and settlings-in were finished. He hung back from the family, drinking in the sight of her, enjoying the way his heart had swollen so inside his chest that he was breathless with his feelings, trying to keep a look of fatuous adoration off his face.

Finally, she stepped back from her last embrace and came over to where he was standing in the shadows. Her face was lit up with happiness. 'This is just like the old days, isn't it?' she said. And then, with a more searching look at him: 'You're very quiet over here in the corner, Master Hans.'

He didn't know what to say. He was still breathless. But it hardly seemed to matter now he was basking in the joy of her presence.

'Oh,' he said awkwardly, watching her hands because he didn't dare go on staring into her eyes. 'I've been working. You know how it is. I suppose I'm tired.' But he felt as though he could stay awake forever.

'Margaret says you've started again, from scratch?' she said, still gazing into his face. 'I'm so looking forward to seeing.'

Perhaps, he thought, with a wild burst of hope, he could take her off now and show it to her. Be alone with her. But he dismissed the thought almost as soon as it came to him. She wouldn't want that. She was being reunited with her family.

'I've done a lot already,' he said hesitantly. 'And I was thinking . . . it would be good to take tomorrow morning off. Have a break. Now that you're here . . .'

Or was that invitation too forward? He felt her eyes drop. Sneaked a look at her face, fearing he'd see it close against him. But all he saw was a faint flush making her cheeks even more beautiful, and a slight, repeated movement of the chin. He could hardly believe it, but she was nodding.

'There's a bumper crop of apples,' she said in a quiet rush, and her voice was light. 'Will says. And Cecily says you haven't been out of your room since she got here. You probably need a bit of fresh air, don't you? We could go first thing. Be back before dinner. Get baskets from Margaret. I'll ask her now.'

She grinned, meeting his eyes for a moment, and flitted off to talk to her sisters. Holbein went to his bed full of anticipation. Tomorrow he'd have hours and hours with her, sitting on a branch in the orchard, admiring the innocent wisps of dry grass on her skirt and the golden sunlight in her hair. He fell asleep imagining the drunken buzzing of wasps and the cidery promise of fallen apples, with laughter in his heart.

I woke up as happy as a country child. There was innocent dawn light coming through my window and someone whistling outside. When I peeped out of my window, Master Hans was sitting under the mulberry tree. He had the baskets. He must already have seen the picnic of bread and cheese and the bottles of ale I'd asked Margaret to put inside. We could stay out all day if we liked.

'I'm on my way!' I cried, and watched joy flush his upturned face, and half-skipped, half-ran down the stairs to meet him. Things were so simple with Master Hans, and so clear. All I wanted was to be alone with my friend, talking over whatever in the world came into our heads.

The day seemed to last forever. It was as hot as August. There wasn't a breath of wind, just that sleepy buzzing and birdsong.

While the shadows were still long, and they were still shy, they walked through the dewy grass, picking up windfalls. Mostly they were too far gone, with fizzy undersides and wormholes. Hans Holbein began taking the apple boughs in his big strong hands and shaking the ripe fruit down himself. He could feel her watching him. He grunted with extra effort as the fruit dropped around him. 'It's raining apples,' she called, more adorably childlike and whimsical than he remembered her; then, indignantly, 'Ow!'

as one fell on her. He stopped, laughing, out of breath, absurdly happy watching her rub her head.

She squatted down, took off her boots, hitched up her skirts and scrabbled into another tree. She braced her bare feet on the lowest branch, and bounced. It was his turn to shelter his head while apples rained on him. 'Now you know what it feels like,' he heard her say playfully as he ran to catch them.

He could have gone on all day, but they filled the baskets in an hour, before the sun was near its peak. He looked doubtfully at her. Was she going to say they should go back now? But she only grinned. 'Shall we eat?' she said.

He told her about the Protestants taking over Basel while she cut cheese into slices and gave him beer to swig from the bottle and flashed smiles and teeth at him in the scented air. 'A useless bunch of bigots they turned out to be,' he said, munching. 'And we'd expected so much of them too.' He guffawed at his own past foolishness and fell cheerfully silent.

He caught her watching him again from under her eyelashes as he wolfed down his third massive shelf of bread loaded with cheese. 'You make everything seem so easy, Master Hans,' she said, and he wondered if she was laughing at him, and, suddenly embarrassed, lowered his meal to the grass. Had he been greedy?

'Don't be shy,' she said gently, curling herself up, arms around knees, bare toes peeping out from under her skirts. 'I mean it. You make people feel happy. Look at Father. He gets quite . . .' she looked down as she searched for the right word, and wiggled her toes in the grass, '. . . playful when you're about. He seems younger. He's not at all like that with the rest of us, you know. I think you two must have the same kind of minds.'

He felt his face burning. Inside he was surging with bashful pride.

'Oh, happiness . . .' he muttered. She looked so pretty and happy herself, in the shout of birdsong, with that halo of cow-parsley waving behind her. He hugged his arms round his own knees, hardly aware of the bread behind him on the grass as he shuffled closer to her.

'I like your little boy,' he said awkwardly, fishing as cautiously as he knew how for information about what her life had become as John Clement's wife. 'Tommy. I can see you must know about happiness.'

'Mmm . . .' she said, and looked down, as if tussling with difficult thoughts. 'You were right, all that time ago. Children definitely are the best thing that ever happen to you.' Then she laughed. A forced sort of laugh. 'Marriage is harder than I thought, though. Once you're into the happy-ever-after bit.'

He hardly knew how to breathe next, let alone what to say. So he just went on looking at her, feeling the golden honey of the light ooze down on them. 'But we all get by,' she added, as if regretting what she'd said. After that she didn't seem to want to say any more. As if changing the subject, she unclasped her knees and lay back on the sweet crushed grass and looked up at the blue sky.

'So hot,' she said slowly, 'a beautiful day.' And she sighed, as if she might want to doze in the sun, and stretched her beautiful long limbs out, and folded her arms under her head, and shut her eyes. Hans Holbein could hardly restrain himself from throwing himself down beside her and raining kisses on her, like apples. But he knew himself well enough by now to know not to trust his baser instincts. So he sat on, bewildered by the sheer beauty of her, and when he was reasonably sure she must be asleep he got up and left her sleeping between the trees, and tiptoed off to the hedgerow to empty his bladder.

*　　*　　*

472

I woke up and he was still sitting there watching me with the gentlest look imaginable on his big face. He stopped as soon as he realised my eyes were open. I could see from the shadows that it was getting late. He'd tidied up the picnic while I was asleep. And when I sat up and started looking for my boots, I saw he'd picked a whole armful of wild flowers and left them lying next to me.

'They're lovely . . .' I said, spellbound, so touched that I almost got up and put my arms around him. 'Thank you. I'm sorry I went to sleep. But sometimes . . . sometimes it's good to be so at ease with a person that you don't have to say anything. I've missed that. I don't know many people this well, anywhere.'

Something about those words seemed familiar as they came out of my mouth. I wondered, as we walked in languid silence back to the house, where I could have heard them before.

Holbein saw Thomas More first. He was standing under the mulberry tree watching the sun sink. He looked as tanned and relaxed as a countryman. 'Lovely evening,' he said warmly, turning to face the returning apple-pickers and looking into the baskets. 'Though they say there'll be a storm tonight. You've got a good crop there.'

Holbein saw the attentive look Meg fixed on her father, so different from the sullen, worried glances he remembered from the garden in Chelsea, when none of them could yet understand the changes just beginning in the world. More smiled down at her. 'I wonder, Meg. Has Master Hans shown you the new version of his picture?' he asked, and suddenly Holbein realised the other man might not have simply been enjoying the afternoon light, but was waiting for them. 'I think he'd love you to see it before everyone else does,' More went on. And, with a hand guiding his surprised-looking ward's waist, he determinedly

473

propelled her – with Holbein in their wake, feeling astonished now that he hadn't remembered even to mention the
picture in that whole long day of happiness, and a tremor
of unease that he didn't know how to explain, even to
himself – into the house and the painting parlour.

More didn't even begin to offer explanations until he'd
shut the door behind the three of them in the parlour. It
seemed dark. Holbein's eyes were still dizzy with sunlight.
He began fussing like a housemaid with candles, eager to
show Meg his picture at its best. The lawyer's voice behind
him said: 'Of course, the light isn't good enough any more
to appreciate Master Hans's full artistry. But you'll understand in a minute why I wanted you to see this before
everyone else does.'

Holbein lit candles at two walls and at his painting
table, and offered pewter candlesticks to his two guests.
Meg's face looked as innocent and bewildered as a child's
in the circle of golden light, he thought. She stared at the
picture for a few minutes without seeing the changes. Then
he saw her begin to take note. Her eyebrows rose. She
moved her candle up to examine the most obvious new
element – his portrait of John Clement. Then she stared
at the red and white Tudor roses in the Fool's cap. Then
she began stepping backwards and forwards, to left and
right, trying to make out more with the little pool of light
she was holding like a weapon against the gathering gloom.

It seemed an age before she turned to her adoptive father
with a silent question on her face.

'Erasmus told him,' More said gently, and Meg's eyes
flickered uncertainly up at Holbein as if, for the first
time, it was crossing her mind that he might represent
danger.

'It's all right for him to know, Meg,' More reassured
her. His voice sounded almost as relaxed as it had in the
old days. 'Master Hans is our friend. He can be trusted.

474

I just didn't want you to stumble on this unawares and be frightened.'

She stared at him, wide-eyed and still doubtful. 'There's no doubt this could be dangerous if anyone outside the family saw it,' More went on. 'But of course they won't. It's private; just for us. It will stay here at Well Hall.'

Holbein nodded, disappointed but reluctantly accepting the wisdom of More's judgement.

Meg nodded too, but Holbein could see she still wasn't entirely reassured. 'But what do you think the others will say when they see it?' she asked her father, and Holbein realised with a stab of shock that John Clement's past was a secret that not even the rest of the More family knew.

'Simple coincidence of features,' More answered glibly; Holbein could see he'd thought the argument out beforehand. 'If anyone asks, we'll just say that John's face happened to be enough like the Plantagenet portrait we all know that Master Hans 'borrowed' it. Why not? He did the same thing with Henry Pattinson,' and More laughed.

Meg smiled back, relaxing at last, and Holbein breathed a suppressed sigh of relief. 'After all, why worry?' she said more light-heartedly. 'They'll probably never even ask. It's astonishing how people don't notice the most extraordinary things, even when they're right under their noses. I've thought that for years.'

The men nodded, understanding what she was talking about, complicit as conspirators in the flickering darkness. Then Meg turned directly to Holbein for the first time, as if realising that she hadn't praised the picture she'd made so much effort to get him to paint. 'You see straight into our souls, Master Hans,' she said with poise; then, more warmly, putting a hand on his arm, 'You're an astonishing man.'

Holbein was grateful for the candlelight now, knowing it would wash the colour out of the tremendous blush he could feel turning his face scarlet with pleasure. He couldn't speak. The best he could manage was to bob his head forward in a bow.

'They'll be sitting down to eat,' he said in a strangulated voice, trying to sound self-possessed. 'Shouldn't we go back and join them?'

But she shook her head gaily, as if she was throwing herself with all her heart and soul into the project of trusting him. 'Oh, wait just a moment more,' she said, and that hand squeezed his arm entreatingly. 'Let me try and make out a bit more of what you've done.'

And she stepped forward again with the candle, moving away from the kings this time and, confident she'd like what she saw, towards the opposite corner where she knew she'd find her own likeness.

He watched her; a silhouetted bonnet very still again behind her candle flame. 'Oh,' she said, then fell silent again. Then, in a less carefree voice: 'You've changed this too, Master Hans. You've put Elizabeth in my place. I'm right on the edge of things now. And how sad you've made me look . . .'

More laughed. 'Everyone looks first at their own likeness, Meg,' he said expansively. 'No one else will notice that, either. Come. Master Hans is right. We're finished here. It's time we ate.'

She came obediently out of the room with them, still holding her candle. But even in the near-dark, Holbein could see the puzzled little frown she'd worn earlier settle on her face again as a new anxiety replaced the old one.

The questioning, vulnerable line stayed on her forehead right through the simple family supper. For once, Holbein wasn't able to do his food justice. He picked at his meat and bread. He was too busy watching.

'Meg,' Elizabeth called from across the room, with

her pretty mouth curling up at the corners. She fluttered over to her sister, put an elegant arm around the taller woman's waist, kissed her with grace. Not a feeling reunion, Holbein thought, with growing understanding; this was behaviour for public consumption. 'It's been too long,' Elizabeth said, with the practised charm of the politician's wife. Her smooth, creamy fingers were playing with her choker of pearls, their jewelled ornament set off-centre on her neck – the new fashion set by Anne Boleyn; they said to hide the dark wen on the new Queen's neck – as if, Holbein thought with hostility, she wanted to draw Meg's attention to them. Elizabeth, in a yellow brocade stomacher that set off the gentle curves motherhood had given her, was dressed far more elaborately than anyone else in this country parlour. 'How lovely you look,' Elizabeth went on, sizing up her sister, 'as willowy as ever. Like a young girl.'

Holbein winced at the spite he saw in the remark. Surely Elizabeth was mocking Meg, with that falsely rueful look down at the swell of breasts and stomach and hips that the birth of her own three healthy children had left on her. Wasn't that a rivalrous woman-to-woman reminder that Meg had borne only one baby? He ached with admiration for Meg's gallantry when she just smiled cautiously back, not responding to the remark's hidden barb, and said, inoffensively enough: 'You're still the beauty of the family, Elizabeth.'

A desultory conversation began between the two women, led by Elizabeth, who peppered her bright remarks (about the calm of country life, her improving ability to play the viol and sew tapestries, and the naughtiness of her tree-climbing children) with inquisitive sidelong looks at her sister. Holbein noticed that Elizabeth didn't mention her husband, or the political career he seemed to be salvaging from the shipwreck that had brought down the rest of the

Mores, by building new bridges to the Boleyns and Cromwells and Cranmers who were now in the ascendant at court. But she did lean forward to say, pointedly and so quietly that no one but the eavesdropping Holbein heard: 'Still, I'm not too much out of circulation to hear how well John's doing with Doctor Butts. The King's physician! It's a great honour for your family, Meg. We're so proud of you. Especially since I know how hard it must be for a man in John's position to negotiate a way through all the intriguing,' and she raised a delicately inquiring eyebrow. 'Of course, one never believes the rumours . . . but I've heard people say Doctor Butts is becoming one of the new men . . . that he's carried messages in his time from university men being investigated for heresy to' – her voice, already only a murmur, dropped to a whisper for the next two words – 'Queen Anne.' She paused significantly. 'I've often thought how tricky it must be for John to be so close to him yet steer his own path.' Her whole body, led by her eyebrows, had become a cunning, curving question mark, inviting Meg's confidences.

'Oh,' Meg said, with blank eyes, rejecting the invitation as though she wasn't aware of it being there. 'John's never been very interested in all that. I never hear about politics at home. All he cares about is doctoring.' Her eyes lit up with sudden interest. Holbein leaned forward to hear more. 'What John thinks about most is whether physicians should still base their work on Galen. You know: heroic doctoring. A lot of bleeding.' Holbein was aware of Elizabeth drawing back with a faintly disgusted look on her face. This wasn't at all what the beauty of the family had wanted to find out. 'He and Doctor Butts have taken against Galen,' Meg was saying. 'John says Galen was a bit of a fraud – a man who got all his knowledge from dissecting pigs and didn't actually know much about the human body at all. He and Doctor Butts have been looking at copies of Italian drawings of the human body – they have public dissections of criminals there, and theatres of anatomy, it's not like England, and artists are allowed to watch. And they're reading parts of the treatise that a colleague of theirs is writing – Vesalius of Padua. It isn't finished yet, but when it's published it will change the way we do medicine. I think that's the only kind of "new man" John wants to know about.'

Elizabeth nodded, but she looked as though she'd rather be elsewhere. Holbein was full of pride in Meg for the effortless way she'd blanked out her sister's potentially damaging inquiry. If diplomacy was what she'd been doing, in fact; her expression was still so innocent that he couldn't be sure whether she wasn't just genuinely interested in the medical theories on her husband's mind.

'You must know all about this, Master Hans,' Meg said, turning to Holbein as if she'd known all along he was listening. 'Have you seen Leonardo's drawings, or Buonarotti's?'

And so intense was the joy Holbein felt at having her dark gaze on his face that he was only vaguely aware of Elizabeth turning away, with a look of relief on her face, to begin a new conversation with young John More.

There were already yawns and sleepy looks around the table. Some of the family had made their excuses and gone to bed. When More and Dame Alice left, the glow went out of the room with them. The shadows were beginning to advance. The wind was gusting against the windows. The Ropers were snuffing out candles at the empty end of the table as if encouraging the stragglers – Elizabeth, comparing notes on children's behaviour with Cecily; and Meg, still discussing Italian discoveries with Holbein, about human anatomy and the moral difficulty of cutting open dead bodies to learn how muscles and veins and hearts functioned. Still with that absent-minded little line of worry scarring her forehead.

Suddenly the tired peace was broken. There was a suppressed giggle at the door. Holbein knew what it meant. When he looked up, there were the bright eyes and dark tousle-heads peeping in out of the blackness. The children, all in woolly nightgowns, had crept out of their dormitory to spy on the grown-ups. Now, seeing they'd been rumbled, they swarmed in: a noisy, cheerful, high-pitched invasion, pouring over to the table, snatching at bits of bread and the dish of apples, gleefully dodging the adult hands that reached out to catch them, hiding behind chairs and under tables.

There was uproar. Rightly or wrongly, all the parents instantly identified their own eldest child as the ringleader. Each of them rushed to grab whichever offending infant they could lay hands on. 'Tommy!' shrieked Margaret Roper. 'Tommy!' shrieked Cecily Heron. 'Tommy!' shrieked Elizabeth Dauncey. 'Tommy!' shrieked Meg Clement.

After a scuffle, Will Roper caught two or three small Ropers under his arms and strode off, weighed down by offspring, back towards the dormitory. Holbein could hear him saying, 'You're a disgrace!' with laughter in his voice as he climbed the stairs two at a time. John and Anne More followed, dragging their children by their thin little arms. Cecily and Margaret trapped most of the stragglers and shooed them off in the same direction, looking forbidding and amused by turns.

That left the room almost empty. Holbein watched Elizabeth (daintily) and Meg (with more energy) reach for the last two breakaways. Naturally it was Meg who caught them. With one collar in each hand, she pulled the two little boys towards her. The fight had gone out of them now; they could see the game was over. They hung from her hands like puppies; two identical sets of penitent pink cheeks and downcast eyes; two identical aquiline noses.

'Tommy,' she scolded, looking crossly down at the slightly larger boy. Then she stopped; looked astonished; and turned from him to stare at the smaller Tommy. 'Tommy . . .' she said to this one, with wild surmise dawning in her eyes.

'I'm sorry,' this Tommy answered, wriggling in shame.

A deathly silence fell. Elizabeth, standing by the fire, was also staring in growing horror at the smaller Tommy. Meg's head was turning from one twinny child to another. Seen side by side like this, you couldn't help but notice that they were as alike as two peas in a pod.

The little boys didn't understand the hush. They began to cry guiltily.

'It wasn't me,' Meg's one whimpered.

The other one piped up, gazing beseechingly at his own mother, frozen at the fireplace: 'It was all Tommy Roper's idea.'

'Shh,' Meg said quietly, leaning down to kiss her child's mouth shut, unable to avoid giving the other little changeling a sick look of recognition.

Then she looked at Holbein's appalled face. And what she read in it seemed to answer the question her anxious little frown had been asking all evening, ever since she'd seen the painting.

She nodded at him – a cold, determined nod. 'Will you take them up, please?' she said. It was an order, not a request.

As he walked out of the door behind the children's twinkling little legs, almost as eager as they were to escape the atmosphere of enmity at his back, he heard her voice – flat, accusing, and full of certainty – break the silence.

'Our boys look like brothers,' the voice said. 'My husband is the father of your son, isn't he?' And then the door shut, leaving him outside in the darkness.

* * *

481

She came to him soon afterwards, in his parlour. He was standing at the window in the dark, watching the wind sweep through the vines on the other side of the glass and toss more clouds across the sky, like hay being pitchforked, obscuring the stars with the storm to come, when he heard the door click. He didn't turn. He knew who it was.

'All she said was "I have nothing to tell you",' Meg said in a monotone.

He didn't dare answer. She was carrying a candlestick. She glided across the room to the picture, to the corner where Elizabeth was depicted pushing her out of the way and giving John Clement that lascivious look as she stripped the glove from her hand. Meg put down the candlestick on the table and stared at the painted scene again. From behind, Holbein could see her head slowly nodding as if all her suspicions were at last being confirmed.

'You knew,' Meg said, still with her back to him. 'You saw them both and you realised. That's why you changed the picture, isn't it?' She turned round. A worse thought had come to her. Her haunted eyes searched his face. 'Or perhaps Elizabeth told you,' she said accusingly. 'You used to be friends.'

Holbein felt crushed with guilt. He'd always known this would be a dangerous picture, but this wasn't the secret he'd meant to reveal. 'I saw the boys when I got here. I just guessed,' he said helplessly. 'I thought you knew already.'

And all at once there was no more place for words in his heart; just the tingling urgency of his need to put his arms around her and spin her round and put his mouth to hers.

Twined together, with his body crushing hers inside his, and his leg pushing hungrily between her skirts, against the dark shifting vine leaves and the dapple of clouds and the stars, he was transported back in time to that first kiss

482

long ago under the mulberry tree. Only this time she didn't pull away. This time he felt her respond; felt her hands on his back, clawing him closer; felt her breasts moving against his chest; felt her breath quicken.

Her open eyes were fixed on his face, full of knowledge. His heart was bursting. Still crushing her against his chest with one arm, he untwined the other just far enough to pick up the candlestick and then began drawing her slowly towards his mattress in the little back room, still kissing her wetly, almost bursting with desire, murmuring incoherent endearments as he negotiated the door with an elbow and eased her back to the ground.

Afterwards – just afterwards, when he was still sighing and sated and happier than he'd ever known a man could be, with one of his big master-craftsman's hands still possessively on one of her pale girl's breasts with its childishly pink nipple – he whispered fuzzily: 'I love you.' It was what he'd always wanted to tell her. Always, for as long as he could remember. It was why he'd left his wife a second time, and why he'd lived like a monk for the past year. This was his dream coming true. Safe in the darkness, with the sounds of the storm only faintly audible through the window, he felt faint with the joyous release of it.

She whispered something back, nuzzling his neck. Holbein couldn't make out her words but he wanted them to have been 'I love you too' enough to believe that was what he'd heard. It was only after a few minutes that he startled awake, suddenly uneasy, suddenly thinking that what she'd actually been muttering might have been: 'I hate him'. But it was too late to ask. Her eyes were shut.

20

I tiptoed out of Master Hans's room before it was light. Very gently, I wriggled out from under the thickset arm pinioning me to the mattress, as if by moving too quickly I might hurt it, and kissed his cheek, and dressed my crumpled self as best I could in the dark. I wasn't shocked by where I found myself when my eyes opened, just by my calm. I knew I'd committed a sin but I was full of a terrible lightness. My mind was shying away from what I now suspected must be the reality of my past – John coming to Chelsea not to court me, but to pursue a secret affair with Elizabeth. Of me being the second-best almost daughter, the wallflower who was still there, available to be married; his only practical way of cementing his ties with the family of the man who'd helped him most in life. I'd go mad if I let myself think about that final betrayal. I was going to stay in the sunlit, innocent world I'd discovered in the orchard instead. After all those years of struggle with the imperfections of everyday life, the idea that I'd at last found a way of creating my own idyll just by making love to Hans Holbein was enough to make me feel euphoric. For the first time I could remember, I felt free: beautiful and dangerous and free.

I felt my way up the stairs in the grey pre-dawn with my nostrils full of the smell of him and my muscles warm with remembered embraces, avoiding whatever creaking boards I could. I needed to shake myself out of the languid, selfish, pleasurable way my body and mind were behaving; shake my memory away from the fire of the night. I wanted to be back in my room, washed and fresh, before Tommy woke up and came to me. I needed to stop feverishly comparing the quiet caution that making love with John had become and the hot wet passion I'd felt under in those big new arms. I needed time to think.

Then I saw a gleam of light through a doorway. A candle was burning in the chapel. Father must be at prayer already.

I darted up the last few steps, suddenly terrifyingly aware of my bonnet in my hands and my hair flowing down my back and my unlaced stomacher. No one must know.

It was only once I was safely on the other side of my door, watching the catch click into place, that I breathed again. I leaned against the wall. My legs and arms were shaking so I could hardly move. I could feel bruises on my neck and breasts. But my heart was bubbling with laughter.

Thomas More let himself into Hans Holbein's parlour soon after sun-up. He found the painter, looking rumpled and puffy-eyed, staring at his picture from the window seat. The light wasn't good enough to paint by. The sky was still sullen and overcast after the night's storm. Holbein leapt up as soon as he saw More. He bowed, then looked at his feet, then knocked over the empty cup at his side.

The painter retrieved it from the floor, cursing under his breath, and set it on the table next to his clean paintbrushes.

'I was born clumsy,' he said, looking ashamed. 'My father always said so.'

'I'm sorry to interrupt,' More said gently. 'I was hoping you'd let me take another look at your masterpiece. I woke up thinking about it.'

Holbein, already full of chaotic guilts, found it almost stopped his breath when More stepped up to the left-hand side of the painting to look at the likenesses of Elizabeth and Meg.

But he didn't comment except to say rather sadly, as he stepped back a long moment later, 'This picture tells more stories every time I look at it. You have an enviable talent for the truth.'

Holbein hung his head, not knowing how to reply.

Sir Thomas looked older this morning, he noticed, unable to stop observing line and texture despite all the mass of worries weighing on him. The luminousness of that dark skin had thinned, refining the shapely strength of More's features, as if a rich oil painting was turning into an etching of thin lines before his eyes. Perhaps it was the cold grey light. Or perhaps it was Hans Holbein's own uncertain mood. He'd woken up and reached happily for Meg and found her gone. So he didn't know whether he was the happiest man in the world or the most wretched. He could still smell her skin and feel her breasts under his lips, but would he ever be alone with her again? He urgently needed to find her and see how she reacted to the sight of him. He could hardly just walk in to where he could hear the family gathering and calmly start eating breakfast next to her in front of everyone. But his belly was rumbling with hunger. And while he was stumping around in his quarters, not knowing what to do with himself, he'd started looking at the picture and found himself thinking again – despite the wonder of what had happened in the night – that maybe he'd committed the sin of pride by putting into it everything he'd thought he knew about the Mores. He'd seen so much of the truth; but, as he was only now beginning to realise, he'd understood so little of what he'd seen. It might have been the biggest mistake he'd ever made to stir up all this trouble.

'Have you ever been in love, Master Hans?' More asked unexpectedly, with his eyes on the picture again. Holbein goggled and gulped, but the older man didn't wait for an answer, just went on, almost to himself, 'I don't know why, but I woke up this morning thinking about my first love.'

Holbein couldn't believe what he was hearing. More was a man of great public grace who never spoke about his private feelings. This couldn't be happening.

'I was sixteen . . . just out of university . . . starting at New Hall as a barrister . . . full of hope and promise . . . when I saw her. The most beautiful girl I'd ever imagined, standing opposite me at a dance with the most beautiful smile in the world on her face. She was up from Norfolk to stay with an uncle. It was as if I'd been struck by lightning. I was on fire from head to toe. I'd have married her right there and then if I could.'

More stopped, as if choosing his words. 'Nothing came of it, of course,' he went on. 'A snatched kiss or two. A few meetings and letters. Her uncle saw me off as soon as he noticed. He'd brought her to London to be betrothed to someone else. A better man than me: a young neighbour of hers from Norfolk who'd just completed his education. My father was told in no uncertain terms to stop me meeting her. I thought my heart was broken for a while, but I survived. I never saw her again, though of course,' he nodded at the likeness of Elizabeth Dauncey in Holbein's picture, as if explaining why he was telling the story now, 'much later, I named my pretty second daughter after her.'

He turned his gaze away from the painting and looked

straight into Hans Holbein's eyes. 'I was a young fool, of course. I overreacted. I tried to become a monk. But they married me off too, a year later, and I found in the end that I could love my wife perfectly well. And my second wife too, if it comes to that. I had no idea back then of the lasting happiness you can get from your family.' He laughed – softly, but in a way that Holbein, still trapped in a gaze as intense as the look a beast of prey hypnotises a rabbit with, felt might easily contain menace. 'Nothing ever does come of these storms of emotion, does it? But I was still too much of a child then to know what adults all find out sooner or later: that you only find real contentment by doing the decent thing.'

There was a sudden shiver of rain against the window. Gratefully, Holbein turned his shamed eyes away and fixed them on the spurts of water running down between the drenched vine leaves. He was trying to will the heat out of his flaming cheeks. With no more success, he was trying to stifle his hot memories of tongues and muscle and breasts and Meg's body harpooned under his on those guiltily rumpled sheets that he knew to be just behind More's back, through the bedroom door he'd forgotten to shut. If he didn't know that More couldn't possibly know how he'd spent his night, it would be only too easy to think he'd been discovered, and was being subtly warned off. He doesn't know, he told himself. He can't. But he'd have found it easier to pretend innocence if he hadn't known More to be at least as good as he was himself at intuiting other people's secrets.

'It's good to be able to open my heart to you, Master Hans,' More said, turning, like Holbein, to watch the rivulets of rain. 'I like knowing there are no secrets between us.' Then, politely: 'Have you had breakfast?'

Holbein nodded. He couldn't speak. However hungry he was, there was no way he was going to walk in on the family's breakfast with the man making these knowing, playful, half-accusing, guilt-inducing remarks. They were making his stomach churn worse than ever. For once, he felt, he needed peace and solitude even more than bread and ale.

More made his last enigmatic comment from the doorway: 'Meg's family is from Norfolk, you know. That was partly why I adopted her. She's very dear to me.'

As soon as he was alone, Holbein slumped back down into the window seat. He leaned one red cheek against the glass and stared unseeingly at the raindrops that were beginning again, letting the heat out of his body, and feeling the cold seep in like fear.

She bobbed up out of the drowning greenery outside and tapped on the steamy window, startling him out of his reverie. She had no cloak on. Her hair was stuck to her head. Her clothes were clinging to her body. But her face was lit up with laughter as she beckoned him outdoors.

Holbein rushed out into the garden, stopping only to grab his own cloak as he raced for the door.

He couldn't believe his happiness. He pulled her under a tree, rejoicing in the yielding softness of her, covering her face with relieved kisses that quickly turned hard and urgent.

'You'll get as wet as me,' she whispered, pulling at the cloak he'd still got slung over his arm, and laughing teasingly up at him again.

He'd forgotten the cloak. He laughed, delighted, and pulled it playfully over both their heads. In the rough darkness underneath it, he nuzzled his nose softly against hers. 'Meg,' he whispered, with a blissful smile practically splitting his face, staring down at the perfection of the face he'd always loved as if seeing it for the first time. 'I can't believe this is happening.'

She didn't answer, just looked unblinkingly back up at him until he touched her eyelids shut with gentle lips and moved his mouth back to hers and went back to kissing her in earnest.

When he began to shake it was she who, leaning into him with the whole of one side of her body, as if their flesh was melting together, led him off down a path to a clump of elder trees behind the deserted barn. She spread the cloak on the relatively dry ground at their feet and drew him down next to her on it and, clinging to him as though she were drowning, pulled him on top of her. He looked down at her and opened his mouth as if to speak. He was torn between delicious desires; there was so much he wanted to say to her. But she muttered, urgently now, 'Not now. Don't say anything now,' and shut his mouth with her lips.

As soon as his breathing had returned to something like normal, he propped his head up on one elbow and gazed at her with eyes full of dreams. There was a leaf in her hair. He picked it out. The rain had stopped. The leaves were dripping quietly. The world was at peace.

'I could stay here all day with you, like this,' he began, unable to think beyond their embrace. He wanted to go on, 'I love you', but she wouldn't let him.

'Tommy might be looking for me. There's no time,' she said wistfully. Her face set, and she added: '. . . and John will here before nightfall.'

That thought seemed to sober her into action. She wriggled out from under him and sat up, brushing herself down, smoothing her skirts back over her legs, rearranging her bodice, self-consciously regaining her poise. 'I'll come back and find you again when I've seen to Tommy,' she promised. 'After dinner. We'll talk. I promise.'

'But . . .' he whispered, and felt his mouth puckering, like a great baby's about to cry. It was just sinking in.

490

'Clement's coming . . .' he muttered, beginning to understand the great dread filling him. He couldn't be in the house with that man. Nor could Meg, now she was his.

'I know. But I can't think about it yet. I don't know what to do,' she said, somewhere between briskness and desperation. 'Let's not worry now. We have hours still.'

'And then?' he couldn't help blurting, hating himself for nagging at her to pick her wound.

'I don't know. I don't know.' She shook her head, and he wished he could read her mind in her distracted expression. 'Whatever happens, we can meet sometimes,' she added, and he thought he heard a note of pleading in her voice now. 'In London. I could come to you. You could be my secret. That's not what I want. You know it's not. But it's the best I can think of for now.'

His first instinct as he got to his feet and pulled her to hers was to angrily refuse the offer; to plead with her instead to come away with him, dissolve her empty marriage, leave her husband, leave her family, leave England, find a new life somewhere else, anywhere else. Anything. He'd come to unravel the More family secrets, not become another secret himself. But there was no point in protesting. He had nothing but daydreams to offer. She'd only say no. And by now a picture of the alternative future she was suggesting was already insinuating itself seductively into his head: a barefoot and tousle-headed Meg getting up from the bed in his rooms in Maiden Lane and padding towards the window to look at whatever was on his easel and kiss him and whisper compliments in his ear. It would be a future of brief moments of happiness in the darkness. But even that would be better than the utter darkness of life without her.

They turned back home, carefully not touching. Holbein drew what comfort he could from the way her footsteps slowed as the house came closer. He didn't want to go inside either.

'Do you remember your first family?' he asked, trying to stretch out the parting; hoping to elicit a confidence and have a new kind of intimacy to savour when he was alone again. 'The parents from Norfolk?'

She stopped and looked curiously round at him. 'Not really,' she said cautiously. 'Only my father, a little. Nothing about my mother. She died when I was born. Why do you ask?'

So Holbein found himself telling her about More's visit to his room that morning, spinning out his story to keep her hovering on the path beside him.

'He said he'd come to see the picture again. But he hardly looked at it before he started talking about love. He said he'd once fallen in love with a girl from Norfolk who was betrothed to someone else. He was so insistent that love is dangerous that I almost began to think he must somehow have guessed about us.'

He laughed, hoping she'd reassure him all was well. But she'd gone very still.

'He couldn't have guessed,' Holbein said uneasily. 'Could he?'

But she was thinking a private thought that she wasn't going to share with him. Her answer was too oblique to fathom. 'In this family, Master Hans,' she said, with a strange grin, 'the hardest thing is just working out how many more secrets might be waiting to come to the surface.'

He felt the quick squeeze of her hand on his. 'Thank you,' she said inexplicably. And then she was gone, flying up the path away from him, leaving him standing staring after her with his mouth open in astonishment.

'Father?' I whispered into the thick chapel air. It was so dark that all I could see at first was the blue-robed Virgin

492

rearing up in front of me. But he was kneeling there. He turned round and saw me. I'd never dared interrupt him at his fierce, solitary prayers. I didn't know whether he'd be angry. But as soon as he saw me he started scrambling stiffly to his feet, as if he'd been waiting to be interrupted.

I couldn't wait. Before he'd managed to get his back straight, the words were out of my mouth: the only words that made sense of everything. 'Are you my real father?'

I could hardly see for tears. I could feel the wet trails on his cheeks, too. After a lifetime of scarcely touching, we were suddenly clinging to each other in front of the Blessed Mary in a confused, swaying, weeping, radiant embrace.

My mind was racing as fast as my feet had been. The extra piece fitted so well into the puzzle that Father had always been. It filled the space between the detached irony with which Father liked to be seen treating his family and the world and the furious punishments he inflicted on himself and others in the name of God. He'd had his own secret all along. He'd flung himself into a love he hadn't been able to honour. He'd got a girl from Norfolk pregnant and wanted to marry her but she'd been taken away from him. And he'd never forgiven himself; never quite had the courage to believe in love again.

'You're the very image of her, you know,' he whispered. 'So painfully alike ... sometimes I could hardly bear to be near you. I can't begin to tell you how much I loved her.'

Every other discovery of the past tumultuous day and night was blotted out of my mind by this one: the sudden blinding, absolute certainty that filled me now that I too had always been loved.

Of the thousand questions bursting into my mind, I didn't know which to ask first.

I could more or less guess for myself what elaborate

493

steps he'd have had to take to get me back into the London home he'd started making by the time I was nine and my first father died. He'd have known my mother had died in childbirth. He'd have paid for information about me from Norfolk ever since. He'd have petitioned the King to buy my wardship as soon as my father was killed, and paid whatever extortionate fee was demanded for the right to raise an orphan of means who might later repay the debt by marrying one of his own children.

I'd always thought I couldn't marry into the More family because God had granted Father three daughters and only one, much younger, son. Now I saw that I could never have been brought into the family to marry any of a dozen sons, even if he'd had them; they'd all have been my half-siblings. Father must have had someone from outside the family as my husband from the very start. He'd hired John as our tutor within weeks of my arrival, I recalled; but that was too painful to dwell on now.

'What was my mother like?' I asked instead. When I was a child, I'd always pictured her kneeling in church, but that was just because her effigy in the little Norfolk church had its slim hands crossed in eternal devout prayer.

He laughed. 'Like you. Inquisitive. Impulsive. A bit of a loner. Full of difficult questions.'

I laughed back through my tears, so perfectly happy in the light of his blue eyes on my face and in the warmth of this embrace that I realised now I'd always been waiting for. Every other embrace I'd ever felt – even the passion of Hans Holbein, which had seemed so all-encompassing just moments before – faded into distant memory.

'Why didn't you tell me before?' I whispered.

He waited a second or two before replying, as if gathering his thoughts. But when he did there was a great tenderness on his face. 'I used to think the things of this world were more important than I do now . . .' he said hesitantly, as if he were feeling his way towards a difficult truth. 'Appearances. Public behaviour. Surfaces. But Master Hans has shown us something in the past day or two about the value of honesty. What I know now is that I want my family to be happy in the truth, and to do the right thing before God.'

He paused again, and this time I realised he was waiting for me to speak. He took a half-step back, though only far enough to put his hands on my shoulders, and gazed into my eyes again.

Suddenly I understood something else. By revealing that I'd guessed this secret, I'd also revealed the intimacy between me and Hans Holbein. No one but he could have told me about Father's past. Father had been cleverer than I'd realised. By confessing his long-ago sin, he'd brought mine out in the open too.

He was nodding kindly at the appalled dawning of realisation in my eyes. 'It wasn't hard to guess,' he said gently, but his voice was serious as he added: 'Don't do it, Meg. Please. I was lucky to get you back and have a second chance of happiness. You might not be so lucky. Master Hans is a good man, but he's not your husband. Don't let sin destroy your life the way it nearly did mine.'

'But,' I said, with my joy fading at the unfairness of what he was asking, 'this is different. It wasn't me who broke my vows first. It was John.'

I thought he'd be shocked. But he wasn't. He just went on smiling, still holding me at arm's length, still looking at me as if he were memorising every inch of me.

'You've seen Elizabeth's son, haven't you?' I added, trying to jolt him into seeing my raw pain, and I couldn't keep the betrayed anger out of my voice. But there was no changing the look on his face. Nothing I could say about this could surprise him, I saw. It hardly surprised me to realise that he already knew about John and Elizabeth.

He nodded, as if he understood my feelings. But what he said, as he slipped one arm around my shoulder and pulled me close to him again, was: 'It's irrelevant. It's only now I see my children making these mistakes that I realise how insignificant they are.'

'It's not insignificant to me!' I cried, abandoning any attempt at measured conversation, feeling my hands tremble in his and almost howling with the cruelty of what I'd found out. 'My husband is the father of my sister's child! How can you call that irrelevant?'

But he only smiled an old wise man's smile and put a finger to my lips. 'Hush,' he said, almost absent-mindedly. 'You're doing John an injustice. I'm going to tell you what really happened. We've both had enough of living with secrets, haven't we?'

He waited till I nodded, then delved in his clothes for a kerchief and gave it to me to wipe my eyes. He turned his face towards the window, so his pale, greying features were suffused with watery light as well as kindness as he remembered.

'I married Elizabeth badly. It was my mistake. I chose a man for her whom she didn't really love. I took her away from court as soon as I realised the mischief she was getting herself into. John didn't even know who she was until it was too late.'

I could see the scene he began to describe now so clearly that it was almost as if I'd been there myself. A masked ball; John and a beautiful married woman flirting; a rumple of clothes against the arras; rose petals in his hair. John, idling away his time at court while he waited for a place at the College of Physicians; petitioning Father every day to be allowed to come to me at Chelsea ('He tormented me for months, Meg; there was no doubting who was on his mind,' Father said ruefully); then relaxing for an evening into the whispery, secretive, licentious ways of

496

the court. Afterwards, terrified when the woman he'd so hurriedly made love to giggled and whispered, 'But you don't need to unmask for me to know you,' and revealed herself as a More daughter, but the wrong one. My little sister Elizabeth.

'She'd never have done it if I'd found her the right husband in the first place,' Father said rather sadly, 'and he'd never have done it if he'd known she was your sister. She was a lady in a mask to him. It was part of the mischief of a young king's court. It meant nothing.'

'How did you find out?' I whispered.

'He didn't know what to do. He took her for a walk in the rose garden and begged her not to tell. He told he'd come back to England hoping to marry (though he didn't say who) and threw himself on her mercy. He told me she was dignified about it. She told him it would stay their secret. She was married already, after all. He took her back to her husband and fled off to his rooms.'

Father's face crinkled into the beginning of self-deprecating laughter. 'So the last thing he expected was for me to be at his door the next day, angrily demanding explanations. I'd heard a completely different story. Elizabeth was hysterical by the morning. She came to me and told me she'd realised she wasn't intended for Dauncey. She wanted her marriage annulled so she could marry Clement. She said they were lovers; she said she could make him love her forever. I was struck dumb. After all the years I'd spent making sure he was the right man for you, it was the last thing I'd ever expected to hear. I wasn't far off horsewhipping him.

'But John was even more distraught than me. He was terrified I'd keep him away from you now I knew,' he went on. 'And I had half a mind to.'

I was beginning to breathe again. 'But you didn't,' I said.

'No,' he answered, and twinkled sideways and down at me. 'If I've learned something about sin in my life, I've also learned enough about repentance to know when someone truly wants to right the wrong they've done. The man was eaten up with love for you. He'd have died rather than give you up.'

'So I smoothed things over. I told Elizabeth she must live the life she'd chosen with the husband she'd chosen before God. "You can't look to go to Heaven at your pleasure or on feather beds," I said. And I sent her home to Chelsea. My idea was to send her quietly off a bit later to live with Dauncey's parents in the country, before I let John come to Chelsea to claim you. That would have been the kindest way. But John pre-empted me by just turning up to find you. He surprised me, to be honest. I thought he'd been so hollowed out by his young years that he'd obediently do whatever I told him to. I was wrong. When it came to winning you, it turned out he still had a spark of his old fire.'

I was so full of emotions I didn't understand that it felt as though a whirlpool was churning up my insides. 'He came to you and won your hand,' Father was saying now, from what seemed like very far away. 'He's been an honest husband. He loves you.'

Those words made me feel as though a late ray of sunlight must be breaking through the autumn gloom. But when I looked up at Father, his face was still running with the reflection of the streams of water pouring down the window.

'Don't think,' he added sombrely, 'that Elizabeth hasn't suffered. She had to feel a child grow inside her and watch the man who fathered it in love with you. She's had to make compromises you can know nothing about to go on with her life. And she'll carry her sin, and her punishment, with her to her dying day. It's Elizabeth who lost by loving John, not you. For you to make a quarrel of it now would be wrong.'

Less reluctantly than I might have expected, I found myself nodding. Flashes of memory were coming back to me: Elizabeth running white-faced from the great hall at Chelsea when I told her John Clement had left; Elizabeth throwing herself down the stairs, and stealing my penny-royal, to try and get rid of the baby she was carrying; Elizabeth listening wistfully to Master Hans's stories of mother love. However rivalrous and suspicious our relationship had always been, I thought the feeling starting to stir in my heart at those memories might be pity.

The churning inside me was beginning to subside; a new kind of peace, a warm stillness I'd never experienced, was taking its place.

I stole another look at Father's profile, expecting him to be suffused with the same calm simplicity. I was almost surprised to find him still looking worriedly down at the floor, as if choosing his words.

'They've done their best to atone for their sin,' he said slowly. 'Now you have to be honest about yours, too.'

I shook my head. I didn't even want to think about it. Now the other thing was coming back: the feel of Hans Holbein's body on mine; the whole tangled, beautiful confusion of my future. But he ignored me and went determinedly on:

'No, hear me out. You think you're attracted to Holbein's genius. You think it's more exciting than the quietness John has chosen in his life. And part of me can see why. There have been so many secrets between all of us that you've let yourself be carried away by Holbein's passion for truth-telling. And I agree it's exciting to watch his mind work – in ways he doesn't always understand himself. I feel it too.

'But you're wrong to be so impressed by it that you can

think of throwing everything you've made of your life away for it. You can't live with genius any more than you can pick up ice or fire. Genius is too cruel. Look at what's happened even here, in these few days. Master Hans didn't think twice before putting a secret in his painting that was bound to cause you pain. That's the fire in him. His gift warms people and makes them feel more alive; but it will burn up anyone who comes too close. I'm not doubting that he loves you, but how much good did loving him do the family he's already left behind in Basel? If you went to him, you might be happy for a while. But it would be a flimsier happiness than you think now. You'd be dishonoured. You'd live with shame. And he'd hurt you too in the end, and maybe destroy you – because Hans Holbein's greatest passion is his painting.

'It's different with John. John had his wild side once, but he's suppressed it to make himself the man for you. Even if it still comes out sometimes. You've seen it. I've felt it,' and, ruefully, he stroked the jawbone John had hit. 'But the point is that his passion is you – it always has been. Losing you would destroy him.

'There's as much lasting good in the way John Clement has remade himself for you as there is in genius. You could find true happiness with him if you learned to make the same sacrifice, with yourself, for him. There'd be a beauty and nobility in rebuilding your life together. And, if you found the courage for it, it would transform and reward you as well as him.'

It wasn't just reflections of the rain on his cheeks; he was crying.

'It's only one part of the truth to say that you'll always be more essential to John than you ever could be to Holbein,' he said softly, looking down at me. I didn't think he'd noticed his own tears. 'What's equally important is that you'll be more yourself, too, if you stay in

500

your marriage. John will always enjoy your pleasure in your medicine and your children and your family. He won't swallow you up. He'll let you breathe. You won't be choosing second best.'

I could still feel the heat of Hans Holbein on my body; the scratches, the bristle, the saliva; but the memory was already beginning to seem like a feverish dream.

Father wrapped his other arm round me and we stood, perfectly still, listening to each other's breath. 'It wouldn't be so hard for you as it was for Elizabeth,' he whispered, not seeming to realise I didn't need convincing any more. 'All you'd have to do would be to forgive John. Forgive yourself. Go back to your life. Learn how to love someone who's learned not to fight like you do.'

'Yes,' I whispered back, 'I will,' and now I felt his tears come faster and a great sigh come from deep within him. He put a hand to his face, over my shoulder, and dashed the tears away. 'The wine of angels,' he muttered, with the faintest of smiles; a phrase from my childhood that made me smile. 'I'm being a fool. But it was time for us to be honest, or be lost. Thank you.'

It seemed a long time later that I said, quietly, into the sounds of the rain, 'Can't you give up the other things, Father? Your campaigning, your writing? Your fight? Can't you just be with us and be happy?'

But when he raised his wet eyes to mine I saw I'd hoped for too much. He never would. There was nothing to do but accept it.

'We may not have much more time together,' he said gently, wiping away the wetness on my cheeks. 'Let's try to be happy with what we have.'

Holbein waited all morning in his room, fiddling with details of his painting, in a worsening agony of suspense. He startled every time he heard a tap at the window, but

Meg's face was never there when he rushed towards the light. All he could see were vine stems broken by the fury of last night's storm.

He'd never lost his appetite before but he couldn't face food now. However, at noon he slunk out into the open and braved the family gathering for dinner. It was worth it just to see her, even if he had to brazen out a sighting of the treacherous Elizabeth and more excruciatingly enigmatic observations from Sir Thomas. But Elizabeth wasn't there. More wasn't there. And Meg wasn't there.

'You're not eating anything, Master Hans,' Margaret Roper said worriedly. 'And you've always done our food such splendid justice before. Don't you like chitterlings? Can I get you something else?'

He retreated to his room like a wounded animal and sat staring out of the window into the cold afternoon. When the children came visiting, quieter than on the previous day but just as eager to be tickled and carried and given piggybacks and to stick their fingers into his paints, he tried to get his spirits up enough to play with them. He even gave one Tommy a weary piggyback. But they knew something was wrong. Gradually their manic giggles died down and they began to look uncertainly at each other. He could see they were relieved when they heard the quiet clip-clop of a horse riding into the courtyard.

'It's Father!' the Tommy he'd been giving a ride to screeched, in sudden ecstasy, and the children all shrieked and poured out and away. Holbein followed them as far as the doorway to the yard. John Clement's tired, dark, eagle profile flashed in front of him as an athletic body swung off a horse. And then, at last, there was Meg.

But there was nothing in her of the reluctant, dutiful wife he'd expected to see, all downcast eyes and anxiously hunched shoulders. She was walking fast out of the main door into the courtyard on her father's arm, looking radiantly happy in a way Holbein had never imagined her. 'John,' she cried, and, letting go of More, ran forward to throw herself into her husband's arms. Clement looked surprised by her enthusiasm for a moment, but then he folded his arms around her and kissed the top of her head, and an almost worshipful expression wiped the fatigue from his handsome face.

Holbein knew the look of love when he saw it. But he couldn't bear to see any more. He rushed away from them, into the garden, half-running down the path he'd walked in a different life with Meg to the sodden clump of elders. It was only after he'd flung himself down to the ground under them and seen the pale gleam of a seed pearl that must have been torn off her bonnet that morning that his chest began to heave. He clutched his head in his arms and curled up and gave way to his grief.

He didn't know how long it was before the soft little hand patted his shoulder. For a split second he dared to hope, but when he looked up it was only Elizabeth's lovely, pointed, melancholy face he saw staring down at him. The wrong face. He groaned again and hid his smeary face in his hands.

'Are you in pain, Master Hans?' she asked, with unexpected sympathy. 'Is there anything I can do?'

Holbein tried to master himself. He had no idea what was happening. But he was a man who trusted his instincts, and what they were telling him was that he was staring complete defeat in the face. 'No . . . no,' he grunted, desperately holding back his heaving breath. 'A touch of stomach cramp . . . nothing to worry about.'

She put a gentle hand to his hot forehead. 'I've been out for a walk,' she murmured. 'I could hear you from way back there.'

'It's nothing,' he grunted again, desperate to be alone.

But there was nothing he could do to stop. The sobs kept on convulsing him.

After another long pause she leaned forward and kissed his forehead.

'Well, I'm sorry for your pain, whatever it is,' she said. 'But you're a survivor, Master Hans. I know you are. I am too. You helped me see that, long ago. I'll pray for you.'

He looked up, startled out of himself for a second by that promise; and saw that the lovely dark eyes staring back at his were no strangers to sadness.

'And I for you,' he mumbled as her footsteps retreated.

More watched Meg and John Clement come together out of the painting parlour. He stood stock-still in the deepening shadows of the stairwell.

'Can you ever forgive me?' John Clement asked his wife, and he took her very tenderly in his arms.

'Can *you* ever forgive *me*?' she whispered back, clinging to him.

The former Lord Chancellor of England waited a few more seconds before nodding and tiptoeing away. The kissing couple didn't hear him go.

Margaret Roper looked puzzled when she put her head round the family parlour door. 'I can't find Master Hans anywhere, and it's nearly suppertime,' she said. 'I can't think where he can have got to.'

'He's gone,' her father said, turning round from his place at the window. His eyes were as red as if he'd been weeping but he sounded cheerful enough. 'He had to get back to London.'

'But he's left all his things in his room!' she cried, astonished. 'And he hasn't even shown us his painting!'

'He was in a hurry,' More replied laconically, turning back to the window.

He wanted to watch the small figure hunched on its horse until it disappeared at a slow clop over the brow of the hill. He was saying goodbye: not just to Hans Holbein, a man he'd trusted and respected and wouldn't see again in this life, but to the whole world of the mind that he'd once shared with that fast-vanishing generation of men of genius.

He pinched the bridge of his nose with two fingers and impatiently dashed away the wetness he found there. He had no need of the wine of angels now. He'd done what was best for his daughter.

Hans Holbein stopped his horse at the crest of the hill and looked back at the glade in which Well Hall was built. The animal was walking towards the setting sun, and the sky behind him, above the house, was already nearly dark and prickling with faint stars.

He was very cold, full of a quiet stillness unlike any of the tumults that so often raged through him. He couldn't imagine ever getting warm again. This felt like the death of his heart.

At least it was easier riding without any of the packs he'd been weighted down with as he left London. His only luggage now was the large bag of coins he'd found in his room an hour ago, with a note from Thomas More tucked inside. '*My dear Holbein,*' he'd read, '*it was far too generous of you to try to make us a gift of your painting. Please accept this small sum in payment. And please remember me to Erasmus. You know the regard in which I hold him.*'

Affectionate as it was, he'd recognised it at once as a letter of dismissal. He'd stumbled over to the painting and stared at it through swollen eyes. It was finished. It had come out the way he'd wanted. Then he'd gone to the stable and, ignoring the groom's surprised look, got his horse saddled up to ride away.

Now he took a last look back, wondering briefly when they'd notice he'd gone.

Then he pointed the horse's head forward towards the fading light and London, and spurred it on.

As he clip-clopped dispiritedly down into the next gentle Essex valley, Hans Holbein was already beginning to think about the shape of Thomas Cromwell's narrow eyes and square red face. He was wondering how best to place them in the painted setting he was about to create.

So he never saw the blood-red orb deepen in the night sky behind him, above the rooftops he was leaving behind, or the long tail flaming ominously against the stars.

Author's Note

This story is based on more historical fact than might be expected.

Thomas More's first public role was as a pageboy in the household of Archbishop John Morton, Henry VII's right-hand man, who liked to tell dinner guests that the witty, self-possessed child would one day be a great man.

After qualifying as a London barrister, the young More befriended the Dutch humanist Erasmus and a circle of English humanists including Dean John Colet. The group helped Dean Colet to set up a school for city children in the yard of St Paul's Cathedral – which exists to this day, though in Barnes and Hammersmith – and worked together to set an appropriate curriculum for bright Renaissance children. More later set up a separate home school along the same lines for his own children, who became famous across Europe for their learning.

More had a glittering political career, ending when he resigned as Henry VIII's Lord Chancellor in 1532. He is also remembered for two books. One is *Utopia*, a playful and ambiguous description of a perfect land that cannot exist. He explains in the book that this place has been described to him and an assistant he calls his 'boy John

Clement' during a diplomatic mission by a sailor who likes to tell tall tales. More's second book is an unreliable but gripping history of Richard III, the last Plantagenet king, who was killed in battle by Henry Tudor when More was five. More's history formed the basis for Shakespeare's later play about Richard III, which cast the Plantagenet king as a scheming hunchbacked usurper who murdered his nephews, the Princes in the Tower, so he could steal their throne for himself. More's book has been denounced in modern times as slanderous victor's history but it remains the basis of most people's thinking about Richard III.

More's horror of heretics late in his career is well documented, both through his written denunciations of Martin Luther and his Protestant followers and the writings of contemporary friends and enemies.

His adopted daughter Meg Giggs was interested in medicine and was known in the More family for having cured her father of tertian fever after reading the medical writings of Galen. She married the former family tutor, John Clement, a decade after he left the More household to lecture in Greek at Oxford and then train as a physician in Italy. The Clements began their married life at the Mores' former family home in London, the Old Barge on Bucklersbury Street, from where More (and, briefly, John Clement) was arrested in 1534 before being executed a year later.

The Clement family, along with the Mores' closest friends, the Rastells, later left an increasingly Protestant England for the safety of the Catholic enclave of Louvain in the Low Countries, where they lived out their days.

More's eldest daughter Margaret married William Roper, who hero-worshipped More and wrote an adoring biography of his father-in-law after More's death. Cecily More married Giles Heron, another child adopted by the family, who was executed not long after More. The only one of the children to escape virtually unscathed from the death of the family patriarch was More's daughter Elizabeth, whose husband William Dauncey's political career continued smoothly.

Hans Holbein, a German painter, came to England in 1526 to make his fortune as a portraitist. He spent several months living with the More family at their new home in Chelsea and painted their family portrait. After returning to Reformation Germany in 1528, where the churches were being whitewashed, Holbein was unable to find enough work as a decorative artist to sustain his family. He returned to England in 1532. A second portrait of the More family, which was handed down through generations of Ropers and now hangs at Nostell Priory in Yorkshire, is usually attributed to him even though it is signed 'Rowlandas Lockey'.

Hans Holbein remained in England till his death a decade after this book ends. In that time, he became the King's painter and made portraits of many leading courtiers. He died, probably of plague, in 1542 and is buried in one of the churches along Bishopsgate at the eastern end of the City of London.

Sweating sickness appeared in England for the first time in 1485, just after Henry Tudor's victory over Richard III and his seizure of the English throne. It was widely believed to be God's sign that the Tudors were not a legitimate dynasty. It struck half a dozen times while England was under Tudor rule before vanishing forever.

No one knows what became of the Princes in the Tower.

BIBLIOGRAPHY

My first source for this book was Jack Leslau's website, www.holbeinartworks.org, which sets out the theory he derived from Hans Holbein's portraits about the hidden identity of John Clement.

Also of interest:

ON HOLBEIN
Holbein: Portrait of an Unknown Man by Derek Wilson (Phoenix House 1997)
The Ambassadors' Secret: Holbein and the World of the Renaissance by John North (Phoenix/Orion, 2002)
Holbein and the Court of Henry VIII by Jane Roberts (National Galleries of Scotland 1993)

ON THOMAS MORE
The Life of Thomas More by Peter Ackroyd (Chatto & Windus 1998)
Thomas More by Alvaro de Silva (Catholic Truth Society 2003)

ON OTHER SIXTEENTH-CENTURY FIGURES

William Tyndale: If God Spare My Life by Brian Moynahan (Little, Brown 2002)

Thomas Cranmer by Diarmaid MacCulloch (Yale University Press 1996)

The Uncrowned Kings of England: The Black Legend of the Dudleys by Derek Wilson (Constable 2005)

John Clement and his books by AW Reed. The Library, 4th series, vol 6, (1926) pp 329–339

Life of John Morton by Reginald Woodhouse

Margaret of York, Duchess of Burgundy by Christine Weightman (Alan Sutton/St Martin's Press 1989)

ON SIXTEENTH-CENTURY LONDON LIFE

London: A Biography by Peter Ackroyd (Vintage 2001)

Elizabeth's London: Everyday Life in Elizabethan London by Liza Picard (W&N 2003)

London: A Social History by Roy Porter (Hamish Hamilton 1994)

ON MEDICINE

Medicine and Society in Early Modern Europe by Mary Lindeman (CUP 1999)

Medieval & Early Renaissance Medicine: An Introduction to Knowledge and Practice by Nancy G Siraisi. (Chicago University Press 1990)

Medicine before Science: The Business of Medicine from the Middle Ages to the Enlightenment by Roger French (CUP 2003)

Blood and Guts: A Short History of Medicine by Roy Porter (Penguin 2003)

ON RICHARD III AND THE PLANTAGENETS

Richard III: England's Black Legend by Desmond Seward (Country Life Books 1982)

Bosworth 1485: Psychology of a Battle by Michael K Jones (Tempus 2003)

The Daughter of Time by Josephine Tey (Touchstone 1995)

The Wars of the Roses: and the Lives of Five Men and Women in the Fifteenth Century by Desmond Seward (Constable 1995)

Ludford Bridge & Mortimer's Cross by Geoffrey Hodges (Logaston Press 1989)

Sir Thomas More: The History of King Richard III, foreward by Sister Wendy Beckett (Hesperus Classics 2005)

Richard III: And the Princes in the Tower by AJ Pollard (Alan Sutton 1991)

Various issues of The Ricardian, the quarterly journal of the Richard III Society.